# The Lacquer Lady

# F. TENNYSON JESSE

# The *Lacquer Lady*

*With a New Introduction by*
*Joanna Colenbrander*

LESTER
&ORPEN
DENNYS
PUBLISHERS

This book is dedicated to Sir Harcourt Butler,
G.C.S.I., G.C.I.E., with affection and gratitude
*Frater, ave atque vale*

Published 1981 by Lester & Orpen Dennys Limited
78 Sullivan St., Toronto, Ontario M5T 1C1

ISBN: 0-919630-22-7

# INTRODUCTION

Artists with a proved talent in one genre often set their hearts on triumphing in another, though it may prove to be a will-o'-the-wisp. It is said that Gainsborough, strolling round Reynolds' studio, remarked sourly: 'The beggar's so various!' The same might be said of Fryn Tennyson Jesse's extraordinary diversity. Time and again, she earned her laurels of *succès d'estime*, 'book-of-the-month', or 'all-time-classic', but always went on to other things. 'That is why I have never been a best-seller,' she apologised.

Yet A. C. Ward, in *The Nineteen Twenties*, wrote: 'Tennyson Jesse's novels are remarkable for their extraordinary richness and animation. Her books are more intensely alive than those of any other woman now writing in England. And *The Lacquer Lady* is a threefold success: for the strange beauty and terror of the Burmese scenes, for the first and final chapters at Brighton, and for the character of Fanny, who is good enough to take tea with Becky Sharp.'

It was sheer chance that enabled Fryn to write *The Lacquer Lady*, her most magnificent achievement. When she received a letter, late in 1922, from the first Marquess of Reading, inviting her and her husband to visit him and Lady Reading in India, she found herself in a quandary. Her war-time marriage to H. M. Harwood the playwright had only recently been officially announced. Moreover, she had just become engrossed in the study of the fascinating personality of Mrs Edith Thompson, accused with her twenty-year-old lover Frederick Bywaters of the murder of Edith's husband. She could hardly bear to tear herself away. However, she capitulated, saying: 'We may never have the luck to know another Viceroy; let's go!'

Arrived in Bombay, they found letters of introduction to every Resident Governor and native Prince, including Sir Harcourt Butler, who was about to be transferred from Agra to Burma. With him they struck up a warm friendship, and he urged them to follow on to his new Residency in Rangoon. So, after completing their tour of India and Kashmir, they reached the country of pagodas, striking north from Rangoon into what had been the ancient Kingdom of Ava, with the Lion Throne in the Golden Palace of the Gem City of Mandalay.

Burma is a narrow country wedged between India and China and split north-south by the great river Irrawaddy. Lower Burma, with the entire coastal area, had been part of the British Empire since 1824, but when Upper Burma was annexed in 1885 it had been a kingdom for a thousand years. There the travellers met Rodway Swinhoe, who knew the story behind the Annexation, and gave that story to Fryn; how it was a secret treaty between the French and the dissolute King of Ava – a secret betrayed by Fanny – which impelled the Indian Government reluctantly to take action to protect the great teak forests conceded to the Bombay-Burma Corporation. It put her hot on the scent to find anyone still living from the cruel reign of King Thibaw and his wife Supaya-lat, the Middle Princess. 'I was only just in time,' wrote Fryn.

Having spent two Burmese winters harvesting a rich crop, she carried it home, and allowed it to mature like wine in the cask. 'I am a slow writer,' she has explained, 'and it took me three years. I finished it in a great burst late at night, not having gone down to dinner. It is the book by which I should live.'

By 1929, when *The Lacquer Lady* was published, she had written all manner of other things; she had translated from the French; she had written *The White Riband*, which Joseph Conrad called 'this jewel in a casket'; she had published her first collection of poems, *The Happy Bride*, her first collection of murder studies, *Murder and its Motives*, the prodigious novel of the sea, *Tom Fool*, and two introductions to the Notable British Trials series, the only woman at that date to have been so honoured.

*The Lacquer Lady* was acclaimed everywhere; it was the Book Society's Choice for January 1930. W. J. Locke wrote to her: 'This is a marvellous achievement. Its workmanship is exquisite. Its treatment of character enlightened by irony and warmed by pity. Above all, it has passages of extraordinary, abiding beauty. Your last paragraph is unforgettable.'

\*     \*     \*

Fryniwyd Tennyson Jesse was the second of the three daughters of the Reverend Eustace Tennyson d'Eyncourt Jesse and his wife Edith Louisa James. Eustace's mother Emily Tennyson, before her marriage to the valiant naval officer Richard Jesse, had been engaged when she was seventeen to her brother Alfred Tennyson's Cambridge friend Arthur Henry Hallam, who, dying at twenty-two, became the subject of Tennyson's elegy *In Memoriam*. Edith's father, Henry James, had left Cornwall as a youth to seek his fortune, and had done that so well that by the time he retired from Cory Wright, the coal merchants, he was worth a quarter of a million pounds. But the combination of Eustace and Edith did not prove felicitous. Eustace's High Anglicanism took a beating from the Nonconformists of the Suffolk coast, which drove him to seek gentler treatment in South Africa. Edith, having lost her third child there by meningitis, retired into invalidism and religiosity. She gave away her first-born daughter Stella to the rich relations, as being too high-spirited for her delicate nerves, thus choosing to make two lonely children out of the fond pair remaining. In the nursery language of the time, Stella was 'the musical one' and Fryniwyd 'the one that drew'. So, when Stella was allowed by the grandparents to study music and drama, Fryn was sent to Cornwall, to study art.

In 1911, of age and already suspecting that she would never make an artist, Fryn left for Fleet Street, bearing a portfolio stuffed with drawings and short stories based on Cornish lore. One of these stories, 'The Mask', she sent to the *English Review*, where its sombre power and originality had threefold results, clearing a path before her like some violent explosive. William Heinemann asked her to write a novel for him, which she called *The Milky Way* and which was hailed as 'the gayest novel of the season' when published in 1913. Then H. M. Harwood wrote to her as 'Mr. Jesse', asking if he could dramatize the story; it was the first of many happy collaborations between them, including their eventual marriage. And through the owner of the *English Review*, Alfred Mond, she met Sir Rufus Isaacs, the Attorney-General, later Lord Chief Justice Lord Reading and Viceroy of India, who instructed her in law.

In the years that followed, Fryn lost the fingers of her right hand in an old 'pusher' aeroplane joy-riding over Lake Windermere. After repeated surgery to the nerve-ends, she taught herself to write again with the beautifully moulded little creation she called her 'pandy'. She travelled through America and the West Indies, paying her way with articles for the *Daily Mail*, and at the outbreak of war got herself home on an English ship making a dash with all lights out, and to Belgium as a war correspondent for the siege of Antwerp. She did much work in the war zone, and at sea for the Ministry of Information, and became reader for Heinemann and review-writer for *The Times Literary Supplement*. She was elected a Fellow of the Royal Society of Literature in 1947.

\*   \*   \*

In his last book about the family Tennyson, Sir Charles Tennyson described his kinsmen as 'a unique blend of childlikeness and grandeur'. It is a perfect description of Fryn. She had the imagination of a poet, the training of a painter, and the mind of a lawyer, and it was these qualities, combined in a delicate body with the courage of a long-distance runner, that gave her the sustained creative power for the descriptive passages in which she excelled. Rebecca West wrote of her: 'Her faculty of vision is marvellously intense. She has shown herself a master of descriptive prose. Her style is strong enough to be an inspiration'.                Joanna Colenbrander, London, 1978

*Joanna Colenbrander was for many years F. Tennyson Jesse's secretary and is now writing a biography of her.*

# PREFACE

A PREFACE is a portentous thing and, coming from the author of a novel, may seem to imply an over-valuation, but it would not be honest to issue *The Lacquer Lady* without thanking those people to whose expert knowledge I am deeply indebted.

To the late Rodway Swinhoe, expert in matters Burmese and " The Father of the Mandalay Bar ", I owe my first thanks, for it was he who told me the true story of the causes which led to the Annexation of Upper Burma—how it was " Fanny " and her love affair, and not the pretext (justified as that would have been) of the Bombay-Burma Corporation that drove the Indian Government into action at last. Rodway Swinhoe was one of the earliest dwellers in Mandalay after the Annexation, and knew most of the people in the drama. He had planned to write the story himself, but with great generosity he gave it up to me.

I might, dazzled by the roundness and irony of the story—for, as it is no invention, I can say as much—have launched on the writing of it gaily enough, but I should soon have found it impossible to continue with any sense of confidence in my own statements had it not been for the expert help of others.

Sir George Scott, K.C.I.E., a British authority on Burmese life and literature, and himself author of standard books that will always be vital to the serious student, was my court of appeal. He gave me vivid descriptions of the men of that day who made this particular piece of history.

Sir Herbert Thirkell White, K.C.I.E., one-time Lieutenant Governor of Burma, with his memories and research also helped me much.

Everyone connected with this story is dead so I can mention the real names of the characters, which I could not do when I first wrote the book. Fanny was not the daughter of an Italian father and a Burmese mother, neither was her name Fanny Moroni. She was the daughter of a Greek called Calogreedy, and a Burmese mother, and her name was Mattie.

Selah's real name was Hosannah Manook, and without her

help I could never have written the book. She was the daughter of an Armenian who was the Kalawun, or Minister for Foreigners. Kalā means foreigner (and I put one accent on the word here, so that the reader may know where the stress falls). It also means a barbarian and everyone was a Kalā to the Burmese except the Chinese and the Shans. Hosannah Manook (who eventually married an Armenian cousin) became European Maid of Honour at the Court of Ava, and it is to her that I owe the intimate details of the Palace life. Not even a Burman could have known these things, because only a woman was allowed in the women's part of the Palace.

It is to M. Duroiselle, Master of Ceremonies, that I owe my knowledge of their details. He was in charge of the lacquer palanquins, the court robes and the other paraphernalia of the Palace.

Mattie Calogreedy herself was still alive when I first wrote the book in 1929, though she had lost all her charm.

The French weaver's daughter, whom I have called Julie Delange, but whose name was Denigré, was alive though stone blind when I met her. She died, aged nearly one hundred, shortly before Burma fell in the last war. She, too, remembered very well the old Palace life and was most interesting.

Sandreino's real name was Andreino. His chief source of income was as agent of the Bombay-Burma Teak Company, for his own country, Italy, was in no condition to jockey for position against France and England. The new Consul-General for France whom I have called Maas was really Haas, and the villain of the piece whom I call Bonvoisin had the suitable name of Bonvilain.

The only thing that remains to be said is that I have in every case simplified the spelling of native names as much as possible. I might, to give only one example, have spelt Supayalat (which is a title meaning Middle Princess and not really a name at all) in many different ways: Su-payaw-lat; Su-paya-lat; Soopayahlat; I now realise that I ought to have had no hyphens and I might have spelt it Tsaubhuralat! I hope my readers will think I settled on the simplest version. Both hyphens and accents have been abandoned ages ago, for there is no standard system and therefore most Far Eastern authors avoid them. The only deliberate inaccuracy in this

version of the book is that I have referred to the Alè Namma-
.daw, or Centre Queen, by her best known title of Sinbyew-
mashin. This, which means Lady of the White Cow
Elephant, was a title only conferred on her after the death
of the Chief Queen. But Sinbyew-mashin (here again I
must ask the reader to believe that I have settled on the
simplest spelling—how would he have liked to grapple with
Hsenghbyumasheng?) is bad enough; and to have called
the lady one thing in the beginning of the book and by this
staggering name afterwards would have made a needless
complication. I only mention this inaccuracy lest the pundits
write and correct me. I have kept the accent on Alè
Nammadaw for the greater ease of the reader, as I have kept
one hyphen in Supaya-lat.

In the Second World War we and the Americans, with
the help of some of her people, freed Burma. It was a
tremendous combined operation, one of the most important
of the war, and too little is known about it and this is no
place to write what one does know. But at least we can say
that we have lost among our bravest and best in Burma.
It is a mistake to talk about Myitkyina and Bhamo as though
they were important towns, though Bhamo was centuries old,
but the towns of Burma were little more than big villages
and the houses were all of wood. Only Rangoon was built
of stone and more or less a modern city. Mandalay itself is
hardly recognisable as it was burnt out in the course of the
fighting. The rose brick walls remain but the great timber
Palace with its magnificent wood carving went up in flames.
So Mandalay has ceased to be, it exists no longer save in our
memories, in old prints and photographs. And we English,
too, have all departed. We no longer rule Burma. She is
now a sovereign state styling herself the Union of Burma
which denotes the union of her many peoples, Burmese,
Karen, Shan and Kachin, to mention only the more important. When we left in January 1948, the future of Burma
looked bright. If things have turned out, as alas they have,
not to have that gleam that once we believed in, it is because
civil war between Burmese and Karens followed upon dissen-
sion amongst the Burmese themselves. We can but hope
these troubles will soon cease and that there will be a true
union of her peoples. This will be necessary if—as is likely
—she is overwhelmed by a greater power.

# CONTENTS

# PROLOGUE

THE crocodile walked, as sedately as the blustering wind permitted, along the parade. A dark reptile, sharply articulated, it crawled along the strip of asphalt that separated the pearly wind-blown sky and pallid sea from the greys and duns of the town. To closer view it was plain that the reptile was divided into living sections; two and two the girls struggled along, be-ribboned sailor hats bent forward, brown kid-gloved hands clutching at the rims; heavily-swathed and many looped dresses of blue serge blown against those moving pillars of flesh and bone that were never called legs, but referred to as lower limbs.

Two and two, as alike to a casual and distant glance, as toy soldiers out of a box, all were sharing the same physical sensations of stinging eyelids, swaddled bodies, a slight emptiness of stomach, and the coolness of the wind that blew upon salty lips and made the tongue taste again and again of that sharp little flavour.

A nearer glance, and the toy soldiers could be seen to differ each from each, though a certain unmistakably British look would have protected them—with one exception—from the supposition that they could belong to any other nation. Round faces, pointed faces, blobby faces, dark girls, fair girls, clumsy or graceful girls, all bore the stamp of nationality, so hard to analyse, so impossible to mistake. Only one girl, about the middle of the crocodile, walking with a high-boned British creature whose bright blue eyes of a fierce purity made her almost beautiful, showed traces of strange origins, and that was not so much in her colouring —her hair was no blacker than that of a Highland girl who followed after—as in the slant of her dark liquid eyes, the slight flattening of the nose—not a negroid but rather an Egyptian flattening, purely straight in profile—and in some-

13

thing almost inhuman in the fine bird-like lightness and delicacy of the bones of her face and of her whole frame. Yet even she, to the casual glance, held only a fugitive strangeness, no sooner caught than merged in the blue-serge undulating length of the monster. For though, at close range, the girls could be seen as recognisable individuals, their alikeness still seemed stronger than any difference . . . and yet, beneath each stiff sailor hat was that sharp point of consciousness which is *I*, that in every one of them would persist inescapably for a lifetime. . . . And with, yet beyond, the general shared sensations of the moment, there went on, behind the different faces, the knowledge of that *I myself* who informed each one. Each one was conscious, within the varying degree of her capacity for awareness, of the same physical sensations. . . . I feel the wind and the heavy clothing and emptiness, my nose is cold, how good tea will be, even the thick chunks of bread and butter old Patterson gives us, and perhaps there will be potted meat, Lazenby's, I hope. And the ringleted, pretty, rather chinless Maude: Perhaps I shall get a few minutes' talk with Miss Simpson. . . . I can think of some excuse. . . . I'd rather own up to something I haven't done— I can invent something—so that she scolds me, than not talk to her at all. It's rather thrilling being scolded by Miss Simpson, it makes me go sort of queer and trembly. . . . I wonder if Milly will help me with my prep. sums if I help her with her history and English? . . . And Milly: I wonder if Maude will help me with my history and English if I do her sums for her? She will if only she's not too taken up with Miss Simpson . . . how anyone can rave on a music mistress! Anyway, let's hope there'll be something extra for tea.

Thus the *I myself* that was Maude and the *I myself* that was Milly, while that of Ellen said, through her present physical sensations and her preoccupation with tea, something slightly different. . . . And perhaps cake, but anyway I do hope I get a few minutes at " Under Two Flags " afterwards. I can carry it to the lavatory in the folds of my polonaise and read it till there've been two rattlings at the door-handle; it's not safe beyond that. I wish it didn't make my heart beat so, I know my cheeks are scarlet when I

come out.   But Ouida's all right, I can't see why people make
such a fuss over her.   Everyone knows people fall in love.
I know I shall fall in love simply tremendously myself.
It's much better to read Ouida, even if it's forbidden, than to
read all the bad parts of the Bible like that little beast Minna
does, looking as though butter wouldn't melt in her mouth.
And then to talk about it afterwards like she does.   I wonder
if it's true what she says.   I don't think I want babies if it is.
But I'm sure Father and Mother can't have been like that.   I
expect Minna's got it wrong somehow.

And Minna, the demure reprobate, walking along with
that perpetual sneer on her full lips. . . . I hope Mother
lets me leave and come out soon; they're all so stupid here.
But it was great fun getting that note from the boy at Dr.
Hargreave's . . . if I can manage to meet him it would be
something to amuse myself with and to hint about to the
other girls.   Oh dear, how stupid they all are!   It's a shame
to keep me here; I'm a woman really, I know I am.   I have
to wear real shaped corsets, and the others only wear Rational
bodices, except Molly, and she's so fat it doesn't count.

If only, thought Agatha Lumsden, the fair girl walking
with the dark Francesca, I could convert Fanny, how wonderful it would be!   I *do* think religion the most important thing
in life, and I can't help it if I know I'm the most spiritually-
minded girl in the school.   It's all very well for Fanny to say
she's a Roman Catholic, and of course I know the Roman
Catholics are a branch of the Catholic Church, though in
schism, but I don't really think she's any better than a heathen.
She doesn't mind which church she goes to, and often she
pretends to have a headache and gets out of going to any.

And Fanny?   Fanny walking along so demurely, managing
her unruly draperies with so much more skill than was
achieved by any of her companions.   What thoughts went on
behind that ivory face and lay in those sleepy eyes?   Her
vague musings were perhaps even more shapeless than those
of the other girls.   Not one of them had been taught how to
think; it was a mere stream of more or less gently-rippling
consciousness that flowed through their undeveloped and
undirected brains; a series of pictures in which each saw her-

self in thrilling or picturesque situations. Fanny was no exception. Her strangeness was physical and moral rather than mental. Her dreams were bolder, cruder, more rapacious, more vivid, but not more coherent than those of her schoolmates; her chief preoccupation was to snatch the greatest possible amount of attention and approbation from life as she went through it, and many were the little plots she contrived at Miss Patterson's to achieve this end. Sometimes she made mistakes, bad mistakes, because though she insisted on her English blood, she was always finding herself at fault with the strange race. They had an odd way of resenting things that they called cheating, all except girls like Minna; but Minna was a stupid who made a lot of fuss over things that everybody knew, and even so got them all wrong. . . .

Fanny still had a bitter aching, like a sudden blow on her chest, whenever she remembered that dreadful time she had bought a piece of Oriental embroidery from the curiosity shop in Ship Street to give Miss Patterson on that august lady's birthday. She had escaped from the other girls and, running into the back of the shop, had bought the embroidery privily, with much haste. It would seem so much more important to give a present from herself alone, instead of subscribing to the cut-glass rose-bowl that was the school's offering.

"From Mandalay, Miss Patterson. My mother got it from the Palace, the King gave it her . . ." said Fanny, tending her gift, and feeling an Oriental princess herself as she did so. Miss Patterson had been impressed, and though she felt it her duty to imply that she preferred the girls to share and share alike in the matter of present-giving, still she called the others around her to point out the beauties of the embroidery and give a sketchy little lesson in geography deduced from it. To tell the truth, no one, not Miss Patterson herself, who "took" geography, had any but very vague ideas as to the position and history of Burma, till Fanny came to the school, and Fanny herself, daughter of an Italian father, and a mother half English, half Burman, was too much a child of no man's land to assist much in the clarification of Miss Patterson's ideas. Yes, Fanny, though accused by some

of her schoolfellows of " showing-off," had certainly scored a
success with that piece of embroidery . . . and then the shop
went and spoiled everything by appealing to Miss Patterson
for payment when Fanny's promised money from Mandalay
failed to materialise. Fanny was disgraced before the whole
school, and she had never forgotten or forgiven it. Only
Agatha had been kind to her, although Agatha had been
shocked. But Fanny knew she could always fascinate Agatha
whenever she chose.

" Fanny," said Agatha, struggling with the wind, her
words almost blown from her lips, " there's the house where
Constance Kent lived before she confessed. She was con-
verted by Father Wagner of St. Paul's, you know, where
I want you to come to church."

" Your church is so odd," said Fanny; " only you and
two of the others go to St. Paul's. Miss Patterson thinks it is
wrong."

Agatha flushed up even through the redness the wind had
brought upon her too-thin skin. She did not feel equal,
tired and hungry as she was, to explaining for the hundredth
time to Fanny the whole importance of the Anglo-Catholic
position. She said instead :

" Anyway, the religion of Father Wagner was able to do
what all the Roman Catholic convents abroad hadn't been
able to, though of course it's true they were French. It
made Constance Kent confess to the murder."

" What murder? " asked Fanny, interested.

" Why, didn't you know? Constance Kent murdered
her little half-brother because she was jealous of the second
family."

" Did she kill them all? " asked Fanny.

" Goodness, no! What a dreadful idea! She murdered
this little boy, and everyone in turn was suspected, the
nursemaid and even the little boy's father, and they all lived
under a cloud for years, till Constance went to confession to
Father Wagner and he wouldn't give her absolution till she
confessed publicly. Then she was sent to prison, and she is
very, very good there, quite saintly, they say."

" How silly to confess when nobody knew," said Fanny.

"But, Fanny, don't you see that she couldn't have gone on without confessing once she had seen the light?"

"In Burma," explained Fanny, "when a king dies, the next king has all the other brothers killed, so that he shall be safe on his throne.. If Constance Kent had only killed everyone, there would have been nobody left to mind, and then she would have been all right."

"Fanny!"

Fanny looked sideways at her friend and suddenly broke into her high tinkling laughter, the loveliest sound to be heard at Miss Patterson's and probably in the whole of Brighton. Like a peal of fairy bells, so Miss Simpson, the music mistress, described it. Certainly there was something oddly elfin and inhuman in it, lovely as it was. Agatha never failed to soften to it; it knocked at her heart after the loud guffaws or secretive sniggers of the other girls.

"Silly Agatha!" said Fanny, "you never know when I'm joking. My heart is very Christian really." And with a naturally dramatic gesture she laid one small hand over her heart.

Agatha smiled her relief—she never laughed just after Fanny if she could remember not to—and decided against telling Fanny that the word Christian had (rather unfortunately) a Protestant sound.

The crocodile made its last turn for home, and the streams of consciousness flowed on with it; eyes were less nipped by the wind in this street and weary hands could let go of hat-brims, but stomachs were every moment more clamorous for tea. Passion for Miss Simpson, passion for Ouida, passion for underhand experiences, passion for spiritual supremacy, all became merged somewhat in the imminence of tea. Each *I myself*, the most real person in the school, in Brighton, in the world, in all time up to this present year of 1875, wanted her tea, from the two little girls at the head of the crocodile to Miss Patterson and Miss Simpson at its tail. And the *I myself* that was Miss Patterson looked with pride at her lady-like girls, and through her mind flowed the pleasant knowledge that they were pure-minded, obedient, truly nice girls, and did her and their country credit.

There was potted meat for tea, though it was not Lazenby's. Maude had the felicity of sitting next to Miss Simpson, and so, half-regretfully, was able to abandon her plan of self-accusation. Ellen could snatch only a few minutes with her Ouida, but it was her bath night, and she looked forward to an uninterrupted ten minutes during which modesty would ensure her privacy, and as long as she kept splashing with one hand she would be thought to be washing while she was really holding up her book with the other. Minna found a giggling though fearful new girl to whom she imparted the story of the Levite and his concubine, in the broad light of the gas in the schoolroom.

"I'm helping Beatrice with her Scripture, Miss Patterson."

"That's right, Minna; I like to see the old girls give a helping hand to the new."

Fanny, ever indolent, found good excuse in a letter from her mother, of which she kept the actual script to herself, while disseminating, not without a little glorification, its news.

DEAR FANNY, (wrote her mother)

I have joy in telling you your father has been called to the Palace once more by the King and in the presence of the Ministers asked him do you repent, and your father, surprised, remained mute for a second or two for he knew he had committed no fault and only on the whispering advices of the Yenangyoung Mingyi and Myo-Woon U Thah Oh, Mayor of Mandalay, to say Yes, I have repented, so as not to displease the King, as otherwise he would annoy him, only to result in your father being forbidden to trade in Mandalay and sent away, your father was therefore obliged to say Yes, Your Majesty, I have repented. The King was very pleased, and ordered him to attend the Palace once more and next day sent for him and said, Moroni, don't be sore in heart at me. I never hated you, but my Ministers dislike you because you married a British subject and were friendly at the Residency and as there is a saying in Burmese— Thingan ga payah ma san hnain, which, as you know, if you have not forgotten your Burmese, Francesca, means, "Even

God cannot resist the power of the clergy," so I was therefore obliged to send you away to please them for the time being. Your father took the King's above sayings cum grano salis, for you know the craft of Burmese kings, and their manœuvring policy. But now your father has been allowed the revenue of the export tax on Burmese ponies at the rate of 20 rupees per head as well as salary for his work making velvet with Monsieur Delange, which he is now allowed to resume, and to take the Lac, worth about 30,000 rupees, from the Palace of the King's late brother to enrich himself, which is a good thing, because the expense of a Christian family is always more than those of a Burmese. Therefore your father thinks it is time you should come to Mandalay and be presented to the Queens, because it must not be said now your father is in favour that his daughter is with the English, but if you wish for more education you can go to the Convent of St. Joseph here. I have written to the good Miss Patterson and your father is sending money for your fare, first-class. You should travel with some nuns if that is possible, or with another lady, or with some officer's wife.

I am your loving mother,
MAI MYA MORONI.

Fanny looked round the bare schoolroom, where the flickering gas-jets played over the varnished maps upon the wall, and gave a little inner laugh of triumph. She was to leave all this, and take up life in the great gaudy Shway Nandaw, the Golden Palace of the City of Gems. . . . For she never doubted that she would penetrate those inner fastnesses, once she had been presented to the Queens. She would take them presents from Brighton, pictures of the Pavilion, artificial flowers, some woolwork for cushions. Secretly, Fanny considered everything English, except the Pavilion, to be hideous. Everything was so bare, so grey. She could vividly remember the great red walls that girdled the Royal City of Gems and were reflected in the lily-laden moat, could even, so she told herself, remember the red and gold and sparkling glass mosaic of the Palace itself, when she had been taken there as a tiny girl, before her father fell

out of favour. Rangoon had seemed dull after the perpetual excitements of Mandalay, with its processions and
feasts, and she had not minded coming to school in England.
But she had had enough of it; three years in Brighton . . .
and something in her blood leapt to the memory of the red-
and-gold Palace, and the crowded city beside the mighty
Irrawaddy. No going to the Convent of St. Joseph for her·
. . . she was a woman now by Burmese, even by Italian,
standards. She looked round with a sudden savage contempt
at schoolfellows and mistresses, so stiff and contented and
somehow thick-looking; they knew nothing, they never
would know anything—not of the things she knew already in
her blood and imagination. Poor Agatha! so like a rather
nice-looking sheep. . . . Agatha was nearly two years older
than she, for Agatha was seventeen, but what a child!

My father has been called to the Court of King Mindoon
. . . who has given him thirty thousand rupees worth of lac
and gold . . . my father has been given a high post at
Court—(no need to say he had been allowed, after five
years of disgrace, to go back to his weaving)—and I am to
go out and be presented and made a Maid of Honour. I
shall take presents for the Queens, of course—you shall
come with me and help me buy them, Agatha. They will be
sure to give me lovely presents, rubies and diamonds. Maids
of Honour get presents every day. To the best of her ability
Fanny presented these dazzling pictures.

The schoolroom was convulsed with excitement, discipline
was relaxed, Miss Patterson saw herself as the dearly-loved and
never-forgotten schoolmistress of a Maid of Honour. Agatha
said warningly:

"But, Fanny! Heathens!"

But even she could not but share in the general glow.
Only Minna tried to spoil things.

"A nigger court!" sneered Minna. "I don't think it's
much to be a sort of servant to nigger queens, who have only
one husband between them!"

But Miss Patterson, though slightly jarred at this dragging
into the open of the fact that the King of this court of Fanny's
was a polygamist, reproved Minna for speaking so ignorantly

of the friendly Kingdom of Ava.   Of course Buddhists were heathens, which was very sad, but what a chance for our dear little Fanny to carry on a glorious work of conversion. Fanny dropped her long ivory lids, while Agatha's blue eyes glowed.

And, a stuffless sound in that dull schoolroom and to those unattuned ears, did Destiny give a little laugh, lighter and more mocking even than Fanny's own?

# BOOK I

## CHAPTER I

## THE SHIP

NOTHING, thought Fanny, on board the S.S. *Bengal*, is like what you expect it to be. The weather had been rough till Sicily was passed, and Fanny had felt and looked like a sick monkey. Since then she had emerged in the sunshine, and was an attractive young woman, but in spite of her draped and fluted skirts, her hair caught up on the crown of her head save for the two sausage ringlets tied by a bow at the nape of her neck, and her grown-up airs, people would insist on treating her as a schoolgirl. That was partly Agatha's fault, of course. Agatha, who was so absurdly raw in spite of being in reality two years older. It had been a disappointment to hear that Agatha was to come too. She had been useful enough at school, but somehow the fact that she also was going to Mandalay to join her missionary father, who had been transferred there from Southern India, seemed to take the edge off Fanny's uniqueness—though of course it was a very different thing going out to a mere mission school, from going out to join your father when he was a great Court favourite and you yourself were bound to be summoned to Court. Still, there it was—undoubtedly the presence of Agatha, still full of interest in the dead-and-gone school-life and friends left behind, did drag into the exciting present much of the old Brighton atmosphere that had no longer any interest for Fanny. On the whole, how she'd hated it all . . . !

The female missionary—no officer's wife, alas!—who was chaperoning the two girls, was not liked even by the amiable Agatha, and was actively hated by Fanny. Mrs. Murgatroyd

23

. . . a harsh name and an ugly woman with a long pale nose, the end of which twitched all by itself, like the nose of a rabbit, when she was agitated. She said dreadful things, things that made you go hard and fierce and want to kill her. Don't try and show off, Fanny. You must remember that you're only an ignorant little girl. Let me see, Fanny, didn't I hear of a certain little girl who pretended that something she'd got at a Brighton shop had come from the Queen of Ava. . . . And that she didn't even pay for it? . . . I think that girl should watch herself very carefully and pray for grace to withstand the terrible tendency to dishonesty she has inherited. . . . If you were only blessed enough to be completely English how much less you would have of this untruthfulness and spirit of boasting! Of course it's not your fault, Fanny, and Heaven forbid you should be blamed for what is not your fault, that you have this temptation to tamper with the truth; Providence has seen fit to make you very largely a foreigner, and we all know what foreigners are, but it should make you very, very careful. . . .

The only consolation was that there were several gentlemen on board who took Fanny seriously as a young lady. There were the third officer and the stout Rangoon merchant at whom some of the other passengers sneered for being "eight annas in the rupee," but who knew how to amuse Fanny, and there were a couple of young men, going to Ceylon as tea-planters. They had all vied with each other in explaining to her all about the new Suez Canal as the *Bengal* passed through it. Mrs. Murgatroyd could say what she liked, but these people did not think of Fanny as a little schoolgirl. They thought her very beautiful and clever, and Fanny's heart swelled happily. Agatha disapproved, but, then, poor Agatha, though she was quite pretty when her nose didn't get pink, wasn't that sort of girl.

Fanny, coming into the cabin she shared with Agatha late at night, her ivory cheeks flushed, her eyes glowing, Fanny tingling with life, with the lovely sense of power and skill that meant life . . . made Agatha feel envious, yet censorious. She looks quite pretty, although her nose is so flat, admitted Agatha; but she's not *good*, not really, I'm sure. Looks don't

matter, it's the heart that matters; but it doesn't seem right
she should look so lovely . . . she isn't really, not if you pull
her to pieces; her face is too round and flat as well as her nose,
and of course she *does* look·foreign. . . . And the waves of
femininity that came out of Fanny seemed to pass over
Agatha's shrinking flesh, and she felt her mouth going tight
and hard. It was disgusting to be as Fanny was, so that she
made you think, do what you would, of all the things that
weren't nice. Agatha shook with anger at the sense of sex
that filled the little cabin on Fanny's entry.

" You've no business to be so late," she said sharply; " you
know Mrs. Murgatroyd doesn't like it."

Fanny hummed a little tune and broke off to say she didn't
care what Mrs. Murgatroyd liked. Old cat! Fanny
couldn't think how anyone had ever married her.

" It isn't right, Fanny; it isn't really. Fanny, what do
you *do* all this time on deck? "

" Oh, I talk; and they talk. To-night Mr. Jacobs showed
me the Southern Cross."

" Well, he ought to show it you by daylight."

Fanny's laugh rang out.

" Silly Agatha! It's *stars*. You couldn't see it by day."

" Well, you know what I mean. And Mr. Jacobs too . . .
he's so *fat*."

Fanny widened innocent eyes at her.

" What has that got to do with me? "

" Then you don't . . . he doesn't . . ." Agatha stammered.

" Oh, Agatha, what a goose you are! I suppose you
mean do I let him kiss me? "

Agatha blushed a slow painful blush that burned over her
fair skin. It sounded awful said right out like that. Fanny
thought for a second. Agatha would despise her if she knew
that Mr. Jacobs had kissed her, and she didn't like Agatha to
despise her, she liked her to envy her. Impossible to explain
to Agatha that there was something about the expert kisses of
fat Jacobs that was more pleasing than the kisses of the young
and handsome third officer. . . . Stout and middle-aged as
Mr. Jacobs was, he had a message for Fanny's flesh that the
younger man had not. Fanny, at the very threshold of

experimenting, found everything of interest, but it was no good trying to explain things to herself, let alone Agatha.

So—" Of course not, Agatha," she said indignantly.

Agatha stared at her, feeling a curious excitement.

" Fanny," she said, " Fanny . . . you . . . you don't *flirt*, do you, Fanny?"

Fanny nodded, dimpling.

" Oh, Fanny . . . how dreadful . . ."

They stared at each other in solemn excitement.

Yes, yes, thought Fanny, I'm going to have lots and lots of men in love with me. I'm always going to get everything I want. And she felt a lovely warmth that was tingling throughout her frame, she was aware of her flushed cheeks and her shining eyes, she was the most living thing in the whole world, she was Fanny. . . . And Agatha, the first shock of Fanny's avowal over, also felt a stirring of new interest, as though she were recognising something different about life for the first time. Was it possible that flirting— even that " it " itself provided, of course, you were married, mightn't be so very wicked and disgusting, after all. . . .? Of course we all had to come into the world somehow, or there wouldn't be any souls to save. It was all very confusing. Agatha was only vaguely aware of " something," the big, looming " something," that was never acknowledged by nice girls, but that was there all the time, in the background, waiting. . . . Of course if he were a good man that might make it all right; you had children and brought them up to be good Anglo-Catholics. . . .

Fanny broke the spell by beginning to let down the masses of her shining black hair. Agatha saw its silken folds slip like water over Fanny's slight shoulders and pour down below her waist, with a contraction of the heart. But——

" Oh, Fanny, your hair ! " she ejaculated generously.

She never could help it. Fanny's hair was magical. Fanny did not tell her that all over Burma peasant women might be seen by any wayside well with tresses as amazing. Perhaps Fanny had forgotten it in the wonder that her hair was to Brighton.

But the next night, when Fanny slipped into the cabin

with her hair already about her shoulders, the old anger welled up in Agatha. Fanny was disgusting, horrible. No nice girl would have . . . Agatha knew quite surely that a man's fingers had been playing with those soft silken strands, that must be so deep, so different from her own thin locks, to plunge into. . . . She found herself trembling, speaking icily, contemptuously. Fanny, ever wishful to avoid blame, tried to justify herself. The pins had slipped out, her hair was so heavy, it hadn't happened on purpose, and then it wasn't worth while putting it up again.

" You're lying," said Agatha furiously.

" Oh, well then," said Fanny, " what does it matter? You make such a silly fuss, Agatha. And anyway, you needn't pretend you're always so pi. What about the drawing you have in your Prayer Book? "

" Fanny ! What do you mean? Why . . ." Agatha began to stammer in her indignation as she remembered that her Prayer Book was always kept locked away in her glove-box with the Crystal Palace on the lid. Fanny must have deliberately stolen the key from the handkerchief sachet where it was kept and made an examination.

" It's easy to see you're not English ! " cried Agatha. " You've been prying in my things. What a dishonourable thing to do ! "

Fanny shrugged her shoulders.

" You shouldn't always pretend to be so good," was all she remarked.

Agatha rummaged in her handkerchief sachet with trembling fingers, found the key and unlocked the glove-box. There, under the gloves, lay the Prayer Book with the brass clasps; she seized it and opened it. The precious drawing was still there. It was a pencil drawing made by Agatha's own not too skilful fingers, and represented a young man in a clerical collar, over which drooped a long fair moustache. Beneath was written—" My Confessor."

Fanny, proceeding with her undressing, laughed a little maliciously.

" Did you think I had taken it? I don't want your young man, Agatha ! I can't bear clergymen."

"It's not anyone," said Agatha indignantly. "It's not my young man. How can you be so vulgar? It's just a drawing I made of someone I imagined."

Fanny, who knew that Agatha always spoke the truth, thought this still sillier. Not even a real clergyman!

"Don't you see," went on Agatha, "if it were real he wouldn't have a moustache? Priests shouldn't have moustaches. I only drew him with one because I've always thought of Sir Galahad with one."

"Who's Sir Galahad? I didn't know you knew any titled people, Agatha?"

"Oh, you don't know anything!" said Agatha impatiently; "it's no good being cross with you."

She tore the pencil drawing across and across and, going to the port-hole, dropped the fragments out into the darkness. Fanny, who disliked unpleasantness, cuddled up to her.

"I'm sorry I looked in your Prayer Book if you didn't want me to," she said, skilfully gliding over such matters as abstracting the key from the sachet and unlocking the glovebox. "I was hurt at your keeping it a secret from me. I thought it was a real young man, you see. And I have no secrets from you, Agatha . . ."

Agatha, wishing to believe this, felt her face first melt and then re-set into its mentor look.

"You're such a child, Fanny," she murmured, feeling that to treat Fanny's triumphs as the harmless escapades of a child was the best way to get out of having to envy her as a woman. "You're so dreadfully thoughtless and unwise."

"Oh, am I? Everyone doesn't think so, I assure you. Gentlemen don't think so."

"Don't be so silly and conceited. None of the gentlemen worth anything talk to you, only a vulgar merchant like Mr. Jacobs and those silly boys. You couldn't get anyone like Mr. Danvers to talk to you if you tried."

A dreadful pang shot through Fanny as she thought of the grave, clever, important Mr. Danvers and realised the truth of what Agatha said. From a sense of power she fell swiftly upon a knowledge of utter futility, of an inescapable cheapness. Her lips quivered. Her eyes brimmed with tears. Aloud she said :

" Oh, he's dreadfully dull, Mr. Danvers. I should not bother to talk with him ! "

And to herself she vowed that Mr. Danvers should be seen talking to her as soon as, she could manage it. Mr. Jacobs, whose thick hands had trembled so in her loosened hair, the young planters, the handsome third officer with his uniform, ceased to interest her, they were nothing, she felt. Mr. Danvers was in the Indian Civil Service and an important man. Agatha should see . . . but in her heart she felt that Mr. Danvers would not care twopence about her, and she hated Agatha for having made her face such a disagreeable truth.

## CHAPTER II

# THE DHOW

THE scorching rocks of Aden lay twenty-four hours astern, and the S.S. *Bengal* was well out into the Indian Ocean, the bleak, dry mountains of Arabia making a faint purplish pattern away to port. A storm had only been missed by a couple of days, and the sea still ran with a long swell; it was the hour before sunset, and the shadows lay long and dark upon the decks, whose whiteness was tinged with gold by the evening light.

Suddenly, in the telepathic manner in which things become known on board ship, word flashed round amongst the passengers that the course had been altered, that " something " had been seen . . . the *Bengal* was making for it, whatever " it " was. Field-glasses were fetched, ladies asked a dozen questions of any man within sight, touchingly confident that gentlemen know everything at sea. Fanny, running to the rail, stared with the rest.

A dark dot marked the sunlit waters far ahead, and people stared alternately at it and at the navigating bridge, where the Captain directed matters. What is it? Can you see it yet? Is it an open boat? Oh, I wonder if there are people dying in it. . . . Presently the *Bengal* slowed down, and it became apparent that the object was not that romantic thing, a ship's boat laden with castaways, but a native dhow, her sail down, rolling on the swell. It was, however, still permissible to hope that all on board her might be dying, and as the *Bengal's* engines stopped everyone redoubled the effort to see all that was to be seen. Fanny, small and fragile, was being elbowed out of her place at the rail, when a genial voice said:

" Too bad, little girl. Let me give you a helping hand."

And Mr. Jacobs, breathing down the back of her neck, placed his two hands about her waist and lifted her up so that her feet rested on the second rail.

"Lean over. I won't let you fall," he advised.

Fanny, giggling, left herself in his grasp and leaned well forward. The dhow was now rolling on the pale burnished green of the swell about a hundred yards away. Although an open vessel of not more than fifteen tons, she was crowded with people. As the *Bengal* hailed her, two negroes, naked save for their loin-cloths, dropped from her gunwale into a tiny dug-out, and started to make for the steamer. The negroes, paddling with long, strong strokes, called in English:

"Water! Water! We wanting water!"

Water . . . Water! The classic ever-dramatic cry rang thrillingly through the evening air.

"Water! Poor things! They want water . . ." said everyone, much gratified.

The inevitable passenger who knows everything declared that the crimson flag fluttering from the dhow was the flag of Zanzibar, the passenger who always contradicts maintained it was merely a signal of distress. In the bows of the dhow a tiny boy sat huddled up, twelve other people, one a woman, crowded the thwarts, a tall, bearded man clad in flowing white robes gave the impression of being in authority.

An accommodation ladder had been swung overboard from the *Bengal*, the first officer, down in the waist, leaned over the bulwark, a crowd of deckhands and coloured third-class passengers around him. The tiny dug-out reached the ladder, but there it rocked so upon the swell that it perpetually filled with water, and there was no possibility that it could bear back a cask in safety. The end of a hawser was dropped overboard and the two negroes started to paddle back, towing it to the dhow. But the heavy hawser dragged at them, acting like a sea-anchor, so that they could make no progress. Suddenly a man on board the dhow, not troubling to remove his scanty dress, dived into the sea and swam to their assistance. The hawser was made fast and the dhow pulled alongside the steamer. All this had taken the best part of half an hour, and it had become increasingly and disappointingly plain that the occupants of the dhow were in no distress whatsoever. The man in the white garment took it off and changed it for one of pale blue, the solitary woman cunningly pulled her veil to one side the better to see and to be seen. A skin of water and a great sack of rice and two of bread were lowered into the dhow. The occupants called out their thanks, the first officer replied curtly, and the dhow hoisted her lateen sail and drifted away on the darkening swell. The *Bengal's* engines began to throb once more.

At first Fanny had thoroughly enjoyed the episode. It was fun being held up by Mr. Jacobs, and fun wondering whether the people in the dhow were all dying. Then something had happened to spoil her pleasure. She suddenly realised that the quiet man next her at the rail was Mr. Danvers, and that she, who wanted to impress him, was being practically cuddled by the Jacobs man, and that she had squealed and enjoyed it. As she wriggled forward to watch the dug-out at the foot of the ladder, she had pressed against her neighbour, who had drawn a little aside, glancing down at her as he did so. It was then that she saw it was Mr. Danvers, and she fancied she saw contempt in his grey eyes.

" I'll get down, it is all silly," she told Mr. Jacobs curtly. " I don't believe they really want anything at all."

" I expect they wanted to look at you, little girl," said Mr. Jacobs, retaining his clasp about her waist, and holding her where she was, " or maybe they've got out of their course or something like that. What do you think, sir? "

Fanny hated him for saying " sir " to Mr. Danvers, but she felt excited when Mr. Danvers turned his head and spoke pleasantly.

" They often do this hold-up in these waters. These dhows trade and carry passengers between the east coast of Africa and Arabia, and they count on this sort of pick-me-up assistance. They'd probably got plenty of food and water stowed away under the thwarts, but . . ." and Mr. Danvers broke off with a shrug. He caught Fanny's puzzled gaze and his face relaxed into a smile.

" What are you puzzling your head over? " he asked her, speaking as to a little girl. Fanny realised with a rush of relief that he was of the class of men to whom she would still be a little schoolgirl, nothing but a child. How silly she had been to confound him with those others! . . . Why, it was even all right Mr. Jacobs holding her like this; she was only a nice forward little girl.

"It seems funny a big ship like this bothering to stop," she answered in a voice that was like a little child's, half-eager, half-shy. "They're only negroes, and this is a mail-ship with heaps of important people on board."

Mr. Danvers paused a moment or so before replying, as though he were thinking how to put what he wanted to say in the simplest language.

"That's not what matters," he explained at last. "It's the law of the sea never to refuse assistance to another vessel. A handful of niggers can hold up a ship of the line if they want anything. How important you are doesn't matter a bit. Life is life. It's taken nearly an hour of our time, and perhaps they could have got along without food, but we mustn't risk that. The law must always be obeyed for its own sake."

"Is it a law like in Parliament?" asked Fanny, bewildered.

Mr. Danvers stared at her and then laughed, and Fanny had an uncomfortable feeling that they were talking different languages. Yet at the back of her mind new ideas were struggling towards the light. Vaguely she became aware, through the very fact that she did not understand, of the existence of modes of thoughts and conversation unknown to her. She thanked Mr. Jacobs for his help, still in that childish voice, and slipped away. Perhaps, thought Fanny gropingly, there are plenty of people like Mr. Danvers and perhaps they're better than the other sort. . . . She struggled painfully with the notion. She knew he would not have asked her to let her hair down in the shadows of the boat-deck . . . the awful cheap feeling came over her again. Yet he hadn't thought her cheap; all her experiences since she came on board were hidden from him, she was a nice little schoolgirl. Pretty, he must think her that. But he was in the Civil Service . . . did he . . . did he think of her as coloured? She thrust the idea away; it was not one that the circumstances of her life had forced unkindly upon her notice. Hitherto her " difference " had been a source of distinction.

That evening she went to bed when Agatha did, and mentioned casually as she undressed that she had had such a pleasant conversation with Mr. Danvers.

" He's not a bit stuck-up really, Agatha. He told me all about the boat and why it stopped."

" They wanted water."

" Not really. It was us that *had* to stop. That's the law of the sea. He explained it all to me."

Fanny went to bed, proud that she had impressed Agatha. If only she had left it at that! The shame and misery of the next day she always tried to forget, but it was a long time before it ceased to come up in her mind, like that dreadful day when she had been found out about the present for Miss Patterson.

Mr. Danvers was lying in a long chair close to hers, talking politics, dull government stuff, with a judge who wore grey whiskers. Fanny listened, but idly, just for the pleasure of hearing Mr. Danvers' cool, quiet voice.

" Lytton ! " Mr. Danvers said doubtfully. " I can't believe he is the man for India, or that Salisbury is the right man for Secretary of State. It isn't that they aren't both clever, they're brilliant, but even that may be a danger."

" Lytton's charming," said the judge, " perfectly charming. I met him when I was home last time—the most delightful fellow, and his essays are really good. I do a bit in that line myself, you know, Indian stuff, and I think very highly of Lytton's."

" Well, we shall see; but I was a great admirer of Northbrook's common sense. He never flew off at a tangent; he relied upon facts and on his own experience, and he acted accordingly. He saved us from another war with Afghanistan. Lytton and Salisbury will be more go-ahead, and I don't believe that any good comes out of these Afghan wars."

The judge snorted rather indignantly. " Got to keep these people in their place, you know," he said.

"And what about our place?" asked Mr. Danvers. " I

don't see that by any possible argument you can make ' our place ' stretch as far as Kabul."

Fanny's thoughts wandered, but she pricked up her ears again when the talk veered to King Mindoon, though it was dull stuff, all about the King and some French statesmen, that they discussed. Fanny, in a crisp white muslin decked with rose ribbons, was lying back on her wicker-chair, her usual little court about her; Agatha, sitting on its out-skirts, hardly shared in the glow. Often afterwards Fanny wondered what on earth had taken hold of her; part of her mind told her she was being stupid, and yet she couldn't stop. She heard her own clear loud tones beating about like birds, forcing themselves on the attention of Mr. Danvers. Perhaps it was that she felt no longer the little girl that day, but instead knew a return of that swelling confidence, that exhilaration, she had felt when admitting to Agatha that she was a flirt. She knew just what she must be looking like, her small, dark, sleek head against a scarlet twill cushion, the bangles dangling on her small, fine wrists, as she gesticu-lated with her little ivory hands, her long dark eyes, glancing upwards from beneath her thick upcurving lashes. She knew she made the pretty girls, the fair-haired, pink-and-white English misses, seem thick and clumsy, and the knowledge pleased her. She knew that this particular morning she was looking at her best and had the delicious feeling that every-thing was just right about her, that her finger-nails looked bright and shining, and the brilliant light of the Indian Ocean could find no flaw in her pale skin, that her frock fitted her slender bust and small waist and flowed out below in just the right way. All conspired to give her that sense of excitement in which hitherto the voyage had been so disappointing. Her eyes were shining, her voice was animated, her light-hearted laughter charmed her own ears, she was holding the little group of men enthralled. The story that had had no encouragement since leaving school came to her lips once more. She built up by vivid touches that life at the Palace which she had been far too young on leaving it to remember.

"Of course, it'll be easy for me," she said lightly; "my father is such a great friend of the King's. Only the other

day the King gave him sixty thousand rupees, and he goes
to the Palace every day.   Of course, they'll want me to be a
Maid of Honour, but I'm not sure I should care about it.
There'd be so little freedom, rather like going straight from
one school to another, wouldn't it be? "

And Fanny screwed up her face and gave what she felt
was a delightful pout.   The heroines in the books that
Fanny read drove men to despair by the simple art of pouting.
None of the gentlemen seemed affected other than pleasur-
ably, however; they laughed and the Rangoon merchant said
something to the effect that he would turn schoolmaster if
Fanny would be his pupil.   Fanny pouted again and went on
happily :

"I suppose if the Queen insists on it I shall have to live in
the Palace, but I think I'd rather stay with Papa; after all I
expect he'll be able to manage it, he is a sort of Minister, you
know, not quite Prime Minister, but something like that, and
enormously powerful."

" What nonsense you talk, Fanny," said Mrs. Murgatroyd,
the female missionary, suddenly appearing round a ventilator
like a bad fairy in a pantomime.   " I'm afraid you're a
very boastful, untruthful little girl.   Your father is a weaver,
and works at his looms all day.   I've a good mind to keep
you in your cabin for telling such untruths."

The world, the beautiful blue-and-gold world of sea and
sky, the snow-white and pearly shadows of deck and awning,
the white suits of the men and their laughing eyes, all seemed
to turn black about poor Fanny; her heart thudded as
though it would choke her, her slow burning blush seemed to
smother her like a hot blanket; in the agony that she went
through she would willingly have seen Mrs. Murgatroyd
struck dead upon the planking.   Even Agatha, who thought
it wrong to exaggerate, let alone tell lies, was sorry for Fanny
and indignant with Mrs. Murgatroyd.   Agatha, forgiving
Fanny all the snubs the latter had inflicted on her when
things had been going well, gathered the poor, damp,
hysterical little creature in her arms and comforted her in the
privacy of their cabin, but it was days before Fanny felt she
could laugh and joke again, and the consolation that she

eventually found in the arms of Mr. Jacobs on the boat deck was short-lived, for even there Mrs. Murgatroyd, the very shadow of doom, found her out.   As to Mr. Danvers, Fanny avoided him for the rest of the passage.

Altogether she was relieved when the ship entered the muddy waters of the Irrawaddy mouth and steamed up through the thick, yellow wavelets between the flat and ugly shores to the port of Rangoon.   And, with a catch of the heart, Fanny saw again the incomparably fluent line of the Shway Dagon, a burnished gold against the paler gold of the sky.   Christian as she was, at sight of that, some deep sense of inheritance in Fanny told her that she had come home.

## CHAPTER III

# THE RIVER

RANGOON seemed very large and busy and important, full of warehouses and shops and bungalows, its streets crowded with lacquered rickshas, in which Fanny delighted to ride, the frightened Agatha clutching her by the arm, while Fanny called to the boy in Burmese to go faster. There are few sensations of superiority as intense as being able to speak a language that one's companion does not understand.

At the Custom House at Rangoon Mr. Jacobs was claimed by a large, determined-looking wife, and Mrs. Murgatroyd handed Fanny and Agatha over to a teacher from the Church of England Girls' School, and in that uninspiring spot they passed their night in Rangoon. Fanny was all eagerness to visit the Shway Dagon, for she remembered as a tiny child the delightful feast days when she had been taken there by her` mother, although Mrs. Moroni was nominally a Christian. However, a glimpse of the lake from a ricksha the next morning, with the golden pagoda reflected in its waters, was as near to heathendom as was allowed. Then the girls were put upon a train in charge of the guard and sent up to Prome, beyond which the railways did not run. At Prome they were transferred to the river steamer of the Irrawaddy Flotilla Company, in which they were to journey to Mandalay.

The days of that trip up the river went by very pleasantly for Fanny. No more missionaries and school-teachers, only the guardianship of the Captain, Silas Bagshaw, a great, burly, red-faced individual, huge in frame, with a stentorian voice, husky from much bawling of orders. His vessel, the *Nemesis*, was a side-wheeler, very broad in the beam, but she carried with her, lashed along her starboard side, a huge two-decked

flat, roofed with canvas, which looked rather like Agatha's
notion of the original Ark. The flat was laden with ngapee,
dried fish which has been allowed to go bad, a great delicacy
beloved of the Burmans. Luckily it was cool weather, but
even so the smell of the ngapee was overpowering. Vegetables, live cocks and hens and large families of itinerant
vendors filled up what space the ngapee had left both on
board the flat and over most of the *Nemesis*. The vessel
acted as a travelling stores to the whole of the riverside
population, and every few hours the *Nemesis* would turn her
blunt nose towards the bank and make fast and throw out a
gangway, and the inhabitants of the village would swarm on
board; laughing, prosperous, good-natured people, apt at a
joke and a bargain.

" Very different up in the King's country," grunted Captain
Bagshaw. " All just as jolly, but they haven't got the money
to spend up there that our people have got in Lower Burma.
Up there each official gets a district to look after, and, as the
country folk say, he ' eats ' it. But you two young ladies
won't be interested in politics."

Fanny tossed her little head.

" Why not, Captain? I suppose you think that all ladies
care for nothing but dress; but, you see, my father is in
a high position at the Court, so naturally I'm interested in
anything to do with the Government."

" Your father's the Italian weaver, isn't he?" boomed
Captain Bagshaw. " An old friend of mine. I brought
*your* father up-river, young lady," with a nod to Agatha,
" when he arrived a month ago. Don't take much stock of
sky-pilots, but he seemed a good one."

Agatha flushed with pleasure; she had built up, in the
years of absence, and by dint of talking of him to the other
girls, a romantic notion of the Perfect Father, and she was
more than half in love with him already. Fanny, who had
no intention of letting the conversation be diverted in the
direction of the Lumsden family, leaned her elbows on the
rail and, cupping her chin in her hand, gazed up at the huge,
red-faced skipper.

" Tell me all about Mandalay," she begged.

Captain Bagshaw scratched the back of his bright red neck reflectively.

"Tell you all about Mandalay? You're asking something, young lady, it's the devil of a place, begging your pardon. The King's all right for an Oriental, but if he's not so bad as the others, he's not as good as some people make him out. I don't have anything to do with Courts, thank the Lord, I'm a simple sailorman, but I tell you I'd sooner navigate this river blindfold in the dry season, sandbanks and all, than I'd try and steer a course in that Palace. Everyone jumps about as though they were on hot bricks waiting to see what's going to happen. Oh, it's a lovely place and no mistake. Even the King blows now hot, now cold, and as to the others . . ."

"My father was out of favour for some years," said Fanny.

"I know he was, and for nothing at all; somebody made trouble and told a pack of lies. Your father's all right, if he *is* a foreigner, Miss Fanny. I used to see a lot of him down at Rangoon when he was in banishment. More fool he to have gone back, if you ask me, but of course there's pickings to be had in the Palace that you can't get anywhere else. Ah well, you'll find it all out for yourself."

"Shall we enjoy ourselves in Mandalay?" asked Fanny. "Will there be parties?"

The Captain screwed up his face.

"Well, there's not what you'd call much young society, you know. There's all kind of dagoes—excuse me, Miss Fanny—Frenchies and Italians and Greeks and Armenians and goodness knows what, and a fair amount of British. But there's not what you'd call much give and take, except among the missionaries. They give a few parties to each other."

Fanny wrinkled her nose in disdain, but Agatha said seriously :

"I don't want gaiety, I'm to help my father at the mission."

"Ah well, they all begin like that," said the Captain philosophically. "Look, young ladies, if you want to see a crocodile, there's one on that mud-bank."

That was an excitement indeed; they could not at first

believe it was not a log, but as the steamer went churning
past, the creature lifted up an ugly lip at them and crawled
into the yellow wash of waters with an angry flirting of its
scaly tail. Agatha was sickened at the evil that a crocodile
seems to exude, but Fanny was fascinated by the very horror
that it gave her.

It was certainly great fun, that trip up the Irrawaddy.
You soon got used to the dried fish after a few days of it.
Fanny loved it all; she loved the faint incense-like smell of
the little villages of an evening, the limpid glow of the river
and sky, the chattering of the cheerful people, the men with
pink and blue and green head-dresses and bright lungyis—
skirts of silk or cotton; the slender, pretty little Burmese
women with their oily black hair swathed in a high tower
round their heads. She loved the wailing cries of the two
natives of Chittagong who stood in the bows of the flat,
sounding the depth of the water all day long, with two poles
painted with bands of scarlet and white. Ceaselessly they
chanted the varying depths of the water in wailing voices
that sounded to her like the Catholic chants which she had not
heard for so long.

It was the spring of the year and already the jungle was
festooned with masses of flowers of a faint, dead pink and of
brilliant purple. Then jungle would give place to the
gleaming squares of water, pierced by thin emerald flames,
that meant paddy-fields; or here and there along the river
bank a pagoda would gleam whitely, looking to both the girls
like a gigantic wedding cake, and the sound of its bell would
come clear and distinct across the water. Then whenever
the *Nemesis* was heading for a village, six men, so dark as to
be a purplish black, almost decent even to Agatha's eyes,
although they were naked except for a tiny loin-cloth,
would spring over the side, one of them with the ship's
hawser between his strong teeth, and they would swim with
powerful overarm strokes to the bank and haul the *Nemesis*
in till her stern was on shore. Then would come the chattering natives, swarming round the little booths on board, and
sometimes the girls would stay and watch, sometimes, if
Captain Bagshaw could accompany them, they went for a

little walk in the village and saw the merry, brown babies
playing in the dust, saw the youths playing chin-loon with
balls made of basket-work, their laughter going up into the
still evening air with the sweet smell of the wood smoke.
Back to the *Nemesis* and to supper by the light of a kerosene
lamp, in whose rays big moths and little moths fluttered like
scraps of silver. The chain would be grindingly wound in
once more, the paddles would begin to revolve, threshing the
black water into a gleaming pallor, the leadsmen would
take up their melancholy chant and the *Nemesis* feel her way
into midstream, where again the anchor would be let go with a
noise like thunder, so that she could lie safely for the night.
For those merry, pleasant people could not be trusted, once
the northern border of Lower Burma was passed, not to
attempt a little dacoity in the night-time; and vessels found
it more prudent to anchor in midstream.

So at last they came to Mandalay, and the six men swam
ashore once more with their dripping burden, the stern was
hauled in-shore and the anchor-chain ran through the hawse-
pipe, the gang-plank was thrown out and Fanny's journey had
come to an end.

Papa—as Fanny thought it genteel to call him, though he
himself preferred the homely Italian Babbo—was waiting
at the top of the high mud-bank. Fanny recognised him at
once by his dark, pointed beard, and pointed him out to
Agatha. There was another European with him, a thin,
white-faced man, who wore coloured glasses and had slightly
prominent front teeth. Agatha realised with a pang of disappointment that this was her father; she had managed to
forget those teeth in the years she had been away. . . . Both
the Reverend Arthur Lumsden and his daughter were a little
shy; not so Fanny and Mr. Moroni. Agatha envied them
the naturalness of their embrace; perhaps there was something in not being altogether English, after all. . . .

The moment arrived when, the luggage duly separated,
the girls had to get into their respective bullock-wagons.
Agatha parted from Fanny with a little pang; she would
rather have gone with her, she felt, than with this father so
unlike the idea she had built up of him. But Fanny, all

excitement and readiness for the new life, climbed skilfully,
with a wriggle of her supple little body, over the backs of
the bullocks, into the brightly-painted cart. Agatha was
helped into her conveyance with much more difficulty.

Mr. Moroni's bullocks were first away and set off at a
brisk trot over the atrocious road, a mass of holes and dried
ruts a foot deep, that led from the river bank through the
straggling town. Immediately a cloud of dust rose into the
air, a cloud that accompanied everyone who moved about
the town of Mandalay during the dry season, as though each
vehicle belonged to the Israelites (many of them did), and
the pillar of cloud was once more performing its useful
function. Fanny, her little hand through her father's arm,
looked out eagerly, and now it was her turn to be disappointed. How sordid and shabby it all looked! Little
one-storied wooden houses, great patches of waste-land,
masses of cheap little booths . . . Mr. Moroni noticed her
expression.

" You mustn't mind all this, Francesca; this is the town
of the kalās. We're kalās," he said, with his fine, dry smile.
" All foreigners are kalās to the Burmans. English, French,
Italians, Indians, everyone except the Chinese and Shans.
We all have to live outside the walled city."

He spoke English almost perfectly, but with slightly more
precision and care than an Englishman.

" Your friend seems a nice girl," he observed. " Though
quiet, like all the English."

" Agatha? Oh yes," said Fanny. " Look, Papa, there
are some poongyis; I remember them. Oh look, they're
holding up their fans so that they shan't see me."

" Buddhists are very like Catholics in many ways," remarked her father dryly.

Fanny gazed back at the group of orange-clad monks and
laughed.

" In Agatha's church the priests are allowed to marry,
though Agatha says she doesn't approve of it. I'm sure
that she'll marry a clergyman, all the same. What is her
father like, Papa? "

" He's a good man. He has come to take the place of Dr.

Marks. He will never be a great man as Dr. Marks is, but he may be easier to get on with because of that."

"Papa, tell me, has the King been nice to you? Is Mamma going to take me to see the Queens? Tell me."

Mr. Moroni shrugged his shoulders.

"He has forgiven me for something I never did, yes. That is to say, he found that Monsieur Delange and his daughter could not produce all the velvet and silk that he needs. But I do not complain; he is a good King as monarchs go. Even as a Garibaldino, I admit that."

Fanny, whose sympathies were instinctively anti-republican, made no reply, but continued to gaze about her. It was the time of the noonday rest, and quietness had begun to settle over the town of the kalās; in the shadow of a rest-house, ochre-robed priests were sitting in meditation, Indian shop-keepers were curled up on their straw mats, or lay pulling at their hookahs.

From a side road, heralded by a faint jingling of bells, appeared a caravan from China, some twenty-five shaggy, rusty, stocky little mules, laden with great bales; they passed the bullock-carts, their hoofs making a pattering sound like heavy rain on the thick, white dust of the road. Arrogant-looking men the Chinese were, beneath their huge pyramidal hats of golden straw, which cast a finer, clearer yellow glow over their bronzed faces. They stared in-solently at Fanny with their sidelong eyes, deep-set above high cheek-bones. Their lips, vermilion with betel-nut, looked as though slobbered with blood. Beside them ran their fierce chow dogs, shaggy and panting. The procession turned off on to a piece of waste-land and the men began to unsaddle.

"Oh!" cried Fanny. "At last . . ." and pointed.

"Yes," said Mr. Moroni, his eyes also resting on the great rose-coloured walls beyond the wide, lily-laden moat that Fanny had seen. "Yes, there it is. That's the true city, Francesca; not this town of kalās. That is the Gem City of Mandalay, and in the heart of it is the Golden Palace, and around it we all sit, waiting, hoping and struggling."

Fanny hardly heard what her father was saying, she was

gazing with the whole of what soul she possessed in her eyes, and indeed nothing stranger and lovelier than the Gem City of Mandalay could be found upon the earth. The high rose-red walls, crowned at intervals by soaring spires with upcurving pagoda-like roofs, stretched all along above the moat, which shone in limpid patches between out-flung masses of pink lotus. And moored all along the gleaming leafy mile of water were golden barges with high prows, decked with golden dragons that sparkled and glittered in the sunlight till they were mere twinkling points of light in the far distance, points that gleamed like flame against the soft blue of the Shan mountains. Beside the moat the turf was a vivid strip of green, dappled with shade from the dark clumps of mango-trees that hung their heavy pointed leaves in the still air. Farther down the moat a bridge, washed a dazzling snow-white, spanned the lily-strewn water. As Fanny gazed, the deep notes of a gong sounded from beyond the rose-red walls.

"That's the watchman striking the hour on the clock tower opposite the Palace," said Mr. Moroni.

"And you go in there every day?" whispered Fanny.

"Every day. Don't worry, my little Fanny, you'll get in too. You'll be in good company. Catholics and Pro-testants, priests and nuns and clergy all spend hours every morning sitting there in the hopes of getting something out of royalty. But now, Fanny, we must turn away and go on to our own home."

The bullock-wagon lumbered down a side-street and then passed in at the usual shabby compound, though it was gay, as many of them were, with tamarind and mango trees. Mrs. Moroni, large, brown and overflowing, in rather a dingy wrapper, was waiting on the verandah steps.

## CHAPTER IV

## JULIE

THE days that followed were a disappointment to Fanny. She was not, and never had been, accustomed to luxury; the Brighton school, apart from the much-ornamented parlour in which parents were received, had been plain and uncomfortable enough, but even so the standard set had been higher than that obtaining in the Moroni household. The bungalows for kalās in Mandalay were simple wooden buildings standing in compounds of trodden earth, where tamarinds and mangoes might grow, but where nothing more solid than a frail fence gave any privacy or sense of a garden, for no house was allowed to be so enclosed that it might be capable of being fortified.

The roads, though well designed in that they were straightly laid out at right angles to each other, and shaded with trees, were mere rough tracks pitted with great holes, and the bullock-carts that were the only means of conveyance were the most painful affairs, with rude wheels often worn quite out of the round, and axles that screamed and wailed for lack of oil. All day long this wailing of the bullock-carts rose and fell, till the ear grew so accustomed to the noise that the nights seemed mere empty spaces to echo the dreadful intermittent barking of the wretched pi-dogs. Fanny was young and healthy, her nerves were excellent, but the sordidness of her surroundings depressed her. Her mother, in that perpetual wrapper and bentwood rocking-chair. The messy meals of curry and rice. The flies that buzzed everywhere. The Indian servant, a Madrassee, whose black face never lightened from its gloom, so different from the cheerful bumptiousness of the Burman who acted as bullock-driver. Yet perhaps, observed Moroni, in his usual dry manner, a Madrassee was less likely to be a spy in the pay of the Palace than a Burman. In no household were the kalās able to rid themselves of that ever-present dread. . . . Foreigners, above all the English, who had already, in the second Burmese war, wrested the rich Pegu province from Pagan Min, Mindoon's deposed brother, were suspect at the Court of Ava, although they were welcomed also for what they could bring of Western knowledge and arts. Moroni was an Italian, and Mindoon was for ever playing off the Italians against the French, and Moroni was at the moment high in favour, but his wife was half-English, and his daughter had been sent to England for her education. Besides, favour ran oddly at the Palace, he who was exalted to-day might be cast down to-morrow. Mindoon was not the bloodthirsty maniac that his brother Pagan Min and his father, Tharawaddy, had been, but he was of the unstable race of Alompra, quick-tempered for all his genuine piety and kindliness. The foreigners who came to Mandalay did so at their own risk, even when, like Delange and Moroni, they had come at the invitation of the King. An atmosphere of intrigue was all very well, Fanny felt her own mettle quite equal to that, but it must be amidst the traffic of the Palace, not in the straggling wastes of the town-without-the-walls.

On the third day of her stay Moroni brought back a note from the Palace for his daughter, who fell upon it with avidity. Her father watched her with his amused look that could not be called a smile and that always made Fanny feel faintly uneasy.

"It's only from Mademoiselle. From Julie Delange," he observed dryly.

Fanny felt a little pang of disappointment, but kept the bright excited look upon her face without faltering.

"From Mademoiselle Delange! How nice! Is she young, Papa?"

"Very old. Quite thirty!"

"Oh, dear! Still . . ." and she opened the note. "She invites me to come and take coffee with her this afternoon, Papa."

"Shall you care to go? They live very quietly, you know, she and her father. Just a little French ménage."

" Oh, yes, yes.   Can I take Agatha? "

" Better not.   The French keep very much to their own people everywhere.   And the Delanges are Catholics.   They know the priest and the nuns from St. Joseph's.   The great Bishop Bigandet himself has stayed with them.   They have Burmese friends, too.   Although they live without the walls, they are in great favour at the Palace."

" Oh, of course I won't take Agatha.   She'd asked me to go round to tea to-day.   I shall send a note to say I have an engagement."

And Fanny went dancing off, happy for the first time since she had arrived in Upper Burma.

It was impossible not to feel the charm of the Delange house after the bungalow.   It was a brick building, cream-washed, built round a courtyard, with green shutters, and might have been transported straight from southern France. A vine grew over the walls, throwing upon them a delicate tracery of blue; cocks and hens walked in and out of the long, low living-room.   On a table covered with a checked cloth of white and yellow there was a coffee service of Sèvres ware and plates of pastries.   Two cobwebby bottles of wine stood beside a dish of oranges.   The evening sun shone in on all these pleasant things, and found bubbles and splinters of light on rounded surfaces and sharp edges.   Against the whitewashed walls hung brightly coloured prints of the Sacred Heart of Jesus, of the Empress Eugénie at the height of her glory at Compiègne, and of the Stabat Mater, her breast transfixed with a perfect galaxy of swords.   A photograph of the saintly Bishop Bigandet, the great Buddhist scholar and Catholic missionary, was upon a side table.   In the middle of the room Julie Delange stood to receive her guests.

She was not pretty, was Fanny's first thought, but she was very elegant.   She had had small-pox, and her colourless skin was slightly thickened and the outline of her fine features a little blurred.   Her eyes, soft and brown, looked weak, and she kept her lids screwed up, as though to see better.   She had a lovely smile, showing small even teeth, and she held herself erect save for a slight poking-forward of her head, which added to the impression she gave of peering. Her simple dress of fine grey silk woven by herself was beautifully cut and fitted her slender figure perfectly. Fanny felt suddenly gaudy in her frills and flounces of pink muslin.

Julie Delange was an important person in her quiet way in the strange cities both within and without the walls. Outspoken, with a flashing temper, yet supple and secretive when she chose . . . there were people who said that you never really knew Julie. She had the strength that comes of being able to eliminate oneself entirely from the conversation save as a listener; she was fearless but respectful in her dealings with the incalculable royalties, and she had never married, saying that she had no right to do so because of the perpetual menace of blindness that she felt creeping ever nearer. So much had Moroni observed to Fanny, talking to himself rather than to her, after his wont, as though he did not expect her to follow any subtleties of his thought. He had lived long with his wife. Fanny felt a little thrill of gratification when her quicker comprehension drew a more personal regard from his eyes.

Julie welcomed Fanny kindly, holding her hand between her own soft palms for a moment, when she introduced her to Delange, a white-haired, stout little Frenchman from the Midi. Two Sisters from St. Joseph's were there, Sœur Thérèse, the Superior, and Sœur Sophie. They talked among themselves, paying little attention to Fanny, and she listened eagerly, although she could not always follow their French, for all of their talk was of the Palace, of the illness of the Chief Queen; and of the Alè Nammadaw, or Centre Queen, Sinbyew-mashin—that, Fanny knew, was the Queen who befriended her mother—of her three daughters, the Big Princess, the Middle Princess and the Little Princess.

" Sinbyew-mashin will be Chief Queen yet," observed Julie. " There is no manner of doubt about it."

" Ah, and then she will start marrying off the Princesses," said Sœur Thérèse; " Sinbyew-mashin frightens me sometimes. She can be so gracious—only yesterday she gave me a ruby ring for my poor—and then next time I may sit for hours and word will come the Queen is not seeing anyone that day. She is a cruel woman; I saw her a few days ago in a rage with a Maid of Honour; she tore her hair down and beat her face with a slipper."

" She will do a great deal worse than that if she gets the chance," said Delange, handing the little cups of coffee that his daughter had poured out. " Heaven send that the King has a long life. After him . . .! " And he gesticulated with the tray in a manner that drew a reproof from Julie.

" Who will be King after him? " asked Fanny innocently. The others looked at each other.

" My child," said Moroni, " that is not a question we ask here in Mandalay. Not aloud, that is. No one asks themselves anything else in private. Who indeed? It's not a case of the eldest son, as it is in Europe; the King can choose whom he pleases, and he has many sons."

" And many daughters," said Delange. " Since the King must marry his sister, that is of importance too."

Fanny, who had been too young when she left Burma to have assimilated this fact, was shocked. Moroni smiled.

" They only follow the custom of the greatest civilisation in the world. The Egyptian rulers did the same thing. Whether it's a good plan, considering the madness in the Alompra dynasty . . ."

" The Salin Princess is the King's favourite," said Sœur Thérèse; " he believes, in his heathen fashion, that she is the re-incarnation of his mother. They say that when she was taken into the room of the King's mother, which has been kept sealed ever since her death, she was able to tell them where everything was kept, where the silk dresses were, and what jewels were in the jewel-box. Since then the King has been certain it is the voice of his mother speaking."

" She's a strange little thing," said Julie; " so grave and quiet. But it's certain that whoever is King afterwards, she is to be Queen."

Mrs. Moroni, who had maintained her customary placid silence hitherto, and had occupied herself in disposing of a great many little cakes, now broke in with unusual finality.

"If Sinbyew-mashin becomes Chief Queen, then the little Salin Princess will never be a Queen. It is the daughters of Sinbyew-mashin that will be Queens, perhaps all of them. You do not know the Alè Nammadaw Queen as I do. People will have to do as she chooses if she outlives the King, I know."

"Perhaps, perhaps," said Delange nervously, for Mrs. Moroni had spoken in Burmese. "Julie, perhaps Mademoiselle Moroni would like to look at some of your silks, eh?"

While Fanny was thus engaged, the nuns took their departure and a new visitor arrived. He was introduced as Monsieur d'Avera, and Fanny felt at once that, elderly though he was, he was much better worth her attention than Monsieur Delange. This was no little bourgeois, but a French aristocrat, and even his shortness and excessive stoutness did not detract from his dignity. His grey imperial was neatly trimmed, a red ribbon was in his buttonhole, his manner as he bowed over her hand made her feel she was already at Court. No one with any knowledge of the world would have mistaken M. d'Avera for anything than the finest type of French gentleman if he had met him in the middle of the desert, and that even if, as at the present moment, he carried under one arm a couple of bottles wrapped in old newspaper.

Was it imagination or did Fanny see the tiniest little glance of dismay pass between Julie and her father? M. d'Avera, with a beaming smile, laid the bottles on the table. "A little present, Mademoiselle Julie," he announced, "from my own vineyard."

A resigned look appeared upon the faces of father and daughter, but it was only for a moment. They thanked him warmly and with every appearance of sincerity. The three men began almost insensibly, despite their courteous manners, to talk amongst themselves. M. d'Avera had had a mail from France.

"It is my belief, my friend," remarked M. d'Avera, who had by now removed the cork from one of his bottles, and filled from it several glasses that Julie had brought him with an expression even more inscrutable than usual upon

her pale countenance, " that the Assembly is soon going
to break up. What is this?—the beginning of February.
Soon, you see, we shall hear of trouble. Ah, if only the
Legitimists and Orleanists could have settled their differences,
we should have had a king on the throne of France by now."

" A king!" said Moroni, in his dry voice charged with
scorn, " the Comte de Chambord! A man with a mind as
narrow as his nose. I can't believe that even your MacMahon
would support him, or the Comte de Paris either."

" You must not forget, Monsieur," replied d'Avera rather
stiffly, " that MacMahon, although, like myself, to serve
France he fought under the Empire, is a Royalist; and that
the hope of all of us, when he was made President, was that
he would be able to hold France together until we could
present a king. He is a man of strict honour and will endeavour, I feel certain, to continue the policy with which he
has been entrusted."

" He will continue it to the best of his ability," remarked
M. Delange, " and, after all, our new constitution, our
famous constitution of only last year, combines the Republic
and the Monarchy and the Empire. Napoleon's administra-
tive system, republican principles and a constitutional ruler
subject to the deputies, will be the result of it all. It is already
the result. What does it matter what you call your figure-
head, king, emperor, or president? It is the constitution that
matters."

" No, no, my friend," said d'Avera, " we," and he tapped
himself lightly on the breast, " in France have been planning
a constitutional government, but it was to be a monarchy like
that of England and Belgium."

" Bah!" grumbled Moroni, " you might as well frankly
adopt the Austrian ideal : temporal power, absolute monarchy
and the domination of the clergy. You succeed in nothing
because your factions all work against each other. When we
made United Italy we all pulled together, Royalists, and
Republicans, Piedmontese, and all."

" Yes, and we helped you," remarked d'Avera, " don't
forget that. I agree with Delange that the new constitution
may solve everything. I regret, naturally, the passing of

things that I and my ancestors have fought for, but MacMahon
and the Duc de Broglie have at least the right principles.
They are not like that wretch Gambetta."

" In Gambetta is the only hope for France in the long run,"
said Moroni.

" Permit me to disagree with you.   He gives himself all the
airs of a king without being one.   We should at least have the
advantages of a king if we have to have the disadvantages.
Pomp and colour,· everything that gives beauty to life, will
soon be gone, for there will be no more kings or emperors in
France."

" And a good thing too," grunted Delange, " what do
they ever do but bring about wars ? "

" Republics have been known to shed blood," observed
d'Avera dryly, " and there was always the Commune. . . .
But at least, my friend, as an honest tradesman you must
have admired the Second Empire for its prosperity."

Delange made a gesture of blowing something away from
between a snapped thumb and finger.

" Bah, the pasteboard prosperity, shattered by impossible
dreams of grandeur abroad and squabbles of politicians at
home.   Maximilian in Mexico and the Spanish woman in
the Tuileries—these two made an end of the tinsel.   That's
what the prosperity of your Second Empire was—tinsel."

" Very like the prosperity here," observed d'Avera.
" Perhaps that is why I am happier here than I should be
at home.   We have to come to the East for the pomp of
courts nowadays.   But my dear Delange, M. Moroni, you
are not drinking your wine," and the old gentleman lifted
up his own glass, and with a bow towards the ladies, emptied
it at one essay.   His friends bowed towards him, but only
sipped their wine.

Fanny thought all this sort of talk extremely dull, and
she was glad when Mr. Moroni made his farewells and took
his family home.   He laughed a little to himself as they
picked their way gradually down the uneven road.   It was
Sky-shutting-in time, and they wished to get home before
Brothers-would-not-know-each-other time descended with
its attendant dangers upon the kalā town.

"Why do you laugh, Papa?" asked Fanny, stumbling along to keep up with her father, and clasping both her little hands round his arm.

"I was only thinking," he told her, "of M. d'Avera. He is the finest and most honest man in Mandalay, with the exception of M. Delange. We have all quarrelled together for some years now; but, oh! saints in heaven, that dreadful wine of his!"

"What's the matter with it, Papa?"

"He makes it himself," groaned Mr. Moroni, "from his own vines. The last bottle he gave me I used instead of vinegar in the salad."

"They all seem to talk a lot of politics," observed Fanny. "I shouldn't have thought, Papa, that it mattered out here— what happens in France, I mean."

It was almost dark, but she could see her father's fine, quiet smile to which she was becoming accustomed, although it always made her faintly uneasy.

"It is what happens in France and perhaps in Italy, or even in Germany, that will determine what happens in Mandalay," said Mr. Moroni.

Fanny shook off such tiresome predictions. She was more interested and amused in the little story about M. d'Avera's wine than she was in the fate of European cabinets. She had met a lot of people; she had observed polite admiration in M. d'Avera's elderly but gallant eye. She went to bed happier than she had been hitherto.

CHAPTER V

# SELAH

THE following day Fanny went to tea with Agatha in the bungalow attached to the school of the English Mission. Any gaiety was better than none to Fanny just then, and the evening spent at Julie's had stimulated her social senses. She was quite excited as she walked along, the servant behind her. She was at the age when any chance to exploit her own personality was what mattered; a handful of missionaries, male or even female, might prove as admiring as anyone else. Indeed, it might even be that she could prove dazzling to missionaries. She had often had the delicious tingling that meant she was being a success, among the girls at school, or in the family of some girl who had taken her home to spend a half-holiday, and whenever she felt it she was happy. She walked gaily along, watching carefully where she placed her feet in their shoes of French kid, her parasol of scarlet throwing a rosy glow over her head and shoulders.

Agatha came running out to the verandah to greet her, and Fanny was struck by her prettiness. The warm climate suited Agatha's thin skin, which at Brighton had been so apt to turn red with the cold wind. Here her face had lost its pinched look, and the colour on her high cheek-bones was just enough and not too much.

I didn't know Agatha was so pretty, thought Fanny, and she felt a little sense of envy for Agatha's honey-and-rose colouring. Anyone could be dark out here. She, Fanny, had been distinctive in Brighton, but out here in Mandalay it was the blonde Agatha who might get the greater share of notice. Agatha's blue print gown softened the rather fierce flax-blue of her pure and candid eyes. Fanny stared at her a little resentfully.

" You don't look like a lady missionary," she observed.

" Oh, Fanny," said Agatha in distress—up till then she had been quite pleased with her appearance. " I do hope I don't look very unsuitable."

Fanny laughed, she couldn't help it, her slight ill-humour gone.

" What a goose you are, Agatha! Surely you don't want to look like a missionary? I mean that you look much too nice, that's all. Tell me, is there anyone else here? Do you know anybody yet? "

" Dr. Marks is still here; he goes on the steamer to-morrow morning. He's coming to tea to-day to say good-bye, and we're expecting the Kalawoon, that means the Minister for Foreigners, and his daughter. I expect he'll help Papa at first if there are any difficulties. And there's young Mr. Protheroe, who's assistant here; he'll be under Papa now."

It certainly sounded gayer than the Moroni household, and the house, too, was more imposing, for the King had allowed it to be built with a triple roof, a thing usually only permitted to Princes and poongyis. That was, explained Agatha, whò had already absorbed a mass of information about missionary affairs, to show the honour in which King Mindoon held Dr. Marks, founder of the school, whom he called Poon-dawgyi, which meant High Priest or Great Priest.

" Thank you," said Fanny rather tartly. " I know Burmese a great deal better than you do, Agatha."

It was quite a comfort, after the glory of the triple roof, to find that indoors Agatha's home was even barer than hers. Mrs. Moroni had at least collected a mass of ornaments that overflowed from every little table and bracket, of which there were many. Tinsel girdles and hair ornaments, paper flowers, china models of old boots, leaden kittens playing the violoncello, pink porcelain pigs with a slit for coins in their broad backs, woollen mats, bunches of dried grasses, strips of satin, hand-painted with sprays of pansies, old Christmas cards, and such like bric-à-brac caught the eye and frequently the careless sleeve or skirt as well. Agatha's living-room could only boast of three stiff, unnatural-looking pictures of saints that she referred to as " Arundel prints."

Dr. Marks was talking away in his curiously persuasive voice when Fanny arrived. He was a small, stout man, very Jewish-looking and completely bald, but with a heavy, dark beard, turning grey. His dark eyes beamed from behind gold-rimmed glasses. He was dressed in clerical black, and the front of his coat was rather stained with tobacco ash. A huge cheroot was sending up a cloud of smoke now as he talked. He seemed somehow to fill the quiet room with his personality; the emphasis which his flexible, almost insinuating voice, already gave to his words, was added to by his manner of striking the air with his right hand. An eager, a dominant, and yet a supple man, almost as though there had been a trace of the East in him. Mr. Lumsden looked more neutral-hued than ever in this powerful presence.

Mr. Protheroe was a thin, pale young man, with a clean-shaven, slightly concave face, delicately modelled about the sensitive mouth and slightly protuberant jaw. It was the sort of face that Agatha told herself was " Burne-Jonesy." Fanny, with one glance at him, decided he was the most interesting man there. He was the only one who, from her point of view, was a man at all. And he would never be interested in her . . . her instinct told her that. For her he was another Mr. Danvers. He was the sort of man she would like to captivate and couldn't, the sort of man who wanted at least the illusion of intelligent companionship, of what Fanny called " booky talks."

All three men were kind to Agatha's little friend and pressed cakes and sweets upon her, but it was Agatha whom they treated as grown-up as she sat there behind the teapot, looking, thought Fanny, very much as she had been used to look at school when in charge of some of the younger girls and trying to improve their behaviour. Fanny, not sure of what to say in this company, wisely held her tongue; and gradually, as she listened to Dr. Marks, who held the floor completely, she began to admire him. Fanny always recognised power when she saw it; also it was interesting to hear what he was saying about the difficulties of life in Mandalay. Fanny's Burmese blood made even the discussion of intrigue intensely interesting to her.

"Don't let yourself be dragged into anything at the Palace, my dear Lumsden," urged Dr. Marks. "That's my advice. H.M. will pretend a great interest in the Christian gospel, will ask you to discuss it with him; he's done the same time and again with me and with Bishop Bigandet and with the Armenian Bishop. He's helped us all in turn and hoped that Bigandet would help him with the French and that I would help him with our people. He can't understand, or he didn't for several years, that a missionary must set his face against being exploited politically. You see, the Buddhist priesthood is enormously powerful; they have their finger in every pie, even the King can't go against it. He no more understands Christianity than my little dog Jacko does. No, that's wrong, Jacko's a good little Christian according to his lights. I've known many worse. But I tell you, Lumsden, that I've come very regretfully to the conclusion that he had me up here in the first place, not because he wished to know anything about our religion, but because he wished to ingratiate himself with the British. He got me up here and promised to build a school and church and send his sons as pupils, which I must say he did. But I assure you if I hadn't been bald already, my hair would have gone grey trying to get the money out of him for the upkeep of the school. He's always trying to get me to accept presents of money for myself, and when I refuse he gets very angry. Yet I couldn't get the fees out of him for all the pupils he sent from the Palace. I'm not much good at money matters, I'm afraid, and it's been a hand-to-mouth existence; your daughter will look after you better, Mr. Lumsden, I expect. Some more of that cake, please, Miss Lumsden; it's delicious; I can see you're a splendid housewife. The long and the short of it is, Mr. Lumsden, that the King's got one idea of what we are here for, and we've got another. In the early years, when he thought he could make use of me, nothing was too good for me. You should have seen the Princes coming to school. It was enough to make a cat laugh."

"Why was that?" asked Mr. Lumsden in his precise little manner.

"They used to come on an elephant apiece, as many as nine of them at a time, two golden umbrellas held over each one and forty followers in attendance. That might make a procession of as many as three hundred and sixty people, to say nothing of the elephants. They were nice lads, too. The Palace pages used to attend also; they're called Lapetye Dawtha, which means Sons of Tea, because their office is to hand tea to the King; they each had a little yellow umbrella and about a dozen followers. They were good pupils. You'll find all Burmese boys are good in school. Burmans have a great respect for learning and for schoolmasters. You'll find that part of your job easy. It's the politics that are fatal."

"I don't intend to have anything to do with politics."

"I didn't intend to either, and, what is more, I succeeded in keeping to my resolve, though I never can get certain members of the Government at Rangoon to believe it. You've no idea how difficult it is, and how everyone misinterprets your actions. A Political Resident here and I got badly at loggerheads. Not Sladen, but the man after him, MacDuff. He wrote and complained to General Fytche that I visited the King too often, though as a matter of fact I'd only been nine times in ten months. He told the Burmese Minister that I wasn't to be received in the Palace again. I couldn't let the matter drop there, and referred it to the Governor General and to the Bishop. You see how foolish it was of MacDuff. If I'd had to consult him and obtain his permission every time I went to see the King, it would have made me an agent of the British Government instead of a Christian clergyman. Of course I won. Headquarters impressed on me I had no political status and had nothing to do with MacDuff, but that's the sort of thing that's always happening. Then the Bishop came to see me. We're under the Bishop of Calcutta here, as you know —more's the pity, we want our own See of Rangoon—and of course the King wanted to see him. I think he had got it into his head that if he could influence the Bishop, the Bishop would influence the Viceroy so that the province of Pegu might be given back. The King was apparently willing to

see the Bishop without the Political Agent and to treat him
with all honour as Poon-dawgyi, or if he came with the
Political Agent to give him political honours, but MacDuff
wouldn't hear of either. The result was H.M. withdrew
his sons and they have never been to the school since. As a
matter of fact the school is filled with paying pupils and we've
really been more efficient without the royal patronage than
with it, but my position has been getting more and more
difficult. Of course, we shall never get free of this taint of
politics, it's bound in H.M.'s mind to be connected with the
See of Calcutta, until Burma has a bishop of her own. That's
what I'm going to work for now. The finishing touch as
far as I was concerned came about eight months ago, when
H.M. sent for me and disclosed what he wanted me to do.
If you please, I was to go to England in his own private
steamer and take two or three of his sons with me, and see
the Queen and ask her to give back one of his sea-ports,
Bassein or Rangoon! That's the sort of thing they think is
possible; they have no notion of what the world outside is
really like and how countries are run. I explained I couldn't
do anything of the sort, and he got very angry and said,
' Then you are no further use to me.' Then he pulled himself
together and laughed and joked as usual, but I've never
seen him from that day to this. I went again and again to the
Palace, and my subsidy ceased and I couldn't get any of the
arrears owing, and at last H.M. sent me a message telling me he
didn't want me any more, that I was to leave his capital
because my life would be in danger if I stayed. Of course, I
didn't pay any attention to that. My plans didn't allow of
my going for another six months or so, and I wasn't going to
alter them for the King. I wish you joy, Lumsden; you'll
have an interesting time, I can promise you that. You've
only got to remember never to ask the King for money, and
never to take any from him unless you send it to the S.P.G.
secretary at Calcutta. H.M. will respect you all right if you
keep independent, but don't you let yourself believe any
of his promises. I don't doubt you could be in high favour
for a few months if you chose, but if you let yourself get
involved in politics, sooner or later you'll have to eat dirt,

and that's not good for the prestige of our religion or our country."

"I think I understand," said Mr. Lumsden quietly. "My talents, such as they are, do not lie in the direction of Courts, and that is not the sort of thing that I aspire to."

"Good Lord, man!" exploded Dr. Marks. "Do you imagine anyone aspires to it, anyone of our profession, that is to say? He'd be unworthy of the cloth if he did. No, what I'm telling you is that you may get caught in spite of yourself. We foreigners are on a hair-trigger here, my dear fellow, most of us are here for what we can get; and the missionaries, who are here for what they can give, find themselves in a very difficult position."

Fanny sat watching both men from beneath her thick eyelashes. Fanny was very aware of what people were like; she couldn't read through a book of Dickens, she couldn't have picked up a newspaper and understood what anything was about except the police-court cases, she couldn't have held an impersonal conversation on any subject whatsoever, but she had a sensitiveness, within her limitations, to human beings, that amounted to a talent, whenever her judgment was not obscured by her personal wishes. She was aware that she knew what the three men in the room were like far better than did Agatha, who had been seeing them for several days past. She didn't think consciously about them, for her interest in human beings began and ended with her own relationships with them, but she held in her mind the knowledge of certain aspects of their selves. She knew that young Protheroe was the sort of idealist who might imagine later on that he was "in love" with Agatha—if only Agatha would be clever and know what to do. . . . He was nice, and yet he was the sort of man Agatha would like, thinking she understood him. I should like him too if he'd like me, thought Fanny, but he never would. Mr. Danvers . . . he's like him that way. He's got much more in him than Agatha will ever guess, because he'll respect her too much to let her know . . .

Fanny's calm eyes turned their gaze on Mr. Lumsden. He, too, wasn't quite what he looked, not just a timid,

dyspeptic parson. He looks silly and he isn't, thought
Fanny; he's thinking and feeling all sorts of things, things
he's afraid of. He minds things. He minds not being
as powerful as Dr. Marks, and he knows he can't be because
of the way his face is made, but he understands about things.
I believe he understands lots of things better than Dr. Marks.
I wonder why they are all missionaries? What's the good
of believing in something as much as that? I don't understand it.

That was quite true—Fanny herself always did things
with a reason, not because of something she believed in.
She did things because of something she hoped for. To
her it was extraordinary that all these three men were doing
something because of what they believed in. . . . And
Fanny, refusing with her pretty little manner yet another
pink sugar cake, gazed limpidly at her hosts. And Agatha,
dispensing the hospitality of the teapot, also had her thoughts.

How pretty Fanny looks, but she doesn't seem able to
talk intelligently about anything. After all, gentlemen
do like to be talked to about their work. Of course, Dr.
Marks is frightfully important and has made the Mission
here, but I see what people mean when they tell Papa that
he's been difficult. I'm sure Papa will be much better,
because he doesn't get excited over things  Dear Papa does
want looking after; I'm so glad he's got me ; and I suppose
Mr. Protheroe needs looking after too, gentlemen always do.
He looks as though he were a poet, you really wouldn't think
he was a clergyman if you didn't see the way he was dressed.
I'm sure he's a splendid missionary. How Dr. Marks does
go talking on ; I'm sure Papa would know exactly what to do
without his advice. Dear me, who is that on the verandah?
It must be the Kalawoon. These foreigners seem to have no
idea of time. And Agatha rang her little brass bell that stood
on the tea-table, for her housewife's mind was already thinking
in terms of fresh hot water.

It was indeed the Kalawoon and his daughter—a girl of
about Fanny's age, round-faced and glowing, with a certain
thrust of the chin and direct glance of the brown eyes that
told of character. She had flashing white teeth and a fresh

rosy colour in her round cheeks. She was dressed in a
yellow muslin gown, with black velvet trimmings, and a
little hat covered with loops and bows of magenta ribbon.
She carried with slightly-conscious pride one of the new
sunshades that one held upside down by a tassel attached to
its ferrule. Her father, the Armenian minister, whose duty it
was to placate the foreigners in King Mindoon's dominions,
was a pleasant-faced man with dark eyes that gleamed from
behind large spectacles. As Fanny soon discovered, he spoke
little, preferring to encourage conversation in others; a
certain carefulness, born of the circumstances of his life,
seemed to overlay the natural spring of his talk. He gave
nothing away in speech, and his part in any discussion consisted chiefly of spreading his hands and smiling deprecatingly.
Dr. Marks plunged into a conversation about the mission and
the Court, and the Kalawoon, spreading his palms forwards,
denying this and not-quite-asserting the other, flattering and
placating and yet yielding no ground, gave a pretty exhibition
of verbal fencing.

Mr. Lumsden listened gloomily. If this is the sort of
thing I'm let in for! Where is the message of Christ in
all this? And Edward Protheroe, burning with a zeal
that tended to absolute directness, listened in dismay, every
now and then trying to break in, but though the Kalawoon
always waited politely to hear what he had to say, Dr. Marks
brushed him aside like a fly, and himself boomed into the
attack again.

The three girls were left looking at each other. Fanny
soon took the lead; she talked airily of the evening before
at Julie Delange's. Selah sat nodding and smiling, and
not until a quarter of an hour had passed did Fanny realise
that Selah knew Julie a very great deal better than she did
herself. Fanny saw at once that she had been stupid, but
Selah's ever-pleasant smile and her own happiness in indulging
in the small chit-chat that passed for conversation in Mandalay,
put Fanny at her ease again.

Presently the whole party went out for a walk in the golden
cool of the evening, the ostensible reason being to take
Agatha's little friend Fanny home to the Moroni bungalow.

The three girls walked ahead, their shyness beginning to thaw, chattering amiably, as they went past the Gem City, past the rose-red walls which in the still evening air reflected into the moat, without a ripple to jar the illusion of reality. Here and there the pagoda-like pyathats reared up their curving roofs, dark against the glow of the sky, and walls and towers and the snow-white bridges that arched the moat and the heavy blots of darkness made by the mango trees that stood along the far bank, all went down into the clear water as if into infinity. A great golden barge, rich with carven dragons, seemed to float in the heart of a crystal. It was an evening when the clarity of the air made everything at once shining and oddly dream-like.

Edward Protheroe, walking with the older men, found his eyes drawn ahead to the three girlish figures, so gaily coloured, beneath their flower-like parasols, that seemed to float ahead along the turf of the moat. Suddenly he heard himself speaking aloud, and his cheeks grew hot, but having begun in a voice that rang out more loudly than he had meant, he continued firmly:

" What about women, sir? " he asked Dr. Marks, who gazed at him in surprise. " I mean the Burmese women. Coming from India, *you* must notice the difference, Mr. Lumsden. It is not only that there's no caste in this country, but the women seem to *run* the place far more than they do even at home. It seems to me "—here he began to hesitate, to feel around in his mind for just the words he wanted to express the shade of his thought—" that the whole country is in the hands of women. This sort of thing "—and he jerked his head towards the Palace—" is sort of steeped in women, if you know what I mean. It's—it's oppressive."

" Women! I've never been able to be interested in women," said Dr. Marks. " It's better not, for a missionary."

" I didn't mean that," began Edward, but then felt the impossibility of explaining himself properly. He didn't *like* this over-feminised atmosphere, but he was acutely conscious of it, nevertheless. " I mean I don't think it's safe to ignore the question of women here," he began again.

Dr. Marks fixed him with a belligerent eye.

"Unfortunately, in the way you mean, we cannot ignore them; only too many young Englishmen have their Burmese 'wives,' as they call them. Of course the tie is not permanent, and when the white man leaves, the girl goes back to her own people with any children that have been born of the connection. It is shockingly immoral."

"But that wasn't the way I meant," began Edward once more. Then he gave up. How explain that what he was conscious of was a sort of hot, heavy insistence in the very air of the country, an insistence that was somehow female in its pressure? He hated it, he distrusted it, he felt the whole nation had the danger of the female in its essence. A convinced celibate himself, Edward had the nerves that told him of danger, and this danger that he feared was not some entanglement, no gross snare of the senses, but a thing purely mental in its insidious attack. He felt that this Kingdom of Ava stood for feminine domination, for feminine guile and points of view, in a way that was new to him. He fell upon silence, and the others, startled by his outburst, were silent also.

They all paused awhile beside the lotus-laden water, and Dr. Marks, that little, bald-headed, bearded, rather overpowering man, gazed at it, knowing that it might be the last time, and feeling as though it were the first. The self-conscious beauty of the place seemed to him almost monstrous in its perfection, gross in its subtlety, too fantastic to be good; he felt that one ought to be able to fold it all up like a painted fan, to run golden pagodas and red reflections one over the other, clap the white bridges together, merge tamarinds and mangoes into a scented whole, and put the entire affair, smelling of incense and orange blossoms, into a lacquer chest. It had been everything to him for the past six years and he was withdrawing from it, vanquished. It smote him, with an almost unendurable pang, that it could continue to exist without him; and that he left it, for all his passionate faith, almost untouched by the religion for which he would have given his life. He shifted his feet a little in their hot European boots, and for a moment brought his umbrella down sharply between his eyes and the painted vision that was Mandalay.

It should all go out like that . . . he thought. But he twitched his umbrella upwards, and the cruel beauty before him again brimmed his eyelids and his very soul. A breath of wind blew across the moat, the leaves of the trees rustled faintly, and more faintly still the pyathats with their curling roofs and the proud, angry dragons quivered in the water beneath their canopy of lily leaves. It was as though a giant hand had very slightly, very capriciously moved the sticks of the painted fan. The breeze died away and once more Mandalay was spread out shining and clear, painted on stretched silk. In front of him, at the water's edge, Dr. Marks saw the three girls, the one fair and the two dark heads together as they gazed and chattered. Pretty little decorations he thought them, but nothing more . . . they were of no real importance.

He stared for the last time across to where the golden seven-tiered spire, the Centre of the Universe, stood proud and graceful against the golden sky. It seemed to him that in that moment he gathered up all the memories of the past years. It was as though he were standing alone, steeped in the glow about him, and the persistent tonk, tonk, tonk of a coppersmith bird in a mango tree near by sounded like the blows of a hammer upon a coffin.

## CHAPTER VI

# THE CITY

PAPA, sorry for Fanny's disappointment in the matter of the Palace summons, took her and Agatha one evening up to the top of Mandalay Hill. The endless flights of stone steps cut into its rocky flank were tiresome to lazy Fanny, but once at the top she felt it had been worth it. For there, stretched out before her, the City of Gems lay open to her eager eyes. The four-square moat edged it about with gleaming silver, and within its rose-red battlements, among lawns and trees of fresh green, were clustered its myriad houses, its golden spires, its scarlet palaces, its gold and white pagodas; and there was the great central pyathat, the brilliant beacon that marked the Lion Throne of the Arbiter of Existence, the Lord of the Rising Sun, the Lord of the Celestial Elephant—King Mindoon. Exquisite and insolent, that great seven-storied pyathat stood gleaming as though afire in the burnished light of the evening sun. Fanny fixed her eyes upon it, hardly heeding the spectacle of the white Incomparable Pagoda, of the lovely curves of the distant river, the Sagaing hills soft and purple beyond the further banks. Agatha also drew a breath of amazement and stood gazing. But when Fanny at last turned her shining gaze upon her, something naked and avid in the younger girl's look disturbed her.

"Fanny . . ." she said, "Fanny . . . it's like when the devil took Our Lord up on to the high mountain and showed Him the kingdoms of the world."

Fanny nodded absently, then laughed.

The next day when Mr. Moroni disappeared as usual through the great gates, Fanny watched him go with wistful eyes.

"Won't they send for us soon?" she asked her mother,

who was lying back in her dingy wrapper, rocking herself placidly.

"Wait, wait. You always want things in such a hurry, Fanny."

How Fanny envied Mademoiselle Delange, tall, calm, business-like, who disappeared through the great gates every day, generally bearing a little present for the Queens in a basket over her arm. But then Mademoiselle was over thirty and had already been there several years. She was well known and liked at the Palace. She had plenty of character and was afraid of no one. Fanny could pretend not to be afraid, but she knew only too well how liable she was to sudden panic, that stripped her very soul and laid it bare.

At last, without any warning, the great day came. Mr. Moroni arrived home one evening and announced that his wife and daughter were to call on the Alè Nammadaw Queen, Sinbyew-mashin, the following morning.

Fanny slept little that night, and next morning, lazy as she usually was, she was dressed in her freshest white muslin, a new one with a bustle, and a polonaise with yellow ribbons, long before she could induce her mother even to take her bath. Fanny was in a nervous fret by the time the old lady was finally corseted and got, with many complaints, into a European gown. Mrs. Moroni much preferred to revert to the costume of her nation, in which she looked a pleasant old lady enough, but now to please Fanny she wore a grass-green satin, straining very much at the seams of its close-fitting bodice. The useless little bonnet of white lace was tipped coquettishly forward on her black, oily hair and was tied with green ribbons under her ample chins. The parasol lined with green, which Fanny had brought from England, was clasped in a podgy hand clad in a lavender-kid glove, over the fingers of which she wore the rings that from time to time the Queens had presented to her.

Fanny gazed despairingly when all was done, and the feeling that everything was not well depressed her. Perhaps the old lady would have looked better in one of her beautiful silk tameins with the white muslin jacket and the silk neckerchief that make the Burmese look so bright and fresh. However, it was too late now; besides, Fanny was determined that they must look as European as possible, and if Mrs. Moroni looked none too well, she, Fanny, could draw all eyes to herself without misgivings.

Fanny stood and admired herself in the small, spotted mirror and longed for the day when she would be able to see herself full length in a great mirror with a gilt frame. Papa had promised that next time he went to Rangoon he would buy her one. Meanwhile, she must do as best she could in this ridiculous little postage-stamp of an affair. Fanny drew on a new pair of kid gloves with two buttons each, settled the velvet ribbon with the gold locket round her neck, tilted her coquettish little straw hat, from which bright red cherries dangled, further forward over her forehead and picked up her scarlet parasol. Yes, whoever else was wrong in Mandalay that morning, there was no doubt that she was perfection.

She waited impatiently while two servants heaved and pushed Mrs. Moroni's bulk into the brightly-painted bullock-cart, and then, with a lithe movement of her apparently boneless little figure, she too disposed herself upon the mattress on the floor of the cart, the servant with the tray of presents followed, and the bullocks started off at a brisk trot over the rough road. A very few minutes of this and Fanny wished with all her heart that she had walked, even in the high-heeled French slippers that hurt her feet, but it was too late for lamentations now; the springless cart bounced and crashed over the holes and hummocks in the road, and Fanny held her hat with one hand and clasped the side of the bullock-wagon with the other, praying that by the time they reached the Palace her hair might not have come down. But soon the red battlements came into view, and everything except eager anticipation left Fanny's mind. At last, at last—she was driving over the curved bridge, dazzling white as snow, and the next moment the bullock-cart had arrived at the great gateway and was being challenged by the barefoot sentries. Then the cart passed through, and Fanny found herself within the Shway Myodaw, the Royal Golden City.

Ridiculously there ran through her head a line of the hymn she had sung so often at Miss Patterson's—"Once in Royal David's City . . ." She peered out eagerly from the arch of the bullock-cart. A group of soldiers in tin hats that glittered in the sun, and long, red cloth coats embroidered with white, over ballooning white breeches, stood and stared at the bullock-cart and its occupants. Fanny saw that beneath the tin hats they wore red velvet caps with wing-shaped ear-pieces edged with gold and silver tinsel.

The next moment an officer came up and spoke to her mother in Burmese. His tin hat was trimmed with a great roll of twisted gold tinsel, and his long flowing coat of crimson velvet, that fell to his heels, was bordered with gold, while on his shoulders epaulettes, like the fantastic wings of a great bird, made a sort of little cape edged with gold. He was a pleasant, impudent-looking young fellow with the high cheek-bones of the Shans, and a bright roving eye which settled admiringly on Fanny. As ever, at the hint of approbation her spirits rose again.

This City of many thousand souls was a very different place from the dusty town-without-the-walls! True, there were masses of wooden houses here as there, but the grass was green about them and everywhere there was movement. Her mother, falling naturally into Burmese, explained to her that here lived shopkeepers, merchants, courtiers, officials and Ministers, and that through the next barrier, in an inner enclosure, lived the greatest and most important, the Prime Minister, the War Lord and such god-like beings.

" See," said Mrs. Moroni; " look quickly, Fanny; here comes a Minister in his carrying chair."

" Where, where? " cried Fanny, and followed the direction in which her mother's finger pointed. Towards them there advanced at a swinging trot a huge red lacquer chair with panels of carved gold; it hung on two scarlet poles and was borne by sixteen panting men. Sitting in it under an orange umbrella was an old man with a pale Mongolian face and drooping black moustaches. He was dressed in apricot velvet trimmed with gold braid that glittered in the sun, his high hat glittered with thin beaten gold, his fine, pale yellow hands lay upon his knees. His eyes, serene, inscrutable, gazed calmly in front of him.

"It's the Kinwoon Mingyi," whispered Mrs. Moroni reverentially as the bullock-cart drew aside to let King Mindoon's Prime Minister be borne past, with a thudding of bare feet and the sound of heavy breathing from the bearers. The huge scarlet lacquer conveyance passed them and went on down the straight white road.

At the next gate Mrs. Moroni and Fanny dismounted, not without much groaning on the part of the old lady, who was stiff from the cramped position in which she had had to sit and from the fierce jolting, but Fanny leapt out lightly as a bird and stood arranging her muslin flounces. Then they were conducted through the gate into the next enclosure. In this enclosure also the straight streets cut across each other at right angles. Before them on their left was the Tooth Relic Tower, the carvings on its white walls making faint blue shadows in the strong sunlight, and on their right was the great Clock Tower, white also, from which the drum was sounded at every third hour night and day. Fanny stood still, gazing about her, so entranced she might easily have been run down by one of the many horsemen who seemed to gallop perpetually up and down the road with a whirl of flying draperies, but Mrs. Moroni, who was accustomed to these things, drew her to the side of the road, saying:

"My goodness, Fanny, do you want to be run over? You silly girl, come now."

They passed the Hloot-daw, the Supreme Court of Mandalay. Like the Palace, it had great teak pillars, lacquered red below and gold above, and the tent-like curves of its roof were massed with carvings of strange figures and beasts and flowers, all very different from the buildings in the town-without-the-walls. In front of them was the famous Tagani or Red Gate, through whose massive wooden portals only the King and Queen, the Princes and Princesses of the blood royal, chief Ministers and the Ambassadors of foreign Powers were allowed to pass on state occasions. Mrs. Moroni headed for a little postern at the side of the Tagani, a postern so low that even she, who was not a tall woman, had to bend her head to get through it.    Thus did everyone who entered the precincts of the Palace have to pay reverence by bowing his head, whether he would or no, towards the great golden throne of the Monarch of the Universe.    But little Fanny was so small she passed through head erect.

## CHAPTER VII

# THE PALACE

THERE, beyond the great stretch of roadway, which seemed to Fanny's sight to be covered with prancing horsemen, hurrying messengers and elephants decked in golden trappings, there rose flights of white steps, and above them the scarlet and gold pillars of the Great Audience Hall. Above that again the golden spire reared its seven tiers up into a cloudless blue sky. Not for Fanny, either then or later, was there any horror in the fact that all the many roofs of the Great Palace were made of corrugated iron; to her eyes they looked silvery and splendid, as indeed they did to the eye of King Mindoon, who had chosen them as being peculiarly fitting to his purpose. For royalty was supposed always, according to ancient Indo-Chinese custom, to roof its palaces with silver or lead, and the Burmese, who are the most conservative race on earth, finding lead and silver impracticable, had considered the problem well solved with corrugated iron, which had the great advantage of being obtainable very cheaply from the Europeans. And indeed, such was the splendour of the whole effect, the curving tent-lines of the roofs themselves, the depth and richness of the carving on gables and eaves, the stateliness of the vast pillars, each made of the trunk of a towering teak tree, lacquered scarlet and exquisitely patterned with gold leaf, that Fanny was not far wrong in not noticing the corrugated iron. The stretch of white steps and the glory of the Great Audience Hall were not for women, and Mrs. Moroni turned off to the left, Fanny at her heels, casting many glances over her shoulder. Past the soldiers' quarters they went, and then turned up towards the shed of the Saddan, the Celestial Elephant. There was a crowd beneath the trees, and Mrs. Moroni gave a little ejaculation:

"We are lucky, Fanny," she said; "the Lord White Elephant is being fed."

In that moment, when she saw what was taking place, Fanny realised with a sudden vivid shock of surprise that her mother had remained at heart always a Burman, that her English blood and Catholic upbringing had had no real effect at all.

The Lord White Elephant, who was still very young, had been led forth from his house, which was decorated with a royal golden spire, and was receiving his breakfast of milk, drawn by himself from the breasts of Burmese women, who daily presented themselves at the Palace, eager for the honour. They were waiting now in a row, some young and slender and pretty, some, though still young, fatter and less comely, but all with their eyes shining with their ardour and their devotion.

The Sacred White Elephant was an ill-conditioned beast, lean in the flank, in spite of the care lavished on him. He was only white in the technical sense; that is to say, when his scented bath-water was splashed over him, his mouse-coloured skin turned a reddish colour instead of black. He had twenty toe-nails instead of a mere sixteen, and his bad-tempered little eyes were rimmed with red. A hundred soldiers in scarlet and white guarded his Palace, and a row of dancing-girls, in their little white muslin jackets with wired tails, and their pretty silk tameins, were waiting to dance to him after his meal should be finished. Two attendants led him down the line of young mothers. A speckled trunk would come waving out and seize upon the proffered breast, pulling it up and outwards. The women awaiting their turn trembled with eagerness. One woman fell upon the ground in a fit before he reached her, the milk already spurting from her breasts, and her lips foaming; her ecstasy had proved too strong.

Mrs. Moroni watched with a placid eye, remarked that she thought the process must be rather painful, and went on, nodding at the guards who stood between the elephant's Palace on the right and the servants' houses on the left. They let her pass, and she and Fanny went on down the southern side of the Palace platform into the inner enclosure, towards the buildings that sheltered the Queen they sought.

The Alè Nammadaw, or Centre Queen, though the mother only of daughters, was, so Mrs. Moroni declared, the most important person in the Palace. The Chief Queen, the Nammadaw, was old and ailing, and occupied herself little with politics. The King loved her and she stayed quiet and as content as the perpetual Palace intrigues allowed her to be.

Here in the western half of the Palace, there was nothing to be seen but women and little page-boys, brilliant as butter-flies, that tripped about the lawns, dabbled their thin brown fingers in the fountains and pools, and passed perpetually through the bands of sun and shadow made by the great red pillars of the Palace buildings.

The sleeping-apartment of the King, crowned by a small seven-roofed spire, was pointed out reverently by Mrs. Moroni. In the passages surrounding it some ladies in white were sitting with their toes tucked under them, their slippers and umbrellas left on the outer step. Fanny was allowed to peep into the Glass Palace, a vast apartment entirely covered with mosaic, of mirror-glass to represent diamonds, and of green and red to represent emeralds and rubies.

" My, Fanny," said Mrs. Moroni, " you should see this room on a feast day at the New Year.' Oh, it's splendid. I came here when the young Princesses had their ear-boring ceremony—that was before your father fell out of favour. That's the Chief Queen's apartment behind there. Who knows, Fanny, perhaps you'll be in waiting there to the next Queen? "

Again they turned to the right, round the Chief Queen's apartments, and at last found themselves at the rooms of Queen Sinbyew-mashin.

Fanny's heart began to beat more rapidly. Following her mother's example she took off her shoes and, leaving them outside, passed into the Central Hall, which was the unofficial place of reception of the Queens. On feast days the Chief Queen received in the beautiful Lily Throne room, loveliest of all the throne rooms of the Palace. The hall was open, as were all the Palace rooms, except the enclosed inner chambers, to the out-of-doors, but it gave a welcome impression of coolness and dimness to those coming in from the glare of the Palace platform. The great red and gold pillars soared up and up to the dim gold roof, the floor was covered with carpets which were all thick and soft, antique Persian lay side by side with the modern product of France covered with roses and bunches of blue ribbons. Little Maids of Honour were sitting about; they nodded and smiled at Mrs. Moroni, but kept very quiet, for the Queen had not yet emerged from her room. Mrs. Moroni sank to the soft thick-piled carpet and doubled her feet under her in the regulation style; Fanny's swift drop and swirl was as easy as if she had been practising it all her life; her supple little boneless figure was pure Burman. As Fanny sat and waited, her nerves calmed down, soothed by the quietness, by the dim splendour of the room with its delicate red-and-gold lacquer.

Suddenly the gilt door at the end of the hall was thrown open, and the figure of a woman advanced into the room and stood there for a moment without speaking. It is polite to sit, that being considered the most humble attitude, in the presence of Burmese royalty, and Fanny copied her mother as the old lady bent forward and brought her folded hands up to her forehead in a gesture of obeisance. From the shelter of her hands Fanny peeped up at Sinbyew-mashin, the Alè Nammadaw Queen.

Sinbyew-mashin was of the direct blood royal, being a daughter of King Bagyidaw who died mad, and first cousin to her husband Mindoon Min. Like him she had the retreating forehead that marked the arrogant but unstable Alompra dynasty. Like him also she had a royal and commanding air, though untempered by Mindoon's benevolence. In repose her face hardened into lines of determination and ill-temper, but when she smiled, as now at Mrs. Moroni, she had a certain charm which consisted not so much in her expression as in the way her mouth opened over her white teeth.

Mrs. Moroni produced the presents that Fanny had brought from England, and Sinbyew-mashin, seating herself on the low gilt-legged couch, sacred to royalty, studied the gifts attentively. She seemed particularly pleased with the little tray on which the Pavilion of Brighton was embroidered in coloured wools, decorated with spangles set under plate-glass, upon which the other presents, which ranged from a gold thimble to a box of Bryant and May's matches, were laid out. She cross-questioned Fanny, who found some difficulty, in spite of Mrs. Moroni's lessons, in coping with the elaborate Palace Burmese, to which she was unaccustomed, but evidently the girl's modest replies took the Queen's fancy, for she smiled at her again, and suddenly pulling off a ruby ring from her little finger she handed it to Fanny, who blushed crimson with pleasure. The fairy story had begun to come true. . . .

At that moment there came a quick pattering footstep on the platform without, and the figure of a young girl, a year or so younger than Fanny herself, appeared in the doorway. She stood staring at Fanny and Fanny stared back at her. Neither could see very much, the newcomer because she was looking into the dimness (although she had at once noticed Fanny's European clothes), and Fanny because she was looking at the strong sunlight, but she could see the graceful shape that the young girl made against the brightness. Small and slight as Fanny herself, she carried her little head with its sleek black hair, decorated with flowers, very high. Even against the light as she was, her dark eyes, much larger than Fanny's, seemed to glow. Kicking off her little velvet slippers, she put a beautiful little naked brown foot over the raised sill of the door and entered.

" Who's that? " she asked in Burmese, pointing to Fanny.

Mrs. Moroni, bending her head and folding her hands in salutation, replied that Fanny was her daughter. The girl stood looking at Fanny, swinging the skipping-rope she held backwards and forwards in one hand.

" I like her," she said. " Tell her to come and play with me."

" Go, Fanny," whispered Mrs. Moroni; " it is the Middle Princess, Supaya-lat."

The Queen laughed and bade Fanny rise, and the little Princess held out a hand and seized Fanny's.

" Come along," she said; " you may use my swing with

me if you like.    Nobody else is allowed to sit upon it, but you may because I like you."

She dragged Fanny along to the end of the hall, where a large swing, upholstered in red plush and hung on crimson cords that passed through silver rings, was hanging.   Fanny felt terribly nervous and watched the Queen anxiously to see how she would take this familiarity, but Sinbyew-mashin was in a good mood that day and chose to approve of the daughter of her old favourite.    With one agile movement the little Princess had swung herself up on to the red plush seat, and Fanny, no less agile, took the place beside her. They swung gently side by side, studying each other.    There was a curious likeness between them in spite of Fanny's European clothes.    Supaya-lat's eyes were bigger and more lustrous than Fanny's almond-shaped orbs, but she was not as pretty, for she too had the Alompra forehead, which gave her an adder-like aspect; and Fanny's mouth was the true cupid's bow, small and arched with full lips, while Supaya-lat's was thin.    Yet it was at Supaya-lat that an acute observer would have looked the longer.    Her tense vitality, her brilliant eyes, the flash of her teeth as the thin lips parted in a smile, the quick waving of her long-fingered brown hands, all combined to give her a flickering quality as of flame.    Fanny seemed quiet, like a delicate little painting upon lacquer, beside this uneasy brilliance.

## CHAPTER VIII

# FANNY AND SUPAYA-LAT

THE life at the Golden Palace absorbed Fanny thenceforward. She was not taken to live within the flame-and-gold enclosure, but hardly a day passed that she did not visit them, as the bee visits the honey-laden blossom.

The Middle Princess had taken an aggressive liking to Fanny. Exclaiming that she loved her at first sight, she proceeded to talk to her at great length day after day about herself, Supaya-lat. This was a new experience for Fanny, who was used to being the bestower and not the receiver of confidences. Yet the adaptability of her mind, as supple as her slight body, accommodated itself with ease to this new order of things. For was it not a Princess who asked of her this change? And oddly enough the rôle of confidante gave to Fanny a feeling of superiority. She realised, with that unfailing instinct of hers, which was her only talent, that it is weakness which has to talk, and that it is strength which can listen, and listen without comparative references to self. For Fanny had never been, in the true sense of the word, a confider. She had talked about herself, she had been the brilliant and attractive person who held the centre of the stage, but she had never given a true confidence in her life. Her stories had been but stories, a fine spun-glass fabric woven of her wishes, and not actual truths. Supaya-lat was inferior, or superior—according to the point of view—to Fanny in this matter. She did not see herself as an enchanting little figure in the midst of a set scene, she felt and thought with an astonishing naïveté, violence and actuality, which Fanny could not approach.

Boring as it had been to her, Brighton had yet taught Fanny that there were different points of view in the world and different civilisations, but behind that retreating Alompra forehead, Supaya-lat had room for only one idea.   And that idea was not so much the importance, the greatness and the uniqueness of the Kingdom of Ava, as the conviction that there really did not exist anything outside it.   She was as completely innocent of the imaginative conception of other strange human beings, let alone civilisations, as a rabbit in its burrow would have been.   She was a person of immense importance, and she knew it.   She and her two sisters had been declared Tabindaing, which meant that they were of the royal blood, pure and uncontaminated, and were fit for marriage with whatever king inherited the throne.   Who that king might be lay in the lap of the gods, or in the hand of Mindoon, or more likely still in the hands of the Palace plotters, but whosoever he might be, the Great, the Middle and the Little Supayas had a claim on him as his predestined wives.

Supaya-lat, though the germs of ambition were already beginning to flourish within her, had not formulated her desires very expressly as yet.   She had determined some day to be Queen, and had but a small opinion of her older and plainer sister, known as the Supaya-gyi or Great Supaya, who was really only fit to be a nun; and an even smaller opinion of her meek, good-natured youngest sister, Supaya-gale, or Little Supaya; while her half-sister, the plain, uncanny Salin Princess, worried her not at all, in spite of being King Mindoon's favourite daughter.   Supaya-lat felt convinced that if lack of priority prevented her being the Chief Queen, she would yet contrive to be the most important.   After all, was not her mother, the Centre Queen, the most important person in the Palace, while the Chief Queen was of no account?

As to Fanny, it was sufficient for her, for the time being, that she had gained the Golden Palace friendship.   Perhaps later on she might become a Maid of Honour; now it was enough for her that she was the spoiled child, the petted playmate, the only kalā on terms of lighthearted intimacy, who went as a matter of course three times a week to the women's part of the Palace.

Summer came and burned its relentless way onwards, but while Fanny mocked at its red-hot pressure, Agatha lost the apple-red that was wont to lie on her high cheekbones, and became wan and listless under her triple roof. Fanny spent the days playing in the Southern Gardens amongst the Queens and Princesses in a temporary palace erected against the heat, and there sometimes would come King Mindoon himself, that large, grave, kindly man, with his upward-slanting eyes and the thin, black, down-curving moustache that lay across the pallor of his face like a strung bow. Surrounded by his Queens and his many children, by the giggling, bright-hued little Maids of Honour, and the mischievous pages, the King threw off the grave and weighty air which he assumed for audiences, and revealed the child that lies so close beneath the skin of most men and of every Oriental.

The King's idea of a joke was as simple as most of the ideas obtaining at the Palace. Great merriment was excited one day by the discovery of a dozen or more turtles crawling about at the edge of one of the canals in the Water Gardens; all the little brightly-coloured ladies ran forward with little screams of pleasure, and started looking for eggs, which they discovered, in satisfactorily large quantities, buried just beneath the sandy soil. There was much discussion as to how the turtles could have found their way into the garden, and the turtles' eggs were cooked and eaten at that day's picnic. Then Mindoon explained that he had caused the turtles to be brought to the city and the eggs to be buried, ready for their discovery by the ladies. Everyone was very gay and happy over this, the most harmless of all Palace plots.

Fanny and Julie Delange were not the only foreigners who passed freely in and out of the Palace. Indeed, two kalās lived in the Palace itself and were allowed freedom to come and go—the King's Minister of Forests, a German called Dr. Tarfels; and an old Manipuri Brahmin, Raj Singh, who was astrologer and horoscopist at the Court. The fat German doctor, who had left a not too flourishing practice in Rangoon for the greater emoluments which he felt he could pick up at the Court, did not interest Fanny; but old Raj Singh,

who cast her horoscope for her, impressed her profoundly.
Not that he told her anything very definite, but there was
much talk of important happenings ; Fanny herself was seen
in a very lofty position, a long life was promised to her,
though the old Brahmin refused to tell her of her latter years,
but this did not worry Fanny. A high position in the immediate future was too exciting for that. She felt that Raj
Singh was really telling her the truth, not making up pretty
fairy stories as he did for the little ladies of the Court. It was a
strangely superficial and simple life that was led in the
women's quarters of the Golden Palace—little jokes of a
personal character, little ripples of laughter, little jealousies,
little heart-burnings and griefs went to make up the days.

And Fanny accepted this gay and careless living, this
butterfly fluttering over the surface of things, with rapture.
For although her desires and her passions, with which she
had as yet only trifled ever so slightly, were strong enough,
her mind was of the slightest. She knew that there was
something that she wanted, something that she was following
in this airy maze, but as yet her youth made her content with
the brightness of the passing moments.

These moments lost no whit of their brightness from
Fanny's description of them to Agatha, on those rare occasions
when Fanny passed from the glittering play-hours at the
Palace, to spend a quieter and less luxurious afternoon at the
Mission House. There, in the hot, dark room where the
heavy air was hardly disturbed by the punkahs, lazily pulled
by Indians who were apt to fall asleep, Agatha would be
sitting, pale and peeked and disapproving. Poor Agatha,
indeed, found life as a lady missionary far less romantic than
she had anticipated. Her father, excellent man, with a
thwarted and delicate imagination that might have flowered
into beautiful words and ideas had his upbringing and the
mode of life which he had imposed upon himself not in-
hibited such a thing, was irritable to live with, fussy over
trifles and occasionally afflicted with violent headaches.
Agatha, laboriously learning Burmese, was still unable to
instruct the native children except in the use of the needle,
a matter at which she had never been very adept herself.

Her correspondence with the girls at Brighton, which had begun in such a flourishing manner, had died. What indeed was there to tell except Fanny's triumphs? Mr. Protheroe had been sent for to Rangoon, the headquarters of the S.P.G., and Agatha's maiden fancies, that had begun to endow him, moustacheless as he was, with the glamour of Sir Galahad, languished and died. The French kept themselves to themselves, the Greeks nobody wished to know, of English there were none save a few adventurers who would have been laid by the heels for debt had they remained in Lower Burma, and who fled to Mandalay to see whether they could not manage to fleece the innocent Buddhist in his own fastnesses. The nuns of St. Joseph's were always friendly and pleasant, but Agatha resented the fact that they did not consider her a Catholic and treated her with pitying benevolence. Though Fanny irritated her, she could not but feel pleasure at her gay entry, that high fluting voice, that fluttering of fresh muslins and ribbons and of explanatory hands that meant Fanny telling of her latest adventures.

"How can you care about it, Fanny?" said Agatha, "playing about like that all day like a lot of lower-form children; worse, kindergarten children! Don't you ever want to read a book, a *serious* book, I mean?"

"No, indeed," cried Fanny. "I had enough of that at Miss Patterson's, thank you! Why should I want to read? Oh, Agatha, we had such fun yesterday, the Princess and me. She took me out in a little boat in the Southern Garden, and fancy, I nearly upset the boat! Wouldn't it have been dreadful if I had? You can't think how lovely the lotuses were, just masses of them, like a pink carpet, and I screamed out ' Oh! ' just like that, and leaned out to pick them, and the boat nearly upset, only the Princess seized hold of the root of a tree and prevented it. My, she was angry for a moment, Agatha! I was frightened. She stared at me with her big eyes, and they looked all cold and different somehow, and she said : ' Do you know that if I were drowned my father would kill you? You would be beaten on the throat with a club till you were dead, then you would be thrown into the Irrawaddy.' "

" What a dreadful girl ! " said Agatha.

" Oh, I didn't mind, really," said Fanny, tossing her head. " I said, ' Oh, Teik Supaya, I am not afraid of the King killing me, because if the boat had upset we should both have been drowned, and he wouldn't have been able to.' Then, what do you think? She burst out laughing and said : ' You're a very smart girl, and I love you, and you shall always come and play with me.' And that evening she gave me some ear-rings, but I can't wear them, they're the real big amber ones, as big as cigars, but I like having them. They're the last things she's got that are real, as the Queen found she pawned all her jewellery to have money, so she's taken it all away and only gives her imitation things."

" Doesn't she mind very much? It's such an awful disgrace ! " asked Agatha, interested in spite of herself.

" Not a bit; she doesn't care about wearing jewellery, anyway. She only likes it so that she can get the money to spend. She gets all sorts of things done for her when she has money. What do you think she's done now? She's bribed one of the Maids of Honour to get a whole boy's outfit from one of her brothers, and she's going to dress up as a boy."

" Why? " said Agatha.

" I don't quite know why, she hasn't told me, but I think " —Fanny lowered her voice anxiously—" I think she means to go over into the Northern Gardens and see one of the Princes, but you mustn't breathe a word. Of course, it's a dreadful thing to do. I don't know what would happen if it were found out."

Agatha was really impressed at last, almost too impressed to be shocked. After all, Supaya-lat was very young and had no notion, no idea save that of a childish prank . . . In Agatha's mind the whole thing savoured rather of schooldays at Miss Patterson's and of innocent little affairs with the boys from Dr. Hargreave's school, when the whole excitement had consisted in passing surreptitious notes from one crocodile to another.

That evening when Fanny arrived home she found her mother very important with news from the Palace, having just returned from a visit to the Centre Queen's apartments.

Supaya-lat, dressed as a boy, had managed to get into the Northern Gardens in search of one of her half-brothers, Thahgaya, for whom, at the moment, she was suffering the sentimental throes of first love.

" Only fancy, Fanny," said Mrs. Moroni, awestruck and speaking English for fear of listening servants. " She could not find him, and she met the Thibaw Prince ; you know, the one who is called the poongyi's son——" Mrs. Moroni whispered the scandalous words—" his mother is the Shan Princess who was disgraced. Well, she met him and asked where the Thahgaya Prince was, and because he didn't answer at once, for he took a minute or two to recognise her, she hit his head with her hand."

" What did he do? " asked Fanny, interested.

" Do? Why, nothing. He is of lesser birth-rank than the Princess. He pointed with his finger, so, and said, ' He's in there.' But when she went in to look for Thahgaya, he was *non est*, so she had to come away again and back to the Southern Garden ! "

" Well, there wasn't any harm done," said Fanny practically. " How did anyone find out? Did the Thibaw Prince tell about it? "

" Gracious, no ! " cried Mrs. Moroni, shocked. " No, but one of the Queen's sycophants—you know what *they're* like, all over the Palace—watched and found out. Oh, my, there is trouble ! Supaya-lat is shut up in her room, and the Queen is going to the King about her. It is indeed a disgraceful thing for a young girl to have done. Mark my words, Fanny, that girl will land them all in trouble yet. Her mother's heart is sorrowing for her behaviour."

All agog, Fanny went to the Palace next day, but Supaya-lat was still shut in her room, and Fanny was only the wiser by the gossip of the excited Maids of Honour. The Queen had suggested to the King that Supaya-lat had better be married as soon as possible, as she caused too much anxiety as she was.

" Perhaps they will marry her to Thahgaya," suggested Fanny. But this was met with a chorus of shocked disapproval.

" No, no, how could that be? He's a Prince of the pure

blood, and she has disgraced herself. No, they say now that she will be married to Prince Thibaw, the one that she hit on the head."

Mrs. Moroni shook her head when Fanny repeated this conversation.

" The Queen would never marry one of her daughters to Prince Thibaw. He is the least of all the King's sons, his mother is the Shan woman and disgraced. No, no, Fanny, you will see that that will not happen."

" The Queen might have some reason for doing it," remarked Fanny.

" What reason could she have? " demanded Mrs. Moroni. " Supaya-lat is Tabindaing. She could wait to marry the next King."

Fanny shrugged her shoulders at her mother's simplicity.

" And the next King, who do you think he will be? "

" That no one can tell."

" Besides, they say the Thibaw Prince is studying very hard and well at the Monastery, and if he passes his examination well, the King will be pleased with him."

" He will never be King, all the same," said Mrs. Moroni, " and the Queen wishes her daughters to marry a king. I tell you I know, Fanny; I have known her for years."

" Well, we shall see," said Fanny. " But I'd like Supaya-lat to be Queen, of course."

Supaya-lat was released from confinement, though still under severe supervision. She had declared that nothing would induce her to marry the son of the Shan woman, and the Centre Queen ceased to press the matter. Supaya-lat was, after the Salin Princess, Mindoon's favourite daughter, and he was incapable of harshness towards her. Prince Thibaw disappeared into the Golden Monastery to study for his great examination.

The person who came worst out of the whole affair was the innocent Fanny. Mindoon Min took it into his head that it must have been the free-and-easy manners of the West, as inculcated by Fanny, that had led Supaya-lat to the performance of her mad prank, and, taking advantage of the rain, which provided a good excuse, he bade the

Alè Nammadaw Queen, Sinbyew-mashin, intimate to Fanny that it was too difficult for her to continue her visits to the Palace. The Alè Nammadaw Queen, who, like her daughter, had taken a liking to Fanny, and, more than her daughter, was able to appraise the use that the clever little Fanny might be to her as a link with the outside world, was furious, but thought it better for the time being to acquiesce. So those delightful visits to the Palace ceased, and the gay hours that had hovered, drunken of honey, and slept with folded pinions within the red walls and among the enclosed gardens, fell, broken-plumed, into the dead past. Fanny, desolate in the Moroni bungalow, listening to the thunder of the descending skies upon the iron roof, had to content herself with surreptitious notes that occasionally arrived from Supaya-lat.

And then, in October, news came flying round the kalā town that the Nammadaw, the Chief Queen, was very ill. King Mindoon, who was devoted to her, childless as she was, was frantic with alarm. When physicians, even the doctor from the British Residency, failed to allay the fever, he set free sixty-nine prisoners from the gaol, one for every year of the Queen's life, in the hopes that this pious act would be of avail to the patient. The prisoners went off rejoicing, especially five dacoits who had been under sentence of death, but the sentence on the Queen was not lifted, and in November she died.

There was true mourning throughout the city, for King Mindoon had often sought her advice, and it had always been given on the side of charity and mercy. The King mourned inconsolably in the Palace, and Fanny received news that Sinbyew-mashin was now going to try to become Chief Queen. Fanny's heart bounded up—that would mean her own recall to the Palace. But apparently all the other Queens petitioned the King with tears in their eyes, telling him that if the violent-tempered and arrogant Sinbyew-mashin became Chief Queen their lives would be unbearable, and Mindoon promised them that no one should take the vacant place of the Nammadaw. So Fanny continued to languish in the kalā town.

One evening, Captain Bagshaw, big, red, clumsy and beaming, came to call. Fanny, who had forgotten all about him, greeted him with demure enthusiasm. The booming tones of his voice, as he sat in a rocking-chair in the Moronis' drawing-room, made her forget the depressing evenings when the rain had beaten on the roof. He brought with him a little offering which he presented with clumsy good-humour —twelve dear little handkerchiefs embroidered by the nuns in Rangoon. Fanny clapped her hands with pleasure. She would send six to Supaya-lat—it was time she gave the Princess a present—and would keep six for herself. She would take one next time she went to Agatha's.

## CHAPTER IX

## AGATHA

" Oh, Fanny, where did you get that lovely handkerchief?
What beautiful embroidery . . . you are a lucky girl ! "

" That? Oh, Agatha, do you like it? It's nothing much.
Captain Bagshaw—you remember him—brought me a dozen
like that from Rangoon. It *is* rather nice, but nuns always
embroider so well. If only they didn't charge so much ! "

It ought to have happened like that . . . but Agatha,
intent on her own life, that (strangely enough, she being so
ordinary) occupied her as profoundly as Fanny's important
life occupied her, never even noticed the dainty handkerchief
that Fanny flourished so assiduously. Fanny had to say:

" Agatha, what do you think of my new handkerchief? "
which was not the same thing at all. And even then Agatha
only said: " Oh, yes, how pretty. Fanny, do you think
one ought to allow family ties to interfere with one's own
inner convictions? I mean, if we did, where would the great
saints have been? After all, there is that saying, ' he that
loveth father or mother more than Me is not worthy of
Me . . . ' " which really had nothing to do with Fanny.

Agatha, walking to and fro in the dark room beneath the
triple roof, looking out at the wet green of the trees, smelling
all the fresh scents awakened by the rain, her skin damp
and hot, her body languid, yet conscious all the time that she
was I, I, I, Agatha Lumsden, me myself, within this warm,
damp envelope of flesh, felt her mind as alive and irritant with
her thoughts as her body would have been beneath the
crawling of ants.

The only important thing in the world is religion. *What*
we are here, as long as we *do* right, matters not at all. Mr.
Protheroe said . . . never mind what he said, he's only a

young man, after all. I want to be good, to be good.
Where did I read that sentence . . . *to be a saint, a great
saint, and to save many souls* . . .? That's what we ought
to want. Protheroe . . . a nice sort of name. A saint
is like Saint Teresa. Of course she was a Roman Catholic,
but . . . or Saint Francis of Assisi . . . so was he. But
their saints are ours too, before they broke away . . . of
course they're ours too. Saints are saints. *To be a saint,
and a great saint, and to save many souls.* . . . But can they
have been *quite* like us? I mean . . . to send clothes to the
wash, to have to do all the things one has to do every day . . .
cleaning one's teeth . . . and the other things. . . . It
doesn't seem to fit. Did even our Lord have to . . . no,
that's blasphemy. I mustn't. But everything *is* so mixed
up. Mr. Protheroe . . . but how beastly, how horrid of
me, of course he doesn't . . . but of course he *does*, or he'd
die. How beastly of me, how hateful I am! Oh, Lord,
I want to help Thy Kingdom. Lord, help me . . .

And Agatha, pulses drumming, scrupulously honest,
anxious, the colour flickering on her wan cheek-bones,
wrestled throughout the rains, clinging on to all she had
been taught, to all that would always catch warningly at her
skirts, grow away as she might.

Fanny, pretty, insecure Fanny—odd how the word " insecure " seemed to fit Fanny quite fairly and to bring solace
to Agatha, who would consciously have hated a friend to be
insecure—flitted, bright and charming, through the slanting
rays of sunlight that visited Agatha's kalā-town days. But
Agatha knew that in herself, in Agatha, not in Fanny, lay the
focus of existence. There had been great missionary saints,
there was Saint Francis Xavier, who was martyred by the
Japanese. Agatha's whole soul melted and fused into ecstatic
brightness at thought of that crown to love and devotion
which was martyrdom. And yet I am such a coward;
it's only conceit makes me even think of martyrs in relation
to myself. I can't bear even to burn my fingers when I'm
lighting the lamp.

Agatha thinks she's so good, thought Fanny resentfully—
unaware as the birds flying about the eaves, of Agatha's

intense humility and earnestness—and yet she's selfish. I always thought to be interested in other people instead of yourself was what made people good, but Agatha isn't a bit interested in my new handkerchiefs.

And Agatha, watching Fanny go, caught a glimpse of the lovely curve of her slightly flat cheek and the tender line of her chin and neck against the doorpost as she went, and felt, with the sudden catch of her heart that pure beauty was apt to give her,—Ah, how lovely . . .! I know somehow what a man must feel when he sees someone like that. . . . I wish I could paint, really paint, not just satin table-centres.

Agatha had been brought up with the oblique Puritanical bias which the shades of Catholicism involve, that distrust of beauty which the monastic spirit holds no less than the Protestant, and Keats had always been presented to her as " too lush," just as Shelley had been " too pagan," while a broad-minded literary tolerance was applied to both. . . . They just *weren't* Tennyson, or even Browning. Thus the echoes of sudden joy and satisfaction that had reverberated through Agatha's youthful mind at first meeting—" *Beauty is truth, truth beauty* " had been turned into echoes of disapprobation. Only goodness was truth, beauty could, unfortunately (owing to the devil's adroitness at turning the choicest gifts of God to base uses), be a snare. And a snare was not truth. What Agatha's singing instinct told her of Fanny's curve of cheek and jaw, no sooner echoed through her mind than she tried to cast it forth. Only the soul mattered. *To be a saint, and a great saint, and to save many souls.* How hot it was . . . and how short and irritable poor Papa was when he came home from school.

That evening Agatha stood before her little wavy-surfaced mirror and stared at her own reflection. She pinched the flesh of her thin cheek till it whitened, sure proof of her own actuality and the reality of the whole world. Deep throughout her being, knocked the knowledge that, for good or ill, this was her only life on this earth; that, though not Helen of Troy, she was quite pretty; that she was young; that she had to do something about it all soon; that she was Agatha Lumsden, I, I, I. Her finger-nails, her hands, the aspect of her knuckles, the texture of her skin, the flushing that came upon her cheeks, the gloss of her hair, its greasiness when it wanted washing, were all herself, all I. This enforced intimacy, these almost shocking terms of knowledge on which she lived with the fabric of her own being, would let her have no rest. She seized the handkerchief from Captain Bagshaw's set that Fanny had given her (driven to such a measure by the impossibility otherwise of fastening the importance of the occasion on Agatha's mind) and fastened round her brow the soft fold of linen. I should look like that if I were a Sister. . . . And again Agatha heard her mind saying : To be a saint . . . to be a saint. . . . Clear as the repeated notes of a bell it sounded.

From the leper settlement managed by the Sisters came the tones of the bell ringing for the evening Angelus. And, like an echo, from the distant trees, floated the deep voice of a prayer-gong, as a devout mendicant passing through the world on what was but one, as he knew surely, of his many pilgrimages, struck it to the honour of the Lord Buddha.

Fanny arrived home from the unsatisfactory Agatha's a moment before Captain Bagshaw, red and perspiring, and assuming a look of casual chance, descended from his hired bullock-wagon. Fanny passed into the Moroni compound without apparently observing him. She was acutely aware of how somehow pathetic and touching her slim back-view, with its provocatively waggling bustle and the tiny white muslin train that went jerking up the verandah steps after her, must look, as the slim little white-clad figure, so young and fragile, passed into the gloom of the bungalow. And she was truly touching and pathetic and fragile, just as Agatha was truly agog with the desire for saintliness, for each was young and overburdened with the weight of her own insistent life.

## CHAPTER X

## TOWARDS SILAS BAGSHAW

THE cold weather lay like the benison of a temperate hand over the life in Mandalay. People who had sworn they could never bear the climate a week longer—and these were chiefly those kalās who could not, by reason of their debts or crimes, leave even though the temperature of hell had overtaken them—drew deep breaths and went about their dubious business once again. But Mr. Moroni languished and seemed to grow yellower and more desiccated every day.

He had caught a fever that nothing seemed to allay, and now in the bright sunshine and in the cool of the nights, his teeth still rattled in his head or his limbs burned with the fire that consumed him. Mrs. Moroni tried dosing him with unsavoury compounds she obtained from the bazaar—from the wezas, or wise men, who undertook the curing of sickness. The simple remedies derived from herbs, that often proved efficacious when the art of European doctors failed, were of no avail, and the little cylinders of bamboo, painted scarlet and gold, yielded of their perfumed and harmless contents unavailingly. Moroni, who knew of many cures from the herbs and simple oils used by the native doctors, took of these remedies uncomplainingly, his opinion of the European medicines was not so high that he scorned to try the local wisdom, and the deep scepticism in matters spiritual that was his followed him also into more material regions. But when it came to the nastier panaceas of magic, Mrs. Moroni had to be more cautious. Moroni lay upon his bed, tossing with fever, his splitting head wrapped in wet rags, his tortured limbs racked with swift pains that shot to his fingers and toes, alternately thrown outside the sheet in the effort after coolness, or smothered under heavy wraps as he tried to get warm in the midst of the ague fits that shook him. And, outside on the verandah, the wise men cast his horoscope, to find out under which planets he had been born.

Moroni might, argued the doctors, be ill in any of the four dats, or elements, the dat of earth, that of water, of fire or of wind. It was all-important to discover which of these dats held the largest proportion of his life, and this could only be done by the knowledge of the planets ruling at the time of his birth. Even apart from these four elements, it was always possible that his sickness might be caused by derangement of his mind, which was called seit, or by food, which was called ahaya, or through the influence of the seasons, which was called utu. And there was, of course, always the horrid notion that he might be suffering from his kan, the accumulated influence of all his good and evil actions in all his last lives. If that were so, and the evil predominated, then nothing could save him.

It was, of course, of vital importance that the patient should not eat of any food the name of which began with the same initial as his own name, and, having discovered from Mrs. Moroni, who produced his birth certificate, that he had been born on a Sunday, he was not allowed to eat eggs, or other food spelt with an initial vowel. There was little save eggs that Moroni cared to eat, for the chickens were tough through much exercise. Some extremely unsavoury remedies were provided by the wezas and cunningly advanced by Mrs. Moroni, but her husband, who suspected the draughts, did no more than smell at them disgustedly.

Poor fat Mrs. Moroni, more unkempt than ever, terrified at losing her white husband and the provider of her life, sobbed and shook like a jelly, but she did not dare to suggest to the sick but violent and arrogant man that he might be possessed by an evil spirit, and consequently ought to be beaten with bamboos and have red pepper rubbed into his eyes. So the ancient Garibaldino was allowed to die in peace, with only his daughter Fanny and his partner Delange by his bedside.

"I must be dying because of my kan," the dying man

murmured dryly, with his familiar twisted smile. " My
evil actions are evidently the strongest. I always suspected
it. Yet I fought to make united Italy . . . Fanny, I do
not tell you to look after your mother. She will always
have enough rice and curry, and her rocking-chair. Your
dresses are another matter . . . but I do not worry over
you. You will always choose your friends well . . . you
had better marry Captain Bagshaw ; he is rich and should
not live too long. His kan will see to that, though the
white man will call it apoplexy . . . Delange, don't let them
cheat you up at the Palace like they did me. My respects to
the old King ; I bear him no grudge. Fanny'll have to learn
weaving now if she doesn't marry Bagshaw . . . Julie will
teach her . . ." for a minute the sick man's eyes turned on
Fanny, who knelt, in tears, beside him. That quiet, shrewd,
dark gaze took in the round, sorrowful face, the fine olive
hands, so soft and unblemished from any work, that delicately
dabbed at the frightened eyes. " No . . . I do not think you
will choose to do weaving, Francesca mia . . . it has been
much my fault, I took no trouble over you. But you were a
girl and I did not know how . . ."
 A livid shade passed over the weaver's face, he struggled
to raise himself in bed, and the Frenchman, with an exclama-
tion of grief, slipped his arm beneath his neck, and lifted him a
trifle. Moroni's eyes glowed with a sudden passionate fire—
the only time that Fanny had ever seen them thus illumined.
 " Vengo . . . vengo . . . Generalissimo mio ! Avanti ! "
 Fanny, in the sordid wailing, the hateful but necessary
arrangements that followed her father's death, found herself
leaning both figuratively and literally upon Captain Bagshaw,
for the Nemesis chanced to be up in Mandalay just then.
Monsieur Delange may have been a great friend of Papa's,
but he did not know how to treat Fanny ; he spoke of work
and of learning from Julie . . . Captain Bagshaw knew that
Fanny was too fragile for treatment such as this. Agatha,
melted by Fanny's grief, talked of a life shared with her at the
Mission, even while knowing in her heart of hearts that it
would never be a success. Fanny, between the sobs that shook
her little person, shook her glossy head.

" It's what I'd like better than anything, Agatha darling, but dear Papa . . . dear Papa . . . wanted something else for me.   I don't know yet that I can . . . but I'll try, because of Papa."

And Fanny, with a fresh burst of tears, dried her eyes on one of the famous Bagshaw handkerchiefs.

## CHAPTER XI

# WEDDING DAY

So Fanny was married to her huge, red Captain of steamboats, and Agatha, revolted but excited, was her bridesmaid, while Mr. Lumsden, assisted by Mr. Protheroe, newly returned from Rangoon, performed the ceremony. Fanny was no purist to insist on marriage by a priest of her own faith, and time pressed, for the Moroni bungalow had to be sold. A dispensation permitting Fanny to marry a heretic would have delayed matters.

A Captain Doyle of the Irrawaddy Flotilla Company was best man, and Fanny was given away by the Italian Consul, Mr. Sandreino, an important personage, in that he was also the agent for the Bombay-Burma Corporation; an enigmatic person too, who some said worked for Italy alone, some said was willing to work for France and others declared would side with England if affairs ever came to a crisis. It was popularly reported of Sandreino that he had only one handkerchief, but upon that one a count's coronet was embroidered. He used to speak in a large manner of his estates, but all the land he possessed, he kept, said unkind tongues, under his finger-nails. Unlike M. Delange, he had never been a great friend of Mr. Moroni's, and it was really in his capacity of Italian Consul that he took her father's place now. Fanny recked nothing of all this, but she thought his moustaches were splendid and wished her Captain had such a slim figure. Sandreino wore consular uniform, and Fanny felt quite a flutter as she went up the nave on his arm.

Fanny wore white muslin and a white lace veil and looked like a tiny drift of snow beside a large rock with a bonfire on top of it, and no one who saw the bridal pair could have imagined other than that the drift of snow must soon melt and be absorbed by the rocky, fiery consort. . . .

Agatha, standing behind Fanny in the little mission church, felt at least more important than the other guests, than Julie Delange and Selah Aratoon, who merely sat in a pew alongside. When Fanny took off her new kid gloves, it was Agatha who put out a capable hand from behind her and took them quietly from her clasp. Agatha stood looking at the back of Fanny's bent head, at the delicate dark down on the nape, just visible through the veil of blonde illusion.

"*I require and charge you both, as ye will answer at the dreadful day of judgment, when the secrets of all hearts shall be disclosed . . .*" What were the secrets of Fanny's heart? She couldn't be "in love" with him, with that huge, red, bald man. . . . Agatha's heart suddenly began to beat with a heavy insistence; to her own surprise she found herself shaken with a strange emotion. Fanny was going into something unknown, for though one did know about it with the back of one's mind, it was a place into whose deeps the imagination did not dare to follow. . . . Fanny didn't, she couldn't, "love" Captain Bagshaw, and it was impossible to guess at what a strange man felt, or, indeed, at what a man felt at all at most times. . . . But, suddenly, Agatha knew what a girl would feel—not Fanny, more remote now than ever before—but what girlhood, as Agatha understood it, felt in circumstances such as these. . . . This was the climax, the end of everything for which a girl was brought up; this whiteness and drift of muslin, this focusing of all eyes and all emotions, this almost indecent underlining of what usually was glossed over or not admitted . . . Captain Bagshaw was not Agatha's idea of what was romantic, even of what was permissible, but suddenly something stronger—could it be that it was also more real?—than Captain Bagshaw and Fanny, struck at Agatha's heart. A mystery beyond them, but yet which they, at the moment, were embodying—which was so much bigger and more important than the element of repulsion that this wedding held, that it swamped it. Something impersonal, something that lay in wait, something that was life. . . . Agatha shook all over, while Fanny, calm and rather simpering, lifted the veil from her face and threw it backwards over her shoulders.

The Lumsdens gave the little wedding breakfast in the triple-roofed bungalow, and the huge, red bridegroom, who was in the Royal Naval Reserve, cut the cake with his sword. A terrifying figure, thought Agatha, so big and looming, wielding the heavy, shining sword, but Fanny gave a little cry of admiration at the sight of the naked steel, and, taking the sword in her tiny hands, touched the blade lightly with her fingers.

" Take care ! " cried Agatha.

But Fanny laughed: " I'm not afraid of swords; I like them."

" Fanny, you're a mad girl," observed Mrs. Moroni complacently, biting into a large slice of cake. " Now you've a husband to look after you, it will be his business, and oh my, I am thankful."

Everyone laughed and Fanny dimpled prettily up at her bridegroom.

Agatha, after she had helped Fanny to change into her white cashmere travelling suit and the little white bonnet suitable to a married woman, felt another up-welling of emotion, and as she said good-bye she clasped the bride to her for a moment.

" Oh, Agatha, my ribbons ! " Fanny gave a little scream and smoothed the end of her satin bow carefully.

Then Fanny was stowed away in the bullock-cart by the large hands of her husband, and he ungracefully crawled in after her, and the pole came down heavily upon the yokes of the bullocks, who rocked a little on their feet and spread their hoofs to brace themselves against the weight. A little hand fluttered a handkerchief—embroidered by the nuns— and that was the last Agatha saw of Fanny for many weeks. The bullock-cart creaked off on its slow progress towards the river bank where Captain Bagshaw's steamer was waiting to take the bridal couple for their honeymoon in Rangoon.

The other guests began to say good-bye; the last to go was Mrs. Moroni, who was rather lachrymose by now, but she was consoled by being allowed to take the rest of the wedding cake away with her. When her bullock-cart had jolted and creaked out of the compound, Agatha, who had been standing at the top of the verandah steps, turned, the glow of her unwonted emotions still upon her, and met the glance of Mr. Protheroe's grey eyes, which were looking at her for the first time with a personal interest. Some of that quality of sex, so strong in Fanny, seemed to have invaded Agatha, welling over the barriers of distaste and suspicion which usually protected her. She was aware with a leaping of the heart of this new thing within herself, and somehow it didn't shock her in herself as it did in Fanny. She knew she was looking her best in the soft blue ruffled gown and the white straw hat trimmed with blue ribbons, that her cheeks were pink and her eyes shining; but after all, she had looked her best on other occasions before now. This little tingling feeling that ran through her was something different; it made her more alive.

"Would you like to come out for a walk?" asked Mr. Protheroe. "It won't be too hot now, it's past four o'clock. The house looks so deserted somehow after a thing like this."

Agatha, glancing into the living-room at the table on which lay large derelict slices of cake, was struck by Mr. Protheroe's rather unexpected insight. She seemed to know that if she went back into that room it would be too strong for her, and her glow would fade away. There was a dreadful domesticity about that room, about needing to see that it was cleaned and tidied.

"I ought just to ask Papa," she said, hesitating.

"He's gone to lie down," said Mr. Protheroe. "I'm afraid he felt one of his headaches coming on."

"Well, after all, there's no harm in it, is there?" said Agatha brightly, and started to go down the steps, opening her big Burmese umbrella as she went.

Mr. Protheroe walked beside her and held the umbrella over her. It cast a soft orange glow upon her too-thin skin. Outside the compound their steps led them automatically towards the moat, where, a year ago now, they had gone with Dr. Marks and the others on the evening of Agatha's first tea-party.

" How have you liked your time in Rangoon? " asked Agatha, who accepted without complaint the dictum that gentlemen like to talk about themselves.

" It was very interesting, but not as interesting as here. After all, one hardly feels a missionary in Rangoon. It is up here the work has to be done, and more still up in the Shan hills and amongst the Kachins and Karens and all those wild tribes."

A light sprang into his eyes that were usually so dreamy and vague-looking, and Agatha felt a little pang.

" But if you were to go up there, you would be cutting yourself off from everything ! " she exclaimed.

" I can't cut myself off from ' everything,' no matter where I go. I take it with me."

" You mean you care so much about spreading the Faith? " asked Agatha in a small voice.

" Naturally."

" Oh, so do I," said Agatha. " It's always seemed to me the most important thing in the world."

They were standing on the banks of the moat, but the red walls, the golden barges that lay glittering among the water-lilies, held no part in their minds; they stood gazing at each other. Agatha was against the evening sun, and the trans-parent golden umbrella behind her head made a huge glory about her.

" How wonderful ! " said young Protheroe. " Of course, I have had years of thinking of nothing else, but it s wonder-ful that you, a young girl and pretty and all that, should care about it so much. You are quite different from other girls."

" Oh no," said Agatha modestly, though convinced that he spoke the truth. " I am very ordinary really, but it's a thing that's stronger than ourselves, isn't it? It's given to us from outside."

" Yes, given from on high," he said earnestly.

They started to walk slowly along the edge of the moat, while he poured out his plans and his hopes, and Agatha, listening, sympathising, felt that this at last was life indeed. Passionately they discussed the importance of the Eastward position, the wearing of vestments, and the way that the revival of the confessional in the Church of England was going to revolutionise humanity, more particularly humanity in Burma; and neither knew that it was the excitement caught from Fanny and Fanny's wedding that made their words come so easily,· their hearts beat so hard, and that gave each of them the feeling of having found a kindred soul.

Fanny, sure of herself and of her gift for love, awaited the caresses of her husband aboard the *Nemesis* with far less excitement than that which filled Agatha all the evening.

## CHAPTER XII

# THE RETURN OF THE MARRIED WOMAN

EVERYONE knows—or should know—that married ladies are much more important than unmarried girls. Fanny, back in Mandalay, keeping house for her Captain, when he could be at home between the trips on the river, preened herself before the virgin Agatha. " Of course, Agatha dear, you will understand that I, as a married woman . . ." And Agatha, pursing up her face in the way Fanny so detested and which she always called " Agatha's buttoned-up look," would reply: " Really, Fanny, one would think no one had ever been married before ! " And always at the back of Agatha's mind, ran the words—" Anyway, I *am* white " . . . But Agatha was incapable of meanness, when she knew it for meanness, and no provocation would have dragged that secret thought into the open for Fanny's hurt.

Fanny herself had no such inhibitions. She met Selah, who was glowing with triumph because her mother, the Kalawoon's wife, was running the pandal or festival pavilion for Thibaw. That Prince was going through his Patamabyan examination, at the foot of Mandalay Hill, and it was the custom that he should have a pandal where dancing and feasting could go on all day. His mother, the Loungshay Queen, being in disgrace, her cousin the Kalawoon's wife was hostess of the pandal, a position of great honour, and daily Selah helped her and shared in the honour and merrymaking. But Fanny soon crushed her innocent triumph. Fanny herself was still not on visiting terms at the Palace, although Captain Bagshaw was a favourite with King Mindoon, and many feats of successful trading had been carried through between the two of them, and she was in the mood to decry the patronage of royalty.

" Fanny! But you are well! How glad I am! You
are in your little house now? I must come and see you when
I have time." Selah balanced her glowing transparent umbrella over her sleek head—she was dressed in the pretty
Burmese dress of silk tamein and muslin jacket—and beamed
at Fanny, who looked rather tumbled and creased in a
Rangoon " Paris model."

" Do come, Selah; I am always at home." Fanny's
cleverness deserted her, rather pathetically, in her eagerness
for gossip, and in her strange new loneliness. Selah pounced,
still beaming.

" When I can, I will be pleased to, oh, so pleased to come!
But you know how it is with the Sudhamma going on. . . .
The Thibaw Prince is entered for his examination as Patama-
byan, and my mother has to arrange the pandal for him.
We are there almost all day. They say he is being much the
best in the examination."

For a moment Fanny had to stop and think who the
Thibaw Prince might be. So much had happened to her
since his name had interposed between her and her visits to
the Palace.

" Oh, the boy Supaya-lat smacked . . . ! "

Selah smirked. " He is going to be a very important
person; you have been away in Rangoon so long, you know
little. Did you know the Alè Nammadaw Queen is now
very important and over all the other Queens? "

" No! I thought the King refused—— "

" Oh, he did; she is not yet Chief Queen, though we think
she may be soon. But the King has granted her a white
umbrella and also given her a white cow elephant, so now she
is Mistress of the White Elephant."

Fanny was impressed. She realised that Sinbyew-mashin
would indeed be Chief Queen if nothing happened to prevent
her. And that might mean much to Fanny. . . . Life with
Captain Bagshaw had given Fanny nothing, save, in the
kalā town, the position of mem-sahib, that appealed to her as
had life in the Palace.

" The King is not well," said Selah, " for the first time he
has not gone to the zayat. You were not here in May when

the Atumashi Monastery was consecrated and everyone, all the kalās and all, was invited to the big feasting. The King stumbled as he went up the steps of the monastery, and would have fallen if he had not caught hold of the shoulder of the Salin Princess.    It is a bad omen, and the King has been ill ever since."

The thought of the changes that might take place should "anything happen" to the King flitted vaguely through Fanny's mind and she still stood, not the superior married woman, but the suppliant for news.    Selah continued in her deliberate manner.

"You know, each of the Princes entering for the examination has his own pandal erected and has pwès acted for seven days at the King's expense?    Well, he has to entertain all his own friends at his pandal for the pwès, and the mother of the Thibaw Prince is in disgrace and he has no one to do all this for him, so my mother, being a relation, is doing this for her. We are doing it all at our own expense, and she is attending for seven days and I have to attend with her.    It is such fun— feasting and dances all day.    It is a pity you are out of favour and have to miss everything.    But I will come and see you when I have time and tell you about it."

Fanny, jealous, longing to see the pwès, and listen to the music, and partake in the feasting and games, yet remembered who and what she was in the midst of this triumphing.

"Pooh!    A lot of natives!    Crows, that's what they are! I suppose you will have to marry a crow!"    And secure in the proud consciousness of possessing Captain Bagshaw, that refined and elegant European, Fanny tried to stare Selah out of countenance.    But Selah was not easily bested and she laughed in Fanny's face.

"Crows!    You will be glad to get back among the crows, Fanny!    You may not have married a crow, but you have married a turkeycock!"

Selah and Fanny parted in anger.    Fanny found more comfort in Agatha, but not much.    Agatha, giving tea that afternoon, seemed, most unfairly, to be more superior than ever.    She was getting on well with her Burmese, and dismissed her class of cheerful-faced children with great

fluency and skill in front of Fanny, not looking at her for
approbation, but doing it as though it were the easiest thing
in the world. And later, in the Mission bungalow, dispensing tea—why did one always think of Agatha " dispensing " tea, as though she were a druggist's assistant?
—she, though not even engaged, seemed to disseminate a
successful atmosphere that was most trying and hard to
combat. A photograph of Mr. Protheroe stood unabashed
upon her dressing-table, an almost immodest boldness that
genuinely shocked Fanny. Yet everything seemed so spiritual
with Agatha; when she mentioned the man it was as an
enthusiastic fellow-worker. . . . It was all very difficult,
Fanny decided. Fanny tried to derive satisfaction alone at
her bungalow that evening from counting and rearranging
the garments of her trousseau, but she dropped several tears,
that welled up she knew not quite why or how, among the
folds of the linen.

Two days later the news that, of all the Princes, Thibaw
had done the best in the examination, flew round the kalā
town. Thibaw had passed in the Three Baskets of the Law,
and King Mindoon was so pleased with him, for the first
time in his life, that he presented him with four yellow
umbrellas, next in grade to the sacred white umbrellas, and
invested him with the paraphernalia of a Prince of the higher
grade.

Fanny ran into Selah taking tea with Agatha, for Selah,
as a member of the Armenian Church, was in communion
with the Anglicans, and Agatha felt this a relief after the
sensation that the nuns gave her of being beyond the Catholic
pale. Fanny would have felt out of it indeed, if she had not
been the triumphant recipient of a message from the Palace
telling her to go up and spend the day with the Middle
Princess. Evidently it was true that the King was ill and that
Sinbyew-mashin was virtually the ruler. . . . Fanny was all
agog at the thought of the pleasure awaiting her next day.
Selah laughed at her.

" You will find your Middle Princess will not turn up her
nose now at the Thibaw Prince; everything has changed up at
the Palace."

"It seems so terribly sad," said Agatha, "that this young man who attended Dr. Mark's school for several years should have relapsed into his heathen ways."

Selah stared at her. She might be a member of the Armenian Church and a devout, not to say bright, Christian, but the whole background of her life had been the Palace, and it was impossible for her to regard Buddhism in this unfriendly fashion; heathens were Hindus and Mahomedans, not Buddhists. To Agatha, Buddhists, Hindus and Mahomedans were all heathens, and the American Baptists very nearly so.

Fanny, to whom all such classifications were as empty wind, said :

"Don't be silly, Agatha."

But all the time she was thinking, not of Thibaw's religion, but of what was going on in the Palace.

## CHAPTER XIII

# LOVE IN ·THE PALACE

OH, what a lovely day it was! The clear sun travelled through a cloudless heaven, the water tinkled and fell in the Palace garden, the little ladies ran gaily about in their brightly-coloured silks—Fanny absorbed it all through every bit of her consciousness, her eyes were bright and she was filled with a care-free lightness that had not been hers for weeks. It was as a European that Fanny visited the Palace, but yet she was never so Burman as when she found herself in this enchanting atmosphere.

"How glad I am to see you," cried Supaya-lat, running forward and seizing her by the hand as Fanny bowed her head and put her two palms together in salutation. "It has been so dull without you."

It was delicious to Fanny to hear again the rippling Burmese, and she made an effort to respond in the Palace language which visitors were supposed to use to royalty, although royalty might respond as colloquially as it pleased.

Supaya-lat laughed. "Don't talk like that. You'll never be able to say anything and I want to talk to you, oh, so much. Fanny, do you know the Thibaw Prince is sending me letters, real love-letters? At first I took no notice, but my mother is so cross that I think I'd better; besides, they're such lovely letters. You shall see them, Fanny."

The two girls crossed the sunny stretch of garden, passing under the dappled shade of the mango trees, and mounted the Palace platform. Supaya-lat led Fanny into her own sleeping-apartment, the walls of which were of cream panels, painted by an Italian artist with little posies of flowers. Running to a red-and-gold chest, Supaya-lat opened it and rummaged among the silks it contained, and pulled out half a dozen envelopes. Fanny gave a cry of admiration when she saw they were made of pure beaten gold.

She had some difficulty in reading Burmese, so Supaya-lat read them aloud to her. They were exquisitely written in gold lettering on fancy pink paper, and Fanny admired them enormously.

"You see," said Supaya-lat, "does he not exalt me? You see how he expresses his devoted love and humiliates himself before me."

"You don't think any more of the Thahgaya Prince, then, Teik Supaya?" asked Fanny, and in a moment knew she had made a mistake.

Supaya-lat knit her brows, and the dark cloud that so often shadowed her mother's face, came upon hers.

"How do you mean, the Thahgaya Prince? That was when I was a child. My mother says the Thibaw Prince is going to be King."

"He has done marvellously in the examination," said Fanny hastily.

"Yes, indeed," said Supaya-lat, "and you see how humble he is before me. But how can I answer his letter, Fanny? I can't get anything better than gold leaf; what am I to do?"

"I know," cried Fanny. "I will send to my husband in Rangoon to get me the best English letter-paper and envelopes, and I will get you some flowers of scrap paper, which has gum on the back of it. One can buy whole sheets of them, and one cuts them out and pastes them on a corner of the letter."

"I can paste them on all four corners," said Supaya-lat eagerly. "You must telegraph, Fanny; letters so often take such a long time."

Fanny was in high favour for the rest of the afternoon, and she went back to the kalā town and sent her telegram, feeling very pleased with her day's work.

Captain Bagshaw brought the letter-paper, which was a chaste mauve and smelt of violets, with him on the next passage of the *Nemesis*. He brought also a sheet of coloured flowers, yellow, pink and red roses and one of butterflies. Supaya-lat, enchanted with these, made Fanny cut them out and paste them profusely round the borders of her letters to Thibaw.

The engagement of the Thibaw Prince and Supaya-lat would have been announced, but the King fell seriously ill in July.

Sinbyew-mashin knew that she had entered upon the critical weeks of her career. Mindoon Min was a sick man, and it behoved her now to make all the arrangements possible for ensuring that Prince Thibaw should come to the throne after his father's death. There were many Princes with a far better right to inherit than Thibaw, but they were all men who might give Sinbyew-mashin trouble; Thibaw, she knew she could mould to her wishes through Supaya-lat.

Agatha, to whom Fanny talked freely, though with more discretion than might have appeared, of the state of affairs at the Palace, was reminded freakishly of the games of musical chairs that they had been used to play on wet half-holidays at Miss Patterson's, " to amuse the little ones." The music was still playing at the Palace, and round the one gold chair everyone was circling feverishly, but when the music stopped, who was it that would slip successfully into that vacant seat?

## CHAPTER XIV

# IN THE KALĀ TOWN

THE kalā town could not remain unaffected by the intrigues at the Palace and by the new spirit that emanated from there, now that Mindoon was practically helpless and Sinbyew-mashin was free to pursue her arrogant and ambitious way. Agatha, as well as Fanny, knew the thrill of listening to grave talk about affairs of state, when Mr. Shaw, the new Resident, came in one evening. Mr. Protheroe was back from a preaching tour amongst the scattered mission settlements, and he and Mr. Lumsden sat and listened to Mr. Shaw's account of what had been happening, while Agatha made coffee.

Visits were rare from Mr. Shaw. Indeed, from a social point of view, the Residency was singularly little use to the English in Mandalay. Mr. Shaw himself was a strange choice as Resident, for he came neither from the civil nor from the military caste, and he detested officialdom and all its works. He was a great traveller and a great scholar, especially of Turki. He was quiet and dry in manner and intensely reserved.

The Assistant Resident, the tall handsome Pierpoint, very conscious of the fact that he was a heaven-born, would have turned up his nose, had it not been too aquiline, at the modest tea-parties of the kalā town. Agatha was neither pretty nor knowledgeable enough for him. He preferred them married. As to Fanny, hers was the sort of existence of which he would have remained superbly unaware.

The other Assistant, young Phayre, nephew of the good and great Sir Arthur Phayre, was a pleasantly nondescript young man to look at, mid-colouring, mid-height, with very courteous manners—in which he differed from Pierpoint.

The little Irish Residency doctor was pleasant though peppery, but his chief delight was in horse-flesh. There remained only Mr. Rawlinson, the Postmaster, suspiciously dark of complexion, and quite as conscious of his position as head of a department as Pierpoint was of being a sahib.

A certain amount of communication was of necessity kept up between the Mission House and the Residency, but it took place almost entirely between Mr. Lumsden and Mr. Shaw. There was something grave and disappointed about both men which made them friends after a quiet fashion. Agatha was pleased to see Mr. Shaw, although he was hardly stimulating to the mind of a young girl, but any break in the monotony of life in the kalā town was welcome.

On this particular evening there was agitating news. Two days before a couple of dhobies—Indian washermen and British subjects—had been ill-treated by the authorities. The men were merely guilty of being out at night without a lantern, and while they were trying to find their way home through the dark streets of the kalā town, the Burmese police had fallen upon them and dragged them off to the police station as thieves. They were put into the stocks, which were raised by pegs to such a height that for hours the unfortunate men had to support the whole weight of their bodies on their two hands behind their backs so as to avoid dislocating their ankles, so high had the stocks been raised. Mr. Shaw at once lodged a protest with the Kinwoon Mingyi, and telegraphed and wrote to Mr. Lyall, secretary to the Government of India. Now there was another case of tyrannical treatment, an Englishman this time, which agitated the residents of Mandalay even more violently. Captain Doyle, the Commander of the Irrawaddy Flotilla Company, who had been Captain Bagshaw's best man, was going down to the river to join his vessel, and wishing to avoid a peculiarly muddy piece of road, he went on to the river-bund which, although he did not know it, was presumed to be sacred at this spot. There was no notice up to this effect, and when he was shouted at by the Burmese police he at once went off the bund on to the muddy road again; this, however, did not save him. He was dragged off and put standing into some stocks and kept there for two hours in the pouring rain, for the population of the kalā town to jeer at him. The agent for the Flotilla Company—no other than the ubiquitous Sandreino—was informed of the outrage by an agitated clerk from the offices, and he at once went off to Mr. Shaw's. Again the Resident sat down and wrote to the Kinwoon Mingyi. Captain Doyle was released at once. Nevertheless, he, a member of the great British nation, had endured the degrading punishment in public, and it was necessary, if life and property were to be safeguarded at all, that an apology should be wrung from the Government of Ava.

"The King must be very ill," Shaw opined. "He has always been very sticky over some things, like the shoe question, but never definitely anti-British. All this is somebody else's doing."

"My daughter's friend, Fanny Bagshaw, tells her that the King has not left his room for several weeks, and that Sinbyew-mashin seems to be ruling the roost."

"Has she told you anything else?" asked Mr. Shaw, turning to Agatha, who blushed brightly and set down her coffee cup.

"She said that yesterday when she was in the gardens with the Middle Princess, they saw the Queen in a pavilion with the Taingda Mingyi and the Kinwoon Mingyi, and they were all talking very earnestly, Fanny said, with their heads close together, and the Queen doubled up her fist and hit her other hand with it. Fanny said she seemed awfully upset about something."

"Oh—the Taingda Mingyi . . . I don't like that; he's a bad man. He's as bloodthirsty an old ruffian as ever walked. The Kinwoon Mingyi is wily enough, Heaven knows, but he's not a ruffian. I wonder what they were all laying their heads together about. The succession, of course, one must expect that, but I wouldn't put it past Sinbyew-mashin to try and get rid of us altogether."

"What did the Kinwoon Mingyi say about Captain Doyle and the two dhobies?" asked Mr. Lumsden.

"Oh, he regretted it, of course, but said that the police had made a perfectly honest mistake in both cases. The thing will drag on and on, I suppose, and a hundred letters will be written when one would be enough, but we shall get the apology out of them. It's obvious that the King doesn't know anything about what's going on. I have stated that the Burmese Government must apologise to the British Government and that the head of the guard who tortured the dhobies must pay them five rupees each and that the head of the guard who put Doyle in the stocks must himself be put in the stocks for two hours in the same place. It will be done all right, but the Kinwoon Mingyi will go on talking about it for weeks before he agrees. He did release them at once, but so far he's taken no notice of my demand for enquiry and punishment. You don't catch them up to anything like this with the French; they want to keep in with them. The Kingdom of Ava has been flirting with Paris for a good many years now. Of course it's easy to see why. The French want to get their foot in here. They will be able to do a good bit of gun-running from Tonkin. Which means they would get Upper Burma into their hands and we should have them all along our frontiers. But I must be off now; I'm afraid if I go home to the Residency too late I shall be arrested!"

"I will come with you," said Edward.

"Don't do that; it was pouring with rain just now."

Edward went and looked out of the window. "No, it's left off. It's only dripping from the leaves."

Agatha lit the lanterns and the two men set out, followed by their servants.

"You go to bed," said Mr. Lumsden to his daughter. "I'll wait up and let Protheroe in."

But Agatha hung about the room, putting away books, and she was still there when, long before he could have been to the Residency and returned, Edward Protheroe came back, his face pale with excitement and his eyes shining.

"What do you think, sir, when Mr. Shaw and I were leaving the compound, a man, apparently a coolie, stepped out of the bushes, and who do you think it was? The Nyaungyan Prince."

"What?" exclaimed Mr. Lumsden and Agatha together.

"Yes, and his brother the Nyaungoke Prince is with him, both dressed as coolies. They swear their lives are in danger, and they've come to claim the protection of the British. They're on the verandah now with Mr. Shaw."

Mr. Lumsden hastily accompanied Edward to the verandah, bidding Agatha stay where she was. It was half an hour ere he returned with Edward.

"Well, what has happened?" cried Agatha. "Is the King dead?"

"No, he's not dead, but apparently a message came this afternoon from him bidding all the Princes come to his bedside, and they all did except these two. One of the ladies of the Palace warned the Nyaungyan Prince that the whole message was a fake and that they were all going to be arrested, and he and his brother just got away. Shaw's got them at the Residency. He smuggled them in by talking to them like servants. I don't think anyone suspected anything."

"But has nothing been heard?" asked Agatha. "What has happened to the other Princes?"

"Nobody knows yet. Mr. Shaw is going to try and find out in the morning. Your little friend Fanny is more likely to know than anyone. If anything's happened it will be all over the Palace by now."

"Oh, I do hope Fanny comes to-morrow!" cried Agatha excitedly.

A worried crease came above Mr. Lumsden's eyebrows, so that his pince-nez rose up on his nose and nearly fell off.

"Agatha, you will have to go. I must get you down to Rangoon somehow."

"Papa," protested Agatha, "I can't go. I simply can't."

"Nonsense! You'll have to. I can't risk letting you stop here."

"But Papa——"

"That's enough," said Mr. Lumsden with unwonted decision.

Agatha, mutinous, but outwardly submissive, had to go to bed. It was absurd. Either she was a missionary or she was not, and a missionary should never desert in face of danger; besides this was the most exciting thing that had ever happened to her.   Edward's eyes had met hers with the same light in them as on that evening of Fanny's wedding when they had walked by the moat.   Things were apt to be a little dull between them when there was no inspiration from without to light an inner flame.

## CHAPTER XV

## SICKNESS IN THE PALACE

KING MINDOON, the greatest and best of all the Kings of Ava, lay sick unto death in the Golden Palace. He lay in the inner room of the Glass Palace, several of his Queens sat about the bed, the eldest of them reading aloud to him out of the Holy Books. In the outer rooms and in the passages the lesser Queens sat, their hearts bowed down with apprehension, not only at the sickness of their lord, but because of the trouble that might fall upon them if their lord ceased to be.

For many years now Mindoon Min had caused the more elderly and pious of his womenkind to read to him aloud all night long, so that sleeping or waking he heard the holy advice of the law of Buddha, and there, in the core of the hushed Palace, he had meditated on those things which are eternal. Since the death of the Nammadaw, the things of the flesh had ceased to interest him, curiously enough, for with her his relationship had been purely that of a calm affection for many years, but it had meant an intimacy of mind and heart which had taken with it any desire for the physical side of marriage with younger women. More and more his thoughts had turned towards the eternal verities, which to him, as a pious Buddhist, were the only realities, all else being the painted shadows with which the flesh deceived the spirit during the lusty youth of man.

He did not pray as he lay in the dim inner chamber, seeing mere lines of sunlight here and there where the shutters admitted of them from the outside world, because his beliefs made of all prayer a mere futility, a natural weakness to which only the ignorant succumbed. There was no God in the Christian sense, and the Buddha—the just man made perfect—

had reached Nirvana and was wrapped away from the cries of suffering mortals. Yet the instinct of the human being in trouble is to feel upwards and outwards for something stronger than himself, and since, mercifully, no religion is altogether consistent, there sounded through the chambers of Mindoon's pain-befogged mind—so persistently that he almost thought its echoes must reverberate through the corridors of the Palace—an appeal to that something, call it what one may, in which man despairingly hopes even when he cannot credit its existence. King Mindoon was not troubled for himself but for his children.

There is no right of primogeniture in Burma and the Shan States; the heir is chosen by the reigning Prince. Mindoon Min lay with his heavy lids half-closed over his slanting eyes, his long, pale yellow fingers curved upon the silken coverlet, its well-known texture still familiar to the skin of his finger-tips, the slanting rays of light in the room keeping their accustomed places in his consciousness, and yet his mind, leaving its fleshy envelope of material things, was trying to thrust itself forward, urged by the natural love of the human father to catch a glimpse of the future of his children. . . . For to avoid rebellions afterwards, it had for hundreds of years been the custom in the Kingdom of Ava to assassinate all the Princes save the one called upon to mount the throne, and Mindoon himself had been the first of his line to show mercy. He had not even executed his murderous brother, Pagan Min, whom he had deposed ; but kept him in comfort with his dancing-girls and his fighting-cocks in a corner of the Palace enclosure.

Now, turning his head away wearily from a shaft of light, thin as an arrow, that seemed to his failing senses to dance up and down, the King wished that he had long ago done what his English friend, Colonel Sladen, had so often urged on him—appointed an Eingshe-min, an heir apparent. Mindoon, with his Eastern love of putting off from day to day any definite action, had always argued that to declare an Eingshe-min would be to sign the Prince's own death-warrant, and to stir up plotting amongst his other sons, and so he had continued to do nothing in particular, thinking,

after the fashion of most human beings, both of the East and
West, that his own death was a thing that could never
happen; and yet now it was upon him.   He knew beyond a
doubt that his time had come.   Now, in the dim centre of the
Glass Palace, he felt death creeping ever nearer and nearer,
and he awaited it with the calmness of his race and religion,
but what turned to torment in his mind was the knowledge
that death stood almost as near to the figures of his sons.
His tired mind ran over, as far as he could remember them,
the list of their names.   There was the Thonzé Prince—the
eldest, and with a Princess of the royal blood for his mother.
There was the Mekkhara Prince, a mighty fighter, a proud
man, born to be a King.   And there was, dearest to his
father's heart of any, the Nyaungyan Prince, the most learned
and the most pious, and versed in the Three Baskets of the
law, a Patama-byan.   It was true the Thibaw Prince had
also just been made a Patama-byan, but he was not a possible
King.   He was weak to foolishness, and there was no doubt,
thought Mindoon dispassionately—for such things had
ceased to interest him—that his mother had been too familiar
with the poongyi.   There were also, of course, the Thahgaya
and Maington Mintha, neither of whom was of any importance, any more than the rest of the King's sons.   The question
of succession really lay between the Mekkhara and Nyaungyan
Princes.

   All his life King Mindoon had settled the affairs of his
family and state in an autocratic fashion, but now he knew
himself to be helpless in the hands of the women.   Thunder
he never so loudly, the sounds that he made would be
smothered, and word would go forth that the King no
longer knew what he was saying.   By guile alone could he
meet guile and save the lives that were, in spite of Buddhist
philosophy, so dear to him.   The Nyaungyan Prince came
to see him every day and read the sacred book to him, sitting
on the floor beside his couch, and Mindoon's heart yearned
for him.   Also he knew that, apart from any inclination of his
own, the Nyaungyan Prince was the best selection for the
throne that could be made.   Everywhere his name was
blessed, he had the humanity that should be as much a part

of the Buddhist as of the Christian creed, and which is so often not found in the exponents of either.

He had, too, the subtle brain that could split hairs as to the exact definition of Nirvana, even better than Mindoon himself. As far as any human being could describe the calm of the first beginning and convey in phrases the exact meaning of lifeless and timeless, the Nyaungyan Prince could do it. Day after day, sitting by his father, he discussed the recurring existences, the merits and demerits— the sum of man's kan—until Mindoon almost believed that he had himself attained, while still in the flesh, that state in which is utter cessation from all previous existences and from the present one, so that the old King seemed almost to be rid of his fever-racked limbs and to be floating towards freedom from all the series of existences. Buddhism, unlike Christianity, leaves very little room for the active helping of humanity, but among the kindly Burmans charity is of the very breath of life, and the Nyaungyan Prince was no exception to the rule. To this dearly-loved son it was that Mindoon's heart and mind turned at this pass.

For two or three days Mindoon had lost all sense of time, but it came into his mind now with a little sense of alarm that he had not seen the Nyaungyan Prince lately. Sinbyewmashin had put him off with fair words for the past day or so when he had asked for him. Failure to appear might mean something very terrible in the Golden Palace, and through the King's mind a little thread of fear twanged into sentient life. He turned his head to speak to the Queen, who was reading aloud, but before he could interrupt the monotonous cadence of her voice, a stir of movement and of noise from the passages without broke violently into the hush of the sick man's room. Mindoon Min's failing faculties gathered together and rushed up to the surface of his mind, alert at the note of danger.

Something very dreadful must have happened for anyone to dare to make a noise in the Glass Palace. Women's voices, shrill, wailing, lamentable, clamoured without, and the next moment several of the Queens, a crowd they seemed in the dimness and small space, came rushing into the room.

The chief eunuch, U Kha Gyi, a wrinkled and withered personage, besought them despairingly to go back, and dissociated himself with great speed from any further proceedings. The Queens, all elderly women, their faces disfigured with weeping, flung themselves upon their knees beside the low bed, and began all together, crying aloud, to petition their Lord and King. Mindoon, his heart beating with a sickening violence that threatened to destroy him, tried to calm them. Finally he ordered one of them, the mother of the Thonzé Prince, the chief in rank, to be spokeswoman, and between her sobs she obeyed, while the others stayed, their wet cheeks bowed upon their clasped hands. From the broken words of the mother of the Thonzé Prince and the cries and interjections of the other ladies, the King learned what had happened. Somebody—Sinbyew-mashin was confidently named as the person in question—had ordered all the Princes, in the name of the King himself, to come to his bedside, but before they could come anywhere near the Glass Palace they had been seized, fettered and thrown into gaol, where they now lay.

"The Nyaungyan Prince, where is he?" demanded King Mindoon, raising his head suddenly from the pillow.

"He was not there," said the mother of the Thonzé Prince, could it be with a shade of resentment in her voice? "He is clever and he suspected a trap, and he and his brother have fled to the English to protect them, but our sons lie in prison."

Mindoon signed to the childless Queen who had been reading to him and she came and lifted him up on the couch, propping the pillows behind him. Mindoon clapped his hands together very loudly, it was as though new strength had come into him, but he knew that he dared not fritter away any of it in anger, and he spoke calmly when the officer of the guard entered in obedience to his summons. The King issued a stern order that the Princes were to be released at once and brought before him. The lion had spoken with something of the old roar in his voice and obedience was swift. The Queens allowed themselves to be herded out of the room by U Kha Gyi, who reappeared now that he found the matter was going well and that he was not to be blamed for having allowed the inrush of agitated mothers. King Mindoon, a portion of the silken coverlet clasped firmly in each hand, lay awaiting his sons.

Within a quarter of an hour the Princes had gathered in the corridor beyond the bedroom, and the Mekkhara Prince, who was by nature far more of a leader than the other Princes, had been constituted spokesman, and sent into the sick man's room. The King, still conserving his strength, spoke to him in a low voice. While he yet awaited their coming Mindoon had, true to his blood, planned out a plot whereby he hoped to deceive the other plotters in the Palace. He might yet save the lives of all his children, but his especial care was for the three sons that were bound to be endangered after his death because each of them had a tribe of relations and adherents. If he made the Thonzé, the Mekkhara and the Nyaungyan Princes regents, and appointed them to governorships, two of his steamers that lay always in readiness upon the river could take them and their followers away. The Mekkhara Prince could send to the Englishman, Shaw, to tell the Nyaungyan Prince what arrangement had been made. . . .

Even the dim light had now begun to fade, and the Mekkhara Prince, kneeling beside the bed, his head upon his father's hand, listened to his father's wishes and promised to obey them. He too, for all his courage, knew the life of the Palace well enough to be aware of danger in every nerve of his body. Mindoon, his last directions given, laid his hand for a moment on his son's head, and the Mekkhara Prince, his eyes wet with tears and his heart heavy, turned back the coverlet from his father's feet, and wiped them with the hair of his head in token of obedience to his father's wishes. Mindoon's feet, straight and pallid like pale gold, stood up oddly from the couch in the dim light, and he felt the sense of a chill air blowing upon them. The Mekkhara Prince drew the coverlet again over these pale and helpless feet and left the room.

That night Mindoon became delirious, and as the hours, sounded by the great drum from the watch-tower, dragged their way onwards, he murmured little sentences. " My sons are now on the river . . . they have white turbans on their heads . . . they are safe . . . they are safe . . ."

But the Mekkhara Prince and his brothers, on leaving the Glass Palace, had been seized by order of Sinbyew-mashin and, tied hand and foot, were again lying in prison within the Palace grounds.

And this time their mothers, sisters, wives and daughters, and such of the ladies as might be suspected of interest in their fate, were confined to their own apartments, with soldiers on guard to see they were not free to carry their tale of woe to the King.

## CHAPTER XVI

## DEATH IN THE PALACE

THE next morning there came a rustling at the doorway of the King's chamber and Sinbyew-mashin came swiftly in, and, with a lithe movement of which advancing years had not deprived her, sank to the floor by the head of the bed, and waved aside the meek, lesser Queen and her Holy Book. Sinbyew-mashin was a bold woman and she feared no one, not even the lion in his wrath. Therefore, she did not stay away from the King, but went at once with her own version of the story of the arrest and imprisonment of the Princes, and declared that she had been entirely innocent in the matter, but that one of the Ministers was guilty and she was having him punished. Sinbyew-mashin carried in her hands the official tablet, known as the parabaik; she held it up before him without speaking. Mindoon turned his head painfully and looked at it beneath his drooping lids without speaking. He could just see, through the dimness in the room and the dimness that seemed to be coming over his vision, her lined and yellow face, her bright, hard eyes, and he could feel through all the nerves of his being her fierce intentness. Slowly he took the tablet in his thin withered hands, which lay against it like yellow leaves. On the tablet were inscribed the names of the Thonzé, the Mekkhara, the Nyaungyan, and the Thibaw Princes. Against the name of the Thibaw Prince were two marks.

"These marks have been made," said Sinbyew-mashin, leaning forward and speaking slowly and carefully as though to a child, "by the Ministers, the Taingda Mingyi and the Kinwoon Mingyi. We await your mark to show that you wish the Thibaw Prince to be declared Eingshe-min. You have sent the Thonzé, the Mekkhara and the Nyaungyan

Princes away as regents.  They will be safe, and it is better
that the Thibaw Prince be declared Eingshe-min in their
absence."

King Mindoon laid down the tablet without a word.  His
heart began to beat with alarming violence; he was afraid
that he might pass on to his next existence before he could
regulate matters as he wished in this one.  Wave after
wave of a curious tingling sensation that was the beginning
of unconsciousness, passed over him, his hand lay limp and
powerless against the parabaik, he felt he had no strength to
argue, he almost felt as though he did not care now, for he
thought his three favourite sons were in safety. . . . Sinbyew-
mashin, kneeling beside him, saw his drooping lids fall over
his eyes; she leaned forward and listened intently; he was
still breathing very faintly.  Putting the stearite pencil into
his hand, she clasped her own fingers round his and made a
cross, larger and more imposing than the others, upon the
parabaik beside the name of Thibaw.  There was a faint
contracting motion of protest in the limp hand, but that was
all.  Sinbyew-mashin rose silently to her feet and stole out
of the room.  That evening Thibaw was publicly proclaimed
Crown Prince.

During the next week the King seemed to be unconscious,
but he then had a slight rallying of his forces which alarmed
Sinbyew-mashin and the Ministers considerably, for they
feared that some counter-plotter in the Palace might manage
to get word to the King that his sons were in prison; but the
censorship was too vigorous, and no word ever reached the
inner room of the Glass Palace.  The last flickering of the
flame was but short, and the King sank rapidly.

His last dawn came, first pearly pale, then suddenly alight
with the flame of the rising sun, and Mindoon watched the
grey turn to gold through the series of lattices beyond his inner
chamber.  He thought of his favourite sons and his two
steamers sailing up the Irrawaddy in the clear dawn.  He
thought as dying men will, over his past life, in a series of
pictures that quickly formed and faded.  He was back in the
old capital of Amarapura, where he had first wrested the
kingship from his brother.  He saw the great lake there

with the trees that went down so still and quiet into its shining heart, he saw some cocks fighting in the dust at the end of a village street, their bright feathers and scaly legs burnished in the sunshine, the villagers sitting round, in their gaily-coloured clothes, their eyes flashing while they shouted their bets. He saw a young girl whom he had loved he knew not how many years ago, the pink healthy colour on her high cheek-bones and her kind timid eyes. He remembered the name of the great queen of the West, whose red-necked, red-coated soldiers already owned all the lower half of his kingdom, and he realised in a sudden moment of clear vision, as he had never realised before, that these were enemies who might at any moment come knocking on the gates.

He, the King of the World, the Centre of the Universe, the Source of Greatness and Dignity Celestial, whose threshold was as the firmament, whose suppliants, when he placed the Golden Foot of Majesty on their fortunate heads, became blooming as the water-lily, he, even he, the sum of the world's greatness, had a moment of agonised vision when he knew not only that he was a dying man but that he stood for something that was already dead. He wondered whether it might have been better had he never dabbled in all the money-making activities of the foreigners that had so enthralled him, the factories, the gun-making, the things over which he had liked to flatter himself that he was the lord and patron of industry and art. Perhaps the village days that he had known in his youth were worth the whole of these, the youths playing chin-loon, the girls with flowers in their hair, who leaned over the verandahs to listen to the story of love, the merry babies who tumbled naked in the dust, the little wives and mothers who offered flowers on the feast days at the pagodas. Perhaps these things after all were better. But the Mekkhara Prince, the Thonzé Prince and the Nyaungyan Prince at least were in safety. . . . And Mindoon closed his weary eyes and drifted upwards to the Village of the Nats so quietly that no one watching him knew when he went.

# BOOK II

## CHAPTER I

# THE KING IS DEAD, LONG LIVE THE KING

KING MINDOON lay in state upon a gold salun-daw, a royal couch which had six carved legs, whereas the salun-daws for Princes had only four. The salun-daw was placed in front of the Bee Throne in the Glass Palace; the body was wrapped in white, the face and hands covered with pure gold leaf. A gilded railing enclosed the salun-daw at about six feet off from it, making a little apartment in which the King's personal treasures were displayed. His court dress of silvery brocade tinged with rose and yellow hung upon a pole—his many-flounced court dress, its wired and wing-shaped tiers springing upwards like pagoda roofs. His gold shoes, also turned up at the toes in the wing-like curve found in Burmese architecture, and Burmese clothes stood beside the bedstead. On a little plush-covered European table in each corner of the railed-off enclosure, stood a variety of small objects; Mindoon Min had been—amongst many other things—interested in jam-making, and some pots of jam and little jars of marmalade, with the royal factory labels on them, stood beside gold spittoons and betel boxes. His salwès, or chains of nobility, with their twenty-four strands of gold, hung all about the enclosure, a painting of him by a Burmese artist dangled in one corner and a cheap chromolithograph portrait in another; everywhere was a medley of beautiful or tawdry, but always effective, Burmese objects, and equally tawdry but quite ineffective European products. Above the bed and all about it hung banyan leaves of beaten gold so fine that they swayed at a breath, and by the King's head hung a thin piece of gold shaped like a mango leaf in which the leip-bya or butterfly spirit, nearest approach to the Christian idea of a soul admitted by the Burman, had taken up its dwelling until such time as the body should be buried. Night and day four Princesses knelt, two on each side, waving peacock-feather fans. Every day the royal drums were sounded seven times. On the third day of the lying-in-state, just before the body was enclosed in a golden coffin set with precious stones, most of the foreigners— all of any importance—and all the Burmese officials of inferior rank and their wives, were admitted to see the lying-in-state. Throughout the afternoon the procession of people poured up through the gardens into the Bee Throne Room.

Three days later the funeral took place at noon. It seemed as though the new King were going to placate the English rather more than Mindoon had done during the last few years of his life, for a mandut—a special temporary building— was erected for the accommodation of the dwellers in the Residency, and a few other Europeans of note, a building from which they had a good view of all that passed. Mr. Shaw and Mr. Pierpoint were admitted in full uniform, wearing not only their swords but even their shoes. . . . Many disappointments had not made Mr. Shaw optimistic, but it seemed even to him that perhaps the great Shoe Question was settled at last . . . it was chiefly because of the ignominious order decreeing that Ambassadors must come shoeless into the Palace, that intercourse between the Court of Ava and Great Britain had ceased. But in spite of being allowed to wear swords and shoes on this occasion, the Europeans had to enter the City by the ignominious Western Gate, through which corpses were carried out, and which no Burman would have used for fear of ill-luck.

Captain Bagshaw, perspiring freely in his tight uniform, escorted Fanny; and the party from the Mission House, under Mr. Shaw's wing, also occupied the mandut. It was the first time that Agatha had been inside the Golden City of Gems, and her heart beat almost as high with excitement as Fanny's had nearly two years earlier. Away to the left she could see the scarlet and gold of the Palace, standing serene and majestic in the clear sunlight; down the white

steps, lapping over them like a great blood-coloured river, a
scarlet carpet poured itself down and floated on past the
European mandut, on and on to the place amid the trees
where a white pagoda had been erected to receive Mindoon's
body, for he had left special instructions that he should not
be burned according to the usual royal custom, but should
be buried in his coffin.   Sinbyew-mashin, now in complete
authority, was like many widows, and respected this wish of
her husband now that he was dead more than those he had
wished to be respected in his lifetime.

Agatha, dressed in white in token of Burmese mourning,
but with black ribbons as a concession to European custom,
sat next to Edward in the shady mandut and watched with
all her eyes.   Of course the late King had been a heathen,
and all this was heathen show, and it was terrible to think
where his soul might be at the present moment . . . yet
Agatha was grateful for the doctrine of an intermediate
state which the High Church party allowed, and, religious
scruples apart, this was a great occasion and a fine show.

Edward, glancing from the gleaming up-curled gable-ends
of the great pyathat to the stiff up-curved tiers of the dresses
of the hurrying officials and soldiers, thought that there never
was a civilisation more winged in theory and less in practice
than the Burman.   Dresses, pyathats, roofs, thrones, even the
very betel boxes, all were winged, upward-springing as
flames; but the people themselves seemed to have no aspiration save to be happy.   Edward revolted at that—they lived
from day to day, the unthinking creatures of the moment.

Yet he could not but be fascinated by what he saw, struggle
as he might against a lure that he felt must be of the flesh.
This funeral—how like a fairy story it would seem to the
parishioners of Kilburn, where he had been a deacon!   The
colour and pomp, the infantile yet subtle imagery of these
people—how could any Western mind apprehend it?
Edward himself gave up the attempt, and, not without a
guilty feeling that he was being unworthy of his high calling,
he let scruples and all attempts at analysis go from him, and
prepared to revel in the pageantry to be unfolded before him.
It was, it must be, a fairy story—this was a modern world—

the great nineteenth century of Darwin and steam-engines—
but a fairy story let it be, so long as he was of it. After all,
there mightn't be much of this sort of thing in the world
very much longer . . . utilitarianism was killing it. Edward
felt a thrill of excited anticipation when, punctually at noon,
the great drum was beaten in the watch-tower by the East
gate and the procession began.

First came Mindoon Min's palanquin, empty, like the rider-
less charger of a European king; a great affair of scarlet and
gold borne upon men's shoulders, which was carried down the
steps from the Audience Hall; and then from round the
corner of the Palace came six elephants, which paced with their
swinging heavy stride up to the palanquin. The elephants
were hung with royal purple, on their backs were houses of
scarlet and gold decked with scarlet pennants that flickered
like flames in the light airs, their tusks were clasped by bands
of scarlet and gold from which scarlet tassels hung, and on
their great domed foreheads were skull-caps of gold lattice-
work which sparkled in the sunshine. After the elephants
came the horses, with golden saddles and scarlet stirrups and
bridles set with gold and gems. On foot followed the
Mingyis—the two men, who, under Sinbyew-mashin, were
responsible for everything that had happened lately in the
Palace, and in whose hands the future of the kingdom might
rest. They walked side by side—the cruel, arrogant-looking
Taingda Mingyi, the war lord, with his heavy jaw and close-
set, little eyes, and the Kinwoon Mingyi, with his subtle,
carven old face that looked like that of some pictured cardinal.
Both the Mingyis wore their state robes of apricot velvet,
tiered in wing-like flounces, edged with gold braid and faced
with gold tissue, and they wore high mitres glittering with
thin beaten gold. Over their heads attendants carried the
red umbrellas up-reared on long deeply-curved handles that
were the mark of the highest ministers of all.

Then came the band; muff-shaped drums, silver trumpets,
cymbals and a great gong hung on a red lacquer framework
and carried by two men, while a third walked behind it,
beating on it at intervals. Then, not walking in serried ranks,
but coming along as best they might, often jostling each other

for a place, a crowd of minor officials, wearing high white mitres, attendants holding red umbrellas with straight handles above their heads; and after these a great number of pages and women bearing the regalia and the gold betel box and spittoon, and the rest of Mindoon's personal belongings.

The golden-plated coffin followed—empty, for the body was to be placed on it later.    Now it was borne along in a white velvet hammock, swung from a bamboo pole swathed in red velvet from which, tent-wise, hung a pall of white embroidered in gold.    Two long ropes of twisted white cloth were attached to the hammock, and a medley of Queens and Princesses and what few Princes remained—all little boys—who were not in gaol, held the cloths and guided the hammock along.    The Queens were clad in mourning white and their feet were bare.    The eight white umbrellas of royalty, allowed only to the monarch and his chief Queen, were carried above the hammock, and it was noticed that a white umbrella was borne also over Sinbyew-mashin, who followed next with her three daughters.    Over them, as Tabindaing Princesses, bright yellow umbrellas, next in importance to white, glowed arrogantly.

Agatha leaned forward eagerly; she was seeing Supaya-lat at last. . . . She was disappointed; this girl looked nothing out of the ordinary, though she was prettier than her elder sister, who looked like a nun, which was what, Fanny said, she wished to be—a gaunt, withdrawn-looking girl, seemingly far older than her years; the third Princess, Supaya-gale, looked pleasant but stupid.    They all looked rather brown and insignificant, Agatha thought.    Of course, you couldn't expect them to be really pretty like English people. . . .

A little stir ran through the crowd of watchers, rustling it as the wind rustles a field of barley.    With that sixth sense given to a crowd on such occasions it was aware that the dramatic moment of the procession was approaching.    The King was dead, but the new King would now appear.

And, preceded by his bodyguard, Thibaw Min, the monklet taken from his monastery to be a King, came into view. High up in air he sat, in a scarlet-and-gold palanquin, so huge that it was carried on the shoulders of forty sweating men, and in each of the four corners of the palanquin a girl kneeled

in obeisance, her face bowed upon her clasped hands.  Mr.
Shaw leaned forward and scanned the new King intently
as he was borne past high in air above them.

Although he was wearing the crown of a Celestial Being,
young King Thibaw had none of the majesty of his father;
he was slight and looked very pale, not to say alarmed,
and his eyes shifted nervously from side to side.  But he
looked quite good-natured, reflected Shaw, and might make
a sensible ruler.  After all, he had been a satisfactory pupil
both at Dr. Mark's school and at the monastery. . . . He
was borne past to the sound of the padding of bare feet
and the heavy breathing of the men bent under the immense
weight of the litter.  After the litter came sixty-five poongyis,
corresponding in number to the age of the dead King; they
walked with downcast eyes, holding their fans up so that they
should not by any chance catch sight of a woman, their saffron-
coloured robes making a magnificent mass of burning colour.

When King Thibaw's palanquin arrived at the burial-
place, it paused and an official shouted with a loud voice
three times, "Tait-say-ay!"—meaning "Keep silence!"
Another official stepped forward and did obeisance and
informed the King that all was ready for the royal burial.
A silence held the waiting crowd, for it was now that the
new King had to give the order for the last rites.  Thibaw
leaned forward and his lips moved a little, but nothing
could be heard; he seemed to make a great effort to control
his nervousness, and speaking a little louder, though still
hardly above a whisper, he gave the order, "Thin-gyo-zay."

The official conveyor of orders shouted out in a loud
voice: "By the order of His Majesty, let the body of his
royal father be buried in state, as was done to his ancestors,
his great-grandfather, grandfather and father."  That was
the end of Thibaw's ordeal for that day, for according to
custom he then had to be borne to the Palace, and the burial
had to take place without him.  All was done simply and
without further ceremony save the firing of the guns.

Mindoon Min, the pious convenor of the Fifth Great
Synod, was laid to rest, and Thibaw, whom the evil-minded
called "the poongyi's son," reigned in his stead.

## CHAPTER II

## SUPAYA-LAT SENDS A MESSAGE

THE day after the burial of Mindoon saw Fanny, a contented light in her eyes, trotting gaily through the Western Gate, the nearest to the Bagshaw bungalow, on her way to spend the day with Supaya-lat. Captain Bagshaw had gone up the river to Bhamo on a matter of some Chinese trading, and might be gone for several weeks. There was always apt to be trouble on the frontier, and now that the great King's benevolent shadow no longer lay over the land, no man could say what might happen. It was far better, thought Fanny, to spend the days in the beloved Palace than in the lonely bungalow by the river-bund, listening to the derisive tauk-tch! of the lizards on the wall. It would have been even better to spend her days at the Mission House than to have stayed alone, for there was a curious feeling abroad after the burial of Mindoon Min, a sense of waiting and of tension that Fanny, with her sensitiveness to such things, could not ignore.

The hand that, if sometimes capriciously, yet on the whole so well and so wisely, had ruled that mass of differing peoples which composed Upper Burma, no longer held authority in the gesture of the fingers now stiffened beneath a layer of honey and gold leaf. In the hollow of whose palm now lay the supreme power that always emanated from beneath the seven-storied pyathat? In the clerkly hand of the young monk or in that powerful member, so apt to clench itself in sudden rage, of Sinbyew-mashin? She it was who had plucked the monklet from his monastery, as though by the hair—she it was who had moulded to her wishes the ruthless Taingda Mingyi and even the subtle Kinwoon Mingyi, he who knew men and cities. . . . For he had been ambassador

to the courts of Europe, and knew, as no one else about the
Court could know, how different was real power in the hard
Western world from this painted mimicry in an undefended
city.

Fanny, dazzled as she was by knowing "real" Queens
in a "real" Palace, had yet been long enough to apprehend
with a certain unease that there was some quality of childishness about the pretensions of the Kingdom of Ava, but
this realisation was gradually weakening and fading into the
background in her bird-like mind. Fanny's eyes were simple,
for all their effect of subtlety, and spread out before them
there was at least the appearance of immediate power upon
human beings. She had begun to forget the power residing
in a quiescent threat—the power of armies and navies, of
machinery and the whole complex modern thing called
civilisation, that is always capable of turning a threat into hard
performance.

After all, what specimens did Fanny see in Mandalay
of the great white races? She saw Englishmen who were
drunkards, gamblers and swindlers, who could not go back
to British Burma. She saw French and Italian representatives
of religion, who humbly sued daily for the royal favour.
She saw merchant adventurers, French, Italian, Greek and
German, who all, behind the screen of their none-too-scrupu-
lous trading, carried on a strange undercurrent of intrigue on
behalf of their nations. There were Frenchmen and Italians
employed in drilling and organising the light-hearted and very
unprofessional army, and sometimes they had to bring pressure
upon their consuls to obtain their salaries. There was
Sandreino himself, the Italian Consul and yet agent for the
Bombay Burma Teak Co., who put difficulties in the way of
the English officials as much as he could—an easy enough
matter for him, since he was that mysterious personage, the
"doing-duty" man at the Court.

Fanny admired his cavalry swagger and his long moustaches,
and was not too distressed at his black finger-nails. She
knew he admired her, but though he was friendly, his wife
and daughter would have none of her. Perhaps that was
why, thought Fanny with a giggle. . . . She would meet

him fairly often now, for he was the only European official
who went freely in and out of the Palace.  Captain Bagshaw
did not like or trust him, but that did not worry Fanny—
nothing worried Fanny so long as she could be relieved of
the boredom of the kalā town and go on living in the
vermilion-and-gold fairy story.

The driver checked the trotting bullocks at the Palace
stockade, and Fanny wriggled her little person out over
their backs, and, taking her present for Supaya-lat—a European
scarf printed in Manchester—under her arm, set off towards
the Western Palace.  She found Sinbyew-mashin and the
Middle Princess in the little painted Italian room, sorting
out a great mass of jewellery, native and European, that lay
piled up on the bright cabbage-roses of the Brussels carpet.
Fanny, shoeless, making her reverence at the open doorway,
exclaimed aloud at the glittering mass.  It was a moment of
profound emotion for her, that moment of seeing so much
jewellery. . . . Sinbyew-mashin smiled indulgently at Fanny,
always her favourite, while Supaya-lat frankly grinned—a
grin that made her for the moment a little schoolgirl.

" Are they not lovely, Fanny? " cried Supaya-lat, digging
her small avid brown hands into the heap and scattering
gleams and sparkles of light hither and thither.  " I had no
jewellery left; now see all this."

" Oh, Teik Supaya," breathed Fanny, sitting down respectfully, the soles of her feet hidden from the royal ladies in the
correct manner, " they are indeed lovely.  Are they all from
the Treasury? "

Supaya-lat nodded her head in the Eastern negative.  " No,
indeed, they are the jewels of all the Queens and the other
Princesses."

" Oh," said Fanny, rather startled.

Supaya-lat, without noticing her amazement, seized on a
diamond necklace and passed it over her own little snake-like
head.  " There," she said, turning her graceful neck this way
and that, while her magnificent eyes narrowed and gleamed
at Fanny with a sideways look; " am I not a Queen in that? "

Sinbyew-mashin suddenly gave way, after her fashion,
to a rush of temper, and snatched the necklace away.  It

caught in Supaya-lat's smooth black tower of hair, and the girl screamed and pressed both her little hands against her head. Mother and daughter glared at each other for a moment, the winking strands of the necklace binding them together; naked anger looked out of both pairs of eyes.

Then Supaya-lat, controlling herself, disentangled the necklace from her hair and let the bright chain swing back to the hand of Sinbyew-mashin.

"There is only one Queen at present," said her mother harshly, and began to draw the rest of the jewellery towards her.

Supaya-lat sat very still, her eyelids down-dropped, her hands crossed on her tamein, looking like a little image of the Buddha, so motionless was she.

"Fanny," ordered Sinbyew-mashin, "gather all these up, put them in that chest; we have looked at them enough."

Fanny, whose fingers longed to stick to some of the trinkets, obeyed humbly. Sinbyew-mashin let the carved red-and-gold lid fall with a crash, then flung herself on the gilt salun-daw amongst the cushions.

An attendant appeared in the doorway, and in the florid Palace language informed the Queen that the Taingda Mingyi was waiting in the Hall and craved an audience with her. Sinbyew-mashin began an angry answer, then changed her mind and checked herself. She gave the order for his Excellency to be admitted, and Supaya-lat, who had till now retained her rigidity of pose, sprang to her feet and seized Fanny by the hand.

"Come out into the garden," she said, "I want to talk to you."

Fanny, with a humble obeisance to Sinbyew-mashin, who paid no heed to her, followed the Middle Princess out to the white glare of the Palace platform. They descended the steps and went into the Western Gardens, which were strangely empty that morning. There were very few bright-hued little ladies amongst the grottoes of Portland cement and beside the running water, and those that there were, were not as gay and giggling as usual. The very trees, the feathery casuarinas and the dark-leaved mangoes, and the tamarinds

and the bright-flowering shrubs, seemed to hang their leaves
with an immobility that held something of expectancy and
fear. Fanny shook the idea away from her as an absurdity,
but the unwonted quiet of the Western Gardens weighed
uneasily upon her heart.

When they were out of sight of the Palace, hidden by a
grove of trees, Supaya-lat turned on Fanny with that swift-
ness of hers which was like a snake striking: " Get me a
page," she said, " quickly; I want to send a message; I want
Selah Aratoon to come to me at once. Go quickly, do not
stand there like that."

Fanny cast a look around and saw, dabbling happily in
a little canal, a small boy of some seven or eight years.
She recognised him as being the son of the Sawbwa of
Hsipaw. He was being held as a hostage, for there had
been trouble between the Kingdom of Ava and the Northern
Shan States. Fanny picked up her elegant European skirts,
which according to the fashion constricted her rather tightly
about the knees, and ran towards the intent little boy. He
looked up at the sound of her calling, and withdrew his brown
fat little hands from the gleaming water. He had been
trying to catch goldfish, but he was not very disappointed at
having to desist, for experience had taught him the difficulties
of this absorbing pastime. He lifted his round, rosy face
with its bright, sly eyes to Fanny's rather agitated countenance.

" Run quick, quick," said Fanny, " and fetch Selah
Aratoon. Teik Supaya wants her."

The little boy looked suddenly grave with a gravity
beyond his years. Infant as he was, the dangers of life
had not passed him by, neither had the gossip of the Palace.
He ran off on brown twinkling feet, still wet from the waters
of the little canal.

Fanny, watching him, seeing his quickness prompted by
a knowledge of fear, and yet lightened by his childishness
which could not but make of everything a game, burst out
laughing. The next moment Supaya-lat, whose face till
then had remained rigid and sullen, laughed also, showing
her little pointed teeth. Fanny, rejoining her at a more
decorous pace, and settling her skirts as she came, smiled a

little nervously. Jealousy was in her heart, but she bent her head with a show of humility as she asked : "But why do you send for Selah, Teik Supaya? Cannot I do whatever you want done?"

"Not this time," said Supaya-lat, looking grave, and then with one of her swift changes into a childish mischievousness, she burst out laughing once more. "You shall hear what I say," she promised, "and then you will see why you cannot do it."

A little pavilion with tip-tilted roof stood at the end of the lawn, and here Supaya-lat sat herself down on the carpet that was its only furnishing, Fanny beside her, to await Selah's arrival.

Selah, in common with most of the Europeans or semi-Europeans who waited on the favours of the Palace autocrats, was, as Supaya-lat had guessed, in the hall where these patient creatures of every religion sat day after day, tireless and expectant. Within five minutes she stood on the bright sunlit lawn, bending her good-natured, round face downwards upon her clasped hands. Supaya-lat, all amiability, as she so well knew how to be, called to her to approach, and Selah, entering the pavilion, sat swiftly down upon the carpet in the attitude of respect due to royalty.

"Selah," said Supaya-lat, bending forward and speaking in her sweetest voice—and very sweet it was unless it sharpened into anger—"I want you to give your mother a message for me."

Selah raised her palms again and bent her head.

"Will you ask her," continued Supaya-lat, "to go to her cousin, the Loungshay Queen, and tell her that I have a message for her son, the Thibaw Prince, who is now King. . . ."

Fanny, all excitement, listened eagerly; she, too, had now seen Thibaw, and her natural shrewdness told her that where Supaya-lat beckoned Thibaw would follow, only too glad to have a definite authority that he could obey.

"She is to tell him," went on Supaya-lat, speaking slowly and carefully, "that he is to take me away from my mother, away from the Sinbyew-mashin, and he is to keep me with him. He is to say that he wants me to dress his hair for him. Do you understand?"

"Yes, Teik Supaya," answered Selah glibly. "I understand. Thibaw Min is to take you away to live with him,
and he is not to listen when the Sinbyew-mashin is angry;
he is to take you just the same."

Supaya-lat laughed again and nodded her little head several
times quickly.

"That's right, Selah. What a clever girl you are! Now
go quickly to your mother and send her to the Loungshay
Queen, and say that the King is to give the answer I want
before the sun has set this evening."

Fanny remained after Selah's departure, her mouth and
eyes wide open in genuine admiration and surprise. Supaya-
lat, who seemed strangely animated, with an unwonted
colour on the creamy pallor of her thin cheeks, rocked herself
backwards and forwards excitedly.

"Fanny, you have not been here all the time, but you
are a clever girl. You see a good deal and you hear even
more, like everyone else in the Palace. They all hear things,
but to you I tell things; there is the difference. My mother
has made Thibaw King, she has had the two old men behind
her. The Taingda Mingyi is a patriot, he loves his country;
he is not weak like that other one, the Kinwoon Mingyi;
he has been too much among the kalās, that one. I shall
have to send him away."

Fanny gazed at her unbelievingly. The name of the
Kinwoon Mingyi—the most subtle of the beasts of the
field, as she had heard Mr. Lumsden call him—was the most
venerated in the Kingdom of Ava. The Taingda Mingyi
was a great man and a mighty warrior, but the blood of
many men lay thick upon his soul, whereas the Kinwoon
Mingyi had always been upon the side of moderation and
mercy. It was the Kinwoon Mingyi, too, who spoke
French, who was a great traveller and whose wisdom had
been proved by King Mindoon many times over. Even
Sinbyew-mashin, whose ideas and beliefs were those of the
Taingda Mingyi, had realised that she had to win the Kinwoon
Mingyi to her side before her Palace plot to place Thibaw
upon the throne had been possible of achievement.

Yet here, seated upon the carpet in a slanting ray of sunlight, was this thin, brown, plain little creature, young and inexperienced, calmly announcing that she was going to send away the greatest man in the kingdom! And Fanny, gazing at her, suddenly saw something of her father, King Mindoon, in the arrogant poise of her little adder head, and something of her strong-willed mother in the firm set of her narrow lips, and something that was entirely herself in the gleam of her beautiful deep eyes. It was that third something, passionate and intent, steely-hard but alive like a flame, which suddenly showed Fanny that Supaya-lat was not talking nonsense. Within this tiny frame and burning behind that plain, vivid little face was a flame that could lick up the ambition of Sinbyew-mashin as a thing of no account.

" Teik Supaya," asked Fanny softly, " do you then love Thibaw Min? " Fanny was not conversant enough with the Palace language to refer to Thibaw in the elaborate phrase that she should have used, " Poon-dawgyi-paya," meaning Lord of Great Glory.

Supaya-lat's eyes, that had been narrowed, and with what Fanny thought of as a sort of inward look in their depths, opened widely and looked at her with quite a different expression from any that Fanny had ever observed before. It was not exactly a softening—there was something too eager, too possessive, about it for that—but it carried to Fanny's blood a message of intensity that there was no mistaking.

" The Poon-dawgyi-paya is my own," said Supaya-lat softly, and dropping her hands in her lap, she looked past Fanny out at the gardens that were turning from green to a molten gold in the blaze of the midday sun.

" Oh, Kodaw," said Supaya-lat to herself, so gently that Fanny hardly heard her, " between us we shall rule the universe."

Fanny bent her head. She knew that Kodaw was the expression a Queen used in addressing her husband, and that it meant Royal Body. . . . And in Supaya-lat's sudden and strange use of the phrase, shot, as it were, into space and futility, Fanny realised something new and strange had come into the life of the City of Gems. A little thrill ran along her nerves, a thrill of sympathy for this other girl who was yet a virgin.

Supaya-lat continued to stare out beyond Fanny at the sunlit garden, and suddenly her beautiful eyes—the only beautiful things about her except her supple grace and her royal air—were misted over with tears. With a quick gesture she placed her thin yellowish fingers against her face, over her closed lids. Fanny, rising to her feet and creeping away, left her so. A feeling of wonder stirred in Fanny's shallow little mind, and with it a vague pity.

For Supaya-lat thought she only had to give orders to obtain what she wanted—and what she wanted, she wanted passionately. Fanny even in her short, crude contacts with reality, had found that not so was life arranged. . . . But Supaya-lat, dropping her hands upon her lap once again, stayed happily gazing out over the cement grottoes and the little canals, dreaming dreams not only of power and success, but of a young love that, although set in motion by ambition, was none the less sweet to her imagination.

## CHAPTER III

## AFFAIRS OF WOMEN

KALĀ town days began again for Fanny, for with Captain Bagshaw up at Bhamo and Supaya-lat actually in the men's part of the Palace with Thibaw, there was no niche for Fanny in the Palace life. Therefore the Mission House and the Aratoon bungalow and even occasionally the quiet home of the Delanges', or the less quiet abode of M. d'Avera, saw Fanny's eager, slightly peevish face, and heard her outcries on the boredom of life. Agatha was not allowed to visit at d'Avera's house—there were many pretty daughters, all wearing the tamein, and one or two older ladies, also attractive —and the fact that in Burma no wedding ceremony takes place, and that open living together in the same house makes marriage legal, was no salve to the feelings of the Lumsdens. Yet M. d'Avera was the most popular figure with the English of the kalā town, everyone respected his honesty, laughed at his wit—he had a great theory that Shakespeare was a French-man, and proved it by stating his name to have been really Jacques·Pierre—and appreciated, in short, everything about him save his wine.

Fanny enjoyed going there. All the charm of a French household was there as at Julie's, but with so much more gaiety, and with conversation, thanks to the tamein-wearing little ladies, such as Fanny could enjoy. And once she met there a newcomer, a young French engineer, a M. Bonvoisin. Fanny dimpled and sparkled for him. He had finer mous-taches than Sandreino and his finger-nails were manicured. It was rumoured he was to be employed by Thibaw Min in extensive operations. When M. d'Avera saw Fanny into her bullock-cart he observed quietly : " You think well of my compatriot, yes? "

Fanny laughed and dimpled, nodded after the European manner, meaning assent, which was the more naturally hers, and looked up at the Frenchman's jovial face for approbation. But she did not get it. M. d'Avera suddenly gave her the impression, she could not have told why, of being like Mr. Danvers. He seemed suddenly, in spite of his irregular establishment, to be terrifyingly correct and very much the aristocrat.

"One must, of course, try and be of assistance to one's fellow-countrymen, as long as it is possible," was all he said, with a slight shrug of his shoulders. But suddenly Fanny had that cheap feeling she so detested, and she felt she shared it with the gallant Bonvoisin in the eyes of M. d'Avera. . . .

She went on to see Julie in the hopes of getting some news about Supaya-lat, and in the vague belief that if she could only establish relations with the Court, that sudden odd little cheap feeling would disappear. But Julie Delange, with her calm poise of mind and her poor, peering eyes, was as useless for purposes of imparting the gossip of Mandalay City as she was for that of Mandalay town. Julie seemed to care so little for Court favour, thought Fanny enviously, and yet seemed always to have it. There had even been one dreadful day when Julie carried in as her present a little pastry cake, cooked by herself. There was a terrible outcry, for presents of food to royalty were not allowed for fear of poisoning. Officials had tried to take her cake away from Julie, but she had stood her ground and flashed out at them with the full fire of her southern temper, and Sinbyew-mashin, coming in, had demanded to know the trouble. Julie, who feared no one from the Pope downwards, bent her head in graceful obeisance and raised her hands, but still kept her little basket firmly clasped in them. Sinbyew-mashin, who was in a vile temper that morning, looked at her and laughed, and taking the cake out of the basket, proceeded to eat it. That had indeed been a triumph for Julie, a triumph Fanny grudgingly, but honestly, admitted was due to her personality.

It was not from Julie, but from Selah, that Fanny heard the result of the hairdressing experiment. Fanny had gone to tea at the Mission. Mr. Lumsden was down at the Residency, and Agatha was busy planning a new dress. Fanny looked doubtfully at the rather sickly green limp material in Agatha's hands. Agatha glanced up, a worried crease between her fair eyebrows.

"Fanny, do you think this æsthetic fashion is going to last? I simply can't afford more than one frock, and somehow even out here modes do seem to change so, and then one looks all wrong. But there's nothing to *be* wrong in these artistic things. Just a long straight dress with puffed sleeves and a lace ruffle round the neck. The only thing that matters is that the stuff should be soft and hang well. I could make this myself if you'd pin it on me."

"Of course I'll pin anything you like," said the good-natured Fanny, "but I think they're perfectly dreadful, Agatha. You should see the new dress Silas brought me from Rangoon last time. All pleats and puffs and frills, and the polonaise tied back with a gold cord and a huge bow of gold ribbon behind. It's rather a nuisance because it's where you sit down and it does get crumpled, but that can't be helped. And there's the sweetest little demi-tablier in front, of plush, all rucheings. They say plush is going to be used for everything."

"I'd be sorry to wear plush in this climate. This soft surah is much nicer. I *have* got rather tired of perpetual pink and blue ginghams. And I think the æsthetic style is right for me . . ." And Agatha managed to convey by her voice, in the manner that always infuriated Fanny and left her feeling helpless, that there was, something extraordinarily superior about being able to wear the æsthetic style, that it denoted a finer mind as well as a rarer type of body.

"Oh, well, if you like looking as though you had run in the wash and been hung out to dry, and as though you hadn't been able to afford any trimming . . ." countered Fanny; "have you any new fashion papers, Agatha?"

Agatha, her mouth full of pins, nodded towards a copy of *The Young Ladies' Journal* and another of *The Queen, The Lady's Newspaper*, that lay upon a side table. Fanny pounced with glee. At that moment there came the tap-

tap of high heels on the verandah, and Selah put her round, cheerful face in through the mosquito-door. There was nothing æsthetic about Selah, for she was wearing a European dress thickly covered with puffs and pleats, and was as tied-in and pushed-out as Fanny herself. Only Fanny's little pointed, boned bodices and her many folds of material always seemed to enhance the grace of her tiny figure in such an unfair way. On her the Parisian arrangement of pleats, cutting the perpendicular line across, somehow assumed the rightness of grave Grecian draperies. Selah brushed aside as uninteresting the great question of whether æstheticism was right for Agatha. She was in the superior position of newsbearer, and, with her usual expansive candour, told all she knew to Fanny and Agatha.

" It has been a great success, the hairdressing," cried Selah. " You remember, Fanny, that day that Teik Supaya sent me to tell my mother to go to the Loungshay Queen? "

" Let me see," said Agatha, knitting worried brows, " which one is that? "

" Thibaw's mother, of course," said Fanny impatiently.

" The cousin of my mother," explained the more placid Selah; " you know, Agatha, my mother managed the pandal for Thibaw when he was taking his examination, because then the Loungshay Queen was in disgrace. Now the great King is dead she has become a nun, and she gave Thibaw the message that he was to go to Sinbyew-mashin and ask her for Teik Supaya."

" To marry her, do you mean? " asked Agatha.

Selah and Fanny burst out laughing.

" It will come to that," prophesied Selah. " Already I can tell you nothing like this has happened in the Palace before. You know it is a shameful thing if a man tries to come into the women's part of the Palace, or if a woman goes through to the young men. Now, this is the second time that Teik Supaya has done it. You remember, Agatha, when she disguised herself as a boy and went to see the Thahgaya Prince? That time she smacked Thibaw on the head? Now she has gone again, but not in disguise, and she is living with him. To dress his hair, she says! Lame

excuse! But it will work very well, you will see. Already
Thibaw Min has sent to Sinbyew-mashin saying that he
wishes to marry Teik Supaya, and Teik Supaya only—none
of the others. Think of that!"

"You mean," breathed Agatha aghast, "she is living
with him when she is not married to him?" Agatha's thin
fair skin became suffused with blood up to the roots of her
hair. Even her pale, too-large ears reddened painfully.

Fanny looked at her curiously. "My, Agatha, what a fuss
you make!" she said. "He will marry her, what does it
matter?" Yet even she was amazed by the change that seemed
to have come over the life in the Palace. A few months ago
a proceeding such as Supaya-lat's would have been impossible,
or if it had occurred could have been wiped out only with the
life-blood of the person who had so offended against all morals
and custom. All this had the Middle Princess accomplished
in a few short days. . . .

And suddenly in the minds of the three girls sitting in
the Mission parlour, there was projected the figure of a
fourth girl, who, though she was not actually present,
seemed more real than any of them. . . . Supaya-lat, the
Middle Princess. . . . More—the Queen of Ava . . . who
could doubt it? And not because she would be Queen of
Ava, but because of that something in her which had made
it possible, she was present at the moment to the three very
different mentalities under the triple roof of the Anglican
Mission. To Agatha she was a "native"—but a Princess
none the less. Too many difficulties hedged about the
Burmese royalties for them to seem easy money. . . . She
was also that dangerous something, the Unknown. Agatha
only thought of her as a "native" to save her own sanctity
of tenure in the place of the world's thought. Danger . . .
danger . . . the danger to all womanhood of the Eastern
male . . . danger of adventure, danger of experimenting,
in short—danger—that was what was represented to
Agatha by this insolent risk taken by another girl. . . .
Women should, thought Agatha, stand for security, not for
danger.

To Selah, Supaya-lat represented something very different.

She was simply taking the ordinary risks of life and might win or might not. Danger was part of life in the swift and treacherous East. To accept it was a commonplace.

To Fanny the thing appeared different again. Supaya-lat was to her not merely either the Middle Princess or the Queen of Ava. She was power, romance, life itself. What, without her, would silly, facile, eager little Fanny have been? A little dark woman, attractive to bank-clerks but not to " sahibs," instead of a somebody very real and important and alive in this queer medley of civilisations and ambitions that made up the sordid busy life of Mandalay town, and the stately perilous life of Mandalay City. For Fanny would " matter," nobody as she was, she knew that. That sense of springing life and power within her, that she had felt a couple of years ago upon the steamer, had not been for nothing. The secret of power over others was within Fanny's deft fingers. Or so she felt, because not even marriage had dulled within her that sense of potentialities.

A lizard said: "Tauk-teh!" upon the wall, and the image of Supaya-lat, that ignorant little brown creature, vanished. The length of green-yellow material and the numbers of *The Young Ladies' Journal* and *The Queen* once more swam into the first place of importance. All three girls were studying them when Mr. Lumsden, accompanied by the Kalawoon, entered.

Mr. Aratoon's round, pleasant face was much graver than its wont, and his bland eyes were non-committal behind his gold-rimmed spectacles. Fanny's instinct told her at once that he had news. He stayed whispering to Mr. Lumsden in a corner of the room for awhile after he had greeted the young ladies. Fanny pricked her little ears, but was none the wiser.

However, after the two men had spoken together for a few minutes it seemed they had decided that the matter that engaged them might as well be made known. Mr. Lumsden told it gravely.

"All the Queens and Princesses except Sinbyew-mashin and her daughters have been made prisoner. They are in the Win-gin, the women's gaol."

There was a moment's horrified silence; even Agatha guessed that the news might be more serious than, on the face of it, it sounded. Fanny's mind flew back to a few days earlier, when she had seen that heap of confiscated jewellery glittering on the carpet in the painted Italian room, and she remembered how deserted the gardens had been that morning and how silent. Doubtless already the women and their children had been confined in their apartments. Yes, great changes were going on at the Palace. . . .

Fanny got soberly enough into her bullock-cart; even she began to feel the instability of the tenure of property in Mandalay.

## CHAPTER IV

## AFFAIRS OF MEN

AFTER that not a day passed without strange rumours flying through the kalā town. Mr. Lumsden, who, in his quiet way, had a great sense of his responsibility, as a European and a minister of religion, had established a system for obtaining knowledge from the Palace.

A little girl, the daughter of one of the minor Princesses, who was allowed freely in and out because of her youth, came almost daily to the Mission House and reported on the state of affairs. Like most Burmese girls, she was highly intelligent, and not only fearless but—even more valuable equipment—she still possessed a child's love of mystery and mischief, and to her this tale-bearing was all part of a splendid game. Where an older girl might have feared for her liberty, or even her life, had she been discovered, little Ma Thin —a name which appropriately enough meant Miss Learned— quite simply enjoyed being the source of information and savoured to the full the sense of importance that it gave her.

Old Raj Singh also passed freely between the Court and the Residency, protected by the divinity that, even to Buddhists, hedges a Brahmin, and, by checking up the two stories, the little group of English in Mandalay managed to keep in touch with the march of events behind the Palace stockade.

Life at the Residency was further complicated by the presence of the Nyaungyan and Nyaungoke Princes and their wives and children, who had succeeded in joining them. To give sanctuary was all very well but Shaw knew that the Nyaungyan's followers in Mandalay were plotting to raise him to the throne, and his presence at the Residency imperilled the safety of all the English in the town. The Residency compound was enclosed only by a wall of matting, the miserable building itself and the huts of the assistants would all have gone up in flames in two minutes had a torch been flung amongst them. The guard of Burmese soldiers at the gate was really there not for protection, but to spy on all that went on.

Another troublesome affair took up, at the moment, the attention of the Residency. The *Nemesis*, on her way down-river from Bhamo, was, on the last day of October, forcibly seized by Thibaw's men, and some thirty native passengers, men, women, and children, removed. Captain Bagshaw remonstrated and was very roughly handled. He was going down to the steamer when he was seized by a large body of Burmans, some of whom were armed with dahs, and was dragged away just as he was about to set foot on the steamer's gangway. His gold ring was rent from his poor gouty swollen little finger, and, being a heavy man, when his captors suddenly let him go, he fell, badly spraining his ankle. He got away from his assailants and boarded his vessel in safety. But at three in the morning, a flood of two hundred men, all armed with dahs that gleamed in the moonlight, poured on board and demanded the surrender of eleven men and eighteen women and children who had taken passage in his ship. The old turkeycock refused, but he and his men were no match for the force that assailed them, and the passengers were duly and very roughly removed.

Captain Bagshaw sat down and in his large and laborious hand wrote that, in his opinion, redress was due for such an outrage committed on board a steamer carrying Her Majesty's mails and sailing under the British flag. "That our trade must suffer if passengers are to be permitted to be taken by force of arms from on board British steamers without any authority whatever, but that of power, I need hardly point out to you, and I trust that the Government which you represent will not only obtain redress for the wrong already done to the Company, but will also lend its aid to the protection of trade interests in the future." Thus wrote the outraged skipper to the great Aitchison, Chief Commissioner of British Burma.

Aitchison demanded of Shaw that he should obtain redress, and once again Shaw set about his thankless task. He was slightly cheered by the fact that, for the outrage on the two dhobies and Captain Doyle, he had obtained a certain amount of satisfaction. The men responsible for the onslaught on the dhobies ,had suffered ten stripes each and had had to restore to the dhobies twice the sum extorted, while in the case of Doyle, the Captain of the Gateway had been degraded from his post and imprisoned.

A public admonition had also been given at the Criminal Court of Mandalay to the police that they were not to ill-treat Europeans, such gentry being the subjects of friendly Governments. . . . Meanwhile, evidently the powers that ruled in Upper Burma saw no reason why they should not pluck anyone they pleased from the deck of a British vessel, and from under the protection of the British flag. . . . " And, indeed," Mr. Shaw remarked to Mr. Lumsden, " I see no reason why they should not . . . as we apparently will not or cannot prevent them. . . ."

More and more was Mr. Shaw hating life, large as his salary was, at the farcical Residency, with its rotten floors and its leaking roof and its hordes of spies in the pay of the Palace. Rheumatism was beginning to torture him, the other occupants of the gloomy dwelling were getting upon each other's nerves.

One amelioration there was in life at the Residency—it was decided that to continue to shelter the Princes was too dangerous for all concerned, and an armed steamer was sent up to Mandalay and the Princes and their families safely transferred to it at night. In a curious way, Shaw was sorry to see the Nyaungyan go. He was a very intelligent man, with charm of manner and an apprehension of the meaning of the great world really remarkable in one who had hitherto never been beyond Mandalay. The little ladies, with their delight in learning English ways, had given a certain grace to the dull Residency. They had, at least, reflected Mr. Shaw, learned by now not to try and eat ices with their fingers ! And he nearly laughed to himself as he remembered their shrieks of mock dismay, when, on the great occasion of a steamer having brought ice up to Mandalay, they had tried to cope with the finished product of it, cold, creamy and slippery, between their slim brown fingers.

Still, life was less worrying without their presence, and he had good accounts of them from Colonel Browne, to whose guardianship in Rangoon they had been confided. However, news of much greater importance than the education of Burmese Princesses, came to Mandalay, news that meant even less protection for the British from the Government of India than had been theirs hitherto, if that were possible. The long series of mistakes and misunderstandings between Lord Lytton and the Amir of Afghanistan had come to a head, and once again England found herself committed to a war.

More outrages against British subjects took place in Upper Burma, and the Princes and their wives had to be sent from Rangoon to Calcutta, as men were sent down from Mandalay to assassinate them. Shaw, who had made the usual applications to be admitted to the Palace to congratulate the new King on his accession, was met with refusal. The Kinwoon Mingyi, in a web of words, wrote refusing compensation for the outrage to the *Nemesis* and her Captain. Those who were forcibly removed were, he declared, "Royal-money-bought-servants" and should never have been accepted as passengers. The Captain should be brought up before the Hloot-daw and punished.

It was evident that Thibaw the monk considered himself strong enough—or Great Britain weak enough—for him to flout her with impunity. Fanny knew whose fierce little voice was whispering encouragement into his ear, whose arrogance was driving him on and supporting him. Every consideration was shown at the Palace to the French and Italians, especially to the engineer, Bonvoisin, and to Sandreino, who now avoided the English as much as he could.

"It is Afghanistan . . ." said the English to each other. "Who cares what happens to us here? We can all have our throats cut. The India Office hears nothing but the growls of the Russian bear. Who cares what happens in Mandalay when all that is thought of is to get to Kabul?"

Thus life, uncertain, precarious, went drifting on in Mandalay. Edward longed to go and convert the Afghans —they were so much fiercer, would be so much better value, so to speak, than these Buddhists. Agatha could not repress a little cry of horror at the thought. Martyrdom no longer appealed to her as it had done a year ago. She was by now clad in her æsthetic green garment, and looked very lily-like save for a troublesome tendency of her nose to flush occasionally. She wished it were not wrong to use powder. Anyway, there could be nothing wrong about fringes, especially if you didn't curl them, so she cut her soft fair hair in a straight fringe, which suited her very well, for it took away from the length of her face. Fanny promptly followed her example and found that she looked like a Chinese woman, which did not please her at all.

The Delanges were given a large order for scarlet velvet. And still, while the cool fair December weather lay light and clear over Mandalay, beautifying even the kalā town, Supaya-lat stayed rapt away from all knowledge in the heart of the Palace, with Thibaw Min.

## CHAPTER V

## CAPTAIN BAGSHAW SLIPS HIS CABLE

FANNY yearned for Supaya-lat to send for her once more, but except for piteous messages from the imprisoned Queens and Princesses, no word escaped from the mysterious heart of the City of Gems.

And, as it turned out, Fanny would not have been free to go to Supaya-lat even had she been bidden, for Silas Bagshaw never really recovered from that affray with the Burmese brigands, and on his next journey up-river he was carried ashore on a litter. Some strange fever had attacked him, and Fanny could but stay by him, or make fluttering little expeditions to her friends for help and moral support.

The Residency doctor attended him; Dr. Tarfels, himself ailing, came from the Palace on an elephant, looking like a huge white slug in his native dress. He did his best for the Captain, but no medicaments brought any relief to that great red turkeycock.

Although it was the cool weather, Captain Bagshaw seemed for the first time·to find his gross bulk drag unduly at his vitality. Fanny, ever willing to be occupied with the emotions of the moment, nursed him assiduously, but —even to her careless mind it struck with the ominousness of an echo—he seemed to be going the same way that her father had gone. His great red pendulous cheeks lost their rosy hue and became an unwholesome drab colour, netted over with a myriad little winey veins. His pale and rather pathetic-looking eyes seemed to be bolting out of his head, and his gross red hands, covered with dark hair, that, thickening as it went, disappeared up within the white circles of his cuffs, trembled perpetually.

Fanny was a good wife to him, as she had always been. She bore with his tempers and his fears and simply removed herself from their radius whenever she could, though never until she had done all that was possible for his physical well-being. Anything more had never been her province, nor had he demanded more of her—except for the pathetic feeling outwards of a failing elderly man towards youth and health, as though they might have some healing power that could be communicated. . . .

But it was not in Fanny to give help to him, sorry as she was for her old turkeycock. In the third week of November he had some kind of fit, and a native doctor, hastily called, let blood, a heroic measure that undoubtedly saved his life for a time. It was, however, only for a while, and in a few days Fanny was kneeling by her second death-bed in Mandalay.

She experienced no revolt against fate. She was practical, and though she had been fond enough of her old man and had experienced no revulsions with him, she was able without any difficulty to look upon her marriage as a brief experience that had slipped into her past.

She was not given to self-analysis, but she realised that she had always in the back of her mind considered her marriage to Captain Bagshaw an expedient that would in the very nature of things be but temporary. His death occupied her mind little, except that, without being unduly heartless, she found the status of the widow of a European mildly pleasant; her mind was occupied with business in the ensuing weeks. The newly-bought bungalow had to be sold, Captain Bagshaw's shares in various ventures, less sound than they would have been had Mindoon not died—for his ventures had been bound up with those of the King, who had loved experiments in trade—had to be realised. Mr. Lumsden and Mr. Shaw were both very kind in settling Fanny's business affairs for her, and Fanny, after thanking them very prettily, gathered together her personal belongings, and on receipt of a message from Supaya-lat, trotted happily back to the Palace—this time to stay.

In spite of Fanny's precocious awareness of her own body —not so very precocious, after all, considering her mixed blood—its first encounter with that for which it had been made had not proved particularly illuminating. Nevertheless, it had sufficed to quieten her curiosity, and had left her free to indulge in other ambitions. Hitherto, with all its slight and natural prickings of desire, the flesh had not been for Fanny nearly so important as her dreams of success and advancement. The magic of a palace, the glamour of rich presents, the perilous charm of friendship with Supaya-lat had occupied the forefront of her consciousness. To all these bright and beckoning things she now returned, her curiosity satisfied, her body for the time being not only appeased but satiated. The glamour of board-ship flirtations had resolved itself into something that she had hardly ever disliked and sometimes even enjoyed, but that, once attained, had not particularly interested her. Her body generally responded and her mind never rebelled, but the magic union of both remained unknown to her.

It was a curiously untouched and re-born Fanny who went to take up her abode in the City. After all, it was this she had always wanted, and it was at last within her hands. . . . For it was no longer as a casual visitant, but as a duly instated Maid of Honour, and European Maid of Honour at that—for that much she was indebted to her father and to her husband—that Fanny went to live in the Golden Palace.

## CHAPTER VI

# THE HAIRDRESSING IS CROWNED

Supaya-lat's experiment had drawn to a triumphant conclusion.. Though Sinbyew-mashin had raged vainly in the Western Palace, she and the Mingyis had proved powerless. Thibaw had refused to give up the Middle Princess, and so for nearly two months the great scandal of a woman living in the men's part of the Palace had persisted. In vain the Taingda Mingyi, who was all for the pomp of power, urged Thibaw that he should take unto himself at least eight Queens, as all self-respecting Kings had done before him, preparatory to collecting the hundred or so that were his due. In vain the Kinwoon Mingyi urged the same thing, for the reason that he realised that one wife would have much more influence on a man than fifty could have, and the Kinwoon Mingyi distrusted Supaya-lat very profoundly by now. He had thought that he and Sinbyew-mashin between them could rule the young monk and a handful of girl-wives easily enough, but they had none of them really known Supaya-lat . . .

In those two months during which she flouted all precedent—a brave thing indeed to do in that land where precedent is all-powerful—she grew into the heart and mind of the young monk. She was the first woman he had known and in the intoxication of it he got not only the need but the habit of her into his blood. To all protests he simply returned the message that the Middle Princess was to be his Queen.

At last he agreed to one concession for fear the scandal throughout his kingdom should be too violent. He agreed to take the Great Supaya in marriage at the same time. Supaya-lat cared nothing for this. She knew that there would be nothing between him and the plain nun-like Supaya-gyi, and even Supaya-lat was a little afraid, still being young in power, to go against all the Ministers of the Hloot-daw.

There was no actual wedding ceremony, for that is un-necessary in Burma, but the consecration of the two Queens was combined with the public appearance as wives that formed their nuptials. The whole Palace was astir like a hive of bees from early dawn, for there was much to be done. Three temporary little Palaces had been erected and decorated with gold leaf—the first in which the Queens were to perform the ceremonial head-washings; the second where they were to be robed, and the third where they were to wait until the auspicious moment—decided upon by the astrologers—when they were to proceed to the Bee Throne Room, had arrived.

In the head-washing and robing pavilions all the ritual waters were placed in readiness. Muddy water, charmed water, holy water, well water, water from a creek, water from a canal, river water for the bath, all stored in smooth gilded pots wrapped in thin red cloth and placed upon stands of red lacquer. Soaps, decoctions of bark and leaves, pastes of flowers, for the head-washing and bathing, and cotton cloths for drying with afterwards; gilded salvers with ritual cakes and fruit and skeins of black, red and white thread upon them; covered boxes of red lacquer containing the royal combs of ivory and sandalwood; a square flat pillow embroidered with the moon, on which to lean the royal left elbow; a square flat pillow embroidered with the sun, on which to lean the royal right elbow. . . .

Outside the pavilions where all these things were used in the successive rites, rows of musqueteers were drawn up; the Poet Laureate read out a poem suitable to the occasion; musical and dramatic performances were held; while in the Bee Throne Room all the precious stones in the Treasury were arranged in heaps and covered with finest velvet or Chinese felt.

And in the late afternoon of that day, the two Queens put on their crowns and went through the golden carved doors that gave upon the Bee Throne, Thibaw holding a hand of each.

Supaya-lat was as near being a beauty on that occasion

as she ever succeeded in being in all her life. Her magnificent eyes looked darker than ever with the intensity of her feeling. They all three stood there, looking, so thought Fanny, kneeling in the shadow of a great red lacquer pillar, like three divinities. Even the plain and already elderly Supaya-gyi was changed by her dress and tall mitre-like crown with jewelled lappets framing her face, to an impersonal abstraction of pure royalty. With the flame-like gold carvings of the golden doors spread behind them, they stood there in their tiered and wired robes of silvery brocade, flushed through with rose and yellow, stiffened wing-like epaulettes springing from their shoulders, looking indeed like the statues of benevolent Nats carved on the golden monasteries. They were too winged—tier after tier of winged and upspringing skirts and winged shoulders—to seem merely human. Even the shoes upon Thibaw's feet, the upcurved velvet shoes allowed only to royalty, seemed hardly to rest upon the Throne—those royal duck shoes with an arched bird's neck and silver wings that seemed as though they might bear their wearer upwards.

They all three sat down upon the Throne, and the learned Brahmin, Keeper of the Royal Time Piece, called out the hour. The Brahmins on the right and left of the Throne pronounced a blessing and then the Royal Messenger read out three odes, written by the Poet Laureate upon long tender palm-leaves.

Around the Throne the Maids of Honour clustered, wearing, instead of the jackets of every day, tight-fitting little coats of white and silver brocade, bright waistcoats of satin, and skirts like delicate rainbows. As they leant forward in their eager watching, the stiffly-wired tails of their little jackets stuck up into the air like the tails of a fleet of white drakes.

The Taingda Mingyi was there in his gorgeous dress of apricot velvet cut in pagoda shapes, but beneath his helmet-like head-dress of black and gold his face was cruel and set. The Kinwoon Mingyi was not present—it was an open secret that he had begun to repent of having helped to put Thibaw on the Throne and wished he had backed the

Nyaungyan Prince; and the Taingda Mingyi, though of lesser rank, had begun to oust him everywhere. The other great Ministers were there, in velvets and silks, and gold and gems, their wives equalling them in gorgeousness. Even the attendants along the edge of the Palace platform, in their green jackets, their green and gold turbans, and their red and silver pasoes caught up between their legs, gave an impression of true splendour, the dirt and tawdriness of their attire merged in the glitter.

That night the Supaya-gyi was given in all honour the apartment where Mindoon Min's Chief Queen had lived, but she was left there alone, while the Supaya-lat shared the King's own apartments with him and slept with him in his room, instead of occupying, as she should have, apartments in the Western Palace. She was the first of all the hundreds of the Queens of Ava to show such effrontery. Truly, everything had changed since Mindoon had ascended to the Home of the Nats.

## CHAPTER VII

# IN THE SPRING

QUIETNESS lay over Mandalay, Golden City and kalā town, but it was the quietness of a held breath, instinct with apprehension. In the Palace Fanny was the spoilt pet of Supaya-lat, who, rage she never so fiercely against others when the gusts of her temper shook her, never turned against Fanny. There was some quality in Fanny's presentation of her friendship for Supaya-lat that was exactly what that strange termagant needed. Fanny flattered her—but so did other people, so, in fact, did everybody. Fanny occasionally stood up to her—so always did Julie Delange. Fanny loved her—so, presumably, did Thibaw and Sinbyew-mashin. But Thibaw was bullied by her; and Sinbyew-mashin, though with no success, still tried to bully her. Only Fanny mingled her genuine feelings with her skilful presentation of them in just the right quantities, she herself could not have told how, and would not for a moment have admitted even to herself either the alchemy or its necessity.

So Fanny lived happily, though fearfully, in the Palace. Fearfully, not for herself but for others. Fear stalked through the scarlet-and-gold corridors of the great straggling Palace, lurked in its painted pavilions, caused voices to drop suddenly, and heads to turn over shoulders; unexpected cries would make a sudden hush of panic fall like an iron curtain at any moment. The Princes and all their womenkind, some eighty persons of the blood royal, were still kept in close confinement. Thibaw started to build a line of barracks for their accommodation, and this was the only thing that gave a ray of hope for the continuance of their lives.

The Great Supaya, nominally Chief Queen, lived in proud isolation in her apartments—the Middle Supaya, braving

tradition, still stayed perpetually by Thibaw's side in his
room in the Southern Palace.   Sinbyew-mashin sulked and
argued in her old apartments of the Centre Queen, or met
the Taingda Mingyi in pavilions, but even he, she felt, was
meeting her demands with casuistry, his faith really engaged
by Supaya-lat . . . by the girl who, only three months ago,
was a pawn to be moved at will.   Supaya-lat had indeed
grown in arrogance.

Fanny did her best to help the oppressed, partly from her
inborn love of intrigue, but more, to do her justice, from an
innate if facile kindliness.   Many were the loaves of bread
and the bowls of rice that Fanny smuggled into the half-
starved Queens and Princesses in their dungeons, food
provided by Fanny herself, by Mr. Shaw and the Lumsdens,
and by the Delanges and d'Avera.   Everywhere the acts of
mercy had to be carried on by means of bribery; money or
gifts in kind slipped from Fanny's small brown paw into the
broad palms of officers and gaolers.   Apparently all was
more or less settled as it was to continue in the life of the
Palace—prisoners and those free save from fear of offending,
were to drift on through the months of sun and rain. . . .

Even Mr. Lumsden, utterly without fear for himself,
ceased to worry over Agatha's safety, and she remained the
brave, composed missionary, teaching her little Burmese the
truths of the Christian religion.   For over a month this
strange unnatural calm, a calm like that before a typhoon,
held the two incongruous and nightmare cities as in the
hollow globe of one over-arching sphere.

Edward Protheroe was away on one of his missionary
tours, but he wrote letters telling of his progress and of his
thoughts anent the proper dissemination of religion, to
Agatha, who worked contentedly through January—a month
so exquisite, clear and pale, that it seemed steeped in a light
that shone through mother-of-pearl, the light which is
peculiarly the atmosphere of Mandalay in the spring.   The
incense of the villages went up into the golden air, the boys
and young men played chin-loon and courted the maidens,
the gay brown babies, creased and dimpled, rolled and
gurgled in the dust of the bazaars, or sat up contentedly at the

age of some one or two years to smoke large white cheroots or suck their mothers' breasts with equal enjoyment; the little women, their faces covered as with a pale yellow pollen with the powdered thana'kha, attended the pagoda festivals and the pwès, the racing and gaming, the buying and bargaining, the love-making and the dancing that went on amongst the merry, caste-free and carefree Burmese, in spite of grinding poverty from increased taxation, in spite of swift disease, of crimes of dacoits, and of a complete lack of any policy of protection from their Government. The wise men shook their heads, the relations of the imprisoned royalties went anxiously, but on the whole, for some six weeks after Supayalat's hairdressing experiment had been crowned with success, life flowed on very much as it had done in the days of Mindoon the Good. Fanny, living in the Palace, knew how different was the feel of things from the old days, but Agatha at the Mission House, sheltered from suspicion rather than confided in by the men of her own race, knew nothing.

Then Edward came back to the Mission House, and Agatha appeared in a new æsthetic dress, this time of white surah. Edward, greatly daring, said that she looked like Elaine, the Lily Maid of Astolat, and indeed she had long lost her too-high colour. He himself was being very much of a muscular Christian, and teaching his boys to play football. He ran and sweated, his cassock girt up about him, and Agatha felt a curious little thrill at this manliness. Like the Blessed Damosel, she leaned over the rail of the verandah to welcome him back from these exploits.

Edward found Agatha soothing. She did not seem, as he did, to agonise over the question of the pain of the world. She was practical and sensible over sick pi-dogs, but they did not cause her to arraign the Almighty. She merely blamed man and in her mind that did not inevitably lead to questioning the Deity. But though Edward envied this simplicity, at the same time his own simplicity accepted without question the assumption that Agatha was mysterious because she was a woman. Edward believed that no man could understand women. He believed this not because no human being can understand another, but because of something strange and incalculable that he thought resided in a woman by virtue of her sex.    Agatha did not undeceive him. For one thing she very nearly believed it herself.    Fanny would not have been taken in by such a proposition for a moment, but no one asked her opinion, and she was much too inarticulate to have given it.    Abstract thought held no part in Fanny's speech.

Edward, therefore, concealed his self-questionings, and met Agatha on the common ground of belief.    They read the "Holy Grail" together and dwelt lingeringly on that passage where the nun places the belt about Sir Galahad. In a mutual passion of celibacy they walked beside the splendid heathen glittering moat in the spring evenings.

Agatha, strong in her convictions, when she had embroidered Edward a stole, longed for the courage to quote: "I, maiden, round thee, maiden . . ." as she placed it about his neck.    But she felt self-conscious and embarrassed, and Edward, suddenly aware of that within himself which did not chime truly with the occasion, went abruptly away. Edward was perhaps foolish, but he was honest.    Agatha was perhaps not quite so foolish and not quite so honest either, but even she was too ignorant to be consciously dishonest.    They played with their lives in a pathetic ignorance of nature that would indeed have been laughable to the youngest page in the Palace.

Nevertheless, Sir Galahad and the nun between them might have caused Edward and Agatha to realise a certain difference in themselves from these ideal beings, had not the Zulus in Zululand brought this consummation about more expeditiously.    Cetewayo and his followers killed over eight hundred Englishmen at Isandhlwana, and incidentally caused the death of over eighty men, women and children in the Gem City of Mandalay, but they had at least the union of Edward and Agatha to their credit.    And Fanny, unimportant little Fanny, was the agency that brought together all these unrelated incidents and made of them a force. Fanny, who had no idea in her head beyond getting some crumpled muslins ironed by Agatha's dhobie.

## CHAPTER VIII

## ISANDHLWANA

FANNY, routing in the red and gold chests where she kept her clothes, had decided that her muslins were crumpled, and that someone must become busy with the iron if she were to hold with honour her position as a European. She hated to wield iron or needle herself, and besides it was apparent that, even ironed, some of these muslins needed a new sash or ribbons. Agatha was always generous with her possessions. Fanny decided to pay her a visit. The Mission dhobie could iron the frocks while they had tea. Therefore Fanny obtained leave of absence from the Mistress of the Maids, the black-browed daughter of the fierce Taingda Mingyi, and, calling a bullock-cart, was borne through the enclosed City, out of the ignominious Western Gate, over the arched white bridge, to the triple-roofed Mission.

Agatha was quite prepared to be agreeable in the matter of the ribbons and that of the dhobie, but her permission was off-hand and without real interest. Mr. Shaw and Edward were there, talking with Agatha and Mr. Lumsden, and Fanny, feeling at once that it was the sort of talk that did not interest her, went through to Agatha's bedroom with her parcel. When she came back, however, they were still at it. Edward's face was white and shining, both the older men looked very grave. "An unparalleled disaster," Edward was saying, "an English force utterly out-generalled, defeated by savages . . . over eight hundred English killed!" And Edward looked very much at that moment as though he had mistaken his vocation and should have been a temporal rather than a spiritual soldier. On every face there was not only grief but that added touch of strain, almost a sort of exaltation that is natural to those living as a small minority among enemies and potential enemies.

Mr. Shaw, the quietest in any emotion, shrugged his shoulders.

"It is a disaster, a terrible disaster, but of course it will be retrieved. The tragedy of Isandhlwana will be avenged, and the Zulu taught their lesson. Unfortunately these lessons are expensive in more than money. I'm having a pretty trying time with O'Hara since the telegram came. He will trail his coat, says that Bartle Frere is to blame for the whole thing, that Cetewayo is a splendid fellow, and that as usual England is riding roughshod over small nations. That comes of being Irish. It doesn't prevent him serving the Government. Queer race."

A shade of intolerance passed over Mr. Lumsden's narrow countenance.

"Bishop Colenso, I have heard, has long been the only white man to stand by Cetewayo. He drifts towards heresy by sheer force of nature, apparently."

"Nevertheless," observed Shaw, with the ghost of a smile, "he is very good at arithmetic. He's wrong this time about what two and two make, all the same. Cetewayo has some of the savage virtues, but he's a tyrannical brute. You remember the time he massacred all those girls because they'd married men of their own age instead of the men of an older regiment that he'd designed them for?"

Massacred . . . the word sounded very ugly in that room, that was suddenly held by a little spell of stillness, emphasised rather than disturbed by the swift, sharp tonk-tonk-tonk of a coppersmith bird from the sun-dappled greenery without.

"Look here," said Shaw; "there's no reason why we should brandish this news abroad. It'll be a couple of weeks before any newspapers can get up from Rangoon. I only got the wire from there this morning. Unless one of the foreign powers sees fit to wire it to any of their agents here, there's no reason it need get out yet awhile."

"Exactly. We will all keep it to ourselves."

"There's Fanny in the doorway," said Agatha suddenly. The men turned sharply; Mr. Shaw frowned, then his face cleared. Little Fanny looked so harmless and graceful, so almost pathetic, in her hesitancy.

"Mrs. Bagshaw must promise us to keep everything she has heard here absolutely to herself," he said.

"Indeed I will," promised Fanny, and meant it. What were the Zulu to her? All she knew about them was that they lived in South Africa, like those people called the Boers, who were always giving trouble. The English were always being worried about something. There was Afghanistan, there was what they called the menace of Russia, there was Turkey, and now the Zulu. And over eight hundred English soldiers wiped out, defeated. . . .

If it were none of these things, then it would be the respective merits of Mr. Gladstone and Mr. Disraeli. . . . A strange and a dreary world to Fanny! For her, as for everyone else caught within its walls by its strange attraction, all of importance in the world went on within the Palace.

To Agatha that hidden and fabled life partook of the stuffless substance of a dream, and it sometimes terrified her to realise how completely Brighton and all it stood for had ceased to exist for Fanny. For even if Fanny were not interested in the news of the British Empire, there was still the world of missionary endeavour lying before her—a world that was really interesting . . . but that she never seemed to understand.

However, on this occasion Fanny was sorry for the bad news, and sorrier still for those girls of an earlier date who had been killed because they had married the young men they wanted. She stayed talking with the facile sympathy that made her charm till her muslins were finished. Then, the sash and ribbons duly appropriated, she took her leave, glad to see the last of such gloomy friends.

Between the Mission and the City gates she came across that handsome French engineer Bonvoisin. He swept off his pith hat and she signalled to her driver to stop. He came and stood beside her bullock-cart, resting one hand—a long, fine hand, she noticed—on the edge of it. He reproached her with not having emerged from the Palace to see her French friends for too long. Fanny flirted her long eyelashes at him happily. And then, suddenly, for no reason at all, in the irrational way of such things, something in the turn of his head, in the look of his long-fingered hand, struck at her heart. . . . Nothing quite like it had ever happened to Fanny before. A strange excitement pervaded her. Her eyelashes ceased to flutter, her face became grave.

" You come from Mademoiselle Delange now? " he asked.

" No, from the Lumsdens."

" Ah, you care only for your English friends, and perhaps your Burmese. For the latter, I agree, they are charming; but the English! That long-faced clergyman and that tedious Shaw, and that, oh, so English miss ! "

" Agatha is my friend," said Fanny, pleased nevertheless, for slighting of Agatha was somehow praise of herself, " but they are all dreadfully serious. And to-day—oh my, they are worse than ever."

M. Bonvoisin asked why, with a world of solicitude for Fanny's boredom in his voice. Fanny opened her mouth to reply, and then suddenly stopped. She remembered she'd been asked to say nothing of the news from South Africa. Bonvoisin watched her curiously.

" What were they serious about? Is there bad news from Afghanistan? No—I should have heard it."

" Not Afghanistan. South Africa."

After all, they had only meant her not to talk at the Palace. M. Bonvoisin was different. And it was so oddly delightful to be in the position of dispenser of knowledge to M. Bonvoisin. The dissemination of news gives a moment of importance, even of power.

" The English army has been beaten by the Zulus—at a place with a funny name. I can't quite think of it . . ." Then, in an effort to satisfy the question in his eyes—" Wait a minute. Yes, I know now. Isandhlwana, that's it. They were beaten by a sort of king, Cetewayo."

And Fanny leaned back triumphantly. She had a retentive memory for detail.

" Dear me, I am sorry. But perhaps it is not very serious— how many men did you say were killed? "

" Over eight hundred, I think they said, anyway it was all the English army there was there. It is sad because Cetewayo is a bad man, really worse than Bartle Frere. He once massacred a lot of girls because they married young men they loved instead of a regiment of old men that he'd wanted them to marry."

"That was a dreadful crime. To interfere with love!" And M. Bonvoisin made a gesture, showing his horror of such an action, with the hand that had been lying lightly on the edge of Fanny's bullock-cart. The removal of that hand which had so fascinated her gaze, broke the crystal minute for Fanny. M. Bonvoisin again raised his hat, pressed his fair moustache upon her hand, and departed. Fanny was borne on, through the City of Gems, to the Palace.

## CHAPTER IX

# PREPARATION

NEWS travelled swiftly—swelling, snowball-like, as it went, in the Palace. Fanny heard next morning, to her mild surprise, that M. Bonvoisin had had a private interview the day before with the King in the semi-state Morning Levée Room. A little disquiet stirred uneasily in Fanny's mind. . . . Why should Bonvoisin have been to the Palace for a special interview? Of course he had not told Thibaw about the disaster to the British—what had it got to do with him, anyway? Yet she kept the half-guilty knowledge that she had told it him, in her own heart. It might be unpleasant for him with the British if they knew . . . you couldn't tell.

And Fanny—child of no man's land, of Tom Tiddler's Ground, where all felt at liberty to pick up gold and silver—knew no tug of loyalty that was not purely personal. Why indeed, should she? True, she was one quarter English, but it had not been the peculiar genius of Miss Patterson to weld new material into national fibre, as it is of the American nation. She was half Italian, but Italy was to her but a name, and what had been her father's pride was to her but a phrase. To be a European was to her only a snobbish satisfaction, nothing more.

Easily now she persuaded herself that her meeting with Bonvoisin had had nothing to do with his audience with the King. She could picture that so well; in the weeks since his accession she had heard of, had peeped upon, so many! The suppliant arrived, shed his shoes on the platform, was ushered into the Morning Levée Room, and was sat down on the carpet so that he should have cramp thoroughly well set-in to his legs before royalty even arrived. Then Thibaw would appear, bolting through the gold carved door like an

agitated rabbit, and fling himself on his salun-daw. He
would carry on a disjointed conversation with the visitor,
spit straight upon the carpet instead of into the golden
spittoon, and then jerk himself out through the golden door
again. The visitor would then be taken out of doors and
regaled on brandy and water out of a teapot—Prohibition
obtaining within the Golden Palace. Fanny knew all
about it. . . . How could she take it seriously? It did
not seem vital to her that Bonvoisin, who was very much
*persona grata* at Court, and was employed on important
works, should have had a private interview with Thibaw Min.

Nevertheless, a strange feeling ran through the Palace
that there was something astir, something strange and
perhaps terrible . . . but this was probably only because
Sinbyew-mashin was known to have been closeted with the
Taingda Mingyi and with Thibaw and Supaya-lat. Yet it
turned out to be nothing but a pwè—a better and a finer
pwè than Thibaw had yet given. He lived so strangely
withdrawn since his accession, that his people knew little of
him.

During the great Tawadeintha feast in November, he had
been rapt away with Supaya-lat, having his rather scanty
hair attended to, since he was but newly shaven from his
monkhood. The same applied to the Sondawgyi feast, with
which the Tawadeintha was connected. In fact, Thibaw
had never even undertaken the traditional encircling of the
City—he had never left the precincts of the Palace itself.
In Burmese custom, he who could get to sit, even .for a
moment, upon the actual Lion Throne, was King of Ava, and
probably, even with all his relations in gaol, Thibaw Min
did not feel too safe about leaving the precincts of the Palace
for half an hour.

Why, anyway, be anxious, when all the stir and bustle
resolved themselves merely into a pwè? And what a
magnificent pwè it was to be, or rather series of pwès! The
famous Maung Tha Byaw, greatest actor and stage manager
in all Burma, was to present his Company at the Palace, and
the King was, of his generosity, to provide other pwès, not
only for the City within the walls, but for Mandalay town.

All night long the singing and dancing and feasting were to go on. Bands of musicians and troupes of actors and dancing girls were sent for, and began to stream along the roads. Money for the entertainment of the people was to pour from the royal coffers, let what province or trade be bled for it that might, when all was over.

A feverish activity began to infect the very air, and caused the kalās, and especially the English, to stare at each other in a growing amazement and unease. Mr. Shaw murmured uneasily of *panem et circenses*.

By the next day all was ready, the Palace gardens were strung about with thousands of fairy lamps. All night long relays of servants were to run from one to another, replenishing them with oil or setting the touch of living flame to the wicks. The little Maids of Honour anxiously consulted about their clothes, and keen was the anxiety to know what the Queen was to wear, for already it was well known that not only disgrace but much worse would befall any luckless girl who donned a tamein of the same colour as the one Supaya-lat had chosen. Often, of a morning, there was a scurry to change, after a surreptitious glance had been taken through a peephole at what the Queen was wearing. . . . One of the reasons for Fanny's popularity at the Palace was that she, who could enter Supaya-lat's presence in her European clothes, was so good-natured in sending out information as to the Queen's apparel.

On this evening Fanny dined as usual in her room with another of the Maids who was a friend of hers, and then, donning one of the white muslins with Agatha's primrose sash and ribbons, went along to wait on the Queen. Supaya-lat wore one of the beautiful " zig-zag " tameins, woven with many shuttles, of pale pink, green and silver, and Fanny came back with the news.

Among the innovations introduced into the Palace since the death of Mindoon Min was French wine, of which Thibaw had discovered that he liked to drink freely. The King and Queen dined together at about four o'clock off rice and curry. Supaya-lat, as always, drank water, but Thibaw started to drink champagne with his dinner on this particular day, and kept on drinking it at intervals to Sky-shutting-in-time, when the music began from without the room in which he sat. Strange native music, heavy with drums and gongs, wailful with bagpipes and clarions, clamorous with cymbals, and pierced by the thin sweet notes of flutes, and silken-stringed harps; while always the clatter of the castanets, made of split bamboos five feet long, assaulted the ears.

Sky-shutting-in-time was quickly over, its rose and gold died, and Brothers-would-not-know-each-other-time spread its soft greyness over the world. The thousands of little fairy lamps sprang into flame, like crocuses breaking into flower, and Thibaw called for more and louder music. The Palace was ringed about with clamour now. From the far-off kalā town the noise of other bands could be heard, when for a moment the Palace bands paused for breath or to change musicians, and always Thibaw clamoured for more. At his supper at nine he drank more champagne, laced with brandy, and then the pwè began.

The King and Queen and Sinbyew-mashin sat on cushions at the front of the Theatre drawing-room; all of one wall was rolled away, and the theatre, built on a raised stage in the roadway below, was level with their eyes. Behind them clustered, thick as flowers in a bed, the little ladies in their bright silk tameins and the courtiers in their flaming pasoes or gaudy uniforms. The footlights, wicks floating in oil, flickered brightly, picking out here and there the sparkling glass mosaics with which the walls and pillars were encrusted, and shining upon the golden betel-nut boxes and spittoons that were the emblems of royalty.

Thibaw sat, half drunk, with a furtive, scared look on his face, sprawled across his cushions. Behind him the brilliant glass mosaic in the far recesses of the great room flashed and twinkled; before him the footlights flickered and the ceaseless intonations of the posturing chorus filled the air. Only beyond the theatre there was rest, away in the dark soft night, so dark that the plumy drooping shapes of the great trees only showed against it by the blotting out of the rich stars. Supaya-lat sat twisted round on her cushion in the supple

Eastern fashion, her dark eyes intent upon his lowering face.

" Oh, Kodaw, watch," she whispered, " you will see the triumph of Kings and the triumph of love. You will see enemies confounded . . ."

Thibaw stirred and looked at her. A certain animation came into his face as though her intense belief in life went into him.

" To-night we do not see the religious plays, the ten great Birth Stories or one of the five hundred and ten Jatakas. The life of Our Lord is great indeed, but it is not for my lord to-night. He shall see princes overcoming their enemies, and how when a man is born to greatness it must be that he becomes great."

Thibaw, looking at that intent and watchful face, felt a stirring of admiration that was really relief at her superior conviction. She was so sure of what things were worth while . . . and they were none of them the things which he had been taught mattered when he was in the monastery. She was right, as usual. He did not want to-night, of all nights, to see a play dealing with poverty and charity, he did not want to hear of the sharp hell lying in wait for evil-doers, or of the deep-sunk country of the nagas; he did not even want to hear of the possibility of mastering the deadly sins. She was right—he wanted to see princes overcoming their enemies, lovers long-separated triumphing at last; he wanted to be told again and again, with the drugging effect of constant repetition, of singing and dancing, how a man fated to the high places must by force of destiny rise to them. He wanted to see the dancing-girls writhe in their incredibly supple contortions, their arms rippling like thin banners in a breeze; he wanted to hear their nasal voices singing loudly, persistently, to the clamour of the band, in that strange music, so discordant and monotonous to European ears, in which the Burman detects such fine shades of melody.

He wanted all these things as he wanted the wine that the pages poured out for him. He wanted to hear these sounds as passionately as he did not want to hear other sounds that would be going up into the warm, soft air that night. He wanted these sights of make-belief as much as he did not want to see what would be taking place under cover of all this noise, in the deep shadows cast by such a wide-flung glitter.

The play began, the play that would go on all night.

## CHAPTER X

# THE PLAY

THE king upon the stage threw away the large green cheroot he was smoking and took up his rôle. The queen, who did not have to appear yet awhile, went on making up her face at the side of the stage, in full view of the audience. The courtiers, also abandoning their cheroots, gathered about their king.

*Are my subjects happy and prosperous ?*

*Since your Majesty's most happy reign began, religion has shone forth with splendour. The seasons have been propitious—the earth has been bountiful—the rich and poor, men and women, have enjoyed peace and prosperity, and the happy years have been to them as water to the lotus.*

The music, diminished to allow of the actors' speeches being heard, allowed also of a long and dreadful scream that tore across the night . . . it was as though the sky itself had been made of a piece of stretched silk, and the hand of a god had ripped it in twain. . . .

The Taingda Mingyi, his dark face convulsed with rage, signalled to the zat-oke to continue immediately—for in the panic of the moment the actors had checked in their parts. The music crashed out again as the queen ran upon the stage.

*Beloved queen, the constellation of the Orion and the Moon are now near to each other, and the season is cold. When thou wishest to go out into the sun, wrap thyself in this crimson cloak, put this sparkling ring on thy finger, and go forth to enjoy thyself.*

Only a few of these words came to the audience, for now the music blared perpetually. An immense bird entered, and, mistaking the queen's red cloak for a large lump of flesh, flew away with her to a mountain and deposited her in a tree. In spite of the music, another scream was heard as the great bird attacked the queen, and she scared it away by clapping her hands at it. Again the music crashed out and, alone in her tree, the queen wept. The stage directions at this point, read out by the manager, were to the effect that it came on to rain and that the queen gave birth to a son.

Girls came on and danced while the scene was changed to the front of a hermit's cave. The queen's son was by now full-grown. He was a handsome young man and played on a golden harp. His mother, her voice drowned by the clamour of the music, advised him to seek his father's country and gave him the red cloak and ring as proof of his identity.

Thereafter the story of the prince was a story of triumph, and from being the adopted child of a hermit he rose to be king and to marry a princess. It was played to the crash of cymbals and the loud singing of the dancing-girls. In the glittering glass drawing-room the audience sat, half-enthralled, half ill-at-ease. On with the noise, the posturing . . . let nothing from that world so near at hand, yet so much further than even this mimic world of make-believe, strike upon the senses. . . .

On and on went the play, with scenes of broad comedy between clowns, with love-songs and dances, on and on, till the sky was pale with the reluctant dawn. Thibaw drank his wine; the audience kept themselves awake by chewing let-pet; the strong pickled tea that was handed round by the sleepy little pages. Fresh musicians came and began to play before the others had well finished. The play went on, the flames of the oil-lamps sickly in the light of morning.

## CHAPTER XI

## THREE DAYS

FANNY, sick at heart with apprehension, looking far more bedraggled than any of the pure-blooded Burmans, with a wan, grey hue upon her face that matched the dawn, obtained permission to go to her own room.   Once there, she found one of her jaunty little hats, perched it on anyhow, and stole forth into the strangely deserted gardens.   She was ringed about with the noise of the music still, but for a brief space of time it seemed as though the grass and trees were new-washed and clean.   Only for a moment. . . . She crossed to a space beyond the women's garden and ran into a servant, a great muscular man, naked save for his loin-cloth, who was hurrying through the grey morning so swiftly that he did not notice her until he had cannoned into her. . . . He was bearing over his naked shoulder, and holding with a burly arm so wet with sweat that the dawn reflected on it as into water, a scarlet velvet sack.   A sack that bulged hideously . . . a sack through which a dreadful warmth, more dreadful than any chill, still made itself felt to Fanny.

She started back from that contact.   Too late she saw her mistake.   She had been making, by instinct, for the Western Gate, because it was the nearest to the Mission, to that blessed kalā town where lived people with some relation to what at that time was uppermost in Fanny—her kinship with a world where life was regarded as sacred.   And the Western Gate was the gate by which corpses were removed from the Gem City.   It was the outlet of ignominy to the Irrawaddy.

Fanny turned and ran back to her own room.   She stayed there all day, and in the evening again essayed escape.   But she ran into a procession of carts making for the Western Gate—their axles screaming with the noise that was so

familiar to all the inhabitants of both towns, the sound made
by un-oiled axles as the vegetable-carts came into market.
Fanny took one look at the burden these carts bore, and once
again turned back and fled. Her nerves were worn down by
the music that had never ceased to play since noon of the day
before. Everything that was European in Fanny was in
turmoil. The noise, instead of drugging her, was so upon
her nerves she could have screamed. She did cry bitterly that
second day upon her pillow.

These carts had finished Fanny, for there had not been
enough scarlet velvet sacks woven by Delange and his
daughter to cope with this situation, and the carts had displayed their naked horrors. Princes of the blood should lie
dead in sacks of scarlet velvet—not be left to sprawl their
limbs unashamed to the skies. Once again Fanny turned and
hurried back to the sparse sanctuary of her little room.

The third day she started out again. The music, the plays
and the screams were still going on. By now she did not
ask permission of the daughter of the Taingda Mingyi.
People in the Palace were beyond such trivialities. Always
the music went on and on, always it could be heard across
the moat, echoing from the kalā town. The world was
ringed about with hideousness. No one thought or slept—
except the exhausted, sodden sleep of beasts. Everywhere
man was setting up the barrier of noise against his deeds, and
so against his gods. Noise, noise, noise. . . . Where Mindoon had lain through the quiet nights while his Queens read
to him from the sacred writings, the air was striped and zig-
zagged with noise as varied as an intricately woven tamein.

It was never to be wholly quiet again. For all the years
he existed in the Palace, Thibaw was to have such music
made for him night and day. He cried if it left off, the stillness woke him into a dreadful awareness.

Once again Fanny set forth. She had to pass by what
had been the women's garden to reach the Western Gate,
the only one through which she had a chance of passing
without questioning. All seemed quiet, and she hurried on,
she had no sense of whether it were dawn or dusk. She was
simply thankful for the comparative quiet. Noise there

still was, but lights at least were dimmed. And suddenly the quiet was rent and distorted by screams. Scream upon scream that tore the air about her and the frightened heart within her breast. She heard her own name in those screams.

Distracted with terror, she turned and saw the whole earth dug up into a huge pit that had been hastily refilled. As she started at it she saw the ground heave as though with a monstrous and unnatural life of its own. A light haze hung above it. The movement of limp, silk-clad bodies that lay about the lip of the pit, so informed the earth with a shocking semblance of automatic motion, that it caught her eye. For a moment she thought of an earthquake, sent as a judgment of God.

Then she saw that the figures half buried in the soil still stirred with a sentient life of their own. She turned to fly, when again her own name struck upon her ears. Against her will, again she turned.

The figure of a girl came rushing out from the women's gaol on the further side of the pit, and Fanny recognised the young sister of the Thahgaya Prince, with whom she had often played in the peaceful days of Mindoon Min. The girl had seen her and was still shrieking to her by name. The next moment two big naked men had seized her and forced her downwards. Quickly they passed cords about her frantic hands and bound them between her knees. Fanny, too terrified to turn her eyes away, much as she longed to, saw another man force the girl's head back. They killed her after the Burmese fashion, with blows from a club across her smooth young throat. Fanny, mercifully able after the first blow, to cover her eyes with her hands, heard half a dozen more before silence fell, for the girl had been young and strong. Fanny somehow managed to get back to her room and crouched down in a corner.

The play was still going on—by now the prince and princess must have triumphed over their enemies and the wicked have been put to confusion. The singing and music came beating in at Fanny unrelentingly. Again she set forth, after eating the rice and curry a scared servant brought to her. The life of the Palace went on apparently undisturbed in spite of the cries that even the music could not always drown. And at last, on that third morning, there were no more cries and there were merciful breathing spaces in the storm of music. Fanny once more got together a few things and started to leave the Palace. With head averted she passed the burying-ground of the women, but the strangeness of what she saw out of the corner of her eye made her pause.

A dozen of the Palace elephants were being driven back and forth, goaded on by their keepers, the place seemed filled by their vast and swaying bulks, and by their waving trunks that snorted protests. For the outraged soil had refused the martyred flesh thrust into it, and had heaved up and ·disclosed it, thrust it forth in all its accusing misery, its pathos of broken limbs and limp dangling heads, and the elephants were being forced to trample earth and flesh down once again. The sensitive beasts, knowing that they were violating a law by placing their feet upon even these remnants of humanity, their nostrils sickened by the escaping gases, were urged on by the attendants, who cared nothing and encouraged the inferior animals with shouts and goads.

## CHAPTER XII

## AFTERMATH

FANNY, white, draggled, and almost speechless, arrived to find a Mission House already frantic with alarm. No reliable news had escaped the Palace, but everyone in the kalā town knew that murder and perhaps wholesale massacre was abroad. Those cartloads of murdered Princes on their way to the river had been impossible to hide. The whole town was rife with rumours, it was buzzing like bees; it was running hither and thither like ants from a damaged anthill. Fanny, entering on the conclave of English at the Mission, felt a thrill of importance when she saw the eagerness with which the anxious white people fell upon her. She had been seriously frightened, more than frightened, horrified, but she could not help being aware of her own importance now. The quick revulsion of feeling was too much for her, and she burst into tears.

Agatha, who had never seen Fanny cry except after the awful affair with Mrs. Murgatroyd on board ship, and after her father's death, ran to her anxiously. This was not the usual self-assured Fanny who was apt to patronise her from her secure position as royal favourite. Fanny cried till at last Mr. Shaw said sarcastically, " Well, we can't get anything intelligent out of her. I'm expecting old Raj Singh down to-day, and he'll tell me everything. . . . "

Fanny sat up and, drying her eyes, took a sip of coffee and said that she felt better. When she began to tell her tale, the dreadful reality of it rushed over her spirit and she told it simply and well, with a few pathetic, because unconscious, movements of her little hands. Agatha, horrified, stared at her in awe.

" Oh, Fanny, not all the poor little babies too? "

Fanny nodded. "Do you know how many altogether, Mrs. Bagshaw?" asked the Resident; "they say . . . Ma Thin told us . . . about eighty."

Fanny assented. "Everyone, Mr. Shaw; nearly all the Queens and Princesses, and all the Princes . . ."

"That agrees with my information, Lumsden." There was a little silence. Both men realised to the full the gravity of the situation. Already Shaw had received warning from the little Salin Princess, still alive amid the carnage—probably protected by the nun's dress she had assumed on her father's death—that the party in power at the Palace talked of attacking the Residency. . . . The Residency that could not be defended, and that when it went up in flames would be the signal for the destruction of all the English in Mandalay. Apart from the safety of Agatha, Mr. Lumsden felt no personal worries. Martyrdom was all in the day's work to him, an unexpectedly brilliant crown to a dull journey. In martyrdom all his thwarted sense of beauty, all his aching consciousness of failure, would find at once satisfaction and recompense. And martyrdom it would be if a massacre of the English were decided upon by the maniacs of the Palace. A faint unwonted colour burned on his high cheek-bones.

Mr. Shaw felt nothing but distaste. He had not wanted this job of Resident in a country where he did not even know the language, he had not been either in the military or the civil services, he was a traveller and a scholar, and he felt his good taste was outraged by these gross doings. Also he had not felt at all well of late; he had been suffering from rheumatism, which was not remarkable, considering that the Residency roof leaked everywhere. He was as without fear as any man could be; what he felt was resentment.

He left Fanny to the Lumsdens and took his way, followed by his servants bearing over him the umbrellas that were the mark of his official status, back to the shabby, sordid Residency, which looked, he told himself, as though Great Britain cared very little how her servants were housed. The truth was that in spite of all this talk of Empire brought in by Disraeli—though God knew he was a better man than Gladstone, who would let anyone be killed anywhere without

exacting punishment as long as the person was an Englishman—still the greatest days of England were over.  Imagine
an employee of the old John Company being housed as he,
Resident in a foreign country, was housed!

Thibaw would not have dared perpetrate such horrors under
the nose of a British Resident if he did not believe that the
arm of Britain was shortened, so that it could not save. . . .
And why had he suddenly come to that conclusion?

Probably he had heard of the disaster of Isandhlwana—
Shaw felt himself an idiot to have imagined it could be kept a
secret in such a city of spies and factions.

He composed himself to make his protest to the Court of
Ava and to send his cable to the Foreign Secretary at Calcutta.
And as he sat, the pen between his fingers, he began to feel a
tightening about the heart.  He got up and walked his room.
Mr. Shaw did not care about his job, although it carried
a salary of nearly £4,000 a year; he did not by now like
Burma.  But even his scholar's blood could not but feel the
charm of the most delightful and feminine women in the
world.  Many of these murdered Princesses he had met, and
now, as he paced the uneven floor of his miserable Residency,
he could see again their little heart-shaped faces, their thin
delicate fingers, could hear their gay laughter, and all their
grace and charm of manner suddenly seemed to come alive
and fill the room with their own exquisiteness.  Ah! their
flattering politeness, their heady hint of submissiveness . . .!
Dead . . . horribly dead, by violence and brutality unspeak-
able, all of those pliant creatures . . . and their delicious little
children, so plump and creased, so full of laughter.  And
then he realised, with a groan, that not for many weeks had
that gaiety, that soft roundness of either mothers or children,
obtained.  Half-starved, dragged down by heavy chains,
kept in darkness and filth, they must at the time of the
massacre have looked very different from  the darling
creatures of a few months ago.

He wrote and sent off a letter to the Kinwoon Mingyi :—

" The Resident has heard with the deepest horror of the
slaying of the Princes and Princesses of the royal family and

others.  The Resident has not had time to ascertain who are the authors of this massacre, which will excite the horror of every nation in Europe.  But he entreats the Minister to use his utmost endeavours to save the lives of the survivors. Should any further slaughter take place, the Resident would not be justified in keeping the British flag flying any longer here."

Again he took the pen in his hand, and when he had written he sent for Rawlinson, who came, pale yet important through his terrors.  Shaw handed him the telegram, and Rawlinson went off with it, like a cat with its prey, licking his lips as he read it.

"*General slaughter late King's sons with their mothers, wives, children, some eighty souls, took place successive nights at prison by order of King.  No provocation, conspiracy, or otherwise. Ministers supposed to disapprove, people alarmed, horrified.  I threatened haul down flag, if slaughter repeated.*"

Shaw thought over this effort after Rawlinson had dis-appeared with it.  If the slaughter were " repeated " there would be no one left alive who had anything to do with the royal family. . . . It was all true as far as it went;  he had remonstrated with the Kinwoon Mingyi, an old man as help-less and as stricken as himself . . . if they met, with their old eyes they would look at each other across this arid space made by the young iconoclasts . . . and much good would it do.  He drew his pad towards him and wrote again :—

"*I respectfully submit stern remonstrance ought to be made ; and it is for consideration whether friendly relations ought to be maintained with so brutal and barbarous a King, and whether the Resident ought not to be at once withdrawn.*"

Again he sent for Mr. Rawlinson, and this second telegram was hurled off to the Foreign Secretary at Calcutta.  Then Mr. Shaw felt tired with a deadly tiredness that was like the on-coming of doom.  He dragged off his clothes and went to bed. Like Thibaw, he was never to leave his enclosing walls again.

## CHAPTER XIII

## EVENING

FANNY, a sodden little bundle, was at last got safely into bed by an efficient, maternal Agatha. The two girls had really nothing in common, but the accident of a school friendship would always make them unable to free themselves entirely. Like relations, they were bound together more or less, for the span of life, however disagreeable they found the tie. There would always be between them the strong bond of a youth shared, and now there would be also the even stronger one of peril shared. So Agatha petted Fanny and watched her till she dropped asleep.

The golden light was turning to the warm copper of evening when Agatha came out to the verandah and found her father there, stretched out on a long chair and indulging in a very unusual peg. He raised his full drooping lids and looked at her. In his look she felt more than she ever had before. In the emotional and perilous edge on which they were all living, there was a certain danger of over-emphasis but also a chance of getting at the true values that he and she particularly were ordinarily too self-conscious to recognise. How limited, thought Lumsden, was the European family compared with this spacious spilling of seed in the East. . . . Yet nearly all the children of Mindoon could be obliterated in one night's work, and he had only Agatha. . . . A dear girl and a good girl, if rather like her mother . . . poor soul.

And, looking at Agatha now, her face refined by sleepless hours of dread and pity, she was very precious to him, and even, so he thought, to the world. And, as a symbol, he was right. Agatha stood then for the life of the race which if a man ceases to preserve, he is lost indeed. Any sentimental value of the women-and-children-first type, which might be wholly erroneous and founded upon the material for easy tears, was swamped in the hard fact that she did indeed represent young untouched life of clean pure stock.

Mr. Lumsden reproached himself bitterly that he had not sent her away when first he had meant to do so. Agatha stood looking questioningly at him for a moment. He noticed how flame-like her fair hair was in the evening light.

"Fanny?" he asked almost idly, rather more for something to say, to hide the rush of warm feeling that threatened to overwhelm him, than because he really wondered how little Fanny was faring.

"I think she'll sleep now. . . ." There was, he recognised, a something unforced and genuine about the maternal note in Agatha's voice that there had never been before. She was not thinking of Agatha, the selfless missionary. She was thinking of Fanny, and more, of the little dead women, some of whom she had met and talked to with so much stilted politeness and so little real humanity. . . . He began to say something about taking the next boat—if there ever were a next boat—to Rangoon, but it seemed unimportant in face of this real Agatha. Perhaps there was a consciousness of personal danger about her which, with her youth, she shouldn't have felt; she was aware of it as an enhancing quality that gave importance. . . . Mr. Lumsden felt that it was not for him to judge; he had himself been so dreadfully unaware of the reactions of human relations with Agatha's mother, that her daughter had every moral right to take it out of him now. . . .

Agatha paused politely for a moment and then went down the verandah steps. He knew he ought to have called her back, but he let her go. If she were going to use danger as an emotional asset she must take her physical risks. He had, too, a shrewd suspicion that Edward would not be far off.

And Edward was indeed waiting for her by the gate. The shade of a great mango tree was heavy over the entrance to the Mission, but these two took no advantage of it. They went their usual walk by the moat—a courageous proceeding enough with every native peering doubtfully at them, but, as Edward said, excusing the taking of Agatha into danger the Burmese as well as the kalās were terrified. The nightmare noise of Thibaw's pwès was still rolling round the town like a monstrous dance-band that would never stop, a hell designed for perpetual revellers. But it was fainter now, the fear of those who listened and the natural exhaustion of those who played began to lighten the burden of that dreadful noise.

Edward and Agatha stood by the shining moat and looked across to the rose-flushed walls of the City; they saw the glittering golden barges and golden spires, and, marvelling that so much beauty could hide such horror, turned to look at each other. The golden air lay smooth upon their young skins; the glamour of immediate danger lay upon their glances. They knew it was not a mere idle thought that a few hours might set an end to their days, days that had hitherto been so bare of love-making. The pressure of danger had lit within them that excitement which could not but drive them towards each other. Neither spoke, but suddenly she was in his arms.

In the Mission House Fanny slept on.

## CHAPTER XIV

# MORE ABOUT THE CLEARING AND
## KEEPING-BY MATTER

LUCKY Agatha, thought Fanny, when she heard the news
next day.   Lucky Agatha. . . .  For Edward had always been
something of a Mr. Danvers to Fanny.   And as for Agatha,
she glowed.   Celibacy had given way to the really superior
claims of a partnership in God's work.   What would they
not accomplish together, he and she?   When Burma had its
separate bishopric there was no reason why, after Edward
had done the magnificent work he would be enabled by
her help to perform, he should not sit on the episcopal
chair.   Agatha was proud of Edward, and of herself for
being engaged to Edward.   Proud of what she termed the
refinement of his looks, of his spiritual discernment, of his
charm, which instinctively she recognised as greater than her
own.   She firmly believed herself to be in love, and the old
unconscious patronage was back in her manner to Fanny—
no one could pretend Fanny had been in love with Captain
Bagshaw.   Fanny was still too upset to resent this attitude.
Indeed, it was a relief to see anyone in Mandalay town who
carried a glow about like a light.

The Kinwoon Mingyi's answer to Shaw's remonstrances
was hardly cheering to the kalās, insisting as it did that the
massacres had been according to custom, and therefore
perfectly legitimate.   Mr. Shaw read the translation out to
Mr. Lumsden, when the clergyman paid his visit to the
Residency on the day following, with an even drier note
than usual in his voice.

"They obviously think they can flout us with impunity,
Lumsden.   Listen to the insolence of this : ' Having received
and carefully perused Resident's letter, dated 19th February,

1879, the Minister intimates that the Royal Dominions of
Burma are governed by a distinct independent crowned
head . . .' That's one for us! And he goes on to say that
should there be reason to fear a disturbance in the country,
the crowned head has a right to act according to the custom
of the State. He even adds that it would not be right to
take thought as to whether the action will bring praise or
blame from others, but that it is proper to act according to
custom, for the interests of the Church and State! And he
ends up with the remark that ' this business '—I like that
expression to describe bloody murder—has been ' done
according to custom.' And ' this is intimated in conformity
with the Grand Friendship, for Resident to note!' Grand
Friendship between us and these barbarians! "

"He's certainly telling you politely but firmly to mind
your own business. Yet by all accounts the Kinwoon
Mingyi had no hand in the massacres and disapproved of them
strongly."

"I believe that's true; but he's a wily old bird and is busy
trying to retain his own precarious footing. He sees the
execution yard unpleasantly close to himself. But he'd
come right over to our side if we backed up the Nyaungyan
Prince in an attempt to get the throne. I wish Calcutta—
to say nothing of the India Office—could be made to see the
advisability of that. Everyone seems to be nervous at
home lest we're pushing them towards annexation. No
one wants that, we've more than we can manage already.
But they're just uninterested; all they can think of is Afghanistan and, in a lesser degree, Zululand."

Mr. Lumsden agreed. " It certainly would be a righteous
act to place the Nyaungyan Prince on the throne. Mindoon
wanted him to succeed, and anyway the other elder brothers
are now dead. I suppose there's no doubt that they are dead? "

" None. I had a letter from Raj Singh last night. It
appears that the executioners were the worst ruffians from
the gaol, who were let loose and promised their freedom for
the purpose. The Thonzé Prince seems to have behaved the
best. He went to his death with a swagger in the best
Burmese tradition."

Mr. Lumsden looked rather shocked, but Mr. Shaw went on calmly.

"He laughed at the other Princes who were bewailing their fate, saying: 'See, I told you we should have no release but death!' The rest squealed rather, I gather."

Mr. Lumsden could not suppress a shudder. He was an imaginative man.

"Sandreino came to see me last evening," pursued Mr. Shaw. "He hadn't been near me for weeks till this. He says the Kinwoon Mingyi wrote his answer to me under direct orders from the King. I expect that means the Supayalat or that old harridan, her mother."

Mr. Lumsden sat thinking deeply. The Resident looked very ill this morning, pale and drawn. He moved with difficulty and was evidently in considerable pain. What would happen if Shaw got really ill, if he died? One of the younger men would take over or someone would perhaps be sent up from Rangoon. Shaw was powerless to protect anyone; yet his name and presence stood for integrity, he was respected, and any change might precipitate a disaster. Hadn't Edward and Agatha better be married with all speed and sent down to Rangoon? God knew there was no work left to do in Mandalay, and what little there was he could continue to carry out. It didn't matter what happened to him. He spoke his thoughts and told Shaw his news. The Resident seemed mildly surprised that anyone should take any interest in marrying and giving in marriage, but expressed conventional congratulations. With more warmth in his voice he strongly urged that Agatha should be got away as soon as possible.

"We mustn't forget that the next thing may be a massacre of the whites and Eurasians. I've already had several warnings. And I have now written again to the Kinwoon Mingyi—Sandreino has taken the letter in person—offering to take charge of any of the royal family that remain alive in the Residency. I've swallowed my feelings and begged that the King should spare the lives of any that remain, especially the women and children, as a favour to the British Government. If they do as I ask and send the poor wretches here, then we may be attacked before I can get them away. And once a light is set to this house, it's the end for all of us."

Mr. Lumsden, looking round at the frail timber-and-thatch structure, agreed with a sinking heart. He sat gnawing his under-lip with his prominent teeth, feeling elderly and helpless in the face of all this weight and force of immediate danger. He felt no fear, but the first glow of hope and excitement about martyrdom had ebbed away, leaving him profoundly depressed. He felt that he and Shaw must look old and played-out as they sat in the shadowy bare room, with the green light from without filtering in and reflecting wanly on the white papers and their own white faces. The persistent call of the coppersmith bird was getting on his nerves, sounding ceaselessly from the world of dusty sunlight without. A step sounded on the verandah, and Sandreino was announced, looking very robust if rather dirty, in comparison with the two older men. He bore with him a letter from the Kinwoon Mingyi, and after greetings had been exchanged, proceeded to read it.

"He's distinctly favourable," he assured them, " distinctly. Listen—' Since the Grand Friendship Treaty entered into during the reign of his late Majesty between the Burmese and the British Governments, there has existed a real Royal Friendship, and in conformity therewith the Burmese Government always desires and hopes that the Dominions of the British Government may be in peace and without disturbance; and the Minister trusts and believes that the British Government do also desire and hope the same with respect to the Dominions of the Burmese 'Government. In regard to the clearing and keeping-by matter. . . .' "

"In regard to *what*?" interrupted Mr. Shaw, " what did you say?"

"It's the correct translation," said Sandreino, with a flash of his teeth under his heavy moustache: " ' Clearing and keeping-by '—otherwise killing and imprisonment. Where was I?—oh, yes. 'In regard to the clearing and keeping-by matter, the Minister would remark that such action is taken in consideration of the past and the future only when there exists a cause for disturbance. It is not

desired to clear away or keep-by those whom it is not feared
would cause a disturbance. The wish towards them is that
they should live happily and contentedly . . .'"

"Humph . . ." ejaculated Shaw.

"And," continued Sandreino unmoved, "'with reference
to the clause contained in Resident's letter that those whom
it is. not desired should dwell within the Royal Dominions
should be made over to the Resident for safe-keeping, this
sentiment is exactly in accord with the Grand Friendship, and
the Minister most cordially thanks the Resident.'"

Sandreino ceased and laid the letter on the Resident's
table, then looked slyly at both men.

"And that," he said softly, "is, in my opinion, all you
will hear on that subject. They've no intention of letting you
take charge of anyone."

"So I should imagine," said the Resident. For a minute
all three men sat in silence, only punctuated by the tonk-tonk
of the coppersmith bird. Again Sandreino's smile flashed
under the lifting of the dark moustache.

"Do you know what the people have nicknamed the
Kinwoon Mingyi?" he asked. "You know how quick and
apt they are at a label! They now call him the Tamat
Yay-poolah Sha Hlweh-de-lu."

"And that means?" asked Mr. Shaw, who knew that
Sandreino knew he didn't speak Burmese.

"It means: 'The man who swerves his tongue to one
side when the hot congi water flows into his mouth!' We
must look after ourselves as best we can, we kalās. And as
for saving the imprisoned royalties . . .!" and he shrugged
his shoulders expressively.

He made his farewells, and Shaw drew a tired hand across
his brow after the Italian had disappeared with a final flash of
teeth.

"He's altogether too supple, that fellow. 'We kalās!'
Yet it's true that at a time like this we all feel knitted together,
and yesterday he was really distressed when he came to me
and consulted as to what more I could do. He's entered his
protest at the Court. But this is Tom Tiddler's Ground,
Lumsden. Everyone is here to pick up gold and silver

except those born catspaws, the English. Sandreino wouldn't side with the Burmese against the whites for nothing, but if he can get concessions for Italy he'll leave us all in the lurch. And who can blame him? He's a commercial Consul and bound to do his best. If it suits his country to work in with the French or English he will; and if not, he won't. There's that glib fellow Bonvoisin—have you met him? He's out for mischief, or I'm a Dutchman. He's up at the Palace even now they tell me. Yes," repeated Mr. Shaw, who was pleased with his phrase : " this is the Tom Tiddler's Ground of the nations. Do you know what the Nyaungyan said to me before he left? He was talking to me about his mother's brother, Maung Toke, who was Viceroy of Pegu and lost it to us in the last Burmese war. By the way, Maung Toke was murdered the other day up at the Palace— I've just had his name sent to me on a new list. They stuffed gunpowder in his nostrils and blew him up. Well, after the fall of Pegu he bemoaned himself, as well he might, since he had to make his excuses to Mindoon. He explained that he had sinned through ignorance. ' I had all my life met only Greeks, half-caste Portuguese, and such like; they were the only kalās I knew. They all came to me crawling on their knees and offered me bribes. When the English officers came to Pegu I imagined they must be the same, and I left the whole affair in the hands of my underlings to arrange at the usual rates. I had no idea that there were any gentlemen among kalās. I thought that no kalās came to Burma except to avoid the starvation that would be their lot in their own countries. And so I made my mistake and Pegu was lost ! ' "

Mr. Lumsden smiled wanly and rose to take his leave. Mr. Shaw shook him by the hand with his usual quiet, almost inhuman courtesy. There was no literary touch of two Britons and white men in a tight corner, with women-folk to protect; no We'll-stand-by-each-other-till-the-death,-old-fellow, about Mr. Shaw, and it would have deeply offended Mr. Lumsden's taste had there been.

"Get the young people married," advised Shaw. " The river steamers will go on running off and on, I expect. At present I'm against having an armed vessel sent up, in case it only irritates the Palace party without being strong enough to afford any adequate protection. Come round to-morrow, Lumsden. If anything happens you ought to know about before then, I'll send a message. Any stand, if we have to make one, will have to be made here. It won't be any good, of course."

Mr. Lumsden left him busy with a new dispatch, and himself walked under the shade of his poongyi umbrella towards the triple-roofed mission that had been built by order of good King Mindoon. All the way, through the thick white dust that rose and settled about his boots, the noise of the coppersmith bird or others of its kind pursued him, and from the far and hidden City came floating on the warm air the sound of music.

The missionary was not nearly so "high" in his views as his daughter and prospective son-in-law, but it was with a feeling of deep relief, as when a man long among strangers catches a phrase of a familiar language, that he heard the midday Angelus chime out from the Convent. He raised his hat and stood for a moment in prayer. As he neared the gates of the Mission he met one of the American Baptist ladies shepherding along a little flock of Burmese girls. She was stout and plain, and panted in the noonday heat. An unbecoming dew was upon her broad face, but it looked as cheerful as ever. She nodded briskly to Mr. Lumsden and, somewhat to her surprise—for he was never as a rule able to keep his belief that her creed was outer darkness from his manner—he stopped to speak to her.

"How are you getting on, Mrs. Harker?" he asked her.

"Fine, Mr. Lumsden. I'm just taking these children to their scripture lesson."

He smiled a little. "It seems hardly worth while, does it? God only knows where we shall be—or how—this time to-morrow."

"But God does know it, Mr. Lumsden, so what does anything else matter? My class is doing Joseph and his brethren, and we left him right there in the pit yesterday.

Guess I've got to get him out for them; they're all worked up over it!"

And she nodded cheerfully and went on. Mr. Lumsden's ready humility took the lesson to itself. That's a brave, good woman in spite of her wrong beliefs, he thought, as he turned in at the Mission gate. What a pity she's not a Churchwoman.

## CHAPTER XV

## POLITICS AND FANNY

DAWN of each day brought to the dwellers in the kalā town the same relief that it brings to a sick man—the feeling that it is easier to bear anything in daylight—it meant a twelve-hour respite from the fear of the worst horrors.

Yet the days were strange enough. The suspense was so protracted that the excitement perforce wore off, and only a depression and a dread remained. Always the sun shone, the coppersmith bird gave out his cry, the dust rose and hung in columns in the air and slowly settled, always the axles of the carts creaked and wailed, always the music sounded from the hidden City. And every day fresh rumours ran about the town and died and others were born. And always Mr. Lumsden and Edward said their services and the nuns their offices, and the American Baptists progressed with Joseph to the high places of Egypt, and the yellow-clothed poongyis went about with their begging-bowls and meditated on the futility of existence and the excellencies of the Perfect Man.

Beauty there was in abundance even in the kalā town. The walls of the City shone rose-red in the waters of the moat, the neglected royal barges—for Thibaw never left the Palace—glittered in the sun, the Shan hills and the Sagaing hills showed a soft blue burnished to amethyst at sunset, the very air was filled with a translucent quality, as though the light refracted from infinitesimal particles. The Chinese caravans came more rarely; more rarely, too, the Shans and Karens with their wares, while from the south came no traders at all. But the outward show of prosperity prevailed, for still Thibaw kept the people amused with pwès, and song and dance went on with an appalling unremitting energy. There was beauty of flower and leaf and light, of silk and gold, of the whole bright barbaric way of life, of the incorrigibly gay Burmese race, but it was a beauty that hid fear, as a bed of brilliant flowers may hide a snake. The flowers are seen to move a little, the leaves rustle though there is no breath of wind, and the onlooker knows that the movement comes from the hidden evil life stirring amid the roots, and concealed by the flowers as by a delicate coverlet. Such was life even in the kalā town—how much more then did the simile hold true of life in the hidden City of Gems, and in its heart, the Golden Palace?

Yet Fanny was beginning to yearn again after that life, the horror was fading in her facile mind, and the Mission House, full of Agatha's concerns, was becoming more and more tedious. Every day she cut out and sewed and fitted dresses on Agatha. Every day she heard about the wonders that Agatha, with Edward and the help of the Lord, was going to perform. Julie had resumed her daily visits to the looms in the Palace, life was apparently going on as before, but Fanny cut and basted and stitched, and turned over the latest numbers of the fashion papers—some six months old— and thought of the gardens of the Palace and the delightful games and the pwès, and of the fun of really being a personage and of managing Supaya-lat when no one else could.

Agatha was more content than Fanny. The immediate scare of the first massacres over, everyone had settled down to that acceptance of abnormal conditions to which human nature so soon accustoms itself, and she was loth to leave Mandalay. For one thing, she was of that peculiarly English type that likes being engaged, and knows instinctively that it will prefer betrothal to marriage. She had now everything she wanted and nothing she did not. The sentimental interest attaching to her was, on the whole, preferable to that attaching to a young bride, for it carried with it no drawbacks, actual or potential. She was on ground that she knew from much reading of Edna Lyall, Mrs. L. B. Walford, Rosa Nouchette Carey, and even Charlotte M. Yonge. This was the best part of " being in love "—all aspirations and long talks in the golden evenings and reverent kisses. Later—well,

of course it was all right, especially in her case, because her
love would refine anything, but still you wouldn't be able
to think about it ; it would always have to be a thing not to be
mentioned even to yourself. And the thought of children
out here in this country, perhaps far from doctors and nurses,
was rather terrifying.

But this golden time was perfect, and instinct, backed up
by her peculiarly persistent and obstinate will—a quality
unsuspected in her owing to her rose-and-honey colouring—
made her put the whole dead weight of her resistance against
Mr. Lumsden's efforts to get her down to Rangoon. The
first steamer up from Rangoon after the massacres was too
soon for her, as the marriage could not be arranged in time,
and after that steamers became uncertain quantities. M.
d'Avera, burning with wrath, had cast the dust of Mandalay
from off his feet, and departed by that first boat to join the
Nyaungyan Prince in Calcutta. His Burmese wife and
daughters were perfectly safe, he being of the nation highest
in favour at Court, but he himself was too honest and peppery
a man to stay on in amity with Thibaw. Also he was too
used to the good days of Mindoon Min, that had now begun
to assume the apocryphal aspect of a golden legend to those
who had known them. A good many people left by the
same boat, and a few, such as adventurous newspaper corre-
spondents, came up by it, and then Mandalay town held its
breath and awaited further events.

News came of trouble in Bhamo, up by the Chinese
frontier—for already Thibaw's lack of grip was being felt
in the far provinces—and Edward and an American Baptist
missionary undertook to go up and bring back some women
missionaries who were stranded there. Agatha, sincerely
anxious as she was, could not help feeling that she was
sending her knight on a high mission, and had no notion
that she was also glad of the respite for herself. And Edward,
living as though suspended in a sphere of burning light, was
glad of it too. More direct and primitive in his emotions,
less overlaid by all the muffling conventions and inhibitions
that had surrounded Agatha, as a girl, from her birth, he was
aware of a certain clamour and impatience within himself

for that thing which all his life he had sternly eschewed, but which he at last had admitted.

And yet a certain regret also . . . for not lightly are the convictions of a lifetime overborne. . . . Edward was not truly happy ; he was dazed, almost drugged ; he was exalted and yet was aware, though he refused to admit it to himself, of a fit of remorse awaiting him in the back of his own mind.

He went off on the expedition to Bhamo, glad of the necessity, and was able to take with him the memory of Agatha's flax-blue eyes looking into his with that light in them that excused everything. She was a wonder, and he sometimes felt with a feeling of awe that it profaned such purity as hers to think of her as a wife. But that look in her eyes that were so fiercely blue made everything seem all right for the time being ; it caught him up, he told himself, to that higher plane on which she lived, and enabled him to forget all else. So he went off happily with the Baptist—whom, to his surprise, he found to be a fine scholar—and devoted himself to watching the life of the birds in the jungles, when they disembarked and went on shore. He adored birds and wrote long and accurate descriptions of them that would have bored Agatha, only they did not arrive before Edward himself, when it seemed unnecessary to read them at all—except those few sentences which told her of herself.

At the end of the first week in March, Mr. Shaw received a warning from the Salin Princess, whose nun's robe had saved her from massacre, saying that an attack on the Residency was planned for the twelfth of that month. He was a little tired of telegraphing to the British authorities and getting no reply save that he should remonstrate against barbarities and try and prevent more by dint of reasoning with the Burmese Government, but nevertheless he wired to Mr. Aitchison at Rangoon : " Secretly warned mischief intended us twelfth given for what it is worth." Aitchison, as in duty bound, wired this on to the Foreign Secretary at Calcutta, who replied illuminatingly : " What steps would you propose under circumstances? Consult Shaw."

It was idle to advise Calcutta. Aitchison had urgently wired to the Government that there was no time like the present for introducing a better policy in Upper Burma, that further massacres were feared, that the Ministers were longing for a change of King, that if the Resident were withdrawn and one European and two native regiments were sent as a precaution, not to make war, Thibaw's power would crumble and the people welcome the Nyaungyan Prince to the throne.

The Viceroy remained unmoved and merely wired back that it would be inadvisable to withdraw the Resident, as such a course might imperil lives and interests. Yet the reputable Europeans left in the town could have been gathered into one small party to leave with the Resident, and of British interests there were none left at all. The Viceroy then offered to send S.S. *Irrawaddy* up to Mandalay in case Mr. Shaw might need protection, but that was all. Shaw declined the offer. " In the present temper of the King," he said to the little group of English—Mr. Lumsden, Edward, and the members of the Residency, who daily met in conclave under its roof—" the coming of a steamer would be just enough to irritate him and not enough either to coerce him or protect us. I hear from every source that he's drinking hard and is very excitable. As to the Europeans, none of the non-British want to get away. Bonvoisin, Sandreino and Co. like nothing better than fishing in these troubled waters. I think I ought to be told to haul down my flag in face of the perpetual insults and contempt with which it is treated. But they shall definitely tell me so before I do." And he settled himself, with a little spasm of pain crossing his haggard face, into his dilapidated long chair.

Calcutta, reflecting over the matter of the proposed assault on the Residency, wired again, giving him full discretion to withdraw if he thought this course necessary for his personal safety. Mr. Shaw remained where he was, and the fated night of the twelfth passed off without an attack being made. The Viceroy continued to consider the withdrawal of the Resident undesirable on " political grounds." Even the unworldly Mr. Lumsden could not forbear a snort. Political grounds . . . that meant either Afghanistan, or home.politics, or both. If some overt attack were to be made, as at any moment it might be, against the handful of British in Mandalay, it would be impossible for them to save themselves. They were to be sacrificed to appease a few Parliamentarians. . . .

And they all watched as, day by day, Thibaw's warlike preparations augmented, forts were constructed, and regiments drilled all day long, instructed by French and Italian officers.

And Lord Cranbrook wrote from London to the Governor General of India in Council, that he quite understood the desire to place the relations of Her Majesty's Government with the King of Burma, at present in a very precarious position, on a more dignified footing; but that the grievances tolerated by Great Britain under previous rulers of Upper Burma had not been aggravated by Thibaw, and that there had been no action on his part which called for a distinct change of policy on that of Her Majesty's Government. . . . There might, he pointed out also, occur a change for the better in the King's conduct and demeanour. He was probably in the first excitement of the possession of unbridled power. Anything like an ultimatum based on former grievances would perhaps give Thibaw the erroneous impression that the Government of India was seeking hostilities rather than more friendly relations. . . .

"It is perhaps a little odd," remarked Mr. Shaw, "that the present Viceroy was chosen to put an end to the 'masterly inactivity' policy in Afghanistan and to replace it by a 'forward policy'—a thing former Viceroys and the Council have always opposed—and yet that here we have the 'masterly inactivity' policy firmly enjoined upon us. How well advised I have been to eschew politics in my simple life."

M. d'Avera, jesting wryly, wrote to Mr. Shaw from Calcutta that "nothing but Kabulese" was spoken there, and, indeed, what looked like the success of the Lytton-cum-Disraeli policy in Afghanistan distracted the attention of the Indian Government from Upper Burma almost as completely as disaster would have done. News had come to Mandalay, soon after the massacres, of the death of the

unfortunate Shere Ali in exile, and now came the reports
of Beaconsfield's satisfaction at the British occupation of
Kabul and Kandahar. And at the beginning of May the
wires flashed the news to the British in Mandalay that a
treaty had been signed at Gandamak with Shere Ali's son,
Yakoob Khan, the new Amir.

The Government of India and the Home Government
rejoiced greatly, and at Mandalay the day the news came
the English rejoiced; only Mr. Shaw, tortured with fever,
smiled grimly in his bed at the thought of the pleasure
expressed at headquarters that Kabul was now to have a
British Resident. "Poor devil . . ." quoth Mr. Shaw;
"his troubles are beginning."

The news from Zululand, the other place which was
absorbing all the British reinforcements that could be spared,
was not so good. The war dragged on, and once at least
the British army was nearly outflanked. Chelmsford in
Natal was busy reorganising the forces sent out to him, and
Cetewayo continued to mass his impis and sweep about
Zululand. All thoughts of sending an expedition against
the Kingdom of Ava were done with, and what hopes the
Viceroy had had of establishing a better rule there, were over.
Aitchison's energy and knowledge had been powerless against
the lure of what seemed the greater adventure in which the
Government of India was engaged. A small display of
military strength on the frontier of Lower Burma did, however, remind Thibaw and the Palace party that Great Britain
could still strike, and hence for the time being there was
comparative quiet in Mandalay town.

Fanny paid more interest than usual to the political talk,
for it was about the affairs she knew and saw around her,
and the element of intrigue everywhere stimulated her.
She had sometimes visited the house of M. d'Avera, though
Mr. Lumsden did not approve, for the little Burmese ladies
were gay and friendly as ever, and here too she might meet
M. Bonvoisin. . . . She had never forgotten the strange
thrill that had run through her on that day when he had
stopped her bullock-cart and talked to her, and she had
suddenly seemed to see him for the first time. The horrors

of the massacres had put everything else out of her mind for a
time, but now that life seemed settling down to be ordinary
again, and that Agatha's affairs occupied such a boring
amount of the day, she turned once more to that side of her
life of which she knew Agatha—had she understood it—
would have strongly disapproved.   But she did not formu-
late to herself anything definite that she wanted of Bonvoisin;
she only drifted on knowing that she wanted to see him, and
certain in a fatalistic way that she would.   Was she not
Fanny, wonderful little Fanny, who always got what she
wanted?   An English husband, English widowhood, favour
at the Palace. . . . And now Bonvoisin, for instinct told her
he was of the type of man who would admire and want her.
Nothing of Mr. Danvers or Edward about him.

Fanny was indeed miserable when, at Mr. Lumsden's
request, she had to give up visiting the d'Avera household.
There she could be gay, no one cared for politics, they all
laughed and played and attended pwès and gave tea and
cakes to Fanny as of yore.   And once Bonvoisin came and
found Fanny there, and bent over her hand and told her
she should go back to the Palace.

" It was the old lady," he told her soothingly; " the young
King and Queen did not want the massacres.   Supaya-lat
thinks of nothing but the King; she adores him madly.   You
are the only other person she cares about.   You should go
back before it is too late.   I know that she wants you."
And always after visiting the shady garden of d'Avera's
house, she wanted the Palace more.   The little ladies in their
tightly fitting tameins of gay silk, their kerchiefs, their
snowy muslin jackets, brought back to her the enchanting
atmosphere of the Palace, and again she seemed to see her own
little figure, so noticeable in its puffed and frilled European
clothes, trailing and waggling about the shady gardens and
along the scarlet-and-gold corridors . . .

Oh, but it was boring here in the Mission, seeing hardly
any but English people.   For the French and Italians, it
soon became obvious, considered themselves, and were
considered by the Court, to be on a different and far more
friendly footing than the English.   The sense of opposing

camps became more and more clearly felt. Sandreino frankly gave up communicating with the Residency any more than his position as agent to the Irrawaddy Flotilla Company made it necessary. Any other English people he ignored utterly. Sight of his gallant moustaches would have cheered Fanny, and from him she could have heard of Bonvoisin.

Edward and the American came safely back from Bhamo with the protesting and undaunted lady missionaries whom they had insisted on saving, and once again the question of Agatha's marriage sprang into prominence. Fanny was worse off than ever. For one thing, she could not continue to live at the Mission House once Agatha had left it, and a refuge in the convent did not appeal to Fanny. Mr. Lumsden, simple soul, concluded that she would like to travel to Rangoon with Agatha and Edward, and join her mother there. Fanny shuddered, not unjustifiably. Old Mrs. Moroni, fatter and lazier than ever, living in happy hugger-mugger fashion with her relations. . . . How could she leave Mandalay and all it meant, for that? How could she exist much longer away from the Palace? Away from Supaya-lat and away from all chance of seeing Bonvoisin? No, she must forget the massacres, forget those awful nights of fear, and go back.

Her chance to make the announcement of her decision without shocking her English friends came just before Agatha's wedding. Events, with Fanny's usual luck, seemed to play straight into her hands. There had been further trouble with the Burmese Government—a British river steamer attacked by Burmese coolies and four passengers injured, and another steamer unable to discharge her cargo owing to the violence of the coolies, who were rapidly degenerating into bands of dacoits all along the shores of the Irrawaddy.

Mr. Phayre, the Assistant, was returning from a ride one morning when he was jeered at and insulted by a party of Burmans, and this although the umbrella-bearing retinue, which showed him to be an official, was with him. Some Indians, British subjects, who had been given land by Mindoon and had built themselves houses thereon, were turned out without compensation and their houses given to Burmans. And then news came from the little girl in the Palace that the mother of the Nyaungyan Prince was, with her daughter, put in irons and placed in closer confinement. The little girl and her mother, who had hitherto been keeping these unfortunate ladies alive with the gifts of money sent in by Mr. Shaw and Mr. Lumsden, now feared for their own lives, and went to Rangoon. Communication with the mother and sister of the Nyaungyan Prince ceased entirely. All Shaw knew was that with two other ex-Queens they were confined in a cell bricked up save for one small opening. They had irons on their legs and the thermometer was, in more favoured places, never under 100 degrees in the shade and generally 105 degrees. A Princess managed to convey this information to the Residency before she herself, with a sister, attempted to escape. These two, when their boat stuck on a sandbank, were caught and murdered. After that there was silence from the Palace, for Raj Singh had not the facilities for picking up information in the women's quarters that the girl spy had had. Then it was that Fanny came forward with her offer. She would go back to the Palace and supply the place of the missing women spies.

Mr. Lumsden, who felt himself responsible for her, hesitated, and Mr. Shaw hesitated, for Fanny was a British subject. But Fanny pleaded so earnestly, her eyes were so appealing, her quiet confidence was so touching, that, knowing she would probably be safe, they yielded. Fanny, triumphant, sent a note by Julie, and the next day announced that she had received a summons from Supaya-lat.

"I'm so sorry I can't stay here till your wedding, Agatha darling, but you see how it is. I feel I am really needed, and no one can do this work as well as I can."

So, only a few days before the wedding, Fanny went back to the Palace and, as always seemed to be happening from the days on board the *Bengal* until now, Agatha, who should have been the centre of attention, was quite cast into the shade by the more spectacular Fanny.

Even Edward pointed this unpleasant truth. For the

sake of the proprieties he had stayed at the Residency since
his return—a not too pleasant retreat, as the doctor and Pierpoint were not on speaking terms, and Shaw was so sick of
them that he spoke to neither. Indeed, the two antagonists
had wished to fight a duel in the Residency compound, and
only Shaw's authority prevented it. Poor young Phayre
had the worst time of all, for since Pierpoint and Dr. O'Hara
no longer spoke to each other, and Shaw hardly spoke to
anyone, he was the recipient of all complaints and confidences, an awkward and frequently embarrassing position.

Edward was glad each day, even apart from seeing Agatha,
when the time came for him to pay his visit to the Mission.
But on this evening before the wedding he was very quiet,
and instinctively Agatha felt that the quietness was not
due to thinking about her.

"A penny, Edward!" she said archly, when he had
remained staring uneasily past her for several minutes. He
brought his eyes to her with a start.

"I was just thinking of Fanny," he replied. "I hope she'll
be all right."

"Fanny will always be all right," replied Agatha somewhat
tartly. A gecko clinging to the wall up by the raftered
ceiling gave derisive assent.

"Tauk-teh, tauk-teh!" said the gecko. Agatha could
not but laugh; she knew of the Eastern belief that the
gecko speaks when a particularly true remark has just been
made.

## CHAPTER XVI

## EPITHALAMIUM

On her wedding morning Agatha woke early, and lay for a minute listening to the thunder of the rain and the sudden beating of the wet trees in a great gust of wind. For the rains, intermittent but heavy, had been for some time upon Mandalay, accompanied by a capricious but raging wind, a wind to rend the heart. She lay with her cheek pressed against the pillow, thinking—or as nearly thinking as was possible with her education and upbringing.

She was going to be married to Edward . . . and in a sudden panic it occurred to her that she didn't really know Edward very well. And she fell into one of those awful moments which are like an abyss into which the soul slips and is almost lost. Emptiness encompassed her: the utter negation of all she had lived by. There was nothing beneath her feet, or above her head, or on either side, for her groping hands to touch. She had been drifting down a road she had never imagined to be anything but clearly defined; to get engaged and married and to be " in love " was what all girls did; it must be all right. Now she was uddenly afraid—not of marriage, but afraid that there was something missing in her feeling for Edward.

She almost knew, for a dreadful space of time, whether short or long she could not have told, that she had allowed her whole life to be arranged for her by the Idylls of the King, by Lorna Doone, by the novels of Rhoda Broughton, by all the heroines of all the love-stories which she and the whole race of girls accepted as gospel; the romantic convention which was presented as real and true.

What had she, Agatha Lumsden, alive and palpitating in this bed, the thunder of the rain in her ears, her body damp

with heat, to do with all this assumption of romance . . .?
Life somehow wasn't like that; nothing was as complete
and round as people in books felt it to be. Really everything was jagged, uneven at the edge, not round at all.
Yet she was about to act on this assumption that she had
always accepted; she was going away that day—if no
disaster occurred to prevent it—going down to the bustling
world of Rangoon with Edward. Edward . . . and it
occurred to her to wonder how he was feeling about it.
She sat up in bed and stared at the sky, which was beginning
to brighten with a gleam of sunshine. The rain was lessening; now as it fell the sun struck athwart its arrowy lines of
light. It ceased, and only the heavy drips from the over-
hanging eaves and the foliage of the trees, knocked lightly
upon her senses. Agatha got out of bed and, kneeling beside
it, buried her face in her hands.

In the tiny darkness, personal to her alone, that her hands
made for her, it was as though she felt herself falling, falling.
. . . What was herself? What did she mean by "I"?
It wasn't, certainly, quite what Edward thought it. And
for the first time, in this hollow moment, she felt herself not
good enough for Edward and curiously sorry for him.
Oh, God, make me good to Edward. . . . That figure of
herself as the radiant and condescending angel in which she
had always believed even as a girl at school amidst the inferior
clay, wavered before her mind's eye, and as its bright outlines
blurred and dissolved, she for the first time thought of
Edward as himself instead of in his relation to her. Make me
good to Edward . . . Not as she had sometimes been with
her father, answering his irritation with her own, but always
kind. The image of reality, instead of accepted beliefs,
pressed itself upon her heart and made her humble. She
was nearer to possible happiness with Edward at that moment
than ever before. "There is an hour wherein a man might
be happy all his life could he find it . . ." So said the wise
George Herbert. The pity of it is that such hours are rarely
found, and even then they exhaust frail nature and the soul is
not strong enough to retain them.

Agatha slowly drew her hands away from her wet eyes,

and the light of day poured in upon her.  She felt shaken and tired, and slowly she got to her feet.  Wrapping herself in her dressing-gown, she began to make her morning tea— she did not like the bearer to come into her room—and always used her own spirit-stove.  She was just pouring the tea into the cup when there came a knock at the door and Mr. Lumsden came slowly in.  One glance at his face and she was holding the cup out to him.  He took it mechanically and drank a sip before he spoke.

"I was sent for in the night to poor Shaw," he said. "It's all over.  His heart gave out."  He put the cup on the table and sat down heavily.  "Oh, Agatha, my dear, it was the loneliest death for him.  So reserved, so hating all this sort of thing that happened here!"

"Oh, poor Mr. Shaw!"  But through Agatha's mind there could not but dart the thought that it needn't have happened on her wedding day.  It was to have been peculiarly *her* day; now it would be poor old Shaw's. . . . He had always scorned the facile arts of popularity, but everyone would think of him and remember his fine qualities now—on her wedding day.

"I don't suppose it will make any difference," said her father in a worried voice, chewing the moustache that looked even limper than usual after his vigil, " but I shall be glad when you and Edward are on board."  To himself he thought: I shouldn't like her to see me conducting his funeral just after her wedding.  And he looked at her tenderly.

Agatha delayed over her bathing and dressing.  Some fine mists of her moment still trailed about her, making her movements languid and softening the things of every day.  When she was dressed she looked at herself in the wavy-surfaced mirror.  She had no thoughts of self-pity because she was dressing for her wedding without a woman friend to make a fuss of her; she had a sturdy habit of independence in practical matters, though she had never thought for herself in the realm of ideas.  She studied her reflection now with a new criticism.

The long white folds of the " æsthetic " gown draped her

too-thin form kindly. It's a pity about my collar-bones,
but my hair and eyes are nice. And my complexion, now
I've lost that redness. . . . But my nose *does* shine. And
again she wished regretfully that as a good missionary she
could have used powder. She studied her reflection, then
went to the door and called the bearer. She gave him a
terse direction, and when he had brought what she wanted
she shut the door and started her experiment. How difficult
it was . . . it looked *too* white . . . but if she sort of rubbed
it in and then wiped it off. . . . And that was how it was
that Agatha was married with a dusting of cornflour over her
cheeks and nose. Somehow it being cornflour set her
conscience at rest.

Agatha's wedding was a sadly unspectacular ceremony.
None of the French community was present, not even Julie,
for news had come a few days earlier that the high-spirited,
handsome young Prince Imperial, so admired and senti-
mentalised over by the English, had been killed by the assegais
of the Zulus, and feeling was running rather high as rumours
multiplied as to the circumstances of his death. Vain for the
hypocritical British to protest that they were as sorry as anyone. Deep diplomacy was seen in the occurrence, though,
as every fresh disaster made the tenure of life and property
less certain for the British in Mandalay, they might have safely
been believed for once.

The rescued lady missionaries turned up in full force, and
the good-natured Mrs. Harker, forgetful of previous snubs,
came in before the ceremony to see what she could do to
help, but these kindly ladies hardly added any decorative
quality to the scheme of things. And Agatha couldn't help
feeling that it would have been much more in key with
herself to have had Roman Catholics rather than Baptists
at her wedding. She even hinted such a sentiment to her
father, who replied with unwonted sternness that Mrs. Harker
was a woman that any Christian should be honoured to
meet. And, as it turned out, it was Mrs. Harker's missionary
—and heretic—husband who had to give the bride away,
for owing to the death of Mr. Shaw the Residency repre
sentatives were too busy to spare the time.

Agatha stole a glance at Edward as they knelt side by side in front of her father, and suddenly her heart began to beat thickly. This was Edward, her husband . . . this pale, rather stern-looking man whose shoulders seemed so massive and straight within the close-fitting black coat. Across her mind flashed the thought: *This is my future . . . it lies with him to make my future.* And she was aware, acutely, violently aware, that he held for her the possibilities of pain, perhaps of death, that her children were even now coming towards her, within his power. He was not thinking of anything like that, she knew, but she, who had always avoided such thoughts, was confronted inescapably with them in this space of time while his black firm shoulders held her gaze. He seemed suddenly very much of a man to her, he with whom such power rested. She trembled, and in that moment loved him.

Fanny, turning up all lateness and fuss, radiant with ribbons and the aroma of courts, and the glamour of one coming from unknown dangers, for the little breakfast, was unable for once to disturb Agatha with her greater sparkle. Agatha, her blue eyes blazing, a lovely colour burning through the corn-flour, was in a charmed circle. Selah's good-natured greet-ings and beaming face under a much-trimmed Paris hat seemed pleasant and friendly, but Fanny was only a little stranger. Until the moment of parting came—and then, for a second as they embraced, the habit of years; memories shared, even of irritations and hopeless differences, caught them both up. Fanny, as she stood waving upon the river-bund, while the paddle-wheels threshed the muddy water into foam, won-dered whether after all a certain deep sense of security did not go out of her life with the passing from it of her dowdy English friend. She climbed into her bullock-cart and was carried back towards the Palace, as Edward and Agatha began their journey to Rangoon and their future selves; those selves that Agatha had, in church, been so aware of as awaiting their approach.

## CHAPTER XVII

## MR. LUMSDEN LEFT TO HIMSELF

THERE comes a moment in the life of every man when he knows that he has to a certain measure attained, or has lost for ever, whatever it is that his nature has made him desire most. According to the strength of his power of desiring, so is the measure of his loss. Mr. Lumsden, that unimportant little missionary, who had barely stamped his personality or his creed upon those with whom he came in contact, and of whom posterity would be entirely unaware, had arrived at this dread moment. He had always wanted beauty, he had never caught more than glimpses of the flying hem of her robe, and never had he been able to arrest its passage by more than the brief contact of a clutch as it disappeared.

Alone in the Mission House, the rain thudding and dancing on the triple roof, he was confronted by the strange riddle that everyone is faced with when the hilltop is reached and the descent begins. Only the exigencies of his practical work had kept him from facing it for so long. He had often thought he had met it before—by how many hilltops are we not confronted, always to discover that each is a little local one, before the horrid truth dawns that at last we are cresting the highest!—but now he knew beyond a doubt that he was face to face with it. the riddle of how and when, in heaven's name, he had managed to pass the actual border-line between hope and failure, between the having of desire perpetually in front of him and the placing of it definitely behind him, without even having noticed the moment of the change.

None of us knows the actual passage of that moment; it goes on wings as silent as the down-edged wings of an owl; we pass it over lightly, and only recognise, when we know it has gone for ever, that it is the line between youth and age. It is only after we have lost or won whatever it is that we have lost or won, that we are aware the moment of transition has already slipped into the past. Mr. Lumsden realised it. He was able to realise it because he felt very lonely. There was little indeed that as a missionary he could do, and less as Residency chaplain, when the members of that Residency were on most unchristian terms with each other. Pierpoint discussed political matters with him as in duty bound and was friendly enough after his fashion, but the days dragged along more wearily than they had when Agatha was with him.

He missed Shaw, whose quietness and dryness had suited his own humour. And he missed the glamour that excitement had for the last months thrown about a sordid enough environment. Now that a lull seemed to have come over the face of affairs, the full tediousness of the position became evident. He found he missed, more than he would have thought possible, the feminine element that Fanny as well as Agatha had provided in his house; the discussions on fabric and fashioning, the litter of silks, and the sound of Agatha singing in her small but sweet voice. He felt the desolation, which is like a little death, that comes when any phase of life has definitely ended. For a brief space of time he had sighted the flying skirts of that beauty which all his life he had yearned for and never seemed to capture; in Agatha the love he had missed with his wife, in the gaiety of Burma a lightness not to be found in India; and, above all, in these last few months of strain and excitement, the glow that safety can never give.

Now that he was so alone he missed even this last, for ordinarily he cared little what happened to himself, and the pure emotion of martyrdom, although doubtless its grace would come to him should occasion arise, is too high a frame of mind to be sustained during dreary weeks. He felt old, as a parent must feel when a child gets married; he was now irrevocably left behind, he knew he was unattractive—he had always resented the sight of his own inadequate face in the glass—and he wondered how it was that life, which at starting had seemed so fair and lofty a thing, could so quickly have slipped through his fingers as to leave him old, a failure, and surrounded by ugliness. For a space it seemed to him that everything had been a mistake, that missionary work was futile; he doubted the light that had led him, and there is no worse doubt that can assail a man.

He sat upon his verandah in the still evenings when the rain had ceased, and listened to the tolling of the bell from the convent, to the striking of the bell by Buddhist devotees, the sound of the Mission tinkle for the unattended Evensong still in his ears, and wondered sadly what it was all about. His soul shuddered and drew back from the depths of that pit which his whole life had been spent in avoiding. If his burning faith, the faith that he had often felt was too glowing and glorious a thing for such a futile person as himself, was to flicker and die down, what had he left? And though, in his humility, he felt that it was of no importance whether he had anything or not, yet that persistent thing which is *I*, and which even in the most selfless is the only thing that gets anything done in this world—that thing which is so Western and is the whole reason why Westerners continue to kick against the pricks and why they worry over doing good to others— would not let him be. You matter, it told him, not because you are you, but because if you don't, nobody does. It could not tell him that he did not matter because nobody mattered. He had no peace between this mattering and not mattering.

From the depths of this pit he was rescued, as all his life he had hitherto been lured away from the lip of it, by the resumption of the practical duties which that life involved.

The great question in Mandalay, and in those places which concerned themselves with the fate of Mandalay, was whether or no a new Resident should be appointed. The whole office of Resident had been brought to ignominy by Thibaw's tactics—he had never received Mr. Shaw and would doubtless not receive his successor—and British subjects, English, Indian, Chinese, had been treated with contumely and any complaints met with studied indifference, so that it seemed but to lower the dignity of Great Britain and to attain no useful end if another Resident were sent; and also it would seem to express contentment, or at least acquiescence, in the state of affairs in Upper Burma.   On the other hand, to make an end now would be too spectacular a gesture and one that should be followed up by definite action, such as the Government was not prepared to make.

A compromise was arrived at in the temporary appointment of Colonel Horace Browne, who knew Burma and the Burmese thoroughly, and who had the confidence of the Chief Commissioner, as Resident " on special duty."   The question of replacing Colonel Browne by a permanent official later could be left in the lap of the gods.

## CHAPTER XVIII

# MR. LUMSDEN AND THE RESIDENCY

THE Colonel arrived on board the steamer at Mandalay on the morning of the 22nd of June, and the three Residency Assistants, Pierpoint, Phayre, and the little doctor, met him, and Mr. Lumsden awaited him at the house. Colonel Browne was a very different proposition from Mr. Shaw, big, vital and handsome, every inch a soldier, and his inches were many. He gave one glance of comical dismay at the tumbledown Residency and the mat wall that surrounded it, and a not much more enthusiastic glance at the guard of Madras Sepoys who, twenty strong, were there for his protection and that of all the British in Mandalay.

The first alteration he made in the mode of life of the Resident was that he determined to go out as far and as much as he liked every day, and since it was not fitting that he should be seen trudging over the mud and ruts of the town, he managed to get together a collection of ponies for himself and a few attendants. Elephants, as he remarked, had never appealed to him as a means of locomotion.

He came to Mandalay like a strong gust of wind from the heather of his native moors, and he increased the suggestion by perpetually wearing a tam-o'-shanter, which made of him a personality that otherwise he might not have seemed, in the complete Colonelship of his character and whole attack on life, to be. Westerner of the Westerners, he succeeded in deflecting Mr. Lumsden's mind from the sum of man's kan which had begun to obsess it. " Man's can and cannot is more important, believe me. Leave this hair-splitting to the gentleman of the yellow robe," remarked the Colonel. And yet with all his practical sense, his brushing aside of spiritual values in moments when a decision was necessary, he had a real understanding of and a profound respect for the susceptibilities and religions of all the races with which he had to deal in his life. He had less patience with the Government of India.

He showed to Mr. Lumsden copies of the correspondence between the Rangoon Chamber of Commerce, the Chief Commissioner of British Burma and the Viceroy. The Chamber of Commerce was giving trouble. Serenely untroubled by any considerations save those of business, it addressed a long letter of complaint to the Chief Commissioner, saying that in its opinion the precautionary measure of strengthening the garrison of British Burma, especially at the frontier, was the cause of Mandalay buying less goods than formerly, and practically requested that the soldiers should be withdrawn. Aitchison, whose position between the Government of India, with Lord Cranbrook supporting and even enjoining the let-slide policy on the one hand, and his own profound conviction that now was the time to inaugurate a better policy in Upper Burma on the other, was in no mood to be harassed by the Chamber of Commerce. He had sent the letter of the Chamber to Simla, where the Government of India now inhaled the healthful breezes, and also his own answer.

With the first smile of satisfaction that had come upon his face for days, Mr. Lumsden read : " The Chief Commissioner regrets exceedingly this depressed condition of trade, and his anxiety on this account has led him already to bring the subject to the notice of the Government of India. The Chief Commissioner, however, cannot concur with the Chamber of Commerce in attributing the commercial distress to the reinforcement of the garrison in British Burma. The reinforcements were the result of the precarious situation at Mandalay after the inhuman massacres of 18th February. They were the effect, and not the cause, of the uncertainty of our relations with the Burmese Court, and of the danger to the peace of our own possessions and to the lives of the Resident and the European community at Mandalay, created both by the King's barbarous proceedings and his extensive military preparations."

The letter went on to point out that these military prepara-

tions on the part of the Kingdom of Ava had continued
steadily, and that Mr. Shaw, in answer to a letter from himself, the Chief Commissioner, pointing out the expenses
involved by the unwonted British state of preparedness
and asking whether it would be safe to relax it, had replied
in the negative.  The Chief Commissioner had agreed with
this and added demurely to his letter: " Since then nothing
has occurred to change the Chief Commissioner's opinion."
For, wrote Aitchison: " While sympathising deeply with the
mercantile community in their anxiety and losses, the Chief
Commissioner cannot at present recommend any reduction
of the reinforcements to which the Chamber of Commerce,
erroneously in his opinion, attribute the depression of trade,
and he must consider it his first duty to protect from peril,
or the risk of peril, the lives and property of the general body
of the people."

Browne laughed as he took the letter back.  " Of course
he's right.  The pivot on which trade turns is Mandalay.
If there are no disturbing elements here everything works
smoothly, but if there's any internal trouble here the Lower
Burma merchants refuse to send goods up country except for
cash payment.   So credit is stopped and all trade goes to the
devil.   It's a vicious circle."

" What does Simla say? " asked Mr. Lumsden.

" Oh, even Simla administers a nice snub to the Chamber
of Commerce.  It says: ' It appears to His Excellency in
Council that it would be superfluous to discuss with the
Chamber of Commerce the question of our military dis-
positions for the general defence of British Burma.' "

Pierpoint deigned a smile.  " I detect the Viceroy's own
pen there," he said.  " He has a touch of mordant humour
and of genius about him, though he's not a strong Viceroy.
Even the Chief Commissioner, though he disagrees with
him *in toto* about matters of policy, admires him otherwise.
He certainly *is* a sahib . . ." and Pierpoint seemed complacent as though it were something of a consolation, if
you had to be left defenceless to be murdered, that it should
be by the vacillations of a sahib.  It was one of the moments
when Mr. Lumsden missed the understanding eye of Shaw.

"Aitchison used to be Foreign Secretary to the Government of India," boomed the Colonel; "he only gave it up for Burma—which, after all, is a poor little Cinderella and treated as such—because he differed from Lytton about North-West Frontier policy. He still maintains that of all the Viceroys, Lytton is the genius, the man who can get at the heart of a problem quickest, although he was antagonistic to him. But I'm a simple man and don't know about genius. I say: Oh, for a Dalhousie or a Mayo! The burden of Afghanistan and Burma at once is too much for Lytton's shoulders. The unprovoked massacre of innocent women and children has really only evoked a sort of platonic remonstrance from him, and the murders are continuing on a lesser scale up to to-day. As to the studied insolence to the Resident and the dismissal from office of decent Burmese who are suspected of friendliness to the British, naturally he looks on all that with indifference. The injury to trade does not move him, the fact that all along the frontier line drawn by Dalhousie, the Burmans are encroaching every day, leaves him cold. And as to the danger to which the dwellers in the British Residency are exposed from a sudden burst of rage on the part of the mad Court faction—I can only say he looks on that with seraphic resignation."

Mr. Lumsden could not but agree, as anyone going through those anxious months and not theorising ideally from a home base, must have agreed, with these fulminations, and yet that little voice in him which had always, in spite of his profession, disagreed with most violent opinions, would persist in presenting other points of view now. Persisted only faintly; the immediate pressure of facts was too strong for much else. " Am I my brother's keeper? " was a question that of necessity he had always answered in the affirmative; it was what had decided his profession. He believed in it passionately, and yet sometimes he wondered.

All his missionary years he had been worried, though he would hardly admit it to himself, by the ethics of conquest. As a youth he had readily accepted the dictum that to be conquered by the British must be a blessing to any nation, especially when it brought in its train the added blessing of

Christianity. Now he was not so sure. The business of the Afghan war had worried him; he could see in its whole history and all that had led up to it nothing of which to be proud. The treaty of Gandamak, which had filled the bosom of the Government with such a swelling sense of satisfaction, had, glad as he was that peace was attained, seemed to him like a valuable but mended vase, a thing that looked to casual glance whole and fine, but that was too flawed to stand any test. Oddly enough, it was the Viceroy's own words that had set up this little devil of doubt in Mr. Lumsden's mind. There was no doubt Lord Lytton would have preferred that Afghanistan should have been entirely disintegrated so that she could never have been a nation again, and he gave as his reason that any Amir of Afghanistan would always prefer " the ambitious, energetic and not over-scrupulous Russia " to what he termed " a power so essentially pacific and sensitively scrupulous as our own . . ." What did Sher Ali, he whom Mayo had understood and managed so well, think of the later British policy when, worn out and embittered, deluded by Russia and misunderstood and coerced by England, he had been ground into the dust of death between these upper and nether millstones? Essentially pacific, yes, if submission were duly made. Sensitively scrupulous . . . yes, if things could be arranged by such methods. But, laid down as a description of his country, it somehow did not sound quite correct to Mr. Lumsden.

Yet here he was, grumbling at a too-great scrupulosity in the dealings with the Kingdom of Ava. . . . Really he supposed the Burmans had a right to mismanage their country their own way . . . but it rasped on all his English sense of law and order and his hatred of waste. He did not want annexation, no one wanted that, but surely the solution was to use a certain amount of force in setting the Nyaungyan Prince upon the Lion Throne . . . after all, that was what Mindoon himself had wanted.

He spoke his thought to the Colonel now. Browne looked at him with a twinkle in his eyes.

" I'll tell you a secret, Lumsden. You know the Nyaung-yan and his brother and all their womenkind lived in my

charge at Rangoon after Shaw got them away from here?
Until these beauties at the Palace sent down two men to
assassinate them, when we sent 'em off with their families,
retainers and all, to Calcutta. Well, one fine morning last
April, I was told a Burmese messenger wanted to see me,
and I went out on to the verandah, and there, dressed as one
of his own retainers, stood the Nyaungyan, smiling away at
me. He gave me a letter from no less a person than Eden,
the Lieutenant-Governor of Bengal, who, as you may or may
not remember, used to be Chief Commissioner of British
Burma. That accounts for the Viceroy consulting him about
Burmese affairs. Well, the letter said that he had taken a
great fancy to the Nyaungyan and could conceive of no greater
benefit for Upper Burma than having him on the throne.
So he had allowed him to slip off in disguise, and the Prince
was on his way to Upper Burma and counted on me to
smuggle him up to the frontier. You may imagine I was
staggered at this *coup de théâtre*. Why were these instructions conveyed to me by the Lieutenant-Governor of Bengal,
who has no longer anything to do with such affairs, instead
of straight from the Viceroy to Aitchison? Indeed, Eden
stated that he was acting under orders from the Viceroy."

"What on earth did you do?" asked Lumsden, whose
eyes had opened very wide at this instance of sensitive
scrupulousness.

"For a moment I felt a bit tempted to do as I was asked.
The people up here want the Nyaungyan; he stood a good
chance of success. Then I thought a bit more. It wouldn't
be loyal to Aitchison, who carries the whole burden of
Upper Burma politics, to go and do something behind
his back. And, what was even more serious, it was pretty
evident that the appearance of the Nyaungyan, raising a
standard on the border, would be the death signal for all you
folk here. So off I dashed to Aitchison. He didn't seem
much surprised . . . called the affair a ' dirty trick '—and
wired Calcutta telling them that the Nyaungyan had put in
an appearance and asking for instructions as to what to do!
He pointed out that the presence of the claimant to the
throne was a great danger to the Resident here. Well, of

course, above-board dealing didn't suit the Calcutta book at all. They wanted the affair carried through unofficially as far as they were concerned; they couldn't openly support it. So, seeing their little plot had failed, they wired saying that the Prince must be sent back to Calcutta. And back the poor devil had to go, with a nice idea of British diplomacy."

"Essentially pacific . . .," "sensitively scrupulous . . .," echoed through Mr. Lumsden's head.

"I should be glad enough of a little more here of the 'forward policy' that's in full swing in the North-West, but not if it's going to take such ill-considered forms as that," continued the Colonel vigorously. "The joke is that the whole escapade probably did us good with the Palace party, as they were bound to hear from their spies that the Nyaungyan had managed to get away from Calcutta, but owing to the vigilance of the British authorities, didn't get any further than Rangoon. In a way it was a sad pity we couldn't let him go on and prosper, but our chief duty was the safety of you people here."

April . . . when Agatha was getting together her little trousseau. There would never have been a wedding if the plot had been carried through. Martyrdom for himself was one thing, but for Agatha . . . Her father had a sudden vivid picture of her lying on the dusty boards at his feet, her fair hair dabbled with blood. It had indeed been an escape.

"So it's not much wonder we don't trust the present régime in India, and the sooner it's replaced the better," concluded Colonel Browne.

Mr. Lumsden rose to go when the Colonel stopped him hospitably. "You must have a peg. Yes, just a chota peg, I insist. Let us eat and drink pegs, for to-morrow we may die." He clapped his hands and called out: "Quai hai!" sharply. Mr. Lumsden subsided again and waited while the Indian bearer brought the pegs.

A quai hai wallah! The expressive slang passed through Mr. Lumsden's mind. Perhaps, in his robust belief in plainly-marked values, Browne was the real old quai hai wallah. But it was a breed that Mr. Lumsden sometimes envied for its clear and simple acceptances.

## CHAPTER XIX

# FANNY LEFT ALONE

THERE was no doubt that the temporary Resident knew Burma and the Burmese, and would have been good at his job had there been any job left to be good at. Being an active-minded man, he chafed at the forced inaction of his days. There was really nothing he could do, and, as with Mr. Shaw, a salary of nearly £4,000 a year did not reconcile him to the fact.

He garnered in what information he could, chiefly from Fanny (who thought him, as he was, a very handsome man) and old Raj Singh. Fanny had to meet him at the Mission House, even her position as the favourite who could do no wrong might not have survived going to the Residency.

She brought strange little bundles of news, scraps of information coloured by her own mind and by those who had imparted it in the first place. Rumours, hard little facts, suppositions, threats, a very rag-bag which the Colonel and Mr. Lumsden had to sort out as best they could. Fanny enjoyed these entries into the world of the English far more than she had enjoyed living in it. To her, the occupation she was now engaged in was ideal, and she blossomed. True, Colonel Browne did not respond to her sidelong eyes or the sudden droop of her lashes, but she was used to telling who would re-act to her somewhat artless wiles and who would not, and felt no disappointment. Also for the first time in her life the image of one man, rarely as she had seen him, and though nothing but a pressure of the hand and a few significant glances had passed between them, filled her mind to the exclusion of thoughts of other men. The glances and the flirting of lashes was a mere reflex movement with Fanny nowadays, a thing she could not help.

So she trotted happily to the Mission House and told how Sinbyew-mashin had made searching enquiries about the new Resident, having heard that he was a violent and hot-tempered man. Indeed, the Dowager Queen had been told that it was owing to these defects that the Colonel had not been appointed Resident before, and so she looked on his coming as a bad sign . . . perhaps the British Raj was at last getting tired of the way the Palace party was behaving!

Browne's genial face creased with laughter. " Keep it up, Mrs. Bagshaw, keep it up. Tell her I eat my clerks raw if they annoy me. I shall inspire much more wholesome fear if she thinks I'm bad-tempered—though I think she's been misinformed as to my personal peculiarities."

The next time Fanny came the news was more grave. There had been further executions in the Palace, though of whom Fanny was not certain. The Nyaungyan's mother and sisters had now three irons on each leg, but were still alive. The Salin Princess sent a frightened little note begging Browne not to let it be known that she had been wont to communicate with Shaw and not to mention her name to any of the Ministers whom he might see. Browne sent back by Fanny a small sum of money to enable her to bribe her guards and send a message if it were necessary.

On her following visit, Fanny's remarks smacked more of comedy. She had heard an order given for the shops in Mandalay town to be ransacked for all the tinned tongues, sausages and other English foods they had in stock, as Thibaw's libations were giving him a morning headache, and it was suggested that European foods would enable him to bear up better against European drinks.

Once Fanny brought information of attacks planned against the Residency for a stated date, but this Raj Singh was able to avert by consulting the stars and announcing that the date was unpropitious. Next she reported solemnly that Thibaw was just about to issue an edict that henceforth in the capital a rupee should only be considered worth fourteen annas instead of sixteen, so that the people might have the extra two annas to invest in the state lotteries. . . . Fanny was quite offended by the shout of laughter Colonel Browne sent up, laughter in which even Mr. Lumsden joined. "Of all the wonderful fiscal arrangements I've ever heard of! Oh, I wish someone could explain it to me. It makes my poor brain reel!" And off went the Colonel again.

The next news was that a nephew of the Nyaungyan's mother had been killed, and also the three-year-old son of one of the minor Queens, because he was a "Saturday-born" child, and Thibaw had dreamed that a child born on that day would wrest from him the possession of the White Umbrella. The Nyaungyan's sister sent a beautifully drawn little plan of that part of the Palace where her prison was, for neither she nor any of the captive Queens and Princesses could give up hope that the British of the Residency would rescue them. It went to the hearts of the Colonel and Mr. Lumsden, in their way as helpless as the prisoners, only to be able to send in food and money.

It was while matters were in this state that the Viceroy sent presents to Thibaw. . . . It seemed to the Colonel not a good moment for the Government of India to flatter the King with gifts, and he withheld them.

All this time Sandreino was rarely seen by the British in Mandalay—it was long before he even called on Browne—but he did one day inform him that a rumour to the effect that Thibaw was entering into correspondence with the Tsar of Russia was correct. Browne was amused. "That won't hurt much," he said, to Mr. Lumsden, "France is a much more dangerous element. Mark my words, Lumsden, we are making a great mistake, it may even be fatal, in letting the French get their foot in here. Whilst Upper Burma was shut up in a sort of corner house and we held the key of the front and only door, we could look on her flirtations with all the European powers with equanimity. But now that a back-door is being opened out into French territory, it's a very different affair."

Fanny listened to that unmoved. France meant Bonvoisin, and the more he came about the Palace, the better she would be pleased. Nothing mattered except that she should meet him again and that Supaya-lat should continue to be Queen, and that this Palace life should go on for ever.

Fanny enjoyed helping the poor captive ladies, she enjoyed
being a messenger, but she enjoyed most of all the thought
that somewhere in the immediate future everything would
cease to matter except the fact that life was more golden than
ever before.

And this secret life, the hidden life of the Palace in which
Fanny could sink and sink and drowse away the days—the
complete charmed circle of Palace life, with no pebble
from the shores beyond to disturb its mirror-surface—was
nearer to her than she thought.   For the impossible situation
came to an end at last.   More outrages took place against
British subjects.   A Mahomedan trader from Madras was
dragged off to gaol on a frivolous pretext and there murdered.
Pierpoint, when out for a walk, was attacked by a pariah-dog
which he beat off with his stick.   A hostile mob thereupon
attacked him and he only reached the Residency in time to
avoid disaster by means of using his very long legs to their
utmost—an unpleasant necessity for a heaven-born, and one
that Pierpoint, who was of undoubted courage, heartily disliked.   An unwarranted and brutal attack was made upon the
little doctor.

Again the question arose of withdrawing the British
representative altogether.   Browne, who was by now cynical
on the subject, made himself unpopular with the Government
of India by writing : " With regard to our grievances against
the Burmese Government, I presume the Government of
India would not consider any personal grievances, such as
gross denials of justice to British subjects, sufficient ground to
pick a quarrel on.   We have borne with these so long that
it would seem ungracious and inconsistent on our part to take
them up seriously . . ."

Aitchison kept hammering away at the Viceroy with his
opinion that it was unsafe and undignified to keep a Resident
at a Court that refused to receive him, and that had frequently
threatened to annihilate him, while he wrote to Browne
despairingly that he was kept in ignorance of the intentions
of the Government, and that he, Chief Commissioner of
British Burma, got snubbed if he tried to discover them.

" The fact is," the Colonel remarked to Mr. Lumsden,

" that the Government doesn't know itself. It's trying to gain time and avoid a definite rupture. It comes of having a party politician instead of a statesman at the head of the Indian Empire. His decisions are guided by the political weathercock at home, and he lets matters slide sooner than take any steps on which the Opposition may found misrepresentations—which is the usual way with Oppositions. He's so hypnotised by the Russian bogey in Afghanistan that he overlooks the fact that British Burma is one of the most important provinces of the Empire. It may be important to keep Russia out of Kabul, but it's just as important to keep other European nations from gaining a footing behind our backs here!"

However, the Viceroy at last began to see that the murder of the Residency members and their chaplain would perhaps make a worse stir than withdrawing them altogether and breaking with the Kingdom of Ava, and decided on the latter course, though by a piecemeal process. The Resident was to leave openly, but Pierpoint, who was after all only a minor official, was to stay behind in charge of the routine duties till he could collect everyone in Mandalay town who wished to leave and bring them down the river. This compromise assured that there should not be such a definite official break as if the going of the Colonel had finished matters entirely. It was determined not to give the Burmese any pretext for regarding it as a formal withdrawal, or creating a political sensation.

In spite of having given a formal notice three days before his departure, the Resident was allowed to depart in the launch Aitchison had sent for him, without any message of farewell from the Government to which he had been accredited. He was escorted to his steamer only by his assistants and Lumsden, the former begging him to get a move on Government so that they too could be released from the utter boredom and uselessness of their existence. A week later they had their wish, not so much through the efforts of Aitchison and Browne, as through that of the Afghans. The famous treaty of Gandamak, on which the Conservative party had plumed themselves, became in a

few hours so much waste-paper. The British Resident,
Sir Louis Cavagnari, who had been installed with such a
flourish of trumpets at Kabul, was murdered with the members
of his staff the day after he had telegraphed confidently to the
Viceroy that all was well.

The news, sent by Aitchison, to the Residency at Mandalay,
and a later telegram ordering withdrawal at last, were delayed
by an interruption in communications, and it was with an
agony of mind that Agatha, in Rangoon, waited. If the
Burmese Court got hold of the news first, in spite of certain
steps that had been taken to prevent such a contingency . . .
if it were conveyed by some mysterious agency, as had been
the news of the disaster of Isandhlwana, with an equally
terrible effect . . .! Runners and signallers were sent up,
but no armed vessel, as Aitchison was of the opinion Shaw
had held—that it would be the signal for an attack upon the
Residency while insufficient to protect it.

Fanny, in the Palace, knew even less than Agatha at
Rangoon, for she knew of no sudden urgency for flight.
When she received a note from Selah asking her to go to the
Kalawoon's house for early breakfast next morning, she
went off gaily without a notion that anything beyond the
normal run of events—if events in Mandalay could ever be
classed as normal—had occurred.

She found the Kalawoon very perturbed and Selah busy
packing a large and rather bald-looking trunk that had
once been covered with hair. Briefly she was told the news.
The mail-steamer, *Panthay*, down from Bhamo, was waiting
with steam up in the river, and already the whole of the
small remaining British colony, including Chinese and
Indians, was on board. Pierpoint, once he had received the
news, had carried through his arrangements with secrecy
and despatch. All the Government papers and valuables
had been conveyed on board the previous night, and every
British subject in Mandalay had received early that morning
a note asking them whether they wished to leave, and
telling them if so to get their things together and at once
join the *Panthay*. The Kalawoon and his wife, nervous for
the safety of Selah, of her little sister and a married sister,

were sending them also to Rangoon, hence the hair trunk.
Mr. Lumsden called for them and for Fanny just as explanations were finished.

"But my clothes!" explained Fanny aghast.

"Fanny, we did not dare to let you know earlier, we
could not risk giving you any warning," said Mr. Lumsden.
"You see, you being in the Palace . . ." He did not finish,
but his meaning was plain.

"Come, Fanny, you can get clothes at Rangoon. My, I
should think you would be glad to see Agatha again," said
Selah cheerfully.

But Fanny stayed silent, thinking. If she went to Rangoon
everything was over . . . everything she loved and lived for.
She looked up and shook her head.

"I shan't go," she said.

"Fanny, you must. You're a British subject now. You
won't be safe."

Fanny laughed. She knew better.

"I shall be safe." She searched her mind for arguments
and found the one that would impress Mr. Lumsden.

"The imprisoned Queens . . . I can't leave them. There
is only me now to feed and help them."

It was an argument that was unanswerable to the missionary. Had he had her opportunities of service he would
gladly have stayed. He had only yielded now to Pierpoint's
absolute insistence, though he knew his span of life would
have been short once the Resident was withdrawn, for he
was known as a sympathiser and a helper of the imprisoned
royalties. But Fanny, who could do no wrong in the eyes
of Supaya-lat, Fanny, who was of Italian and Burmese origin,
Fanny would be safe and might still help. It weighed
heavily on the Residency assistants and on Mr. Lumsden
that even now at the last moment they had received piteous
appeals for help from the manacled and suffering women in
the Palace. He ceased to urge flight, and Fanny knew she
had won.

She accompanied the party to the river-bund to say farewell, but declared that afterwards she would go back to the
Palace. "My place is there," said Fanny. She spoke truly—

what place as suitable as the fantastic Palace for the child of
no man's land that she was?

She wriggled into the second of the two bullock-carts with
Selah and they went off down the three long miles of ruts
and holes, everyone keeping a nervous eye open in case of
hostilities.  But so well had Pierpoint, who, for all his airs
of the heaven-born, did know his job, effected the strategic
retreat, that it had not yet dawned on the Palace party that
the English were indeed getting away unscathed.  Fanny
joined the chattering crowd of refugees on the steamer's
decks for five minutes, listening to the arguments and discussions.  Finally the Captain declared that the moment had
come when everyone must make up his mind to go or stay,
and the English and Americans stayed on board, but such
of the French and Italians as had thought of leaving decided
to remain after all.  They knew well they were in no danger.

Fanny was quite an impressive little figure as the members
of the British Residency bade her farewell.

"I expect I shall be seeing you again, Mrs. Bagshaw,"
said dark little Rawlinson, who was looking more full of his
own importance as a Postmaster General than ever.  "I
am going to be Steamer Postmaster now; I shall live on a
boat here and go on board the mail steamer and sort out the
letters on deck and you will come and get all the jollee
letters I shall have for you, yes."

Fanny was, suddenly, beginning to feel very lonely, and
this did seem a link with that side of her nature and her life
which she was deliberately abandoning.  She smiled on
Rawlinson, kissed Selah, and was taken on shore by the
Kalawoon.

The bund was crowded now with Burmans, realisation
that this was a more than ordinary departure had got round
at last.  Fanny gave rather a startled look at their dark faces.
Crows . . . she was throwing in her lot with crows.  She
gave a last look at the diminishing stern of the *Panthay* and
waved her handkerchief rather forlornly.

Mr. Lumsden, leaning over the taffrail, waved back
mechanically.  It was of himself and Agatha, not of Fanny,
that he was thinking.  Three and a half years had gone by

since he had stood on that bund awaiting Agatha's arrival,
feeling shy and uncertain of himself in face of a grown-up
daughter. A year had passed since the death of King Mindoon, a year of a life unbelievably strange for all the British
in the kalā town. What a period of alarums and excursions,
of indignities, of disappointments, of frantic attempts to give
help in circumstances that rendered help impossible. As to
his own special work, it was over. Like Marks, he felt that
the message for which he would have laid down his life had
slipped off the smooth and shining surface presented by these
people.

Again the fluttering handkerchief caught his eye, and this
time he noticed Fanny consciously. She looked very small
and lonely standing on the bund. Who would have imagined,
he reflected, that so much self-sacrifice and devotion to duty
lay in that fragile little frame, in the soul he had always
considered somewhat shallow!

She had turned now and climbed into the bullock-cart,
and the *Panthay* was well away down stream, the wooded
Sagaing hills, studded with white sunlit pagodas, were a
miracle of beauty in the morning light, the ripples of the
broad and shining river were full of faint burnished colours
like a·pearl. The chant of the leadsmen came to his ears
like the sad singing of the Dies Irae.

Fanny felt an unwonted little constriction of the heart as
she passed the empty unguarded Residency and the deserted
Mission. For a brief moment it seemed to her that she had
perhaps chosen wrongly. Then, with that breath-taking
effect it had on less impressionable people than Fanny, the
moat came into sight once more, the golden carved barges,
the golden spire, the rosy walls.

She felt, even more than she had felt when four years ago
she had seen again the glimmer of the Shway Dagon, that she
had come home. And, if by home is meant that place and
those circumstances most fitted to the nature, it was the truth.

# BOOK III

## THE TAMEIN

IN the weaving sheds—mere rush roofs supported on posts—where the girls worked under the direction of Julie and her father, the fine bright strands of silk stretched from sun to shade and to sun again, with transient gleams as the shuttles were thrust upon their way. The girls wove the famous dog-tooth and wavy-line tameins of many shuttles that were worn not by the common herd, but by Queens and Maids of Honour. Pale green and rose and yellow and pearl and crimson, the intricate patterns took shape beneath the slim brown fingers, and order came of a tangle that seemed insusceptible of design to the untutored eye.

It always fascinated Fanny to see the brilliant webs, to hear the faint click of the treadles that caused the warp and woof to rise and sink, to see the shuttles dart on their appointed ways; to gaze from the thin taut threads of many-hued silk to that dividing though steadily advancing edge where the fabric suddenly existed, complete and coherent, a flat silken surface, not a separate web of lines.

Time was not of much import to these light-hearted weavers; it might take long to make a dog-tooth tamein, but sooner or later the day came when it was finished, when the whole process of its creation had slipped into the past and was of no more account. Time itself was oddly different here in the Palace, from time in the West. It went so much faster, though it seemed to stand still. Past hardly existed and the future not at all, in spite of the spirit of intrigue which presumably works for benefits to come. The immediate present was so intensely theirs in the Palace that no one worried over the truth that there is no present, that it is perpetually becoming the past. There was such an illusion of time being static, everything was so changeless, dress, customs, outlook; the very buildings, though new, were so exactly what they had been as far as man could remember or history relate, that no one could notice how swiftly it was slipping away. Fanny's days were ordered as had been the days of Palace dwellers in Indo-China for hundreds of years, days that passed as they had passed in the days of Kublai Khan, whose palace had been of just the same design as was this in Mandalay.

Each day Supaya-lat and Thibaw sleep on till they awaken naturally, for if a man is disturbed in his sleep it may well be that his leip-bya or butterfly spirit does not have time to hurry back from the realm of dreams to its envelope of flesh. But usually soon after the first cock-crowing Supaya-lat calls for her attendants, though sometimes she may sleep as late as nine o'clock. Her Maids, among whom is always Fanny, sit waiting outside the movable screens that wall her room. First the little Pages take in the chota hazri—so-called after the Indian fashion—and then the first of the four dressings of the day begins, and with it Fanny's daily life, always the same, whatever of special rites or violent happenings occur as well. The framework of her days, on which they are perpetually being woven, never varies, ever the present, as the advancing edge of the silk fabric is the same.

First the Queen's bath and the repeating of a pious Pali charm as the water slips in a gleaming veil over Supaya-lat's fine-skinned brown body. Then the shampoo and the rub with soft towels, and the scenting with perfumes from Paris. Next, the hairdresser oiling and combing her black tresses, inter-weaving others, as her hair is scant for a Burmese woman, into its knot or sadon. There is a diamond pin to be placed in the centre of her hair and a fresh flower to tuck into it at the side. Now the scented, powdered, yellow thana'kha, mixed to a fine paste and applied as a cosmetic over her face, the eyebrows and lashes and lips wiped free of it with a soft piece of silk, and rouge from Paris delicately added to cheeks and lips.

The first garment to go upon her body is the skirt—always a rich silken tamein for the Queen—of striped or checked silk on ordinary days, of wavy-line on feast days. It is lined with fresh soft muslin, and this clean lining, the only undergarment worn, is sewn in newly each time before a skirt is donned. Her feet slip into sandals of crimson velvet, and round her bosom is wound a patterned length of silk that passes under the arms. Over this the clean white muslin jacket, and the final touch of the silk scarf or handkerchief, called a pawa, worn in a variety of ways to suit the taste of the moment or the heat of the day. Three diamond necklaces and a large pair of diamond earrings and Supaya-lat is dressed. . . . Not pretty, but oh, how alive, how flickering, like a flame even when she is still! Not pretty, but royal even at her most ignorant or her most cruel!

Three times a day a change into fresh garments for her and for her Maids. Very many new tameins a month are needed by Maids of Honour, for their garments must always look fresh and new, and hide-and-seek, boating, playing at cooking their own meals out of doors, and throwing water all over each other at the Water Feasts, cause skirts and jackets to have but a short lease of life. Julie's looms are kept busy.

The spending of the gold coin of the morning.

A morning in the gardens, amid the streams, the stucco grottoes, and the flowering trees. The sun shining through the leaves and dappling the grass and refracting from off the bright ripples of the water. Hoopoes strutting proudly about, bearing aloft their misty chestnut crowns; the tree-pies flirting their fan-shaped tails up in the bamboos, the mynas, with their self-important airs, rolling bright eyes from the naked, yellow patches surrounding them, and chattering endlessly. In a gilded cage brought out each day and hung upon a branch, a laughing thrush presented by a Shan Sawbwa, and still laughing, though rather angrily, despite its captivity. And above the cage, rising through the air, as Fanny had so often heard them on the South Downs of England, the sky-larks singing just the self-same song that fills the English skies with short almond-shaped notes, fine and golden as the almond-shaped petals of the gorse. And everywhere the bronze-green bee-eaters, flashing back and forth and the insolent crows with their saucy pale eyes and dark coats, and the impertinent sparrows, as like guttersnipes as the sparrows of a London street.

Picnics, eaten off plates of plantain leaves, hide-and-seek among the trees and pavilions—a hide-and-seek where only the newest and most tactless Maids of Honour would dare to find Supaya-lat, even though the tenuous clump of bamboos behind which she has taken shelter show her bright clothing distinctly through its slim shafts; for no one but Thibaw is allowed to find her when she has hidden. Feeding the tame fish, so tame they come crowding and jostling at the lip of the stream, with rice; drawing from a lucky-bag for presents that vary in value from precious stones and gold ornaments to feathers or tobacco-leaf.

After the light midday meal and the siesta, the spending of the second gold coin—the afternoon. King, Queen and their Maids lying beside a little canal. The black-and-white kingfishers hovering, their little bodies curved in tense arcs over the bright water, looking extraordinarily venomous and insect-like as they quiver and pounce and dart away. The calling of birds from the plumy trees, and the butterflies fluttering and recovering in their zig-zag flight as they weave their mazy patterns through sun and shade. The girls, so like butterflies or birds themselves, as they loll on the bright pure green of the grass, their delicate tameins gleaming and their snowy muslin jackets golden-white in the sunshine or soft pearly blue in shadow. Their faces, dusted as with golden pollen by thana'kha, as though they had been nuzzling in the honey-sweet trumpets of blossoms. Away behind the trees, the Palace, menacing because of its bulk and the force of its vermilion attack upon the senses, against a cloudless sky; the only movement from the watchful men perched in the little wooden buildings, like dovecots, on the roofs, ready with slings and mud-pellets to prevent the ill-fortune of a bird of prey alighting upon the corrugated iron in sign of coming calamity.

Perhaps people taking turns to tell stories, or a new con-
juror with magic tricks, or a case of goods from Paris to
examine with little shrieks of excitement. . . . And at four
when the shadows are long across the grass, everyone wanders
in to dinner, taken by the King and Queen alone together,
and by the Maids of Honour two and two in their own rooms.
Later, another bath, a fresh toilet, different jewellery.

The spending of the silver coin of night. Pwès and still
more pwès, with dancing-girls and theatrical companies or
puppet shows, with jugglers and acrobats. Always music
and nasal singing, music going on all night long and every
night from the gardens, music heard by the townspeople
beyond the walls and the manacled prisoners in their dungeons, music drowning the rippling of the bul-buls and the
persistent calling of the night-jars and the uneasy thoughts of
man.

Thus went the time spent in the Palace to Fanny, the patterned dream slipping past her, the fabric always advancing
along the threads that stretched ahead, but so inevitably, so
imperceptibly, that not till her own hand had given that last
throw of the shuttle did she stand and gaze in amazement
and dismay at the finished weaving. It had not been, and
yet suddenly there it was. Like that very different person,
Mr. Lumsden, she was faced with the riddle of how she had
passed the border-line between hope and actuality, and
marvelled, though less articulately than he, how it was
possible for life, that glowing thing, suddenly to be behind
her instead of spread before her feet.

When the weaving was only begun, that weaving which
was to make such a multi-coloured piece of stuff, Fanny
enjoyed the bright threads without thought, her only
conscious aspiration was to meet the handsome young
French engineer again. Supaya-lat, now that she was Queen
and had to be addressed as Ashin-nammadaw-paya, was the
same to Fanny as she had ever been. That alchemy of
flattery and real affection, with a dash of glamour from
years spent abroad, did not fail Fanny now. She and the
Queen both felt rather than knew that they understood

each other.   As a matter of fact, Supaya-lat had the advantage in character.   She could be cruel and courageous as
Fanny could never be, she would shirk nothing in her pro-
gramme, not the annual child-bearing, the ceaseless vigilance,
the murders, that were necessary to keep her husband and the
throne.   Only her ignorance of conditions outside the
Palace, her lack of all communal sense, prevented her from
being a great Queen.   Fanny, though she had not yet had it
awakened in her, possessed as much capacity for passion and
jealousy as Supaya-lat, but for the rest she was of frailer and
less royal stuff.

Selah reappeared one day, and Supaya-lat watched Fanny
with a wicked sidelong glance to see whether she were
jealous.   But Fanny first stared at Selah, then beamed; she
feared no one.   The Queen had ordered the Kalawoon to
recall his daughter, saying that she and her mother had been
good to her before the days of her greatness and she wished
to reward them now, and he had not dared to refuse.   Mrs.
Aratoon was made Hostess to the Wives of Ministers and
Officials, and Supaya-lat received her and Selah graciously,
giving them silks, ruby rings and cups of gold.   Selah,
who was naturally of a bounding disposition, was pleased
to be back at the Palace, life as a boarder at the Convent
of the Good Shepherd in Rangoon she had thought rather
boring.   Now she and her mother spent five days a week
in the Palace and went home to the Kalawoon for week-
ends.
Fanny began to know the Palace as she never had before.
Old Raj Singh, the imperturbable and mysterious, who had
often told her fortune, now seemed more withdrawn from
her, as though, because she was now definitely a part of
Palace life, a shutter had fallen between them.   But she
grew to know better than before the Hairy Woman, who had
moved with the Court when it came from Amarapura.   Of
course she had seen her in the days of Mindoon, but it was
only now that she accepted her as a part of daily life.   She
was so attractive in her gentleness, the Hairy Woman.   If
Fanny had had more knowledge and more imagination, she

would have seen in the Hairy Woman the gentle good earth-spirit that still, through all its false civilisation, guarded the meretricious life of the Palace. As it was, she merely looked on her as an amiable freak, much as the dwarf jesters must have been regarded at medieval courts.

She was old now, the Hairy Woman. No child with silky tufts growing faun-like out of its ears nuzzled at her downy breast, as in the days gone by. The locks that so thickly covered her face, only letting the beaming eyes peer through, were no longer of the soft brown, shading to buff, that had been her glory, but were thickly streaked with silver. Of all the human beings assembled under those fantastic corrugated iron roofs, it might have been truly said that Ma Phoon, the Hairy Woman, was the best. Her voice, amidst all the nasal voices about her, sounded amazingly golden and soft. She laid her silky well-combed forehead on her hands and wept slow tears that slipped down, matting her hair into little dark points, when she visited the imprisoned Queens and Princesses and gave them of her little all. Large, gentle, and blundering, she went her quiet ways about the enclosures, sometimes lamenting in her golden voice the cruelties of man, as a dog endowed with the gift of tongues might so well do.

Mindoon had in her youth promised a large sum to the man who would marry her. Long ago had her husband considered himself fortunate in his furry wife, and her children, accustomed from birth to bury their own smooth cheeks in the silken tangle of hers, had only thought how much more comfortable was their mother than any other. Fanny laughed at Ma Phoon, but found her to be the only person in the Palace who cared as though it hurt herself when other human beings suffered. Perhaps, as compensation, her hairiness bore with it the blessing of a certain amount of the nature of a dog.

Dr. Tarfels, the plump pale Teuton, was dead, or he would, with Raj Singh, that spiritual aristocrat, and Ma Phoon, have made the third in this strange little band of aliens—for Ma Phoon, Burmese as she was, was alien indeed amidst the rapacious or frivolous dwellers in the Palace.

Heavy with her first child, Supaya-lat sat brooding in the sunshine the long days through, only her eyes darting this way and that like the eyes of a lizard. "Where is the Poon-dawgyi-paya?" was the burden of her speech if Thibaw were not within sight. She was even, as the days went on, jealous of the plain nun-like sister who was only Chief Queen and wife in name. She talked of her sometimes to Fanny in broken disjointed sentences, watching for Fanny's agreement. Her thin hands would clench with sudden rage and her cheeks burn at the thought of this woman who divided with her in men's eyes the ownership of Thibaw, her Kodaw. Fanny, seeing her thus shaken by her passions as though a strong wind had blown upon her fragile body, marvelled.

The coming child provided Supaya-lat with the means of disposing of her sister; she demanded that she should vacate her Palace for the purpose of the confinement. It was the custom on the completion of a seven month's pregnancy, that the wives of Ministers and Officials should attend the Queen who was about to present her lord with an heir, night and day, and it was the apartments of Supaya-gyi that were now used for this purpose. Mrs. Aratoon was given charge of the catering, and Selah, very bustling and important, every day made out the list of the attending ladies and presented it to Supaya-lat.

As to the Chief Queen, she retired to Sinbyew-mashin's apartments and stayed there in nun-like seclusion, weeping the death of her favourite old nurse. For Supaya-lat, whether to hurt her sister or whether she genuinely believed in the accusation, which was somewhat unlikely, accused the old woman of conspiracy and witchcraft and caused her to be dragged out of the Palace by her few grey hairs and sent across the river to Sagaing, where she was shut up in a small hut and starved to death. Supaya-gyi and the King never met or spoke with each other again till the enemy was at the gate. . . .

Supaya-lat, free not only from her sister but also from her sister's devoted servant, faced her own ordeal gladly, and triumphantly gave birth to a son.

And while these threads of joy and misery were being interwoven, Fanny's own special gilt thread came and went in the pattern of the fabric. It was the only vital thing— for Agatha's letters telling her the news of Mission life were to Fanny now but as a tale that is told—that bound her to the life that she had known, the life of Europeans and of the hard realities of the West. It was the only thing that was intensely personal and was to herself alone in this fantastic world that she had chosen, and it had the actuality that an acutely personal thing must of necessity hold. Yet it, too, partook to a certain degree of the dream-like quality of all her days.

It was no surprise to her the first time that she met Bonvoisin alone. She had sent a note to the d'Avera household saying that she was coming to tea, and some singing instinct within her told her that the engineer would be there. The chief occupation of the daughters of M. d'Avera was matchmaking. They had little else to think of and they had already teased Fanny about the admiration which M. Bonvoisin had expressed for her.

He was there, and the little ladies made excuses to leave them alone for a brief space. It was late afternoon and the heat had gone out of the sunshine; everyone had drunk tea in the shade of the great pipul tree in the courtyard. For a few moments Fanny and Bonvoisin, after they had been left alone, sat in silence. He was not looking at her but was gazing towards where a grove of palm trees drooped their plumy heads. Beyond them again, thin, clear and exquisite, the seven-storied pyathat pricked the luminous sky.

Fanny devoured him with her eyes and her heart began to beat faster. There came back to her, with all its first freshness, that time when he had stopped her bullock-cart and rested his hand, that long brown hand with its fine fingertips, upon the edge of it. She remembered that sudden aspect of the line of his cheek and jaw, that had for no particular reason caught at her heart. That exquisite falling light of Mandalay, how it had brought out then, and how it brought out now, so much quality of heartbreak on plane and angle!

Heartbreak . . . that was the word. Odd that it should be so and yet it was; something not about this particular soul, but about the envelope of bone and flesh that enclosed it, caught at her heart and twisted it.

He was still looking away from her, and Fanny suddenly buried her face in her hands, shaken by something she had never in her life experienced. This was different . . . this was different . . . something new and strange and fine, something that was unlike, so she told herself passionately, any of the experimental fancies she had had before.

Of course she called it being in love, though it was long before she admitted it even to herself, for Bonvoisin was no eager or insistent suitor. The game at which poor Fanny was a mere tyro, was to him a series of finely graduated steps which he took or not at his pleasure or discretion, with no uncontrollable desire urging him down them. He talked to her, that afternoon beneath the pipul tree, of his parents' home near Paris and of Saigon in French Cochin-China—a little Paris by the sea, he told her—he mentioned that his name was Pierre, and then touched lightly on his work and his interest in it. Fanny could not afterwards have told why it was that she was left with a feeling that his success might chiefly depend on her because she held Supaya-lat's favour in the palm of her little hand. She only knew that Bonvoisin kissed that hand upon the palm, turning it over so that he could do so, before she went back to the Palace.

Sometimes Fanny went to the Delanges', where she heard talk of what was going on in the world beyond Mandalay. Sometimes she heard the same sort of gossip from the English instead of from the French point of view, when she went down to board the mail-boat and met Rawlinson. Rawlinson was more full of himself than ever, because Sandreino in the old days used to have such of the mail as had not already been claimed by its owners sent up to him for disposal, and he had been wont to pick out the letters for the Ministers and take them to the Palace. Rawlinson now organised the distributing of these other letters himself through a Mahomedan. The Mahomedan, who received an

anna for each letter he delivered and was naturally anxious
to make all the annas he could, used to come down to the
steamer carrying a large umbrella which he filled with all the
mail that had not been claimed, and carried it away to
deliver. Sandreino sulked at this curtailment of his privileges,
but Rawlinson beamed all over his plump, dark face.

Mail-day was quite an event and it was fun to sort out her
own letters, as everyone was allowed to do, from the heap
upon the deck, but she really took little interest in the outside
world. It seemed to her unreal and to occupy itself with
shadows. What was it to Fanny that an English general
called Roberts, had avenged the death of Cavagnari by taking
Kabul—though it was true, to Fanny's mild surprise, that
Thibaw had shown much alarm and unease after this news.
. . . It needed tidings of a terrible disaster to the British at a
hill called Majuba to make Thibaw feel quite at ease again.
It was less than nothing to Fanny that Lytton had resigned and
Gladstone replaced Beaconsfield in far-away England; or
that Mr. Aitchison had gone to Council, and a Mr. Bernard
replaced him as Chief Commissioner of Lower Burma.
What was it to her that there were more instances of brigan-
dage and injustice on the part of the Burmese towards the
steamers and their captains, crews and passengers; that the
Chinese had taken Bhamo and the Shans and Kachins were in
revolt?

Yet she liked to hear of the outer world from Bonvoisin
when he and she met. To hear of Paris, of the Bois de
Boulogne, where gentlemen rode beside carriages containing
lovely ladies of the Opera, of the theatres! He talked to
her too of the great French Empire in the East, of French
hopes in Annam and Tonkin: " Soon we shall be established
all along the Eastern frontier of Burma, the province of
Tonkin will be ours for good, and then what a good time
you will all have in Mandalay! The King and Queen won't
have to stay shut up then for fear of a usurper snatching the
Lion Throne, for France will protect them. You will lead
the sort of life that you are made for at last." Golden
visions for Fanny, who saw herself the beloved of the Court
of Ava and of Bonvoisin, saw Supaya-lat receiving the homage

of dandified romantic Frenchmen. A medley of Paris and the Gem City . . . what could be more delightful . . .!

Meanwhile, more and more Frenchmen and a good many Italians and Germans swarmed into Mandalay, and became army instructors, Financial Advisers to the King, engineers, merchants, heads of police, silk workers, munition workers . . . there was no end to them. It made going out much more amusing than hitherto, but it made being in the Palace more amusing too, for Fanny, as European Maid of Honour, was not expected to observe the strict seclusion from males that was enjoined upon the other Maids, and was always with Supaya-lat when some French or Italian soldier or engineer came to have an interview. Fanny generally translated when Supaya-lat argued and planned and studied with the strangers. Always now between the Palace and the stockade there was much life to be seen, horses and war-elephants being tried, soldiers being drilled—and paying very little attention to their European instructors, smoking, spitting and chatting gaily amongst themselves—but looking very brilliant and gay.

Thibaw and Supaya-lat would sit in a pavilion raised above the road, and watch the life and bustle, and the Taingda Mingyi, his heavy cruel jaw out-thrust, would sit with them, but never Sinbyew-mashin or the Kinwoon Mingyi. The Queen Mother, who had advised the first massacre, was now herself aghast at the Palace policy, and often nervously wished for the protection of a British Resident once more; and the Kinwoon Mingyi was entirely out of favour, his counsels of moderation, his wish to keep in with the British, his whole more knowledgeable point of view obtained by two visits to Europe, made him suspect now to the go-ahead policy of Supaya-lat. The Taingda Mingyi's house was in the Palace grounds, the Kinwoon's only just within the City Walls, and he was never allowed in the Palace though he still took his seat in the Hloot.

It would have availed him little, had Supaya-lat decided on his destruction, that he possessed a document given him by Mindoon granting him immunity from all the violently inflicted deaths, which ranged from beheading, to crucifixion, or being eaten by red ants. The oddest thing about his fall was that he and Sinbyew-mashin now tried to support each other, while at the same time trying to keep their own heads in place. The arrogant mother had found her match in her more arrogant daughter, and her favourite child was now the slighted Supaya-gyi.

Fanny was still on good terms with Sinbyew-mashin, and still fed the imprisoned ladies. Something deep within her nature enjoyed being friends with all parties. She enjoyed also the fact that her position was so secure; Supaya-lat was never suspicious of her, and this gave her a swelling sense of power. Fanny needed that sense of power nowadays; she was so often uncertain of herself and her charms, for she was in love for the first time. In love and uncertain of the man she loved. Always before, her unfailing instinct had told her when she attracted a man and when she did not; now she was sure of nothing.

Bonvoisin looked, languished, sometimes thrilled her by a sudden dropping and deepening of his voice, always sat by her when they met and talked to her with his handsome blue eyes fixed upon her face, but never did he say what she was longing to hear. Yet he was always trying to plan further meetings, and her flesh told her that his must also feel the attraction that was so urgent within herself. Sometimes she turned almost faint when he looked deeply into her eyes before lifting her hand to his lips. There were days when her body left her no peace with its crying for him. Yet she felt no impatience or despair. Time was of small account in that Eastern life that was now hers, and she felt that he was only waiting, quite for what she did not know, but the golden tide of the days must surely bring them more and more together. Everything would arrange itself, so her fatalistic mixed heritage of Eastern and Latin blood informed her. And she was still in those early first spaces of love when, even for a body so ready for love as hers, there is a drowsiness and a content that are not troubled by material matters.

As a matter of fact, love-making would be a very difficult thing to arrange in her life. Murder was comparatively easy in the Palace, but adultery was severely reprobated and punished by death. One or two Palace attendants caught in love affairs were promptly executed. Supaya-lat liked to keep her Court as Tennyson described that of Queen Victoria. She was intensely respectable and so, in her heart, was Fanny.

The boy that was to have made life safe for Supaya-lat died of small-pox when he was only six months old. This was, of course, the result of witchcraft. It was said that Supaya-gyi had employed a magician to bewitch the wet nurse—tradition did not allow any Queen of Ava to nurse her own child—and that the nurse's milk had turned to curds, which broke into very small needles. A few executions took place at night of those Maids of Honour belonging to the Queen Mother and Supaya-gyi, who were considered guilty of this sorcery. Already the Queen was pregnant with another child, and in spite of the tragedy, life went on as usual.

Selah was sent, with her aunt, to Calcutta to learn photography, as Supaya-lat took it into her head that she would like to have her photograph taken, sitting beside the King. Selah departed, very pleased and excited, with six thousand rupees for expenses, and Fanny saw her go without much regret for the only other English-speaking Maid of Honour. To be the only pebble on the beach was a situation that had always appealed to Fanny.

All seemed pleasant at the moment in the Palace. The Queen's child, when it came, was to be cared for not only by a wet nurse, but by twenty young girls of good family, who were already chosen and attended the apartments set aside for the purpose every day. No one saw or heard anything of Supaya-gyi, who lived in seclusion with the Queen Mother.

Selah returned more beaming than ever, complete with a camera and a knowledge of how to use it, only to find that the moment was not suitable for taking the Queen's photograph, as her confinement was expected any day.

A common sight in the Palace was the King walking

about with his friend and favourite Maung Toke, a Son of Tea, whom he had raised to the rank of Prince, and who was now called Prince Yanoung. He was of undistinguished birth, a matter of no moment to the democratic Burmese, with whom titles and honours are not hereditary, save in the royal family. But he was a man of a notoriously immoral life, which mattered to the Queen. He would ride at a gallop through the streets of Mandalay town, his lictors striking down anyone who had not already gone on his knees, and if he saw a pretty girl at a window, he would demand her of her parents and carry her away to his house, where he might make her a dancing-girl. This was not the sort of influence Supaya-lat wanted for Thibaw. Fanny disliked the man, partly because she knew that Supaya-lat hated and distrusted him, partly because her own instinct told her he was treacherous. It was Prince Yanoung who taught Thibaw to drink French wine and Scotch spirits whenever Thibaw's nerve was failing him or his conscience would not let him be.

Fanny knew of other things that Prince Yarnoung had brought about in Thibaw's life, while Supaya-lat was ailing and almost laid by before the birth of the baby. After the child was born—a daughter—the King only looked in rarely at the Queen and spent his days in the apartment where the baby Princess was being tended by the twenty carefully selected young girls and the wet nurse. It was Prince Yanoung, hoping to see the exclusive influence of Supaya-lat broken up, who encouraged him to seek one in especial of these young girls, and who always had a bottle of wine at hand to stimulate his flagging courage. Supaya-lat's Maids kept the King's strayings hidden from their mistress, fearing the wide-spreading effects her wrath might have. It was Fanny, who generally nursed the Queen's susceptibilities the most, who at last enlightened her, and it was for the sake of the French engineer, Bonvoisin, that she took the risk.

It was the time when the occasional storms of rain were on the land, but it was a sunny day when Supaya-lat, still weak from the birth fifteen days earlier, was lying on cushions,

Fanny seated beside her, in the little painted Italian room, known as the Fountain Room, for outside it was a pillared loggia built upon the Palace platform, and amidst the pillars a water-tassel played and scattered its diamonds in the breeze. It was the room where the King and Queen were wont to sit alone together in the evenings when there was no theatrical representation to take them to the Theatre Room. It was pleasant in the little cream-walled room, with its painted bunches of artless flowers. Outside, the trees dripped and rustled in sudden gusts of wind; the sun shone and made the outside world sparkle with countless diamonds.

Suddenly there came the noise of a most indecorous commotion from the Palace platform, and the next moment Julie had appeared, changed from her usual calm self to a trembling agitation. It was odd to see how even in the midst of the distraction that possessed her, she became quieter at the glare from Supaya-lat's eyes. She brought her palms up to her forehead and, bowing her head, began to speak with her usual fearlessness, though in respectful terms.

Fanny listened aghast to her tale. It appeared that her father, old M. Delange, had been seized the day before and thrown into prison, he was even now fettered and in the stocks, and with him was Bonvoisin, hitherto such a favourite with the King. It was difficult to discover why the outrage had taken place, the distraught Julie didn't seem to know herself. All she knew was that throughout the night she had sat up awaiting her father's return, and that at dawn she had sought out the Kalawoon and been told what had happened, and told also that it had been at the orders of Prince Yanoung.

At the sound of that hated name, Supaya-lat was on her feet with that incredibly lithe flickering movement of her body. In a second she had seen in this attack on the two Europeans, one the father of her friend Julie, an insult aimed at herself. She did not, as usual, send a peremptory message to the King, but, calling for her umbrella bearer, set off herself to the pavilion where she heard Thibaw was sitting with Prince Yanoung. Fanny was left palpitating and anxious; Julie, who was demented at the plight of her father, fled away again to find Sandreino and enlist his help.

When Supaya-lat came back, her brow was dark and lowering, and she flung explanations at the nervous Fanny, who retained her air of humility and sympathy, feeling her way lest the Queen's wrath should turn against herself.

As far as Fanny could make out, the whole affair was about a couple of golden dahs, such as were sacred to royalty, that Julie's brother, who had been out from France on a visit, had been taking back with him, not for himself but at the request of Bonvoisin, who was sending them to his relations as a gift. The mail-steamer had stopped at Minhla, near the frontier, where she was searched by the Burmese authorities lest she should be taking anything she should not out of the Kingdom. Young Delange had been allowed to continue his journey, but the dahs had been confiscated, and he had written to Bonvoisin telling him what had happened. Hardly had the engineer received the letter, when he was sent for along with M. Delange to go to the Palace. They had gone happily enough, thinking that long arrears of wages were to be paid, but they found awaiting them Prince Yanoung, who had them heavily ironed and thrown into gaol. Poor old Delange, unable to understand why this violence had overtaken him, had tried to resist his captors and had been brutally beaten over the head and back with an iron rod.

It appeared that Prince Yanoung had informed Thibaw that the dahs were being smuggled to Calcutta for the use of the Nyaungyan Prince—though how anyone imagined that the possession of two dahs, even if they were golden and royal, would enable him to come back and seize the throne, Fanny could not understand. But even she saw dimly the part that symbolism played in the outlook of these large children, and how before Thibaw's eyes there must have flashed a picture of an inflamed, triumphant Nyaungyan Prince, waving the golden dahs, not so much as weapons, but as credentials, as he flashed up the steps of the Lion Throne.

That Supaya-lat saw him thus, even as Thibaw did, was clear. She, though no weakling, yet lived in perpetual dread of losing the throne, and for once she considered the Yanoung Prince had acted rightly. For once, too, Fanny could not change her mind with cunning arguments. Fanny could see how the obstinate and ignorant brain—even more ignorant than Fanny's own—had been startled and shocked into a fear that made it rigid. So much was easy to understand, but what puzzled Fanny was the mind of Prince Yanoung, that upstart who disputed, with Supaya-lat, power over the King. This move could not be merely an attempt to annoy the Queen by imprisoning the father of one of her kalā favourites. No, it was that the Yanoung Prince distrusted all kalās, even the French and Italians. His aim was to make the Kingdom of Ava once more a sacred and golden enclosure where he could wax great in power and insolence. Supaya-lat was not enamoured of foreigners herself, but she loved the endless stream of French goods that had begun to pour into the Palace : the chiming clocks, the gilt mirrors, the Aubusson carpets, the perfumes and cosmetics, musical boxes, porcelain, and strange stuffs. And she, too, loved power, but she saw it differently from the way Prince Yanoung saw it. She liked to feel she was using these foreigners, getting the best out of them, bullying them, and she felt, too, that with all their modern arts of peace and more especially of war, that they were enabling the Kingdom of Ava to take a place from which it could defy all its enemies.

Prince Yanoung in his way and she in hers were equally ignorant; neither realised that, whether in proud isolation or in an imitation of modern rivals, the Kingdom of Ava could be nothing to these foreigners but a lucrative comedy. How could Supaya-lat suspect such a thing, when nearly all the foreigners she had met were so obsequious? English, French, Italians, Germans—all that band of cheats and rascals who swarmed in Mandalay—were not likely to make the Burman think highly of the European.

Therefore when any question arose of a possible conspiracy between a kalā and one of the exiled Princes, who all had a better right to the throne than Thibaw, she flew into a panic and even Yanoung, the distrusted, became admirable because he was on Thibaw's side.

Fanny sat humbly before her, considering the problem. Suddenly, though her heart beat thickly with alarm, she made up her mind. The only thing to change the Queen's attitude towards Yanoung and so make her insist on the release of the prisoners, was to rouse her personal anger against him, to show her a perfidy against herself, which would to her be even worse than perfidy to the throne. For, strange contradiction in that arrogant heart, possession of her husband was more to Supaya-lat even than possession of the throne, and Fanny knew it.

" Ashin-nammadaw-paya," began Fanny, and something in her voice, more serious and earnest than it had ever been in addressing her, penetrated Supaya-lat's angry absorption. " You are making a mistake in believing anything that Prince Yanoung tells you. He thinks of nothing but to work you evil behind your back, even as he did when you were last ill and unable to be with the Poon-dawgyi-paya."

Supaya-lat swung round at her with blazing eyes.

" What do you mean, Fanny? "

" I mean this, Ashin-nammadaw-paya, that while you were laid on your couch, Prince Yanoung persuaded the King to take a mistress from amongst the girls chosen to wait upon the coming child."

Supaya-lat was bending forward, rigid as a bent bow, her little hands clenched in her lap, and when she spoke, her voice was very quiet.

" Her name, Fanny? What is her name? "

" Ma Khingyi, daughter of the Kanee-atwinwoon."

Supaya-lat drew a deep breath and nodded her head slowly.

" Ah, I thought he looked at her," she said softly, " I thought I had seen him. . . ."

" The Poon-dawgyi-paya fell in love with Ma Khingyi when he first saw her," said Fanny innocently, but watching carefully from beneath her lashes lest wrath should overwhelm her, " and he asked Prince Yanoung to get her for him from her parents. The Kanee-atwinwoon refused, saying he feared your sword, Ashin-nammadaw-paya, but Prince Yanoung took her privately to the King, who told her he would protect her from all harm. He swore this on a great oath, saying if he failed to do so, might he soon lose his throne and die young, and Prince Yanoung was a witness to the King taking the oath."

" So they gave her to him? " said Supaya-lat, still in the same soft voice.

" They could not help it, Ashin-nammadaw-paya, for the King promised more. He said he would raise Ma Khingyi to be a Minor Queen, and since then he has been meeting her privately in a room guarded by his attendants. He has threatened, too, Ashin-nammadaw-paya's Maids of Honour who come to her about it with a sword, and so no one dared tell of it until I have dared now. He has been happy with Ma Khingyi all this time that the Queen has been with child."

It was at that moment, perhaps fortunately for Fanny, that Thibaw himself came along the loggia, past the dancing water-tassel, whose bright drops blew against him, and into the Italian room. He had grown fat and his hair was carelessly dressed, a bad sign in a Burman whose pride is in his hair, but he looked contented and all unaware of the unpleasantness awaiting him. With one spring the Queen was at him, and two livid scratches sprang out across his face; she pushed him out of the room and then flung her muslin sleeve across her nose: " You smell of slaves! " she shrieked, " you smell of slaves! " She tore the silken band from her bosom and, crying bitterly, beat upon her bare flesh with her closed fists.

Fanny, who had quickly hidden herself in a far corner of the room, saw Thibaw turn and hurry along the Palace platform. From the distance she heard his voice shouting, commanding a servant to bring the Queen Mother without delay. Fanny quietly slipped out of the room and went to her own apartment.

Fanny really suffered that night, anxious over Bonvoisin; she had never agonised over any other human being before. It was a strange sensation, and she was as bewildered by it as a child by its first punishment. Pierre . . . Pierre . . . her heart beat it out all night, over and over again.

The Queen was not visible next morning to anyone but

her mother—the trouble and jealousy between them apparently smoothed over for the time being—and Fanny, as soon as it was possible, obtained leave of absence and hurried out to the Delange house. Julie met her, beaming. All was well. At the first cock-crow that morning the prisoners had been released by the order of the Queen. In a patch of sun in the courtyard, old Delange sat in an armchair, his hands trembling a little and a livid bruise on his cheek, but otherwise none the worse. Julie led Fanny through into the long, low sitting-room after she had greeted the old man.

"Fanny, did you speak to the Queen? Did you plead with her? Sandreino and the Kalawoon were going to see the King this morning, but that would have been no good with the Queen against us."

Fanny nodded. "I told her about Ma Khingyi, and how it was all Prince Yanoung's doing."

Julie gazed at her with sudden horror. "Fanny, she will have them executed, you know she will. You should have waited."

"I could not wait," said Fanny. Julie stared at her and seemed to understand something of the unwonted travail of Fanny's soul.

"Monsieur Bonvoisin is upstairs now. They came back together and he is bathing and changing. I'll send him down to you."

Fanny thought she had never seen the staid Julie so human. A low murmur of voices, Julie's and then a man's voice, came from above, and a few minutes later Bonvoisin, newly-shaved, but looking haggard and with dark circles round his eyes, came into the room. He shut the door behind him and stood looking at Fanny. She stared back at him and suddenly made a curiously pathetic motion with her little hands towards him. "Pierre . . ." she whispered, "Pierre . . ." The next moment he had the hands in his and was looking down at her, his usual cheap assurance missing from his eyes; they were bright as ever, but tender.

"Fanny, you did that for me! You got me out of prison!" And as they kissed, a long, slow kiss, Fanny forgot all about anyone except their two selves. She would almost have burned the Palace down for this.

Sweet and smiling was the Queen that afternoon. She talked blandly to Fanny and Ma Khingyi, and explained to the latter that she was going to treat her kindly and was going to give orders to raise her status so that all might love and respect her. Fanny sat dazed while the scared, pretty young creature came into the room and did obeisance to the Queen. Supaya-lat, her great eyes narrowing, called her up to her and examined her jewellery. With her own hands she took off the girl's necklace and dropped it with a contemptuous air upon the floor.

"It is a great shame for a King to give such inferior jewellery," she said. "Fanny, fetch the box of jewellery out of the painted chest."

Fanny, marvelling, obeyed, and Supaya-lat dipped her thin little brown hands among its glittering contents. A diamond necklace, a pair of diamond earrings, many diamond rings, all far finer than the discarded gifts of the King, she gave to the girl, also a pile of gold bangles and of silk and satin garments.

"Now go back to your room and to-morrow morning attend the Poon-dawgyi-paya and myself, clad in all these things."

The round, rosy face of Ma Khingyi became still rosier. Her eyes brightened, her shy smile showed her gratitude. She bowed herself away and ran off to her room, eager to show the other Maids what beautiful things the Queen had given her. It cannot last, thought Fanny to herself . . . and yet next day the Queen gave Ma Khingyi precedence over what Princesses yet remained in the Palace, treating her as a Queen elect, much to the jealousy both of the Princesses and the other Maids of Honour.

"The Poon-dawgyi-paya has chosen this girl for great distinction, and you must all treat her with respect and give her honour, even as I do," Supaya-lat told them blandly.

One result of the taking of Ma Khingyi under her wing and away from that part of the Palace where she had been in attendance on her infant daughter, was to make it impossible for Thibaw to see her alone any more. Sometimes she allowed the girl to attend upon him in the gardens when

she herself was only a few yards away, but that was very
little good to Thibaw.  Fanny laughed to herself as the days
went on and she saw the King growing surlier.  Such a state
of affairs could not last, and at Yanoung's suggestion the
King took to drinking heavily to give him courage to defy
the Queen, and once he even rushed at her with a spear.  It
was the first time in her life that the greater physical strength
of the male had ever been directed against Supaya-lat, and she
fled in panic.  Thibaw, laughing triumphantly, summoned
Ma Khingyi to his room.

Supaya-lat sat brooding in the Fountain Room and laid
her plans.  Fanny, although her greater preoccupation
was with her own affairs, in planning how and where to
meet Bonvoisin, yet watched with apprehension.  Everyone in the Palace was aware that the Queen was plotting
something, and one execution might so easily lead to a
whole massacre.  It was all very well for Thibaw, perpetually
drinking, to be unafraid, but everyone else was nervous and
ill at ease.

It was not in Supaya-lat's nature to hesitate or to waste
time in attacking unessentials.  She always went to the
root of the matter, which in this case was Prince Yanoung.
She called in the Taingda Mingyi and sat consulting with
him a long morning through.  Then the Mingyi gave orders
for four wooden boxes, gilded and with a slit in the top,
to be made and placed one at each corner of the City walls
after the good old custom of King Mindoon, so that anyone
having a grievance could write it out and place it in a box
and claim royal redress.  Curiously enough, when the boxes
were brought to the King and Queen and duly opened, they
were found to be full of anonymous letters accusing Prince
Yanoung and the Kanee-atwinwoon, father of Ma Khingyi,
of a plot to dethrone Thibaw.  Each letter told different
details, all of which bore out the others.  Prince Yanoung
was to usurp the Lion Throne, and the Kanee-atwinwoon
was to become Crown Prince.  Already, said one letter,
many rifles and much ammunition were buried under the
house of the Kanee-atwinwoon, and indeed this was found

to be the case, though the earth was suspiciously newly disturbed, and Ma Khingyi's unfortunate father had already been held in gaol by the orders of the Queen and the Taingda Mingyi for twenty-four hours.

The King was terrified. He knew that Yanoung was a leader of men and that he himself was not, he knew that soldiers and Ministers were always calling at Yanoung's house. He sat biting his nails feverishly and begged his Supaya to advise him. She soothed and petted him, gave him the right amount of wine and no more, and told him to leave the matter in her hands and those of the Taingda Mingyi.

Thibaw, who in his distress would have turned instinctively to the one wise man in his kingdom, the discarded Kinwoon Mingyi, submitted to her ruling. He waited through three anxious days, varying between a state of mind in which he grieved that his favourite, Yanoung, was in prison and asserting that he must be innocent of the charges brought against him, and wild panics during which he saw in everyone but the Queen an enemy.

On the morning of the third day a rumour flew about Mandalay City and the Palace that Prince Yanoung had committed suicide in gaol, but Thibaw, already remorseful that, in panic, he had flung out the words: "Let him be killed if he has betrayed me . . ." remembered how, when he had so spoken, Supaya-lat had at once left the room and sent a messenger to the Taingda Mingyi. It was too late for remorse now, however; his chief ally and Supaya-lat's enemy was dead, whether by his own hand or by the sword of the executioner, and the next day Ma Khingyi's father followed him.

Supaya-lat was in great spirits and while Thibaw still sulked in his own apartments, she summoned about fifteen of her favourite Maids of Honour to bring Ma Khingyi to her presence. "We will have a game," cried Supaya-lat, clapping her hands. "Let us pretend that it is the time of the Water Feast and throw water at Ma Khingyi."

Word had gone round of the sort of game that Supaya-lat wished, and it was in no playful spirit that the obedient

Maids of Honour not only drenched her with water from
their silver bowls, but beat her about the head and face
with them.  The girl cried and screamed and ran hither
and thither, but always there was a wall of agile Maids
waiting to drive her back.  " You play too hard ! " cried
Supaya-lat laughing.  " You must leave off, girls !  You
will hurt poor Ma Khingyi ! "  But the girls knew better
than to leave off until at length the Queen gave them a
little signal with her hand, and by then the sopping Ma
Khingyi had had her front teeth broken, and her face and
hands and arms were swollen and discoloured.  That night
there was a pwè and Ma Khingyi, beautifully dressed and
heavy with jewels, her swollen face well powdered, was
made to attend on the King and Queen  He cast several
sidelong glances at her, but never again made any effort
to protect her, and soon after she and her mother disappeared
from the life of the Palace.

Yet Supaya-lat did not seem at peace.  A curious thing
was taking place within her mind.  Although it had been
she and the Taingda Mingyi who engineered the affair of
the gold boxes, who had themselves written the anonymous
letters that had brought Prince Yanoung to his hasty end,
yet she seemed to fear that after all there might have been
some basis for the rumours of conspiracy which she herself
had started.  Perhaps that vision of the Nyaungyan Prince
flashing with his golden dahs up the steps of the Lion Throne
remained always with her.  She still brooded and looked
suspiciously at all the world save Fanny.

Selah was quite out of favour, no interest was taken in
her photographs, and again an uneasy feeling began to
spread throughout the Palace.  Perhaps Supaya-lat remembered that it was in Calcutta, where the Nyaungyan Prince
was a refugee, that Selah and her aunt had gone to learn
the art of picture-making.  Perhaps what was worrying
her was that Ma Khingyi's mother was a cousin of Selah's
mother.  Before Ma Khingyi's mother disappeared from
the Palace she was unmercifully beaten by order of the
Queen in front of Mrs. Aratoon and Selah, who, trembling

with fear and horror, held to each other and closed their eyes.

" Your turn may come," cried Supaya-lat to Selah.   " If I think you too have betrayed me I shall write to the great Governor General in Calcutta and get permission to kill you also."

Poor old Mrs. Aratoon lamented loudly all the way back to her house, but the more robust Selah comforted her.

" See, Mother, we have relations who are British subjects; even the Queen doesn't think she can kill us without asking the Viceroy; besides, my father has always done his work well and been a favourite.   Why should we be hurt? "

Nevertheless, even Selah's spirit felt the breath of fear, and she went carefully about the Palace, keeping out of Supaya-lat's sight unless she were asked for by name.

The next death in the Palace was that of Thibaw's own mother, the Loungshay Queen, who had become a nun. A severe attack of conventional morality had seized upon Supaya-lat since she had known about Ma Khingyi.   There was little doubt that the Loungshay Queen's behaviour in the past had not been above suspicion, and it was only Thibaw's adder head that stamped him as his father's son; but elderly and plain as she was now, it took the imagination and address of Supaya-lat to make it creditable that she still indulged in the game of love.   Nevertheless, so cleverly did the young Queen manage, that Thibaw grew to believe that his mother had a lover in one of her attendants.   The man was killed and Thibaw, in a fit of respectability, announced his intention of ceasing to visit his mother's apartments. She, poor lady, had nothing left to live for, and when she contracted blood-poisoning from a sore in the palm of her hand, she refused to allow any healing treatment to be applied. And so alone, except for one faithful old Maid of Honour, she died.

As for Sinbyew-mashin, who had hoped when she was called in to counsel Supaya-lat that her old place was to be restored to her, she soon found that her daughter had merely pretended meekly to accept her advice of conciliation and submission to her husband's wishes, so that she could play her comedy with Ma Khingyi. It might well have seemed to Supaya-lat that the enemies of her own household were all conquered at last, and yet now that it was so, she had to weave fresh webs from within her own consciousness and see trouble where she ought to have seen her truest friends.

Fanny was too absorbed to notice Selah's peril, although it was impossible not to see that she was no longer in favour, but that was too common a thing in the Palace to arouse alarm in anyone except the actual object of displeasure.

Fanny's whole occupation was with her lover. Where and how to meet, that was the difficulty. . . . Life was very public in Mandalay, especially for a kalā; always there would be someone to observe her and say where she had been seen. Now that the Aratoons were under a cloud, Bonvoisin did not wish to visit there—not that at any time their house could have been used as a bower for love, the Aratoons, like Supaya-lat, and indeed like Fanny herself until now, were nothing if not respectable. But Fanny still thought herself respectable. She was half a Burman, and in Burma a marriage is made by the consent of both parties and the knowledge of their friends. Where a Western woman taking a lover might claim loftily that they were husband and wife in the sight of God, Fanny would, with greater simplicity, have observed that she and her lover were husband and wife in the sight of man.

The only thing that troubled Fanny was that she could be a wife so seldom. She could not receive men visitors in the women's part of the Palace, nor might she penetrate to that part dedicated to the men. Even could she have smuggled Bonvoisin into the Western Palace, it would not have been possible for her to shut herself with him into one of the candid pavilion-like rooms. Such a proceeding was difficult enough for Thibaw, with attendants to guard the entrance. Julie, though she winked at decorous meetings in her sitting-room—probably in the benevolent hope of arranging a marriage—was truly dévote and would not have connived at more. It was possible occasionally to drive out to a little deserted shooting box in the jungle, but it was a proceeding that terrified Fanny, who dreaded snakes and panthers, and the drive out and back was hot and uncomfortable and bumpy.

There remained only the house of d'Avera's daughters. Bonvoisin took and furnished a little bungalow lying in a shady garden just behind the d'Avera house, so, to visit her friends the girls, Fanny went whenever she could, and then, after they had peeped out and seen the way was clear, she would slip across from their garden to that of Pierre Bonvoisin. To the simple minds of the d'Avera girls it seemed that Fanny was married to Bonvoisin, and that if they didn't set up house together it was only because they were waiting for a suitable provision to be made for Fanny by the Queen. The need for secrecy that the lovers imposed upon them was no puzzle. Supaya-lat's insane jealousy was too well known to make such a precaution seem unreasonable. Fanny, the little favourite, the trusted European Maid° of Honour, must of necessity be careful not to arouse jealousy or suspicion.

Even so, as the months went on, the lovers' meetings had to be few, and perhaps because of this they retained a quality of freshness and excitement that might otherwise have been tarnished by the inevitable sordidness of the scheming that was necessary to bring them about. Ugly enough, perhaps, the whole affair might have seemed to a dispassionate and unsympathetic observer—on the one side a calculating man who was glad of the convenience and pleasantness of the relationship, and who looked on love as an enjoyable physical necessity like eating or drinking, and on the other side ; a scheming little woman who was all the time hoping to entrap him further.

That was the business at its ugliest, but to Fanny it was the greatest beauty her life had known. Agatha would have been shocked and outraged, Mr. Lumsden grieved, but Fanny would perhaps not have been far wrong in feeling that her simple and natural passion was somehow better than Agatha's carefully fostered and self-conscious love affair. . . . Not that Fanny did not want to be respectable, just as much as Agatha would have done, but to the Burman part of her mind she was indeed married to Bonvoisin, and both to the sceptical Latin part and the intensely respectable part, she always had that answer. Bonvoisin had explained to her that a Frenchman may not marry without the consent of his parents until he is twenty-five, and although at the beginning of their liaison he was already that age, he looked younger with his fair northern colouring. The complete circle of marriage Fanny imagined would be hers when the desired consummation of the union between France and the Kingdom of Ava took place, when British Burma was pushed out into the cold, and the traffic of merchandise and of armies passed from Mandalay through the French Protectorates of Annam and Tonkin—for that Tonkin would soon come under French rule, Bonvoisin did not doubt. By her influence over Supaya-lat she could help Bonvoisin, and that was how Bonvoisin proposed to turn her life in the near future into a fairy story.

Once Fanny got leave to take a trip on one of the royal steamers up the river. She had been a little ailing and made the most of her ailment. Sinbyew-mashin was taking the trip and Fanny, who had managed to remain a favourite with her as well as with her daughter, accompanied her. Bonvoisin was of the party; he was exploring the ruby mines of Mogoke, which had always been a royal monopoly, and for which he hoped, as Fanny knew, to get a concession. Sinbyew-mashin, that worldly-wise old harridan, who was past jealousy, smiled tolerantly upon love-making, and left the lovers free to talk, to exchange glances, to tiptoe down the alley-way between the cabins at night. Always to Fanny that remained her honeymoon—those days spent passing the flowering jungles, where the monkeys swung chattering from the trailing blossoms, and the parrots flew out like streaks of green fire, along the rippling shallows and the broad shining spaces of the pearl pale river.

It was on this trip that Fanny took to Burmese dress. She had always held by the distinction of her European gowns in the Palace, but she had had no new finery for a long time and her things all looked shabby. Sinbyew-

mashin preferred her attendant to be in Burmese garb,
and it made her less noticeable on this trip, where she did
not wish to excite remark. Therefore one evening, when
the Irrawaddy was a broad shining flood of gold and the
distant mountains were a soft amethyst against a sky of
primrose light, Fanny slipped up on deck in a pale gold-
coloured tamein and a gold and pale green swathing across
her bosom. It was not too high or discreet, and the slight,
smooth arches that told of her breasts showed above its
folds, and her tawny skin had a luminous quality through
the fine, white muslin of her jacket. Pawa she wore none,
but carried it in her hand as though her body scorned any
superfluous concealment. On the deck her lovely little feet
were bare, the straight toes a rosy brown against the white
planking. In the sleek black tower of her hair she had pinned
some jungle flowers of a dull soft pink.

Bonvoisin looked at her and caught his breath. Often
before he had criticised her to himself, for he was used to
the women of Paris, and Fanny's gowns were not such
as he could admire, and often, too, it had struck him that
however charming the gown might be, it could not really
become her as would a native dress. Her skin would always
look just one shade too brown and her nose too flat. Now he
knew that his instinct had been right. Just as Fanny's soul
was at home in the Palace, so her body was at home in the
Burmese dress. She felt his admiration vibrating about her
and laughed into his eyes.

Raising her palms to her forehead, she shikoed to him as
though he had been royalty, and then sank to the deck in
the attitude of respect. She stayed there, smiling up at
him, aware that his stiffer body could not have performed
that swift descent and twist.

" You should always dress like that," he told her.

Fanny pouted.

" I feel as though I were in fancy dress. But I don't
mind, if you like it."

" You don't look real. You look like one of those golden
lacquer figures on a screen. A little lacquer lady come to
life—for me."

That was the sort of talk Fanny could understand. She wore her "fancy dress" for the rest of the trip. And afterwards, back at the Palace, she wore it more and more. It saved trouble, and Fanny was lazy. It was much less conspicuous when she slipped through to Bonvoisin's bungalow from the d'Avera house. She still held to the idea of European dress as a mark of her difference from the rest of the Maids, but she wore it less and less. The trip up the Irrawaddy held such glamour for her that the tamein shared in its glow. In every love affair there is a short space of time when the wave is at its full and intoxicating crest, and it was in her cabin on board the little royal steamboat that this was so for Fanny.

She came again to the Palace, more regretfully this time than ever before, and yet with a feeling that never failed her that here, in some odd way, that could never be elsewhere, was her home. The cool dry weather was at its height when Fanny joined the party in the Queen's Gardens. All seemed peaceful and she took no particular note of the absence of Selah, who was often away spending a day or so with her parents. The affair of Prince Yanoung and of Ma Khingyi and her parents had slipped easily into the past, and everything was as it had always been.

This afternoon Supaya-lat, propped on her elbows and made comfortable by cushions, watched Thibaw's face as he sat a little above her, his uneasy gaze wandering hither and thither. Supaya-lat was languid with the approaching advent of her third child, but her face was as alive and vivid as ever, her big deep eyes as burning in their intensity. The King's wandering looks settled on the fresh-hued face of a Shan girl and stayed there. Supaya-lat sat up and clapped her thin, brown palms together.

"A story, Kodaw, we will have a story-telling. You," to the Hairy Woman, "tell us a story."

The Hairy Woman placed her hands to the silky locks that fell over her forehead.

"I have but old stories, Ashin-nammadaw-paya. Yet perhaps the Lord of Great Glory might care to hear the tale of the

young man who made a fatal promise." Her extraordinarily
sweet tones sounded golden after the voices of the others.

Thibaw turned his heavy eyes to her with a flicker of
interest.  "Is it a long story?" he asked.

"Not longer than the chewing of a betel, O Poon-dawgyi-
paya.  There once lived on the banks of the river a young
man called Maung Shway Pan, and he loved a beautiful
maiden.  One day he had to start off on business to a far
distant town—perhaps Prome or Pagan or even Moulmein
by the sea, and before he went, he exchanged deathless pledges
with the maiden."

"What was her name?" demanded Supaya-lat.

"I think it was Mi Meit, for she had a loving heart,
Ashin-nammadaw-paya.  They exchanged pledges of
fidelity, and more, they swore that if one died before they
could meet again, he or she would not be buried until the
other came, a foolish and rash oath.  The weeks went on
and Shway Pan concluded his business favourably and set
forth for his native village.  When he reached the place
he saw, sitting on the bund, his betrothed, but no village.
She would not let him stay his boat, but waved her hand
and called out to him that his mother and everyone else now
lived further up the river.  So, promising to return, the
youth went on home.  And there he found his mother,
and when she saw him, she began to weep and wail.  She
told him that Mi Meit was dead, and that a great misfortune
was feared, for when they had tried to bury her they could
not by any means get the coffin into the ground, for it was
too heavy to lift, so that it had been left outside the village,
and everyone for fear of witchcraft had gone to live further
up the river.  Shway Pan refused to believe his mother, for
had he not seen Mi Meit sitting on the river bank as lovely
as ever, and had she not called out to him and bidden him
return?  So he left his mother wailing and went back to
Mi Meit.  She led him into a hut and he followed her up
the ladder, and they sat and talked lovingly together till
Sky-shutting-in-time.  'I do not look as though I were
dead, Maung Shway Pan, do I?' asked the damsel, and the
youth gazed deep into the dark honey of her eyes and could

hardly refrain from the immodesty of an embrace, so he played upon his flute. But at dusk she suddenly began to swell and swell till she was of unearthly size, and he saw that his mother had been right, and that this was a demon in the body of his beloved. The sweat broke out upon him and his bones turned to water, but he did not lose his head. He let fall his flute through the bamboo floor and then made as though to go down and look for it. But the spectre stopped him and, lolling out a great red tongue that ran out further and further, longer and longer, from her distorted jaws, she picked up the flute with it. Then his heart failed him and he cried upon his mother: '*Amè! Amè!*' And '*Amè! Amè!*' the spectre echoed after him. So he kept silence, but thought: *If only I could get away!* And the spectre echoed aloud after him: '*If only I could get away!*' Then he asked her to make up a bed for him, saying that he felt sleepy and that he must go out and wash his feet. She agreed, first tying a piece of cotton round his toe. From beneath the hut he heard her banging and tearing at something, so he looked through a chink and saw she was banging and tearing at her coffin to make a bed with the pieces. He untied the cotton and made it fast round a post and then hurried off home as fast as he could. But soon she tugged at the cotton to make sure he was still there, and the cotton broke and she rushed down the ladder and found he was gone. Then she snatched up her coffin and started to pursue him and at the entrance to the village, as he was getting away from her, she threw the coffin at him, and it struck him on the head and he fell down dead. Then his mother and the villagers came with lamentations and took up his body. And they found the body of the maiden back in the coffin and now they could move the coffin easily. So they burned it and the youth together on the same funeral pyre."

Ma Phoon stopped, out of breath. Supaya-lat's face was dark. "I do not like tales of death," she said angrily. "The Poon-dawgyi-paya prefers to hear of the triumphs of kings and queens."

The poor Hairy Woman bowed her head ashamed, rather like a nice large sheep-dog that has been chidden.

"There was once a king," began one of the King's own Shan Maids, whom the Queen's Burmese Maids were apt to look upon as half wild, "that had an itching back, and he called a little maid of an exceeding fair complexion, whom he kept near him, and bade her scratch his back, but did not say where. And the damsel scratched aright at once, in the very spot, and this she did again and again, wherever he itched. So at last he said: 'I told thee to scratch, but not where to scratch. How dost thou know so well where I am itchy?' And the young handmaid said: 'Oh, king, the body of royal persons is marvellously soft and fine, and wherever I see a streak appearing I know that there it itches and so I scratch.' The king was much struck by the wisdom of the damsel, and he made her very great—less than a queen but more than a concubine, and she went with him always wherever he went."

Straight at the rosy cheek of the Shan girl went the Queen's slipper, catching it with the edge of the heel. The girl gave a little cry and put her hand to where a bead or two of blood welled up on her fair skin. Thibaw, who had been gazing at her and laughing at her story, looked hastily away.

"A slave-girl's story!" said Supaya-lat scornfully.

"Ashin-nammadaw-paya," said Fanny swiftly, "who are we to know about kings? It is the Queen who can tell us."

"You should all know of good kings," said Supaya-lat sententiously, but her look brightening; "we royal folk have no loves or hates, we give punishment only according to custom. Unless we act like this, our neighbours will not fear us, and unless they fear us, we cannot hope to speed our undertakings. The Poon-dawgyi-paya has driven the English from the country because he made them fear him. If the spur is long and ready to prick, cut the spur. If the beak is long and ready to fight, cut the beak. If the wing is long and ready to fly, cut the wing."

"Maung Maung is hungry and thirsty, Supaya," said Thibaw, using, as always, the affectionate term that is like a diminutive, in speaking of himself to her, "let us go in and have dinner."

So the gaily coloured procession moved across the lawns in the lengthening shadows of afternoon, and the royal pair

retired to eat alone together.    Supaya-lat was the first Queen
in the history of the Kingdom ever to eat with her husband.
She would drink water with her curry and rice and watch
him anxiously as he washed his meal down with French wine.
For she knew that though sometimes wine was her ally,
yet it might give him strength to resist her.    She always
remembered how he had inflamed himself with liquor and
run at her with a spear over the affair of Prince Yanoung and
Ma Khingyi.    She had won, but she had been on the watch,
anxious and tireless, ever since.

And Thibaw, drinking, began to think perhaps he wasn't
as far astray from the true path as at times he feared.    Especially feared it at that lonely hour when the first crowing of the
cocks would tell him that another night of ghosts was over,
and the bright trivial day was to yield the respite that is the
blessing of material things.

*Strive to avert the spreading of evil that has arisen.*
*Strive to avert the arising of evil that hath not arisen.*
*Strive to aid the arising of good that hath not arisen.*
*Strive to aid the spreading of good that hath arisen.*

Such was the Law of Right Effort as preached by the
Lord Omniscient.    And Thibaw, the learned and pious
monk who had passed in the Three Baskets of the Law,
groaned—but gently so that Supaya-lat should not awake
and hear him—as he turned upon his pillows and heard
the perpetual soft singing from the gardens of his Palace.

Fanny was awakened next morning by a little child Maid
of Honour, who brought her, with much secrecy, a long
letter.    For one wild moment she hoped it was from Bonvoisin, but as she rubbed the sleep out of her eyes and sat up to
examine it, she recognised the writing that thickly covered
the pages to be that of Selah.

" DEAR FANNY," (wrote Selah), " this is to say you may
never see me again, but I hope and trust that as we have
always been friends you will do your best for me, my father,

my mother, my aunt and my youngest sister. No sooner had you gone off on your steamer trip than the Queen sent for me and my aunt, and in the presence of the King and the Taingda Mingyi and a few attendants of both sexes, she accused my aunt of having taken a seditious letter from a Maid of Honour named Mah-koo, daughter of Myothit Woondawk, to the Nyaungyan Prince, a refugee in Calcutta, and that we both had met him and his brother there and delivered the letter. My aunt with surprise instantly denied the charge, saying that an open letter and Rs. 30 in bits were given her to give her poor relations in Lait-oo-dan quarter in Rangoon on our way to Calcutta, and that that letter and the money were delivered to the two women who came for them and who had read the letter in our presence and to our hearing, and it had reference to this money for their children and enquiring after the health of her relatives.

"The Queen indignantly replied, 'All lies,' and turned to the King and said my father, the Kalawoon, was 'the cause of having British Residency established in Mandalay during our father's reign, and that he was in the pay of the British Government, and his sister and his daughter, meaning my aunt and myself, went to Calcutta at my expense, and tried to influence the Nyaungyan and Nyaungoke Princes to come and take the throne from us. Well, what would you do with such disloyal people?'

"The King replied that she could do as she liked with us, and turning round to the Taingda Mingyi said the trouble was created among the women and that the Kalawoon knows nothing about all this, and see that he is not ill-treated and don't alarm him and let him live in his own house quietly. So saying, he went away to his apartment. That very morning while we were in the Palace my father and my brother were arrested and sent to gaol after confiscating all our property.

"As soon as the King left us the Queen said that she did not believe all that had been reported about the two Princes in Calcutta, but she hated us because we were related to Ma Khingyi. We were then taken at once and kept, each in a separate room, in the Palace, and the same questions as before put us, and all of us replied 'Yes' to every question, as the Queen had said that we would be put to death if we answered in the negative.

"After two days' confinement, I was taken to a place at about 5 p.m. where I met my father in chains, and I was overcome with grief at the sight and at the knowledge that he was suffering from fever. He told me that this place was his gaol and that he had been there for the last three days; a little while after my aunt was brought in and I heard that my mother, two married sisters and the youngest sister were with my brother in another gaol. Two days after this all of us were taken to the hut just in front of the wooden stockade of the Palace and handed over to Myin-Sayay, who is to be in charge of us while on our banishment journey to Shoay-bo with the only clothing on our backs. Our cousins, my aunt's daughter and son-in-law, hearing of the judgment, have sent sufficient necessary clothings, bedding, oilman stores, ahead on board the launch that is to convey all of us to Singine and then by carts to Shoay-bo. While we were in this hut iron chains were brought in to chain the women-folk, and I being of a fearless nature and seeing my people suffering, my temper getting the better of me, went forward and stretched out my right foot to be chained first, while repeating loudly in anguish that the Queen loves us, and we in turn are not ungrateful but always loved and obeyed her and remained loyal to the Crown, and should this saying be false, may these chains never be taken off my feet. This saying was evidently carried to the Queen by one of her sycophants, and before the chaining of my right foot was completed a man came running from the Palace with orders from the Queen not to chain the women. Those present, on hearing the above order, were greatly surprised, and praising me for my resoluteness and fidelity, and said that this is the work of God. The saving hand of God was made manifest. In consequence none of us were chained, and all of us are now to be placed in two carts, and I am sending you this before we start. I only hope we shall not all be *non est* before this reaches you.

"Your affectionate friend,

"SELAH ARATOON."

Selah, that cheerful companion, and the kindly little Kala-woon, might already have been killed, reflected Fanny, the sheets of the letter shaking in her hand. Often—as in the case of the supposed lover of the Loungshay Queen—the person out of favour was simply shipped across the river and despatched on the far shore. Selah . . . it brought the menace very near somehow. But no more was heard, and Fanny managed to forget and again the days slipped away on their ordered procession. The King, who held the ordinary daily audiences in the Morning Levée Room, sprawled on his golden salun-daw, and to these audiences came Bonvoisin more and more, and a couple of young Italian naval officers who had become naturalised Burmese citizens and were superintending the organisation of the King's navy, officers who did their work well and honestly—a rarity among kālas.

According to immemorial tradition, came and went the ordered events of the Buddhist year. There were Great Homage Days, when all the chiefs and officials of the country were supposed to come in and worship at the Golden Foot. The whole town would be decorated, yelling lictors, stately elephants, officials great and little but each full of his own importance, horses, guns, soldiers, servants, litters with their bodyguards, would go careering and shouting and swaggering through the streets of the kalā town and the City of Gems. Thibaw, in full regalia, winged lappets and epaulettes and gold-stringed salwè, high jewelled crown and swinging sword, would sit upon the Lion Throne while Ministers and Princes and the favoured foreigners would squat in the great Hall of Audience below, and Thibaw would speak a few words to each in turn, ask Bonvoisin about some engineering problem, or Camotto, one of the Italian naval officers, about the river defences.

In the month of Tagu came the New Year's Day and Water Feast, when the King and Queen had their hair washed with great ceremony in sacred water and the people drenched each other all day long. On the night of the moon in the month of Kasone an especially grand pwè was always held. In the month of Nayone four festivals should have been held, but the last of them, the Royal Ploughing, was never held by Thibaw, whereas year by year Mindoon had gone forth in his richest robes of state, covered with jewels, with a plough drawn by white bullocks and decorated with gold and silver, and had himself ploughed a chosen field so as to propitiate the Nats and obtain a good harvest for the whole country.  Thibaw stayed within the Palace; he dared not leave the Lion Throne so long unguarded, and also he went in perpetual fear of assassination.

Boat races were still held on the moat and the Irrawaddy, though without the King's presence.  Monks were still presented in the month of Tasaungmone with the Eight Sacred Necessities, and their new yellow garments were woven and dyed, according to custom, in the space of one night, by the laughing, excited Maids of Honour and the wives of Court officials.  Once a Court lady was found to have smuggled in ready-made cloth so that she did not have to work all night, and yet could produce a beautiful weaving, but the fraud was discovered, and she and her husband, one of the minor officials, were made to dance and sing a song telling of their fault while the honest workers laughed at them in the midst of their own busy spinning, weaving, dyeing and stitching.

Although the King had never speeded the Royal Plough, he sent in the month of Nadaw the first fruits of the grain reaped from the royal fields to the Arakon pagoda.  It was placed in chariots shaped like a buffalo, a bullock, and a vast prawn.

In the month of Pyatho were held the pony races before the King and Queen, on the eastern side of the Palace, and there were also elephant fights and the throwing of spears from galloping horses at targets placed upon poles.  There were many other feasts, and they were all held in due course, except that essential and primitive feast of the ploughing of the earth and sowing the seed.  That was too honest and real a thing for the glittering but pasteboard life of the Palace.

Supaya-lat alone seemed vital and primitive, to her it fell to grow and garner the only seed sown by Thibaw. Each year came the thickening and the heaviness about her flickering presence, and the pain and ignorance of a

tradition-ordered childbirth. Never, after that first time
a boy, girl after girl, adder-headed, bright-eyed.

Always, even at her time of travail, would go out her
cry: "Where is the Poon-dawgyi-paya?" And always
he was there—so much she had accomplished. She even
made the contemptuous gesture of bestowing her youngest
sister, the good-natured, dull Supaya-gale, upon him in
marriage as third wife, so as to stop the scandal of the King
of Ava having only two wives. She was not, however,
married with any ceremony, such as the one that Supaya-lat
and Supaya-gyi had shared; nor was she crowned. She was
given a room to herself next to the apartments of Thibaw and
Supaya-lat, but at night she had to sleep just outside the door
of their bed chamber. . . . Poor plump Supaya-gale was
never treated as a King's wife, or indeed, as a wife of any kind.
Son of Supaya-lat's there should be to inherit the Lion Throne,
or no son at all.

Little to Fanny now were Agatha's rare letters . . . telling
of the death of Mr. Lumsden from malignant malaria, giving
news of the Mission, of two babies, both boys—little curates to
be, Fanny supposed—of Edward working himself to death.
There was a sad note in the resolutely chatty epistles, but
nothing seemed real to Fanny save her own two intertwined
lives of the Palace and the bungalow. What happened to
dim ever so slightly this dream life that was yet the only real
life, Fanny could not have told. Nothing definite did happen, nothing, that is to say, that affected her personally.

There were perpetual murders, but she was used to them,
there seemed no reason why any longer they should poison
her days for her. After all, one did all one could to help
as long as help was possible, and after that there was no
good worrying. Was it just that she was getting too used
to the pleasant side of it all, to the glamour that had a hold
over her? No, for Fanny had not enough imagination to
wish for changes when she was content, and content she
was, except for wishing that the golden future predicted
by her lover should hasten its steps. Even that was coming
true. The French had established their protectorate in

Tonkin, even as he had prophesied. She on her side helped him by praising the French to Supaya-lat and admiring their policy. Gradually their work and that of the band of skilled Frenchmen in the employ of the King had taken more definite form. The Kinwoon Mingyi for a time almost came back to favour, because he who had travelled much conceived the idea of strengthening the Kingdom of Ava by contracting political relations with various great European states, especially France, Italy and Germany.

Seated in the Hloot or in his house within the City walls, the old Kinwoon Mingyi, like a yellow spider, sat weaving his webs of subtlety, planning to play off this nation against that, in the best manner of Oriental intrigue. If, thought he, no one nation had a predominant interest, they would all unite in keeping out England, who would want the chief influence if she were to have any at all. The Kinwoon Mingyi spread out his plans before the Queen and the listening Thibaw in their favourite pavilion, and to their untaught minds it all sounded masterly—as it would have been had the world still been in the stages of simple cunning that the Kinwoon's Oriental mind understood. Fanny, sitting behind the Queen, ready with tobacco for her, listening, was vaguely aware that life wasn't quite like that, that these big nations were not painted toys for Ava to play with, though she could not have told why.

It was interesting to see the old Kinwoon Mingyi and watch him at work. Fanny's instinct told her that he was different from the rest, that he mattered, even though he, too, still lived largely in a world of traditions and dreams. There was wisdom and knowledge on his parchment face, though perhaps not of the kind to fit him to cope with alien and unknown conditions. He brought with him on his visits his clerk, a young man called Maung Yo, whose eyes often sought Fanny's face. Once again she felt through all her nerves that here was one of the men who admired her.

It was so long since she had given a thought to any man save Bonvoisin that she was first surprised, then felt a little thrill of gratified vanity. Maung Yo was no ordinary young clerk, he had been educated in Rangoon and spoke French and

English. He scorned to wear a paso of native weave, costly and many-patterned as these might be; no, his waistcloth was of European brocaded silk in pale yellow. He had heard of Fanny, the European Maid of Honour, and though he found her in Burmese dress, he was filled with admiration for what he considered her cosmopolitan air. She had been in school in England and had married a captain of the Irrawaddy flotilla; to her he could talk, if he could get the opportunity, and tell her of his ambitions, his fine education, his great knowledge of the world. . . . He thought the old Kinwoon Mingyi distinctly behind the times, and often sent an amused gleam from his fine eyes to Fanny, taking her into his confidence, as it were, and producing quite a little feeling that they two understood each other. Fanny was flattered. He was a year or so younger than she, and in any case, she told herself, she would never have thought seriously of a Burmese clerk, but it was not unpleasant to realise that her distinction of appearance had won her this passing tribute. Maung Yo was a handsome young man, though with a weak mouth and too-narrow jaw and Fanny blossomed in the light of his respectful admiration.

What with Maung Yo, and Bonvoisin's satisfaction at the upshot of the meetings, Fanny was well pleased. She felt she herself had not been useless in her championship of the French. It was settled to send a Delegation to Europe, ostensibly for commercial and scientific purposes, and not at all for political ends—as an inquisitive Chief Commissioner in British Burma was duly informed. . . .

This Delegation might, according to the Kinwoon Mingyi, be going to visit impartially France, Germany and Italy, but it was going direct to Paris and it was in the charge of one of the King's French employees—the Comte de Trevelec. Fanny did not care for him, he always looked somewhat over her head, but Bonvoisin was very pleased; de Trevelec was a friend of his and he had had much to do with the appointment.

After the departure of the Delegation, life went on as usual, save that Maung Yo several times sent Fanny little notes that told of a highly respectful ardour such as could not but

be pleasing to her, for Bonvoisin was often very cavalier in
his methods, too lordly over appointments and forgotten
promises to be the perfect lover. Fanny, who had seen his
impatience if she protested, had learned to submit in silence.
She wished passionately that Maung Yo were a Frenchman,
so that Pierre would be jealous of him. . . . As it was she
never even mentioned him, she feared her lover's laughter.

Yes, on the whole, Fanny was content. She lived easy
and languid days. She was not creative by temperament,
and to go on from hour to hour and month to month, so
long as it was a pleasant process, still satisfied her. Perhaps
her uneasiness was due to the fact that, although unknow-
ingly, she was passing the line between youth and that period
not quite so young, when the soul of the most unthinking
begins to wonder intermittently just how much has been
gained and accomplished.

Neither could even Fanny, drugged by the sufficiency of
the present as she was, fail to be sensitive to a curious sense
of increased pace about the whole Palace life. Faster and
faster flew the shuttles of that strange weaving nowadays,
and more and more did the darker threads seem to dominate
the pattern. Like the rhythmic insistence of a machine, the
presence of the foreigners, with all the added stir and action,
hard clear-edged Western action, that they brought with
them, beat through the once idle days. There was in the
very air a swelling sense of great events pending and of
triumphs to come; and in spite of sudden freakish bullyings,
the amazing complacence of the foreigners in the face of
indignity, their gutta-percha resilience after insult and outrage, kept the machine-like beat for ever knocking in the ears.

Few honest kalās were left in Mandalay; d'Avera was an
honest man and he had gone away. Lumsden and the
dwellers in the Residency were honest and perforce they had
had to leave also. Moroni had been an honest man but he
was dead. Old Delange and Julie were honest and in a
curious way maintained intact their life, yet even they,
beyond the sacred enclosure of their French home, had
succumbed to this strange influence that the Court of Mandalay seemed to exert over all who came within its radius.

They, too, forgave the perpetual murders, even the outrage
of the prison and the stocks that had come into their own
lives. Delange was too old a man to leave the place where
he had built up his whole life, and that of Julie was becoming
more and more circumscribed as each year the field of her
sight dwindled and dimmed.

There were arrears of pay due to all the kalās in the King's
service, but on the whole they penetrated life more and
more, gamblers all that they were, they kept on playing for
high stakes. The kalās were no greater gamblers than in a
more candid way are the Burmese themselves. The State
Lotteries continued to ruin the nation, yet if a man were
starving he risked his last anna on a ticket. Everywhere
people were starving, partly because crops had failed (owing,
doubtless, to Thibaw's neglect of the Royal Ploughing) and
partly because, owing to dacoits, rebellions and raids, there
was no security for trading.

In a few months over a quarter of a million people flocked
over the frontier to become British subjects. The Shan
Sawbwas were in open revolt; no longer, for fear of the
Queen, did they send their daughters to become lesser
Queens according to custom, no longer did they come in on
the Beg Pardon days with their tributes of ponies and rolls of
cloth, of gold and silver cups and gold and silver flowers.
A serious Kachin rising caused the cessation of the steamer
sailings to Bhamo, but the whole of Thibaw's strangely attired
and undisciplined troops was sent to quell it and succeeded
in so doing, and Fanny got a passing glimpse once more of the
missionary life that seemed so far away, as the dauntless wives
of the American Baptists, who had perforce gone down to
Rangoon, sailed placidly up-river again to resume their work
in Bhamo and rejoin their husbands. Fanny, who had gone
down to the steamer when it stopped at Mandalay, looked at
them with new eyes. She had been wont to wonder how
they could find it worth while. . . . Now she knew that to
join Pierre, she too would have gone into danger. She
could understand—though the idea of love-making between
these mission people always seemed to her rather incredible
—that the women wanted to be with their husbands. The

thing called "the Lord's work" was beyond her comprehension as a motive for facing death.

The soldiers, such as did not desert to become dacoits, straggled back to the Gem City, but though the Kachins were quelled, other enemies arose; there were perpetual rumours of attempts of various exiled Princes against the throne, and Thibaw sat in his Palace listening to tale after tale. Daily Supaya-lat and the Taingda Mingyi conferred together and urged warlike counsels upon the King; daily there were executions or the threat of executions. The swelling sense of great things impending became more and more a sense of disasters impending . . . as though the very air grew dark with the darkness before a thunder-storm. Faster and faster went the weaving.

Suddenly a scarlet patch that dyed the whole breadth of the fabric of the days. . . . A massacre worse than that first massacre five years ago. It started by a deputation of Mingyis to the King, the Taingda Mingyi at its head. Word flew through the Palace that they had told him the political prisoners in the gaols were plotting against him, and that there were sympathisers outside who were going to join in. Fanny saw much coming and going about the Palace, saw that Supaya-lat was closeted in pavilions instead of playing with her Maids beside the streams, and waited with a beating heart. With sunset the throbbing and wailing of the music and pwès, that had never ceased entirely in Mandalay for five years, swelled louder and louder. . . . Fanny hastily put some things together in a bag and crept out, through the gardens and the Western Gate, and to the bungalow.

Alas, for the years of living on close terms with the violent deaths of others! Fanny did not agonise this time as she had previously. She was frightened, she wept for fear and pity and a sick disgust, but Bonvoisin's arms were close about her, and she accepted massacres now as an inevitable part of life.

She was tender-hearted at the actual sight of suffering, and yet, as all night long a great red pulse of burning beat in the sky, she did feel a certain sense of luxury, a strange

voluptuousness, in the dark and seclusion of the bungalow
and the touch of Pierre's hands. He too felt unwonted
stimulation in that accustomed contact set to the tune of
the leaping flames. This might be the end of them all, of
his fine schemes and himself as well. . . . Whatever his
failings, a lack of courage was not amongst them, and though
with many men danger might have laid passion aside, with
him it merely was, on that first night, a spur.

With dawn, their flames and those that had pulsed in the
sky had left only a sick pallor. They looked at each other
wanly, then Fanny essayed a smile and Bonvoisin, shrugging
his shoulders, called for his servant to make coffee. But
the servant had gone, and the necessity for making it himself
did him good. They went over to the d'Avera house, but
no one knew anything there beyond a rumour that the gaols
had been set on fire by order of the Taingda Mingyi, and
those prisoners who had not been burned alive had been
killed as they tried to escape. Later, at Julie's, where a pale
Sandreino met them, this was found to be true. The fires
that had faintly lit Bonvoisin's face to Fanny's avid loving
eyes had shone more strongly on the harsh face of the Taingda
Mingyi as he had stood, his paso girt up tightly between his
muscular legs, a great dah in his hand, and had himself led
the attack on the defenceless creatures who stumbled out of
the darkness, where they had lain for so long, into the glare
and the shouting. . . .

The next few days Fanny spent at Julie's. Passion was
drowned in such horror as now pervaded life. For Thibaw
commanded that the corpses of the men, women and children
—between two and three hundred of them—who had been
killed should be carted out to the burial ground to the west
of the town but not buried, so that all men might see what a
terrible thing it was to offend the King. There they lay,
mutilated beyond thought, while the pariah dogs and the pigs
feasted and the air stank and quivered above them; while on
the Irrawaddy the royal steamers plied up and down ceaselessly, giving free trips to all who wished, much as a benevolent lord of an English manor might stand free swing-boats
and merry-go-rounds to his tenants. Night after night the

actors and dancing-girls gave their performances, until it seemed the air was as scarlet with their harsh noises as it had been with the flames.

Life had to go on for those who were still lucky enough to possess it, and Fanny went back to the Palace one morning with Julie, and both took up their duties once more. When Fanny next went down to meet the mail-steamer she found Sandreino and Rawlinson conferring long and anxiously. The breach between them was healed, Sandreino could not stomach the horrors he had seen and he wrote asking for British intervention. But the news that came from Rangoon was of indignation meetings held, but of an unwillingness to interfere in the internal government of a neighbouring country by the Government of India. It was indeed an awkward position, for by not intervening at the first atrocities and by holding the other Princes in India, the Government had kept Thibaw upon his throne. To send a protest that would probably have to be followed up by action to be effective, implied a readiness to undertake that action, and therefore Mr. Bernard's recommendation to send a letter of remonstrance was negatived by the Government of India.

So much Fanny learned from talk on board the mail-steamer. At the Palace the little pieces of gossip gradually got themselves pieced together and formed more or less of a pattern. The Taingda Mingyi had filled the gaols with all his political enemies, and to get rid of them had caused a wholesale massacre . . . it seemed likely to be the truth. Probably also the Taingda Mingyi was jealous that for a space the Kinwoon Mingyi had come back to power and was determined to oust him. Certain it was that the saddened Kinwoon Mingyi kept once again in his own house, and Fanny saw him and his young clerk no more about the Palace.

There soon was little doubt that the whole affair of the gaol massacres had been arranged . . . certain prisoners had been told by their gaolers that they would be allowed to escape and their irons struck off. . . . The warders pretended they had been bribed by the prisoners' friends, while in truth it was by their enemies. These prisoners, full of hope, in the disguises provided for them, had left the prisons, to be shot or cut down, simply to start the cry that there was a mutiny in the gaols and that prisoners were forcing their way out. . . . After that the massacres, and a frightened King who sat in his Palace, begging that everyone who had conspired against him should be killed. A few prisoners escaped by being drawn through the burning palisades at the back of the prisons by dauntless friends, who were mostly women. The aunt and two women cousins of the Nyaungyan Prince suffered death—perhaps not unwillingly after so long and harsh a captivity. Of his mother and sister there was no news.

And life went on as usual. The Chinese took Bhamo, and now Thibaw did not dare send troops to recapture it. Once again the indefatigable wives, this time with their husbands, came down-river to Mandalay.

The Parsee Theatrical Company arrived at the Palace and started to give its comedies, its chorus all made up heavily with white powder and schoolgirl plaits to look like Europeans. In the kalā town the Taingda Mingyi and his favoured colleagues swaggered about on elephants, their lictors whipping the citizens into the dust, where they had to kneel with their heads abased.

And, night and day, the music went on and on and on and on.

One afternoon Fanny went down to meet Rawlinson and get any letters or news that there might be, and found him unusually depressed.

"It's all over with us here, Mrs. Bagshaw," he said, blissfully unaware that British intervention, the dream of his heart, was the last thing that Fanny wanted; "we have had the most appalling disaster. Worse than anything that has happened yet."

Fanny stared at him, forgetting, so out of practice was she, that "we" meant the British and that she was a British subject.

"What on earth . . ." she began, her heart pounding,

and Pierre the only thing of importance she could think of in
a hurry.

" Gordon," said Mr. Rawlinson.

" Gordon? " asked Fanny, bewildered.

" Our great General Gordon. In Khartoum. He has
been killed and Khartoum has fallen."

Fanny did not like to ask where Khartoum was, but she
knew at once that it was one of those things of which her
life seemed to have been full, like Kabul and Isandlhwana
and Majuba. This was another of them. The British had
been beaten again.

" They won't think of us any more," said the lugubrious
Rawlinson. " They won't be able to think of anything but
Gordon."

A golden afternoon in March, the birds calling in the trees
and Fanny and Pierre together in his bungalow. Pierre
triumphant, carelessly the lover, very much the elated
adventurer.

" Little lacquer lady, my fortune will soon be made," he
told her, slipping his hand beneath her chin—a chin plumper
than it used to be, but very soft and smooth to the touch—
" I have the concession for the Ruby Mines all drawn up.
Any day now it may be signed. Think of that! "

Fanny did think of it, in all its far-reaching ramifications.
The price of a virtuous woman may be far above rubies, but
it would be rubies that made Fanny a virtuous woman.
Pierre's parents could not object to his marriage when he
had so much money that not only would he be independent
of them for ever, but might even make them an allowance as
well . . . Fanny would not grudge it them. She rubbed
her sleek head against his cheek ingratiatingly.

" Let me see it. Let me see the contract."

" The contract! What a little woman of business. I
see you are of both—of all three—of your nations. I dare say
you will even understand this contract! "

" Of course I shall," said Fanny impatiently, and then,
reverting to coaxing : " Please? "

He laughed and produced the document. She pored over

it slowly, with all the good business brain both of the Latin
and the Burmese woman.

Yes, she understood it.   Bonvoisin and Co.—how grand
that sounded!—contracted to pay the Burmese Government three lakhs a year to work the Ruby Mines, no parties
other than Bonvoisin and Co. being allowed to work them.
Local officials were to give any assistance needed to him and
his men, to help in the question of food supplies and labour,
and his engineers might carry two hundred guns for purposes
of self-protection.   The King was to have first call upon the
rubies, paying the value of any he selected.   Apart from that
the rubies might be sent out of the country and sold to anyone
without tax or hindrance.   It was a remarkable concession
to have made to a French adventurer, for always hitherto
whatever agreements any King of Ava had entered upon, the
Ruby Mines had always been kept as a royal monopoly.
The coffers of the Treasury must be empty indeed.   Six
years of feasting, six years of providing endless pwès and
music for a nation starved of necessities, had taken their toll.

"Now I can go home," said Bonvoisin carelessly, rolling
up the draft of the concession.   Then, seeing her startled
face, added: "Only for a month, chérie.   A month to go,
and a month to be there, and a month to come back.   A
mere nothing.   But I must see my parents and put all my
affairs in order.   Besides, well . . . you know, Fanny, that
it is not all trading that we do here.   There is more in it than
that.   They want me to see Ferry."

"Ferry?" said Fanny vaguely.

"Jules Ferry, little ignoramus.   You have heard me
talk of him.   Our great Minister with the wide vision, the
man who is building up for France a colonial empire as great
as that of England, an empire which will beat England's
before we have done."

"Oh yes, I know.   He wants to see you, this great man?"

"He does.   I have been working all the time I have been
here, you know, Fanny.   De Trevelec went with the Burmese Delegation to Paris but I stayed and worked here.
These lakhs"—he tapped the roll of document on his knee—
"are guaranteed to me.   The work of the Delegation is done

now in Europe, the same work to which I have been bending
all my energies—except those I've spent on you! And a
Frenchman must expend himself on love or he has no energy
for anything else! We aren't like Englishmen who can only
do one thing at a time and neglect the little ladies, the Good
God made us with more to spare than the Anglo-Saxons!"

Fanny, nestling against him, asked what work the Burmese
Delegation to Europe had succeeded in accomplishing.

" Signed a treaty giving us all we want. Now it's in
Rome, making treaties with the Italians, and with the
Germans through their Ambassador. But those will only
be ordinary commercial treaties, ' most favoured nation'
clause and so on. Only last year the Reichstag—that's
Germany's Hloot Daw—declared against Bismarck's colonial
policy, so that's removed the Germans as rivals here. Italy's
too busy with political troubles. France is going to get
everything—make railways and banks, get control of the
army, of all the resources. That's what the treaty is going to
do, Fanny!"

Fanny was delighted to hear the golden vision was appre-
ciably nearer. " And the English? What is the Delegation
signing with the English?"

Bonvoisin laughed. " Nothing, not a single little clause.
The English are right out in the cold! The Burmese
Delegation never even called on the British Embassy all the
time—nearly two years!—it was in Paris, not till just as it
was leaving for Rome! The English have had what they
call a slap in the face. Any other nation would have suspected
something, but the English are finished by all the disasters
that have poured on them the last few years. Afghanistan,
Zululand, the Transvaal, the trouble with Arabi Pasha, and
now the greatest of all—the loss of their General Gordon at
Khartoum. No one thinks or talks of anything but that in
England. They are howling Gladstone down and weeping
for Gordon. They have not long vision and they think
nothing of Upper Burma—of Eldorado!"

He stopped her with a kiss as she began to ask what was
Eldorado. She did ask, a little later, but not with much
interest, what it was that made the treaty with France so

extra-special, so different from any treaty with Italy or Germany.  But Bonvoisin laughed and shook his fair head.

" No, no, those are secrets that aren't for little lacquer ladies off screens.  Besides, what waste of time when soon I have to leave you!  A French Consul-General is being sent out, Fanny, a fine Parisian.  You will forget all about me when you see him."

But it was Fanny's turn to shake her head.  She did not know much, but she knew she was aware of her lover's breath in every breath she herself drew, that in the flowing of the blood within her veins she felt the flow of his, that the fact of his existence was really never out of her mind even in sleep.

And he was going away. . . . She was not unreasonable about it, she knew that it must be, and after all, in the Palace the bright weaving of the days went on so timelessly!  But life was uncertain. . . . She was not imaginative, but even to her came the chill thought of the freakish chances of life. Especially in the Palace. . . .

That afternoon she clung to him in the shaded room and loved him as though it were the first time—or the last.  He was more than her young lover now, he was her husband, her settled life as well, and she was not the woman to know how much less that might be.

The first solace was a large crate from Paris sent by Pierre. Within were presents for Fanny to give to Supaya-lat and a dress and hat for herself—the latest from Paris.  For the Queen there was a mirror, always her favourite present. It had a frame of peacock-blue plush, with bouquets of dried flowers and grasses sewn upon it, and over the topmost bouquet a stuffed humming-bird was poised, its beak at a rustling paper cornflower.  There was also a wastepaper basket of gilt wicker, lined with bronze satin and decorated all round its exterior with a deep band of embroidered velvet cut into points, each point ending in a ball of coloured wool. It was charming as an ornament, thought Fanny, but as a receptacle for rubbish rather inadequate in the Palace, where, for the last year or so, every empty preserved-food tin and

discarded garment and piece of waste paper and packing straw
had simply been thrown into the space between the Palace
platform and the floors of the rooms, where they would
have made excellent kindling had the Palace caught fire.
Fanny was quite used to the smell of the rubbish by now.

Supaya-lat was charmed with her presents, and Fanny
was excited by her new gown and hat. She had worn
Burmese dress now for so long that the thought of wearing a
European dress gave her the half anxious thrill that the
prospect of meeting again an old lover gives to a woman.
Yet when she first lifted it out of its tissue paper, Fanny was
horrified by her dress. Fashion was making a noble effort
towards a drastic change, and instead of the puffs and billows,
the draperies and loopings, that had wreathed women's
forms ever since Fanny had been at Brighton, the daring
spirits of Paris were attempting to bring in dresses that fitted
over the hips, and at the back merely fell in wide flat pleats.
Of course the pleats were not close to the human form, they
were curved out over a " tournure " of stiffly starched frills
of cambric, and if Nature had not given a woman the where-
withal to sit comfortably, fashion would continue to supply it.
But the baldness, the starkness, the almost tailor-made look
it gave to gowns . . .! Fanny thought wisely: They'll
have some difficulty in making people take to *that*! She
didn't herself like it as much as those all-round puffs of draped
overskirt from which the waist and bust rose as from a
flower, although she saw by the fashion papers enclosed with
the gown that this plainness was certainly making an effort to
" come in." Most of the frocks were still a mass of frills and
flutes and puffs and loops, billowing in and out, caught here
and there, covered with edgings and rucheings and bows and
cascades; but evidently Paris was laying down this new line
for the future. And she, Fanny, was probably the first woman
in the whole of Burma, Lower or Upper, to have a frock of
this new kind. . . .

It was made of printed muslin, also of a novel and daring
variety, for all over the ground, of the soft pale grey beloved
of Paris, were strewn little Kate Greenaway boys and girls,
dolls, trumpets, drums, Punchinellos and sad little monkeys,

in bright coloured miniature. The pointed bodice was
fastened down the front by tiny buttons of silver, each
representing a dog's head, with eyes of topaz. There was a
little all-round, stiff, gentlemanly collar of pale grey velvet,
fastened with two dog's heads. Round the hem of the
dress was a pleated frill where the boys and girls, the monkeys
and the Punchinellos, played a sort of grotesque and macabre
game of peep-bo, all mutilated legs and arms and divided
heads and bodies. Here was the round cheek and pudgy
hoop-holding hand of a little boy, and, apparently growing
out of his head on the next flat pleat, the hump of Punchinello;
while beyond, the tiny, smiling face and golden curls of a
little girl ended at a surprising angle in the furry legs of a
monkey. Where the sleeves were set in, where the bodice
ended, wherever a cut or a pleat had been made in the fabric,
a freakish butchery of little lives had taken place; the gown
was a light-hearted massacre, an insane and witty jumble of
feminine and masculine, of human and animal, of toys and
limbs, of arrested action. A mad childish pageant of a gown,
not the brilliant procession of Eastern imagery, but the whim
of a jaded European fancy in search of novelty. Fanny, the
childless, who had never thought of life in terms as elemental
as that, was to be decked out with a thousand symbols of
childhood, with its toys and pictured presences.

With the dress went one of the new " postboy " hats,
high in the crown, with a shallow brim over the eyes, and
none at all at the back, trimmed right in front by a nosegay
of flowers. And what flowers . . . for a minute Fanny
again stared in dismay. They were such common flowers
. . . only ordinary dandelions, yellow blooms and feathery
" clocks " that looked as though but a few breaths were
needed to tell Fanny when her lover could be expected back
again. . . . Yet they certainly looked gay and bright on the
pert little hat.

Fanny tried the frock on, and turned this way and that
before her mirror. And a chill blew over her spirit. Was it
the pale pearl grey that made her look so sallow . . . so
dark? Perhaps, but was it also the colour that made her
look so thick? Or perhaps it was this new severe fashion of

pleats that made her waist and sides look so solid. It must be, because always her body had been wont to seem so fragile and flower-like, rising out of the nest of circling draperies. It was probably this trying fashion of stiff upstanding collar-bands in place of soft lace rucheings, that made her neck and chin seem heavy, instead of fine and tense as she had always known them. She took her hand-mirror and studied herself with a growing dismay. This was what came of wearing the easy Burmese dress and no corsets, of lying about on soft cushions and never walking except a few yards in the gardens. . . . Perhaps also, she had been eating rather too much rice and sweetmeats. . . .

What had happened to her? I can't be old, not at twenty-six, thought Fanny desperately, unaware that the swift doom of her Eastern and Latin blood was upon her. She only knew that somehow she had grown used to seeing herself in the pretty concealing Burmese dress, that this event of trying on a Paris frock for the first time in two or three years had suddenly made her see herself with new eyes. Without her having noticed it, the glow and life which had been her chief charms were gone, and gone too was the thin suppleness that had been her chief beauty. The ivory skin was pasty, the flat nose now looked flat instead of merely unnoticeable, the heart-shaped face had slightly coarsened at all its edges. She stared at herself in consternation and her heart began to beat thickly.

Pierre . . . how did he see her? So fixed in her had been the vision of herself as a little pathetic, attractive figure, the vision she always carried about with her and which informed her very gait, that she could not really credit what she now saw in the glass. And she strove to forget it, and for a time succeeded, pleased by the admiration of the other Maids for her new dress. She put it carefully aside against Bon-voisin's return, and, lest her peace should be disturbed, avoided the glass. But sometimes when she woke, as was becoming more and more her habit in the small hours of the morning, it would be with a vague sense that something was wrong. She would turn uneasily on her pillow, like Thibaw upon his, but instead of a row of grinning piteous death's heads flashing suddenly against the black screen of night, it was a thickened chin and neck and waist that filled the field of her mind's vision.

And next day she would eat less and at evening, when the light was soft, look at herself close, oh, so close, in her mirror so that she saw the matt, still pure surface of her skin and not any effect of altered contours. After all, it was absurd that Supaya-lat, who had borne with all the horrors and discomforts of successive childbirths ruled by native mid-wives, should retain her slim almost meagre figure, and not she to whom these complications were unknown. Fanny did not realise that no such fierce flame as always consumed Supaya-lat licked at her own placid complaisance. The flesh of the Queen was perpetually burned away by her anxious and ardent spirit.

In the dullness of the month that followed Bonvoisin's departure, Fanny took more notice of casual meetings with Sandreino and of the mail-day contacts with Rawlinson. These latter were important, for there might always be a letter from Pierre—but he was a bad correspondent, and when he did write, his letters, she thought resentfully, were not private enough to be worth showing to any of her friends.

Fanny wondered whether the bad news of a French defeat in Tonkin had reached him yet, and was occupying all his attention. Mandalay hummed with the news that had arrived just after her Pierre's departure. It had taken all Fanny's cleverness to reassure Thibaw and Supaya-lat of the power of the big sister France, who was to end all their troubles.

Sandreino was strange nowadays. Fanny, meeting him at the steamer, sounded him about the treaty with Italy of which Pierre had spoken. He seemed despondent and shrugged his shoulders. He spoke to her with candour, not because he trusted her, but because no one minded little Fanny, and it was a relief to speak as though to himself.

"Italy is too much occupied with her own troubles to bother to sign a treaty with the Kingdom of Ava. Your

fine friend, Bonvoisin, could have told you that. His
precious Jules Ferry—who is going to find himself in the
soup over this Tonkin affair—literally drove us into the
Triple Alliance by taking Tunisia when we objected. Oh,
you wouldn't know about all that, Fanny. Anyway, now
we're too busy forming and reforming cabinets to think of
anything else, except Abyssinia. Why any nation touches
Africa or anything to do with Africa, I am at a loss to understand. It always means bad luck—except to these cursed
French and their Tunisian venture."

Fanny heard the hail of strange names rattle round her
head, she made no attempt to disentangle them, but as
usual she came away with the essential truth, which was
that Sandreino was likely to be against the French in Mandalay. . . . Why that should be didn't matter to Fanny, nor
did the actual fact matter at the moment, but the knowledge
of it was there tucked away at the back of her magpie mind.

She was reminded of it by the next piece of news—that
Ferry's cabinet had tumbled down. But that didn't seem
to make any practical difference as far as she could see—the
French activities went on as before, and the French Consul-
General, M. Maas, arrived with unruffled mien and promptly
became a great man in the Palace and the City, and, from
what she gathered from her French friends, in the town also.

He arrived with the Burmese Delegation from Europe—
still shepherded by the triumphant de Trevelec—and naturally
it was this latter's advent that made the more stir in the Palace,
inter-dependent as the two events were. The Delegation,
which had signed an important treaty with France, a treaty
that both Ava and France had desired, that revolutionised
affairs . . . the treaty of which Bonvoisin had spoken to
Fanny—naturally the return of the Burmese members was of
more importance than the arrival of a Consul-General . . . a
kalā. Yet soon that simple state of affairs ceased to exist, and
it was M. Maas who was the most important figure in Mandalay. No one knew what had happened, but a general
feeling of gaiety pervaded the City. The kalās perked up
and went about head in air, the Burmese thought all their
troubles were ended. A golden period of immunity from

trouble and of endless wealth stretched ahead of everyone. There was quite a ceremony and much feasting. M. Maas was asked to breakfast at the Palace with the returned Delegation, and evidently the whole trip to Europe had been both important and successful.

M. Maas was an eager, slim, dark man, who gave a curious effect of brushing aside anything that he did not consider vital to his purposes. And his purposes were those of his country. Fanny did not need her instinct for knowing in what men were interested, to see that for the Consul-General patriotism was all that mattered. He was a man of a single mind, and that mind ran on a single track—a thing that makes for success if all goes well, but that results in broken men, in the discarded martyrs to a cause, if they do not. Such was the stuff of the man sent out to further the plans of France in Mandalay. He was polite to Fanny —she could not help feeling not because he was interested in her, but because word must have been sent him that she was in favour at the Palace and friendly to the French. She had an unpleasant little sensation of no longer being a woman when she met him. She did not see much of him. He was a man of affairs, not in the feminine sense of the expression, but in that of the great world.

He and Sandreino were soon on unfriendly terms, that was plain. It was as though he had expected the Italian Consul to work in with him and was surprised to find it was not so. Sandreino kept himself very much to himself nowadays, and was out of favour at the Palace. He was suspected of being pro-British, and also there came along some tiresome affair of which Fanny could not get the rights, about the Bombay-Burma Trading Corporation, the great organisation for working teak. Sandreino was its agent in Mandalay and he took up the cudgels very decidedly on its behalf. It appeared that the King said he had been defrauded in the matter of payment for logs, which the Corporation denied, and that the King, or rather his Ministers, talked of inflicting a tremendous fine, a fine that would fill the Treasury coffers once more. . . . The argument swayed back and forth and was not of much interest to Fanny. Bonvoisin was not there to explain it to her, to show her that the Corporation's loss might be France's gain. The new French Consul was always busy about the matter and about much else. Fanny waited for Bonvoisin to come back to Mandalay.

After all, it was quite casually that she heard of his return, a mere chance word dropped by a Maid of Honour, who had heard it from a page who had seen him in the Morning Levée Room. . . . Fanny was used to casual treatment; early in their friendship she had had to accept that, but she felt a sudden awful emptiness about her heart, as though it were falling, falling, through space. Then it was caught up again, and beat as though it would choke her. In Mandalay and no word for her. Of course anything might have gone wrong with the letter, but still. . . .

Her hands shook as, back in her room, she began to strip her jacket and tamein from her body. They seemed suddenly horrible to her. She pulled out the frock Bonvoisin had sent her and spread it on the little gilt French bedstead. Then she began to make up her face carefully, delicately, as the women of Paris did. She shook down her magificent hair from its sadon, and tried with unaccustomed fingers to twist it into the fashionable coils and puffs on the crown of her head. She wished the curls on either shoulder that had been the mode when first she had come to Mandalay, were still " in "; this new way of dressing the hair and the person seemed very little help to either, somehow. She sprayed herself with some French perfume Bonvoisin had given her, and then carefully got herself into the pale grey dress, with its boys and girls and Punchinellos, its soundless elfin orchestra of drums and cymbals and trumpets. She pulled the bodice closely and slipped the tiny dog's heads through the button-holes, nipping the flesh of her neck a little in fastening the gentle-manly collar. Then on went the postboy hat with its nodding yellow posy, and a pair of two-button grey gloves that met the narrow grey velvet cuffs edging the three-quarter sleeves. Fanny looked at herself in the glass. What was she to do? She couldn't, she wouldn't go to seek her lover in Burmese dress, she must wear this one. Surely, surely, she looked well in it. After all, she was young still . . . the frock was lovely, the scent, the gloves, the make-up, could not have been bettered by any Parisian. The amateurish hairdressing was hidden by the postboy hat. Her shoes were new and also came from Paris. Her parasol was of black lace, lined with pink that sent a rosy glow over the too-cold grey of the gown. She turned and went out of the little room to the white glare of the Palace platform, through the gardens, past the dimpling streams, away to the ill-omened Western Gate. It was never difficult for Fanny to go in and out, for her the rules had long been relaxed.

She went the direct way to the bungalow instead of through the d'Avera garden. Her heart began to beat heavily as she saw its familiar roof. Of course he mightn't be in, but she could go in and wait for him as she had so often done before. She went up the path beneath the plantains that curved above her, their great smooth green leaves shining with the pale reflection of the sky. She ran up the steps and clapped her hands softly. The pale grey kid split across suddenly, but no answer came from the house. The unmistakable feeling of deadness that there is about an empty house caught at her heart. She went to the window and peered in. The room was unfurnished.

Fanny stood quite still, paying no heed to her split glove. A feeling of intense desolation flooded her being. Of course it was all right, it was bound to be all right, he had moved house, that was all. Now that he was to be a rich man, the little bungalow was not grand enough. If he had only let her know. . . .

She went slowly down the path that led to the d'Avera garden, and through it to their house. Two of the girls were in and greeted her with little cries of pleasure. But was it her fancy, or was there something of restraint in their manner?

" Fanny ! " said the elder, " Fanny, we have been expecting you. What a lovely dress ! You look quite European."

" I am European. Pierre sent me this dress from Paris. I am going to see him."

The two girls shot a glance at each other.

" You are going to the new house? "

Fanny pondered swiftly. She couldn't let them know she
was ignorant of the whereabouts of the new house. . . . She
hesitated, and looked down at her smart shoes.

" I had thought of it, but perhaps it is rather far. These
shoes hurt a bit."

" Oh, Fanny, it can't hurt you to go hardly further than
the old Residency. So nice it is, much nicer than the
Residency, with a garden that slopes to the stream just like
it, but much nicer. They say it is all furnished with things
from Paris."

Fanny's heart leaped up again. How silly she had been.
. . . Of course now it was all as clear as daybreak. Pierre
had taken and furnished a house for her as a surprise.

" The house of M. Maas is nicer than the old Residency
also," she remarked conversationally. The two girls stared
at her oddly.

" Why—we thought you knew from what you said. . . .
It's the same house. Pierre is sharing it with M. Maas."

Fanny's spirits drooped again, then recovered. After all,
the Maas bungalow was big, two lots of people could have
quite separate sets of apartments.

She rose and opened her lace parasol with what she felt
was a *femme-du-monde* air, ignoring her slight mistake.
She made her farewells graciously, and it occurred to her
that the two girls must seem very awkward in comparison.
Really they seemed as though they were reluctant for her
to go and yet still more anxious lest she should stay, as though
they wanted to ask her something and yet weren't able to
get it out. That probably came of never having left Mandalay and mixed in the world. They used not to be like that
though, something had happened to them. . . . But what
did it matter, they were of no importance, it was only she
herself, Fanny, Fanny, Fanny, who mattered in the whole of
Mandalay.

She knew where to go now, and she tripped off in her new
shoes, carefully holding up the grey frock from the con-
tamination of the dust. As she passed the deserted, old,
tumbledown Residency, she caught her first glimpse of the

fine bungalow of M. Maas beyond it, and to her surprise saw
the figure of a woman seated in the shade of the verandah.
She had not known that M. Maas was married, he had
always seemed to her a man who took no heed of women.
Soon she was near enough to see that the woman was really
only a young girl, almost too thin, with a fair head bent
over some sewing, and a rose-coloured dress that spread
about her feet. A black velvet ribbon, a tiny little fine
thin note of black from where Fanny stood, made her head
and face seem blonde as a pearl. She gave an oddly definite
impression of being completely at home; so much so, that
Fanny, standing in the thick dust, hesitated a moment about
going on up to the house and disturbing her.

While she stood hesitating, a man came out from the open
window and, approaching the girl from behind her chair, put
his hands over her eyes. She did not seem surprised or
disturbed, she gave a low laugh that Fanny could have
heard had it not been for the beating of her own heart in
her ears. *Pierre . . . Pierre.* She stood stricken beyond
action, almost beyond thought. Perhaps the urgency of her
agony reached him, for, still keeping his hands over the girl's
eyes, Bonvoisin looked up and saw her. For a moment
they stared at each other and he stayed very still; then he
said something in a low voice to the young girl, and she,
still laughing, allowed him to propel her, blinded by his
hands into the house, as though they were a couple of children
playing a game.

Fanny's immobility broke with their movement. The
angry surge of her blood in her face made the road seem to
whirl round her, but she started forward to the garden gate.
She got no further, however, for Bonvoisin, his sun helmet
jammed anyhow upon his head, came hurrying down the
path and taking hold of her wrists, brought her hands up to
his mouth with an iron grip that hurt her, pushing her
relentlessly backwards as he did so.

" Chère Madame," he said loudly, dropping the conventional kiss of greeting upon the grey kid, " were you going to
call? How charming of you. I regret we are not yet quite
ready for visitors. But you must give me the pleasure of

taking you back." He began to urge her with that iron hand on her elbow, so different from his clasp over the fair girl's eyes, down the road. Fanny stumbled along, kicking up the dust upon the hem of her pale grey skirt, twisting her feet on the deep hard ruts, not seeing where she was going. She was bewildered, she could not understand why Pierre rushed her away from the Consul's wife, but the deep, angry voice in her heart kept saying that Pierre was having an affair with Madame Maas, that he was being unfaithful. . . . She stumbled on, the tears rising hot in her eyes. What a fool she had been, imagining that he would not get a mistress when he was away so long. . . . Her tears blinded her, it was several minutes before she could listen to him.

" You must be mad," Pierre was saying sternly. " How dared you come like this after getting my letter?"

She stared at him dumbly, wanting to say she had had no letter, but her throat was too tight and hard to let her speak. He softened at the dumb anguish of her look.

"I don't want to be unkind, Fanny; I don't mean you may not meet my wife, but you'd better get used to it all first. You're a sensible little woman, I know, and I shall always be fond of you. But just at first, don't you think it's better not?"

The white Mandalay roads, the deeply green fountain-shapes of the great trees, the burning arch of the sky, went round Fanny's head in a mad whirl. For a moment his hard strong arm was the only thing stable, the only thing left to cling to, in the mad riot. Then the world steadied and swung, with an awful dropping sensation, into place again, and she pushed the arm away. He was staring at her anxiously.

" Your wife . . . you are *married* . . . But you can't be, you're married to me. You're laughing at me, you're making a joke . . ."

He flung back his head and laughed; and she saw, as so many times before, his splendid white teeth and the light gleaming upon the taut skin of his upstretched chin.

" Married to you! Even you must have known better than that. I. . . . Why, I have been fiancé for a long while.

It's an old family arrangement. I thought it was a good opportunity to get married while I was home this time." He stopped, struck by her grey look. " Do you mean to say you haven't read my letter? "

" I haven't had a letter. That was why I came."

" My poor little Fanny . . ." He was sorry for her, smiled at her. " I might have known it would not get. to you when I wanted. I sent it last night by the sister of one of the Maids. She was to give it to her to give to you."

" I only heard you were back this morning. I dressed and came out."

She was speaking mechanically, explaining things that didn't matter, that didn't want explaining. She still stared at him. Thinking the worst was over he smiled at her reassuringly. And then the storm broke. Everything that it was possible for a woman of mixed breed who had no one language in perfection, to say, Fanny said. She was the peasant woman of three countries in her vituperation. He was relieved, it was easier to deal with this sort of thing than with that still look of anguish.

" You must have realised," he kept repeating, " it is childish to say you did not. Why, it is done all over the country. . . . A Frenchman does not marry—" he stopped. He could not say " a native " or " a mistress " in the face of that stricken look, apart from the fact that the statement would not even be true! He was sorry for her, he had not known she had so misunderstood everything. They always wanted more than you could give, but he had thought a nice present . . . if only she had had his letter first it would have been all right. He wished now he had written from Paris but there had been all the business of getting married. These other things were always quite easily arranged, especially with little. nobodies of no man's land like Fanny. And he had thought it better to tell it himself so that he could pet her and make it up to her. . . . He had been afraid that she might be angry and break up things so much more important than anything personal, if he wrote it her while he was not there to coax her . . . sure as he was of the solidity of the position he had built up in the country. But she had a certain influence with the Queen in this absurd kingdom which was to make his fortune, which was to belong to France, and for his share in the capture of which he was to get a piece of red ribbon, so he had not taken the risk of a letter till he himself could be at hand.

They were walking on blindly and were at the moat, at that strip of gorgeous loveliness which took the eyes and heart. Fanny was silent now. She accepted the inevitability of what had happened with all the fatalism of her blood, but she was beginning to smoulder with a sick anger. She hardly listened while he told her of his letter, of how it had asked her to meet him at the old bungalow that day. He had been about to go there when he had looked up and seen her.

" I asked you what you would like, Fanny. A trip to Europe, perhaps ! "

Looking at her sideways, tear-stained and swollen, the grey dress dragged tightly about her—stained with dark wet patches under her arms, her face sallow save for the redness of tears, he thought: Might get off with a chi-chi merchant on board. Anyway, give her time to get over it. I really didn't see how she was changing till now. Nothing like going away and coming back again to show you what a woman is really like. And he thought with a pang of sentimental and voluptuous reverence of his pale innocent little bride, who had never been alone with a man in her life until she was married to him.

To his great relief, Fanny parted from him with a sort of sulky peacefulness at the Western Gate, and he thought, as he turned away and mopped his damp brow with a large silk handkerchief, that there was nothing like being firm with them and showing that while prepared to do the handsome thing you were not going to stand any nonsense.

When Fanny, after mechanically kicking off her shoes according to etiquette on the Palace platform, entered her own room, she saw a square white envelope awaiting her on the little table. She pounced on it with a ridiculous hope that it would contradict what she had heard, although she knew what it had been written to tell her. She sat holding it for a moment, unable to open it.

Of course it only told her what she knew, told her charm-
ingly and kindly, but treating the whole affair as lightly as
he had always held it. . . . Thanks for all her sweetness,
promises of whatever she wanted most, tender and polite
regrets . . . not the letter a man would write to a woman
whom he had ever meant to marry.  And over and over
again, Fanny's Burmese method of thought kept repeating
that they had been married. . . . He would probably
hardly bother to deny a Burmese marriage . . . it just
didn't count, that was all.  The letter told her he had married
a French woman to whom he had long been affianced; it
told her they could not go on with their delightful little
friendship, and asked her to meet him so that they could say
farewell and she could tell him what she would like him to do
for her—a *dot* perhaps, to enable her to marry, anything in
reason. . . . She found herself wondering what might have
happened if she could have met him in the bungalow so
steeped with recollection of their passion . . . such easy
passion!  Then she saw herself in the mirror, saw herself
as he had seen her half an hour earlier. . . . Nothing would
have happened . . . nothing. . . .

She flung herself on her little gilt French bedstead and
lay there all day, refusing her curry and rice and pleading
headache.  The grey frock she had torn off, and it lay in a
corner of the room, the smiling rosy faces, the sad monkeys,
the dumb trumpets, were in a thousand new contacts with
each other, but they faded into the grey ground as the swift
dusk brimmed the room like a dark tide.  When, at last, at
Brothers-would-not-know-each-other-time, Fanny arose and
laid the gown away in a chest, nothing but a heap of dark
fabric showed between her hardly-paler hands, as though
all the little scattered lives had sunk into the enveloping
greyness and been drowned.

And the weaving went on, faster and faster, regardless of
poor Fanny and her first real trouble.  More important
matters than the happiness of a little plump, half-caste woman
were in hand, and Fanny's grief, although she was ill with it,
passed unregarded.  Later, when she dragged herself up and

about again, she was glad of that, glad of the egoism that allowed everyone else to ignore her.

Daily Bonvoisin and Maas came to the Morning Levée Room, where mercifully Fanny could not be. There was more and more talk of the Bombay-Burma Corporation, of letters that passed back and forth between the Kingdom of Ava and the Government of India. Sandreino and the Frenchmen were now definitely in opposite camps, and Sandreino wrote perpetually to Rangoon that the whole business was an outrage, that everyone knew it was a put-up job on the part of the Kingdom of Ava to get money.

It was a clear evening, though the period of storms was due, when Fanny came out into the gardens. She was wearing Burmese dress again, and so looked younger and better-looking than in the Paris gown. But she had changed, and changed profoundly. Something unthinking and gay within Fanny was dead for ever, the source of her chatter and her charm. She looked and was, dull—not with the dullness of a dead fire, but with that of a smouldering fire that has one last blaze left in its heart before it burns out and dies. Her face wore a strange inward look, she moved stolidly about as though she were no longer one of the gay crowd of little Maids of Honour with whom she lived. In a few days she had become set, fluidity of movement and thought had gone from her. Supaya-lat had sent her delicacies while she was a-bed, and had even come to see her, faithful in her affection for her favourite, but Fanny looked at her vaguely, feeling she was a fantastic marionette, not a breathing, living woman like herself. The brightly-coloured show of Palace life and Palace people, what was it to Fanny now but a dream? If you pricked them they wouldn't bleed, Fanny would have thought in her egoism, if she had thought at all; Fanny, who had seen them bleed so much. They represented to her now everything that had parted her from Pierre, that had made him look on her as an unsuitable wife for a member of the world's greatest nation.

The day she went into the gardens she obtained leave to go and see her friends, the d'Avera girls, and she went in a bullock-cart, for she felt tired. When she arrived at the house behind the great pipul tree where she had first talked with Bonvoisin, she found the young Maung Yo awaiting her. He came forward eagerly and assisted her out over the backs of the bullocks. He was smartly dressed in an elaborate silken paso and a bright scarf wound about his head, crowning his weak, handsome face flamboyantly. He gazed at Fanny in admiration. To think that she had actually written him, bidding him be here to meet her!

Fanny sat with him under the pipul tree and talked long and earnestly, in English lest the spirits of the air should hear what she was saying. Maung Yo sat petrified with horror. Impossible, impossible. . . . His silk-bound head nodded repeatedly in the Eastern negative. Not even for her. . . . But Fanny raised her eyes, those long dark eyes that were more beautiful for the shadows about them, and looked at him supplicatingly. What harm could come of it? Did she not know practically all about the treaty already? That it dealt with the building of railways, of banks, with other concessions even more important? Was it not known she was a friend of the French and so could not do anything to harm them? Also that she was the greatest friend of the Queen? Well, then . . . it wasn't much to ask for. Just a copy of any treaties with the French, that Maung Yo could so easily write out for her as he sat translating them in the Kinwoon Mingyi's house. . . . And, of course, any letters, as well, that dealt with the affair. Maung Yo hesitated, met the promise in Fanny's eyes, perhaps instead of seeing himself as a lover, less forgivably saw himself as the husband of the great Court favourite—and gave way.

The rain poured down the day that Fanny went to the steamer post-office. She went, not because she expected any letters or cared whether or no she received any, but because she was sure of meeting Sandreino. And indeed, there he was, looking more harassed and anxious than of yore, his fine moustaches limp with mingled rain and perspiration, his brow creased. He greeted Fanny with a cursory nod. She was too much in with the Palace party and the

French for his liking nowadays.  She came up and stood beside him as he was turning over some letters, and told him in a low voice that she must see him alone.  He looked round at her, startled.

"Here, on board," said Fanny, " Mr. Rawlinson will let us have his cabin if you ask him."

An obvious and not too polite gallantry faded on Sandreino's lips as he caught the look in her eyes.  What was the absurd little creature after . . .?  Perhaps she had some really valuable information . . . you never knew in this strange world.  Certainly if anyone were in the way of getting information, it would be Fanny.  And then Sandreino remembered the certain amount of joking there had been in the kalā town about Bonvoisin's return with a bride from Paris. . . .

He drew Rawlinson aside and asked him if they might go into his cabin, as he had reason to believe Mrs. Bagshaw had something of importance to tell. . Rawlinson agreed, and the two found themselves in the dingy little room, with its oil-lamp swinging in gimbals and its bunk covered with army blankets, where Rawlinson, the indomitable little man, slept every night when the boat was moored out in midstream for greater safety.  Fanny closed the door and sat down on the edge of the bunk.  Her legs felt oddly weak but her voice was firm and hard.  Overhead the rain drummed on the deck, it swished past the porthole in long grey lines like the lines of pale silk on a loom.

"Are the English going to war with the King over this quarrel about the Bombay-Burma?" she asked him, watching his face.  He shrugged his shoulders and spread his hands despairingly.

"My dear Mrs. Bagshaw, you know as much as I do.  The British don't want to go to war, they aren't enough interested apparently.  There's this trouble with Russia— it's the usual story.  The northern frontier of Afghanistan— the only thing in their heads.  The dispute about Penjdeh —but I needn't bother you with that."  He smiled at her benevolently.

"What would the English say—what would the Chief

Commissioner and the Governor General say if they saw a copy of the French treaty?" asked Fanny slowly, her eyes upon him. The smile of patronage was wiped from his face, he stared at her in a startled manner.

"The treaty with France . . . they say it's only commercial, the usual most-favoured nation business. There has already been a great deal asked about it by the English Ambassador in Paris. They told him there it was purely commercial. They swore it. Mr. Bernard has asked me to find out what I can . . . but so far, nothing." His dark, bilious-looking eyes never left her face.

"Italy is not getting a special treaty?" asked Fanny slowly and carefully, as a child speaks when trying to tell of something not familiar to it and beyond its ordinary scope.

"Italy can do nothing here. I tried," he added frankly, with a grin that showed her that now at least he had nothing to conceal in the matter, however he may have been working for his own country while at the same time agent for British companies in Mandalay. "We are much too involved in Abyssinia to think of anything else. We have almost as many disasters as the British. Italy refused to sign even a commercial treaty when the Delegation was at Rome; the Italians here have two years' pay owed them by the King, so no agreement was come to. And Italy understands that England could never consent to any import of arms."

Fanny was wearing a green checked English ulster with deep pockets, from one of which she now produced some papers. She flattened them out, watching Sandreino's eager face.

"If the British knew," she began slowly, "that there was a concession to the French to build railways? To run French steamers on the Irrawaddy? To build banks that are to be managed by the French, that they're to lend the money for them? And that there is a letter from Jules Ferry to the Kinwoon Mingyi saying that the French will arrange for the Burmese to import arms through Tonkin——"

"What!", roared Sandreino. He made to snatch the papers from her but she put them swiftly behind her back.

" There's a lot more—the Ruby Mines—the concession to
M. Bonvoisin has been signed. I have a copy here."

" Oh yes, we know about that. I sent a copy of that
agreement months ago, though we were not sure it had been
signed."

" It has been signed," said Fanny, " and here is a letter
from M. Maas to the Kinwoon Mingyi, saying that if the
Burmese can find an excuse to cancel the Bombay-Burma's
lease of the forests, the French will take up the lease . . ."

" You have a letter saying that ! " muttered Sandreino in
an awed voice. He sat down and mopped his wet forehead
with his usual dirty handkerchief, with the coronet embroidered in its corner.

" If you could send all that to Rangoon," persisted Fanny,
" what would happen to the French ? "

Sandreino looked at her and hesitated. This was such a
new Fanny, he could not treat her as a pleasant little simpleton,
he would have to try and explain matters if he were to get
those documents. And he wanted them. They would bring
the British in, and his position as the man who had brought
them in would give him a much more prosperous life than
he had had during the past uncertain years. He would keep
his jobs as agent to the Irrawaddy Flotilla Company and the
Bombay-Burma Corporation, which he would certainly lose
if the French got control of the Kingdom of Ava. . . . The
Palace party were running down a steep place violently into
the sea, they could not be saved. But the French could be
circumvented, even the Government of India would never
allow another European nation to take over Upper Burma.
For then it would only need a flare-up with Russia, causing
all available troops to mass on the North-West frontier, for
it to be the easiest thing in the world to send over trouble-
makers into British Burma; and then a Burmese agression,
engineered and financed by France, could sweep down and
gain all the land to the sea. France would march from
Cochin China to the Bay of Bengal. . . .

Fanny nodded, she knew all about it. Saigon, that little
Paris by the sea, where she had pictured herself . . . she
would never know it now. . . . Annam, Tonkin, the Gem

City itself, where was to have been the magic blending of France and Ava. . . . She had long ago grasped all that. Sandreino watched her anxiously. Women were queer things . . . if she were still too fond of Bonvoisin, in spite of the way he had treated her, to carry this out . . . he hardly dared risk assuring her that when Great Britain saw the papers, especially the letter from Ferry and that other letter suggesting the Minister should make an excuse to cancel the Bombay-Burma leases, the Government would move at last. Then he decided to risk it, and held out his hand for the papers.

"I have been private correspondent to the Government of India in Rangoon for several years now, Fanny. If they get these papers from me the Government will take Upper Burma. They will put up with massacres, even with bad trade, but never with another European nation."

"But the French? If they have made contracts, will the British have to keep the contracts? Like the Ruby Mines one?"

"If they only put in another Prince as they might once have put in the Nyaungyan Prince, they would have to respect contracts made by his predecessor, yes. But we have lately had news that he has died in Calcutta. If the British could have put him in as a protected monarch they might have—on seeing these papers of yours. Then they would have had to stand by any business contracts."

Privately, Sandreino thought that rather nonsense, but it was what Mr. Bernard had said when a question of interference over the last massacres had been mooted.

"But if they annexed the country, no. Then they would make all fresh laws. Maas knows that—it's why he is urging the Ministers to send another delegation to Europe. He knows the Burmese are not in a strong enough position yet, nor the French here, to defy England. He is pressing the Burmese Government very hard to have treaties made by which Germany and Italy will join with France in proclaiming the Kingdom of Ava neutral. England would be helpless if three such powerful nations did that. Maas does not want the Palace party to push the British too far until all that is arranged. And these papers *will* push England too far."

He waited, his eyes on her face. He gave a little sigh of relief as Fanny drew her hand out from behind her back and gave him the papers. His hands shook as he studied them, copied out in a clear clerkly hand.

" *With respect to transport through the Province of Tonkin to Burma, of arms of various kinds, ammunition and military stores generally, amicable arrangements will be come to with the Burmese Government for the passage of the same when peace and order prevail in Tonkin, and the officers stationed there are satisfied that there is no danger . . .* "

Written by Jules Ferry on the fifteenth of last January, after he had assured Lord Lyons in Paris that nothing of the sort had been arranged. . . . And the other letter, from Maas to the Kinwoon Mingyi : " *Should you be able to find a plea to cancel the Corporation's forest leases, I am ready on behalf of France to take them up.*" Telling the Burmese to make an excuse for cancelling the lease was a very different thing from merely saying he would take over in case the Bombay-Burma cancelled . . . though in either eventuality it released the King from the fear of having the valuable forests left on his hands with no one to work them. . . .

And then the railway treaty . . . and the bank treaty . . . Sandreino glanced through them hurriedly but saw in a flash that they gave Burma over into French hands, for the consideration of monies lent to the King. He went to Rawlinson's writing-table, and forgetting Fanny as though she had not existed, he sat down and began to write.

He was recalled to a sense of her actuality by the sound of the door-latch as she turned it. He slewed round on the swivel chair and called after her.

"Mrs. Bagshaw . . . Fanny ! " She halted and looked back at him, her face very pale over the large green checks of the ulster. "When the English come I will tell them. I will not take all the credit. I will say this is your doing."

Fanny shuddered as a swirl of rain came down the companion and caught her averted cheek.

"No, no, I want nothing said. Ever. Promise."

Sandreino, seeing himself as the mysterious and trust-worthy, not to say miraculous, source of news to the powers that were to be, promised.

Faster, faster, cried the Red Queen. . . . It was a pity that Fanny had never read the Alice books, and would only have thought them silly if she had. For life in the Palace was very like them. Faster, faster, cried the Red Queen. . . . But, run as fast as they all could, it was by now impossible even to stay in the same place. They were losing ground daily.

It was difficult for Fanny to find out what was going on in the Palace, for meetings were held between the King, the Ministers, Maas and Bonvoisin, at which she could not be present. But she managed to glean little scraps of news here and there and to hand them on to Sandreino. It seemed oddly like seven years ago, to be telling news to the British, or would have seemed odd had it not been to Fanny so entirely natural to let her personal feelings and predilections over-ride all else. There was, indeed, no reason why she should feel that any European nation had a call on her loyalty. With the Kingdom of Ava it was different. There, in the heart of the Palace she had received unvarying friendship and kindness—and what she had done was going to pull the Kingdom of Ava down about her head. . . . But Fanny, like Maas, had a single-track mind; his ran on the track labelled patriotism, and hers on the track labelled self, that was the difference.

Fanny thought of nothing but the thing she was pursuing—her revenge. Kingdoms might fall, but merely incidentally. That Fanny Bagshaw was going to turn all the schemes of Pierre Bonvoisin into nothing, was all that mattered to Fanny. Sometimes it seemed to her that even now that sleepy Government and that absurdly careful and scrupulous Chief Commissioner, Bernard, were, after all, going to let the whole thing slip into the past as they had let so many opportunities slip for years.

Still, she knew that, however pacific might be the Kinwoon Mingyi—who saw plainly that hostilities with England were

decided upon by the Palace party, and was as horrified as
Maas because it was far too soon to be safe—nothing would
stop the King and Queen, who, confident in the power of
France, to say nothing of that of Ava, were set upon war.
Therefore they imposed a fine of ten lakhs on the Bombay-
Burma Corporation, a fine that would have sent it into
bankruptcy.

From Sandreino, in snatched meetings on the post-office
boat, she learned occasionally how things were going. Mr.
Bernard had communicated with the Viceroy, and the
Viceroy had communicated with the Secretary of State in
England, saying that certain documents had come " from
a trustworthy source "—(Sandreino preened himself)—in
Mandalay, which put beyond the province of conjecture the
fact that France was engaged with secret treaties with Ava,
treaties that placed French agents as the masters of all trade
and sources of revenue in the Kingdom. Even now Mr.
Bernard only recommended that he should be allowed to tell
Ava that any such concessions to subjects of foreign powers
would be regarded as unfriendly acts and contrary to already
existing treaties with England, asking at the same time for
an assurance that such concessions should not be granted. It
was a mild enough telegram, but a very epoch-making one
for Bernard, who had always shown himself as scrupulous
and pacific as Lord Lytton's ideal British Government.

It was apparently Ferry's letter to the Kinwoon Mingyi
that had really brought affairs to a head . . . that letter
written while he was protesting to the British Ambassador
in Paris that nothing beyond the ordinary commercial
arrangements were being entered upon with Ava. That
and the letter from Maas about the Bombay-Burma Corporation. . . . The Bombay-Burma was, Sandreino opined,
going to be the useful pretext. England didn't want and
couldn't afford an open quarrel wih France. It was the
same thing with France as regarded England. Maas would be
sacrificed, as unsuccessful diplomats are always sacrificed,
and France would disown him. That was Sandreino's
opinion, and he thought it was probably beginning to be
the French Consul's also. Cabinets always fell when colonial

policies went wrong,. especially in Latin countries, and how much more lightly were the instruments of those Cabinets thrown upon the dustheap!

Therefore, while the French representatives in London, and the Government in Paris, were denying any knowledge of treaties with banks, railways and steamers, or any knowledge of loans or permissions to import arms, that might have been drafted or signed, Maas, playing by now a gallant and losing battle, kept up the fight.

Encouraged by the seeming impassivity of the Government of India, the Court of Ava pressed its demands and its threats in the matter of the teak forests, and at last Sandreino wired desperately that the Palace was threatening to " act according to custom," which meant confiscate everything and imprison everybody.

Mr. Bernard wrote careful, quiet and well-reasoned notes to Ava; he telegraphed, but all was of no avail. If Britain had discovered that the treatment of the Bombay-Burma Corporation could be used as an argument against the continued existence of the Kingdom of Ava; so the Kingdom of Ava, long used to impunity in matters much more serious, had discovered, or thought they had, that Britain could be once and for all discounted in the consideration of serious plans. The British were blind, dull and stupid, they always had been; they either talked about protesting and then never did so, or protested and withdrew; in either case they were not serious adversaries.

Thus the Kingdom of Ava in its simple Eastern guile, judging nations by their lack of deeds. . . France, in the person of M. Maas, knowing more about the complex candour of Western countries, was not so sure.

Fanny went to Sandreino in a flutter—Maas and Bonvoisin had offered their services to the King as arbitrators in the teak affair, unknowing that their private papers had already found a way to Rangoon, Simla and London. Sandreino laughed.

In Paris it was thought best to disclaim responsibility for Maas and to assure the British that any agreements entered upon had been done by irresponsible French traders. The trouble in Tonkin had been settled, the French war with

China brought to a conclusion, but the time was not ripe for an overt French conquest of Burma, and France knew it as well as anyone. The position adopted by both France and England was that it would be a thousand pities if any difference of opinion had arisen over a matter which could interest France very little, but was regarded as of the gravest importance by England. . . . The English, although late as usual, had yet got there first.

Meanwhile, though news of French treaties had been kept quiet—all that had been promulgated officially was the story of the wrongs done to the Bombay-Burma—yet a certain amount of the truth began to creep out. Agreements, like disagreements, are difficult to conceal.

The French had forgotten to allow for the fact that they were dealing with a nation of shopkeepers. . . . And, to Sandreino's relief, a chorus arose from the Chambers of Commerce. Of course that ever-clamant Chamber of Rangoon—which had considerably changed its tune since six years ago it had clamoured for British troops to be withdrawn from the British-Burma frontier—sent endless notes to headquarters, and the Chambers of London, Halifax and Liverpool (by its President, a Mr. Elisha Smith), Glasgow and Macclesfield, to say nothing of the Salt Chamber of Commerce at Northwich, swelled the strain. All the Chambers of Commerce frankly referred to the French menace and demanded that Great Britain should take steps against it. A perfect orgy of business candour replaced diplomatic cautiousness of utterance. For the last time, Mr. Bernard wrote to the Kingdom of Ava a letter that was an ultimatum. Fanny never forgot the day that letter was discussed. It was almost the last of the intimate pictures of the Palace that was imprinted on her mind.

She knew that the meeting of all the hastily summoned Mingyis was a farce; that war was decided upon; she had seen, as had all the world for weeks past, the steamer-loads of soldiers going down to the frontier, the regiments paraded by the Eastern Gate. All the talk, even among the Maids in the gardens, had been of wars and rumours of wars. The time of rain-storms had ended while the talk went on, the clear, warm, thinly-gold weather was upon the world, the skies were new-washed to a high, fine pallor of blue.  Fanny had lain on her brass bedstead at night and listened to the lessening waterfalls, had seen the clear, bright lines of sunlight break along the edges of the lattices, and had rejoiced to think of war.

Now, in the pavilion where the meeting was held, she sat watchful behind Supaya-lat, with cheroots ready for her as she wanted them.  Behind the Ministers, all grouped about on the carpet beyond the low dais, she saw the pure, clear green of the lawns and the darker trees, the occasional distant, scared flutter of a bright tamein.

She thought, almost without knowing that she did so, of the years these things had made her world, and she felt a sudden aching at her heart, a passionate wish that all could be again as once it was.  For a moment the gold and green world swam about her, then steadied to the harsh sound of the Taingda Mingyi's voice, to the dark thrust of his face, a wedge pushed into the brightness.  War . . . war . . . war. . . . Drive the heretic kalās into the sea from whence they came.  They have already taken from the ancestors of the Lord of All Power and Glory the dominions of Arakan and Pegu, now they would take the heart of Ava.  Let the Lord of All Power and Glory go against them with his soldiers and reign again as King of all the countries to the sea. . . .

Supaya-lat sat, her splendid eyes glowing and her thin hands clenching, regardless of the cheroots she allowed to go out while she listened.  Even Thibaw's eyes brightened. Perhaps he saw at last some outlet for his miseries and his desires, some means of gaining for himself pardon for the matters that so weighed upon his soul at night.

Beside, and a little behind, the King and Queen, sat Sinbyew-mashin, very quiet.  Her tired old eyes met those of the Kinwoon Mingyi from time to time.  Fanny knew how they had talked again and again and had tried to avert what—once Fanny had taken a hand in it—could not be averted.  Fanny felt a little of the old thrill at her own power.  She was Fanny . . . who could make anything happen—except one thing.  Fanny, who always knew what men were like—except one man.

The Kinwoon Mingyi talking, very quietly and persuasively. . . . It was not annexation that the English kalās demanded in their letter. They asked for the restoration of a British Resident, who was to have free access to the King and not be treated as a leper. They asked for the suspension of the proceedings against the Bombay-Burma Corporation, pending an arbitration, though they refused the French Consul-General as an arbitrator. And—even the subtle tongue of the Kinwoon Mingyi could not gloss it over—they said that in future the Kingdom of Ava must regulate its external relations in accordance with the advice of the Government of India . . . in other words, it was to become a protected monarchy.

Such was the letter, and the Court of Ava knew from its spies—not that there was any attempt at impossible concealment—that troops had been moved over from India to British Burma. It was an ultimatum, but it did allow of Ava becoming that protected monarchy that Aitchison and Browne had wished for during the first massacres, and it did allow of Thibaw still continuing to loll upon the Lion Throne. The Kinwoon Mingyi spoke slowly and at length, he advised compliance, he pointed out that delay after delay could be engineered when once an agreement had been come to, but that disaster would be about the heads of all in the Palace if they persisted in defiance. To Fanny's ears, more attuned to the voice of reason than were those of the self-blinded creatures of a golden past, the voice of the Kinwoon Mingyi seemed to go on and on and on . . . only too terribly true.

Suddenly he was interrupted. Supaya-lat was pointing at him with a finger tense with scorn, her whole body leaning forward, taut and angry. Her mother, who had murmured from time to time in agreement with the Kinwoon Mingyi, put a hand upon her outstretched arm. Supaya-lat shook it off and spoke in a shrill, fierce voice, looking from the old Queen to the older Minister.

"You two should marry!" she said. "You are well suited. You are both cowards. . . ." There was a moment's horrified silence, then she spoke again.

"No, you are not man enough to marry any woman, you are less than a woman yourself!" She wheeled on Fanny: "You shall find me a tamein and a fan, and the Kinwoon Mingyi shall go and live amongst the women!"

No woman had ever so spoken to a man, and a great and revered man at that, in public before, no daughter had so spoken to her mother. Even the Taingda Mingyi, though the Queen was on his side, felt the shame of it and his face darkened. No one spoke, for there was that of force and life about Supaya-lat and the violence of her utterance that imposed a shocked silence. Then a murmuring began, and it was a murmuring of agreement with the Queen. The Kinwoon Mingyi was an old man and past his wisdom. He could not understand the glories that were to be.

War . . . war. . . . The King, the source of all greatness and dignity celestial, and whose threshold was as the firmament, should rise and overcome these barbarians. . . .

Again the Kinwoon Mingyi, risking his life and taking no heed of the indignity that had been put upon him, spoke.

"It is easy to say, 'Go up against the enemy,' but how to go, O Poon-dawgyi-paya? Consider the state of the realm, there is no host of countrymen round about the King. They tarry and will not enter the Kingdom. I, servant of the King, spoke of old, but the source of all power and might would not listen. I said: 'Bore not the country's belly, abuse not the country's forehead, pluck not out the country's eye, and break not the country's tusk.' Yet the rich men of Ava, which are as the belly of a country, are rich no more, and the faithful servants and warriors that are her forehead, are no more. The wise monks and hermits, who are the country's eye, have had no part in the councils. The members of the King's own family, who are as the tusks of his country, are no more."

He ceased, and the murmuring broke out again. War . . . war . . . war to protect the religion of Ava, to protect the people's prosperity—no one smiled at this—a war such as was the duty of a king . . .

Thibaw sat in silence after the Kinwoon Mingyi had spoken. He knew too little of the world to know that his

regiments, his war-boats, the defences of his City, built as
they had been built in the days of Kublai Khan, could be
of no avail against the onslaught of the West. It was not
possible defeat that troubled him. He, like Fanny, was
aching for a few minutes with that past-sickness which is
the worst of all.

He saw the Kinwoon Mingyi, old and wrinkled, and
remembered when he had been his father's trusted Minister,
and when he himself had been a youth in the Golden Monastery, and had believed the world to be a troubled and a
painted dream. . . . A troubled and a painted dream in
truth it was, but he could no longer throw it off, he could not
concentrate now on the Beatitudes, his feet had strayed for
ever from off the Eightfold Path.

He stirred and sighed, and spoke.

"My wife, Supaya, and my Ministers, counsel war, and
only by war can I save the honour of my Kingdom. The
English have made improper demands and unlawfully made
demonstrations of war, and the trade and business of all my
subjects have suffered. . . ."

He paused and licked his dry lips nervously. Fanny,
listening and marvelling, saw that he really believed what
he was saying, and she was seized with a sudden little feeling
of pity because of all the lies that had been told to him the
whole of his life.

"Let the arrangements be made and an auspicious day
be arrived at for the victorious army to go forth. . . ."

He put out his hand and held Supaya-lat's hand, warm
and strong and comforting, in his. In the fourth of the Six
Blissful Seats a mere touch of the hand is enough to satisfy
passion, and it was enough to restore Thibaw's belief to
him now. He sat very still, and a more peaceful look stole
over his face. Supaya-lat herself broke the spell by getting
to her feet. She was near her time with a child, and as
she stood up she placed her hands on either side of her vase-
like body with a gesture as though she reassured herself as to
that which she carried. This time surely a son, to sit upon
the Lion Throne and rule over the Golden Palace for which
they were to do battle . . .! She was pale, but her eyes

shone. The King scrambled to his feet and joined her, and together they went out into the breathless afternoon. The Ministers streamed away towards the Hloot, talking eagerly, all very excited except the Kinwoon Mingyi, and he walked off alone with his head bent. Maung Yo lingered behind and looked at Fanny, an anguished question in his eyes. He so wanted to be reassured that all was well, that everything was for the best—but he knew Rangoon and the English and could hardly believe it. If not for the best, he so wanted to know that he and Fanny had had no hand in it. She evaded his eyes and, stooping, picked up Sinbyew-mashin's betel-box and fan, and waited humbly.

"You saw the beginning and you will see the end," said Sinbyew-mashin.

Very fast now, so fast that it seemed to Fanny to go by her as a coloured blur. Each night a pwè, each night the music, the perpetual music. A sudden disappearance of the French who had been going to help Thibaw hold his Kingdom. Maas had been recalled to France "for reasons of health"—a disappointed man indeed. No more Bonvoisin at the Palace; Fanny wondered what had happened to him with a sort of dull languor; she felt she cared for nothing, even for her revenge, any longer.

There was something dreadful about these days, when she heard the King and Queen being given glowing reports of successes by the Ministers; but she herself, when she ventured out into the shuttered, barricaded houses of the kalā town, where all trade was paralysed from fear, was told by San-dreino and Rawlinson of the swift, uninterrupted advance of the British under General Prendergast. A brisk fight with the enemy at Minhla, the only place that offered anything approaching a wholehearted resistance, and the campaign was over. The two Italians surrendered the forts they had been unable to make impregnable, and became prisoners of war, and the flotilla of steamers that carried the expedition sailed on up the river, leaving civil officers already installed at various spots to begin the work of administration.

Sandreino was openly rubbing his hands and expecting

Fanny to do the same as he told her the good tidings. But
Fanny went back to the Palace, to the music and the anxious
faces. No disguising it now, the end was in sight. . . .

The thunder of the English guns had drifted up to the
Gem City on the hot south wind, and the play that was
in progress stopped in panic, just as the chief actor was
making a speech on the greatness of the King and Queen
and the invincibility of their army. The Queen signalled
that the play should go on, but she herself left her place
and went out with the King. They met the Ministers and
this time all listened to the Kinwoon Mingyi. Let them
agree to the terms of the ultimatum, and though the Kingdom
would be humiliated, perhaps it could yet be saved. . . . So
the great war-boat with its forty flashing, gilded oars went
down the shining river, bearing its message of submission.
It came back again with the news that the English General
declined to grant an armistice, but demanded the uncon-
ditional surrender of the army and the King.

The next day saw the end. At dawn (The-time-when-
there-is-light-enough-to-see-the-veins-in-the-hand) everyone
in the Palace was astir. Supaya-lat was bathed and attired
as usual, but no Maid now worried if she were wearing a
tamein like the Queen's—the Queen would not have noticed
or cared. Fanny dragged out her European dresses, but
they had been so long put away that moths had destroyed
them. Only the pale grey frock, sadly crumpled, looked
at her with its thousand eyes, and seemed like something she
had forgotten. She stared at it and put it back. Part of her
wanted to be in a European gown to receive the British, but
the better part of her harboured a strange little feeling that
she ought to keep in Burmese dress, so as to be clearly the
Queen's friend, now that the Queen was cast down from her
estate. It was an unwonted thought for Fanny, and she did
not recognise its purity even though she yielded to it. She
wrapped and twisted the first tamein that came to hand,
pulled on the white jacket and went to join Supaya-lat.

All about the gardens the little ladies were huddled like
birds before a storm. The morning passed in a dull lethargy.
In the heat of midday, Supaya-lat and the silent Fanny climbed

the spiral staircase of the great wooden look-out tower, and from there saw the English steamboats lying on the fair shining of the Irrawaddy, before the purple ripple of the Sagaing hills.   They saw the Kinwoon Mingyi hurrying on an elephant to meet the invaders with words of peace, they thought of the fifty elephants already packed with treasure and goods and arms that awaited Thibaw twelve miles to the north of Mandalay, but which he had delayed too long to use, not crediting that this could befall him . . . besides, his Ministers, fearful lest they should be left to bear the anger of the English, would not let the King out of their sight.

The Queen and Fanny saw and heard the soldiers of the English Queen, red-faced men and Indians, marching in ordered ranks up all the four roads that led from the river bank, through the silent, wondering crowds. . . . Their feet made a strange, regular, scuffling noise, right, left, right, left, not the cheerful, irregular pattering of a Burmese regiment.   Right, left, right, left, as even as the blows of a hammer.

Supaya-lat turned and came down the stairs of the tower, Fanny following.   And at the foot, where the Maids of Honour drew away from her in a scared little circle, she stood for a moment staring in front of her.   Right, left, right, left, right, left . . . the hammer sound came from within the walls of the City now, approaching the great Eastern Gate—sacred to monarchy.   Right, left, hammer, hammer. . . . Supaya-lat flung herself with a loud cry upon her face in the white dust of the courtyard, and tearing her hair from its knot, beat upon her head.

No one stirred towards her.   Fanny felt as though she could choke.   It was she who had done this, suddenly she saw it; all her apathy of weeks, that apathy of self-absorption that had held her, fell away for a blinding moment of regret. It was all over. . . . And Supaya-lat, her friend—more than her friend, her fairy story come true, the only fairy story that ever had or would come true for Fanny, the bright symbol of royalty—lay in the dust, a little Eastern woman, wailing.

It was not for long.   The Queen rose and twisted back

her hair and looked at her Maids. Not so very many of
them remained, they had been gradually trickling away to
their parents and relations. She gave a twisted smile as
she saw them, the poor, clustered, palpitating birds caught
in the storm. She beckoned to them and led them back
to the Palace. Again she bathed and changed into her
richest dress, and then sent for Fanny.

Alas, for Fanny's good resolutions. . . . She had hastily
pressed the Paris frock and was attired in it, the postboy hat
pulled well down over her hair. After all, it was important
she should look European now. . . .

Colonel Sladen, Chief Political Officer—how often Fanny
had heard Selah tell of his friendship with her father!—
was at the Gate, had passed through it . . . was being
received by Thibaw in the great Hall of Audience, the
King seated for the last time upon the Lion Throne of the
Alompra dynasty, with Supaya-lat, hung with diamonds,
and the old Queen Mother, who had originally placed Thibaw
on the Throne, alongside. . . .

There they all were, and there was the Kinwoon Mingyi,
ushering in Colonel Sladen, with his shoes upon his feet and
his sword at his side. . . . The great Shoe Question was
settled for ever.

Colonel Sladen, once friend of Mindoon Min, and himself
of a royal way of doing things, was now too royal in his
lavish kindness to fallen greatness. He accepted Thibaw's
surrender with the provision that he should formally surrender
himself to General Prendergast the following day, and then,
pleased to be able to grant the request, he prevailed on General
Prendergast to allow the women to go freely in and out of
the Western Gate. An English officer and a gentleman—
damn it all! could not be harsh to the ladies. This had been
the request of the Ministers—good fellows who had made no
trouble and were for the most part prepared to work in with
the British Government—and, after all, the Ministers were
responsible for the safe delivery of the King, next day, with
their lives. . . .

Against his judgment the General, when the question
was put to him, yielded, though he pointed out that the

King might try to escape in disguise. Thibaw remained faithful, close by his Supaya-lat, who, even had they escaped, was in no condition to have ridden miles upon an elephant. But of the three hundred women employed about the Palace, only some seventeen, of whom the Hairy Woman was one and Fanny another, remained, and the lowest women of the town, realising what a chance was theirs, streamed all night into the Palace past the English sentries, to whom all Burmese women looked alike. Fanny spent the hours of darkness crouched beside the King and Queen, who sat hand clasped in hand, in a little garden pavilion, listening to the cries of coarse delight as the looting and destruction went on. . . . By morning the interior of the Palace was a vast waste-heap.

By a bitter irony, the only other women in the Palace, save the looters from the town, to whom came happiness that night, were the mother and sister of the Nyaungyan Prince. Even as they had escaped the first massacre of all, so they had survived that second and worse massacre and the burning of the gaol; for they had been latterly imprisoned in an isolated cell of brick. Six years of famine rations and heavy fetters had left them their lives; and even left unimpaired a certain dignity and serenity. But the tears ran down their cheeks as they were carried out of their perpetual darkness, and their shackles removed. The news that these two had been taken to the Convent and treated with all honour, not only as suffering women, but as royal ladies, drifted after the fashion of Palace gossip—although there were but few tongues left to disseminate it—to Supaya-lat, as dawn also stole in. Supaya-lat smiled bitterly but said nothing.

She, Thibaw, Sinbyew-mashin, and the Queen Mother's two other daughters: Supaya-gyi, swathed in the apricot robes of a nun, and Supaya-gale, with her round face blank with terror, were still huddled together in the little pavilion, fearful of what the next moment might bring forth.

Thibaw sent the Taingda Mingyi to claim the protection of the British soldiers, for he feared that his own might at any moment break in and murder him.

Again appeared Colonel Sladen—how Fanny, tired and miserable as she was, admired that martial bearing, that air of being lord of the world which was his, how she realised that despite her Paris dress, here for her was yet another Danvers! He walked in unattended with that fearlessness which was always his greatest asset. All through the Palace, even now in the broad daylight, were streaming the crowds of women, field-workers, big and coarse as men, fishermen's wives, harlots from the river-side, laughing and joking, bearing aloft gold cups, hanging jewellery about their necks, trampling and shouting where the delicate little Maids of Honour had fluttered, a mob let loose.

Sentries were summoned and posted in the rooms, and the King and Queens, and Fanny and the little Princesses, with one or two attendants, withdrew to a summer-house in the gardens where many gay and careless hours had been spent. Abandoned by all his servants, by all the Ministers save the Kinwoon Mingyi and the Taingda Mingyi, who was faithful whatever the rest of his faults, the King sat till he surrendered. It was a bitter and a silent day for these children robbed of their golden toys and their large red-and-gold doll's house. The world had come about their ears, a strange new world in which they had never really been able to believe, and had crushed their own world beneath it.

Thibaw wore a plain white jacket and paso and a pink and white checkered turban, and sat on the carpet as General Prendergast bowed and then shook him by the hand—a liberty of greeting the King of Ava had never known.

Thibaw still tried to temporise, still asked for delays, but the end had come. He walked with the Queens through the gardens, through the red-and-gold corridors and throne rooms, through the Hall of Audience itself, down the steps and so through the great Royal Red Gate, open now for ever.

There bullock-carts were in waiting. There was no other mode of conveyance save the more humble dhoolie, for it would have savoured too much of a Royal Procession for the vanquished to go upon elephants, only allowed to those in authority. . . . The sun was almost setting when

Thibaw turned his head, before getting into his cart, to look his last at the Palace, and the seven-tiered pyathat was lit all along its edges as by fire. He looked, he did not speak, and he allowed himself to be put into the cart. Eight white umbrellas were carried over the cart in sign of royalty, but not the ninth to which he had been entitled as ruler of Ava.

Fanny, more because of a blind instinct to hold by what she knew, by what had always meant so much to her, as long as possible, than from any affection—she was past such an active feeling at the moment—climbed into the next cart with the few other women attendants.

They jolted down the miles to the river, through the crowds that lined the way. For the most part the people stood in silence, but here and there a woman burst out wailing and was echoed down the watching lines. This King had been a bad king, but in his very cruelty and arrogance he represented kingship as these people thought of it. The great lord of their lives was being jolted past them in a bullock-cart, guarded by foreign soldiers, and not he only was thus taken from them, but their belief by which they had lived; their belief that in following and fighting for him they would be going along the way of the celestial regions to Nirvana. . . . This went, too, in the humble bullock-cart, past their straining eyes. The only world they knew was passing away, and with it went part of themselves. He was the symbol of their life and their belief, and he was going.

The swift dusk was on the river, and lanterns had to be lit. By their flickering light the King and his Queens scrambled out of the carts and stood upon the bund to receive the polite greetings of the Captain and officers of the S.S. *Thooreah* —a Burmese word which means the sun. . . .

They went on board, Supaya-lat leading Thibaw, as she had led him for seven years, down ways which had brought him to this pass, without knowledge of how foolishly or cruelly she was behaving. They went on board, and with them went a certain simplicity and arrogance, a lovely unconsciousness of others which soon will be found nowhere on the face of the globe, not even amongst the birds of its furthermost islands.

And Fanny, at the last, never said farewell, the Queen was too occupied in coaxing the King to take his foot from off his kingdom. Fanny stood alone upon the bund, as she had stood when she had seen Edward and Agatha depart on their honeymoon, as she had stood when she saw the British Residency, with such of its flock as it could gather, shake the dust of Mandalay from off its shoes.

A greater loneliness than any she had ever known, even when the girls at school—all except Agatha—had herded together against her and called her a foreigner, came upon Fanny. She felt very tired. She hailed a dhoolie and was taken back to the Palace. She gave the order mechanically, without thinking. At the Western Gate she alighted, but was stopped by the sentries. For a moment she stood and stared at them. The postboy hat was crushed to one side, her hair was straggling, but she asserted herself proudly.

"I live here. I am Mrs. Bagshaw, European Maid of Honour."

The sentry called out to another soldier something about: "Here's one of Soup-plate's little lot . . ." and the other disappeared and presently a young lieutenant came out as from nowhere. Fanny repeated her phrase wearily, she wanted to go to bed. He was very polite, very kind, but he told her she could not go back to the Palace, and asked her if she had no friends to whom she could go.

"It might not be safe for you to try and go to the Palace now, Mrs. . . . did you say Bradshaw? Naturally the City is much disturbed."

Fanny thought rapidly for all her weariness. The Delanges. . . . No, she couldn't go to them, French people . . . she felt ashamed, somehow, when with them. The d'Avera girls didn't seem so completely French, but she hated the thought of turning up at their house, homeless, she who had shed so much lustre upon them as she fluttered in upon them from the Court. . . . The young officer was watching her. Nice enough looking little thing in a way, English name, after all—Bradley. But chi-chi or dago when you really got her in the light. He studied the problem more than her face, however.

" Isn't there a convent, or something? "

Of course, blesséd, blesséd refuge. The Convent of St. Joseph, whither she had not gone for so many years. Fanny gave a deep sigh of relief and assent.

The young officer sent an elderly and very respectable soldier to escort her, his rank or lack of it she never knew, but he handed her safely to the nuns who had remained tranquilly tending their poor, old and young, during Fanny's flaring Palace years.

For the first time Fanny slept without music that night, with only the dim sound of the surge of fluid crowds coming to her ears, till the chapel bell roused her in the morning.

She awoke to an awful sense of loss. Everything was over and done with, everything by which she had lived. The weaving was at an end. The gorgeous and barbaric weaving of the Palace years that had been torn from the loom by the rude contact of the West. The shuttles had ceased to ply, the treadles were still, the pattern indeed was complete, but as the last thread was woven into its fine appointed place, the whole fabric, compact of so many lives and deaths and pleasures and miseries, had been trailed in the dust like a captured banner.

# BOOK IV

## CHAPTER I

## THE ORDER FOR MORNING PRAYER

TONK . . . *tonk* . . . *tonk* . . . went the coppersmith bird. Clear, metallic and persistent, the reiteration of its note sounded through and through the world of green and gold made by the Palace gardens, and struck, like a small brazen gong, on the statements recited within the world of vermilion and gold made by the pillars of the Hall of Audience. *A-a-men. Tonk. A-a-men. Tonk. Tonk.*

*We have left undone those things which we ought to have done; and we have done those things which we ought not to have done* . . .

confessed Dr. Marks, seconded by Edward, and soldiers and civilians present looked into their sun-helmets and agreed. *Amen. Tonk . . . tonk.*

The sacred lotuses, symbols of divine birth, the thirty-two angels and the four guardians of the world, glowed golden from the Lion Throne. On a temporary altar two brass candlesticks and brass vases holding canna lilies on either side of a brass cross, told of other principalities and powers. The supple voice of Dr. Marks was vibrant with feeling. He saw the hand of the Almighty in the march of events at Mandalay.

Almost without bloodshed the Kingdom of Ava had fallen, and as a result, here in the stronghold of Buddhism, the word of the Lord was being read by him, Marks, the famous missionary and great personality of Burma. His disappointment that he had not been offered the newly-created Bishopric of Rangoon was swallowed up in this spiritual joy.

*O Lord, open thou our lips.*

Edward led the answer : *And our mouth shall show forth thy praise.*   And, light and clear from an elfin distance—*Tonk . . . tonk . . . tonk.*

Agatha, kneeling, her thin face buried in her hands, was shaken by emotions that were not entirely spiritual or impersonal.   She had been wrung by past-sickness since returning to Mandalay.   Her father, dead; her own youth dead— for Agatha at twenty-eight, the mother of two children, considered youth gone for ever—and Edward further from her, after a curious fashion, than when they had been here before.

Edward, in surplice and stole, with that withdrawn look about him which she could bear in church as part of the necessary outfit, but that maddened her to such an aching loneliness when he wore it in daily life. . . . Edward seemed, now that they were away from Rangoon and back in the Mandalay " feeling," to be once more that absurd, scrupulous and touching lover of her youth, but set away from her by the husband that he had since become. . . . He was at once further off and yet much more clear, like something looked at through the wrong end of a telescope. She shut her eyes and, pressing her hands against her face, wondered why life was so different from what she had always assumed it would be.   Life had resolved itself into what one had always observed it was for other people, instead of being the strange and exceptional beauty she had expected for herself.   Tonk . . . tonk . . . tonk . . .·

*O go your way into his gates with thanksgiving, and into his courts with praise. . . .*

She peeped between her fingers, and the courts of the House of Alompra with its great red-and-gold pillars, swam up at her, steadied, and settled into place.   The slanting beams of sunlight, the fine dust-motes wreathing about within their clear confines like incense, lit up the tightly-uniformed backs, the red necks, the great round of a pillar,

and Edward's face, worn and lined, but still somehow " clear "
beyond any face she had ever known.

*Endue thy ministers with righteousness* . . .

and Edward responded in his grave, calm voice :

*And make thy chosen people joyful.*

Agatha forgot for a while the more domestic tones of
that voice. Edward was not often irritable—not nearly
so often, she told herself miserably, as she was—it was his
absentness she could not bear. Tonk . . . tonk . . . tonk.
. . . She forgot the service and suddenly grew hot with
anger as she told herself that after all it was she who cared the
more. . . .

*Give peace in our time, O Lord,* prayed Dr. Marks.

*Because there is none other that fighteth for us, but only thou, O
God,* responded Edward. He was used to the slightly
equivocal character of the translation which had puzzled him
as a boy, and this morning his soul was caught up in a chariot
of flame. It seemed even to him, who was so seldom able
to feel the simple and consoling thing, that this was indeed a
great occasion. The romance of his life, which was the beauty
of Christ, was presented to him like a pearl, round and un-
flawed, on the shining platter of the morning.

Only too often it was dull and fretted, but to-day its lustre
was undimmed, it was complete because of its roundness.
The ethics of great Western and small Eastern nations ceased
to trouble him for a space, this bringing of Christ to Mandalay was triumphant answer to any doubts.

Always the beauty of Mandalay had captured him, as
Rangoon, a bastard like all great seaports, had never been
able to do, and now it gave him back the beauty of his
Christ romance, which he was so apt to mislay amid the
worries and jealousies of mission life. Here it awaited
him, a gracious friend, as he always found it awaiting him

in the hills, when he was on a lonely tour. That he could understand—the feet of the Lord were on the mountains and in the lonely places. But that this barbaric mixture of gold-leaf and tinfoil should give it back to him! He wondered even while his soul lifted. For, as soon as the drug of the lovely liturgy ceased and Dr. Marks began his brief sermon, ecstasy was less high within him.

How wonderfully are we led, Dr. Marks pointed out in his beautifully modulated voice. The Lord does indeed move in a mysterious way His wonders to perform. Even the great sin of murder—of repeated murders—had been used to hasten the coming of the Lord's kingdom to this fair spot. All things worked together for good. Tonk . . . tonk . . . tonk . . .

Queer how Edward had been feeling all that himself, and yet now that he heard it being given out in a sermon, it did not move him as the pressure of the circumstances all about him had done. Again there arose within his mind that perpetual trouble which was his—the faculty for seeing rightness on both sides, that his superiors had always told him was his special temptation. It had even been called spiritual pride—the pastors' and masters' version of the " setting yourself up " of nursery days, whereas it was in truth the result of a scrupulous humility.

*And now to God the Father . . .*

A rustling and scraping as the congregation rose to its feet. Fanny, of course, was not a member of it, or perhaps even she, not given to such profitless speculations, might have wondered how Dr. Marks would have dealt with her affair with Bonvoisin, as the cause of bringing the true faith to Mandalay . . .

*Now thank we all our God,*
*With heart and hands and voices . . .*

The hymn swelled, not very fully, for the male voices were a little shy and self-conscious, but loud enough to drown for a few minutes the tonk, tonk, tonk.

Edward never looked at Agatha in church, but now it chanced that their eyes met; perhaps the intensity of her thought drew his own. Something tender and loving that there was between them, even though it had never been true intimacy, lived consciously for that moment when they looked at each other. Their youth was given back to them for the space of a few heart-beats—and it was the memory of that youth, as well as patriotic pride and the stir and glow of great events, and the actual beauty of the world, that had all melted and fused together and gone to swell Edward's master passion and give him his pearl in its rare roundness and lustre.

Edward, kneeling with the congregation as Dr. Marks pronounced the Blessing, let the lovely and simple words sink gratefully through his quiescent mind.

*. . . and be with you all . . . evermore, Amen.*

Tonk . . . tonk . . . tonk . . . tonk . . .

## CHAPTER II

## AGATHA AND SELAH

OUT into the gardens streamed the congregation, as only three weeks ago the brightly-clad Burmese had been wont to do. If the Palace had been a sentient creation, it would surely have thought that the khaki coats of the soldiers and the pale muslins of the few English women, made but a poor show against the memory of all that flower-like brightness.

Most of the people went towards the Lily Throne Room at the west, Supaya-lat's own royal reception-room, now used as a club, but Agatha made for the great flight of steps leading from the Hall of Audience to the sacred Red Gate. She was to wait for Edward, who with Dr. Marks was using the passage-room behind the Lion Throne as a vestry; Dr. Marks was to lunch with the General. She stood at the top of the steps which, until the royal party had gone into exile down them, had never been trodden by a woman's foot. You could look straight through the ever-open gate now, past the Clock Tower and the Tooth Relic Tower, down the long vista of roadway, over massed green tree-tops, slender upcurving pyathats and rippling domes of pagodas, to the grave beauty of the Shan hills.

Agatha stood at gaze, and she suddenly felt her eyes brim with tears. It was long indeed since an impersonal emotion had had such power to move her. The care of a husband and children, the fretting sense that Edward did not see her as the sort of person she would have wished him to, that the mysterious quality of womanhood in which she had been such a believer had somehow failed to survive the rites of baby foods and drying napkins, all these things had loomed so large in her mind, had so destroyed it by their acutely personal preoccupation, that the ready response which had once been hers to visual beauty, had lain quiescent.

She blinked the tears away a little ashamedly, and saw that a cart drawn by trotting bullocks was just drawing up at the great gate. A man and a woman in European dress, he small and feeble in movement, she robust, helping him with a strong arm, scrambled out. They spoke to the sentries, and then one of the young officers strolling past stopped and spoke also. He turned and led the newcomers through the gate towards the Palace steps, and Agatha, as they drew nearer, recognised Selah and Mr. Aratoon. She went down the steps towards them.

The ex-Kalawoon looked older and thinner, with the bleached air of a man who has been very ill. Selah held him firmly by the arm.

"Selah!" cried Agatha, "Selah!" It was her own youth as well as Selah that she greeted, that warmed her voice, the youth which the moment during Morning Prayer and the moment on the steps had brought back to her with such an aching sense of loss, even in the re-capture.

"Agatha! How nice it is to see you, how happy we are to be here!"

"No one really knew whether you were killed or not. Oh, I am glad!"

She shook hands with them both while the young officer hurried off to find Colonel Sladen. Selah smiled contentedly.

"No, indeed, we are not dead, though many times we expected to be. We have been in much danger and my father has been very ill, but now all that is over. You, too, Agatha, are you well? Is your husband here? My, it is fine to be back in civilisation. We have been living in the jungle for nearly three years. We have been sent for by Colonel Sladen. Oh, there he is. . . . Papa, there is Colonel Sladen!"

And indeed, Colonel Sladen, with his air of a *beau sabreur* and his royal lavishness of welcome, was coming down the steps. He took the ex-Kalawoon warmly by the hand, and the poor old gentleman hung on to it for a moment, too moved by his own unexpected emergence from the long, dark tunnel of danger, to speak. The Colonel patted him on the shoulder.

"It's all right now, Aratoon, don't worry. No more exiles or executions. Come along, I'll take you through to the General. He's in the King's apartments. Mrs. Protheroe, I wonder if you'll look after Miss Aratoon?"

"Of course I will," said Agatha, feeling indeed caught in the exciting swirl of great events. "You must come to the Mission for tiffin, Selah. Edward will be coming out in a minute."

So to tiffin at the old triple-roofed Mission House Selah went, very full of talk and news.

"Such a time we have had in banishment, Agatha, you wouldn't believe, but we kept our spirits up. Although the Queen sent us to a very unhealthy part where we couldn't get good food, in the hopes we should die, we thrived corporally, and we were much respected and loved by all the jungle people because of my aunt. You remember my aunt, who went down on the boat with us and the rest of the Europeans? She practised medicine for them and cured sore eyes and toothache and wounds and jungle fever, and I nursed the sick and we took no money for it all, so the people brought us fruit and vegetables and good buffalo milk and butter, and we kept well; and I learnt to weave the native cloth and made all our clothes. Oh, and Agatha, I taught in school too, like you used to do, because there was no one to teach the village children, and the parents were very grateful and used to call Supaya-lat the Biloo-mah!"

"What's Biloo-mah?" asked Edward with interest.

"Biloo-mah means ogress! We were so popular that when dacoits were coming to rob they used to send us warning, so we and all the village used to go out and sleep in the jungle that night and not go back till the dacoits had gone next morning."

"Didn't you ever get ill?" asked Agatha, struck by the invincibly cheerful and successful quality of Selah, who, she thought, would bound up from any situation, however uncomfortable.

"Oh yes, we got fever three times very badly, but as we

had no doctors, qualified or quack, my aunt's medicines cured us. We did not forget Christian worship either, and we had prayer meetings amongst ourselves every Sunday."

Edward was irresistibly reminded of that resourceful family, the Swiss Family Robinson.

"Then one day we got a private letter in Armenian, written on a piece of wrapping paper and used to do up some biscuits in, so that the authorities should not think it was important, and it told us the British were making war on the Burmese, so we were overjoyed, and though we kept the news to ourselves we prayed for British victory. Then one day many people came down the road, and I asked them who they were and where they came from, and they said they were the King's soldiers returning to their homes, and that a new King was in Mandalay, so I asked who, and they said ' the English lord is reigning,' and they went on laughing and joking. And it was true, because half an hour later came a messenger with a letter for my father saying that Colonel Sladen was in the Palace and we were to come back to Mandalay. We were packed and ready to start in an hour, and you should have seen the people of that place weeping bitterly while joy reigned in our hearts! And at Shoay-bo we found the new Government had written saying we were to be given every help to get to Mandalay, and so this morning we got here and went to the house of my cousins, for we have no money or clothes, and this dress is borrowed from my cousin."

Selah looked down happily, and smoothed the flowered muslin appreciatively. Her Odyssey had reached its exciting and triumphant end.

After tiffin Agatha took her to see the little boys, who were having their midday sleep. Very fair they were, with their mother's duckling blondness, and Selah generously admired them as they lay in the deep sleep of childhood, the two-year-old Eddy curled away like a little hedgehog from his paler, thinner brother, the four-year-old John. Agatha stood looking down on them with eyes suddenly misty. The exquisite and terrible trustfulness of sleep struck at her heart.

"My, they are lovely boys," said Selah, "and your husband, Agatha, how gentlemanly! We always thought so."

They had turned to leave the room, when Selah stood still.

"Have you seen Fanny?" she asked, as though talking of Edward had suddenly raised up for her a vision of Fanny's great red turkeycock. Agatha was conscious-stricken. No one had given much thought to Fanny since the capture of Mandalay.

"No, I've heard she's boarding at the Convent; she went there when the Palace was taken. I must look her up, I'm afraid she may be in great difficulties; there can't be any money left of Captain Bagshaw's. But we only got here two days ago, and we've had to settle in."

"The dirt you must have found," said Selah wisely.

"Dreadful. And you can't be too careful. I have such a good ayah, a Madrassee, and a very good bearer as well, but of course I like to overlook everything myself."

"Oh yes, it was the same with me even in the jungle." Selah straightened her hat with its nodding roses, and prepared to depart. "How would it be if I went and saw Fanny, and asked her to come and see you?" she offered. Agatha approved of the suggestion; she did not want to go to the Convent herself, to the Convent where they would persist in considering her a Protestant.

"Do, Selah. And let me know your plans."

"Oh, I expect my father will be interpreter for the General. We have so many relations British subjects, and now we are ourselves. It will be easy for us. Good-bye, Agatha."

Selah passed down the verandah steps and Agatha went into the house to look for Edward, but he was reading with his I-don't-want-to-be-disturbed expression, and she went up to their room. It had not occurred to Edward that you could sleep in another room than your wife's, and for Agatha, it was the only place where he could seem really to belong to her, in that intimacy of common things shared, of being alone at last to discuss the day's happenings; she would have resented the suggestion of separate sleep. Edward belonged so dreadfully to himself as it was.

She went over to the dressing-table, where Edward's hair-brushes lay mixed up with hers in that indecent mingling of inanimate objects which such concepts of marriage involve, and picked up her handglass.  She began to examine herself from every angle in the swinging mirror.

Thinner, paler . . . lines round her eyes and mouth. But surely an interesting face . . . spiritual. . . . People might easily say: "Who is that refined-looking woman? She looks as though she had suffered . . ." when she passed by, not even noticing they were there, her eyes filled with dreams. . . .

Little Eddy lifted up his voice in a wail from the nursery. Agatha dropped the handglass and hurried to comfort him.

## CHAPTER III

## AGATHA, SELAH AND FANNY

Could that be Agatha? That faded, skinny woman, whose colour, such as it was, seemed to have settled in her nose? Who wore such a dowdy dress and who looked somehow so pinched? Of course poor Agatha had never been really pretty, but still . . .

Could that be Fanny, little graceful Fanny? Of course she'd never been really pretty, but now . . . well, squat was the word for her. It might be partly that dreadful dress, so very eccentric . . . it looked like a nursery wall-paper. Perhaps a very young girl—though she would have to be fair—could have worn it successfully, but even so it could never be in good taste to choose anything so conspicuous. . . .

They kissed on the verandah of the Mission House. They had tea in the room where the Arundel prints used to hang and Shaw and Mr. Lumsden discussed events; where Agatha and Edward had held forth so earnestly on the beauties of celibacy, where the little boys were now playing with a wooden horse.

Both women were thankful for the children's presence, for conversation was difficult. Agatha spoke of Rangoon life—not of missionary matters, but of the Gymkhana and Pegu Clubs, of parties given by the Chief Commissioner, of the way even quite worldly people admired and appreciated Edward. Fanny tried to counter with tales of the Palace, but found somehow that she could not do so. . . . Her act of revenge had in its turn taken its own revenge upon her; it had imposed a silence that she felt too numbed even to wish to break.

How could she tell Agatha, the triumphantly married,

of a love-affair that had ended ignominiously? She found it better not even to think, much less speak, of all that had gone to make up her life in the Palace and the town. She felt a worse pang when she thought of the Palace than when she remembered Bonvoisin. The violence of her sorrow and her rage, the almost terrifying success of her answering gesture, had, as it were, torn out of her by its roots, her love. She felt a sore aching, but her life-blood was not ebbing.

The very completeness of the change in all her circumstances, in any hopes for the future, deadened her to acute suffering of a more idealistic sort. Another than Fanny could never have worn the Paris dress, the postboy hat, again. Even she had felt a pang when she had donned it on the day that the British arrived, but she was not the person to throw away the only up-to-date gown she possessed.

She and Agatha looked at each other across a gulf that was not made less by Fanny's secretiveness. Agatha's idea of *I myself*, less naïvely egotistical than Fanny's, more sophisticated, had survived love, though not without damage· Fanny's frail self-pretences were drowned, their butterfly wings waterlogged, in the one love-affair that would ever matter to her. She was stripped to the bare body of her life, and she lay prone, never to rise again.

Fanny hardly suffered any longer, but she would never be happy again. Agatha suffered daily, died a thousand little deaths in her relationship with Edward, but she would never lose altogether that blesséd faculty of seeing herself as she wished. Agatha could protect herself with words from life, but Fanny gave the effect of complete dullness.

She had missed the impersonal philosophy of the East, the violence of the Latin, the capacity for self-deception of the Anglo-Saxon.

She was only Fanny, who had once been so clever with men, had been Maid of Honour to a living flame, and who was now an unimportant little widow belonging to no place or person. How this change had come about was growing misty even in her own mind; she only knew her golden day, that had seemed neither brief nor long, but oddly far from the measure of time, was over.

Little John, whose intent eyes had succeeded in picking out the boys and girls and toys of Fanny's gown, came over to her and began to trace them with his finger. Eddy, pleased to have the horse to himself, got under the table with it. It was a strange animal, rather a symbol of a horse than an attempt at a copy, with bright blue bands painted round a tubular body. It was known in the family as Blue-Ribs.

John began to laugh quietly to himself, after an uncanny habit of his, at the pictures on the gown. Agatha called him to her rather sharply, and then put her arm round him. Eddy, seeing this, crawled out from under the table and rushed to her other side. Eddy was so loving and human, thought Agatha thankfully, as he rubbed his round, fair head against her knee. John just stayed quiet in the circle of her arm, still looking at Fanny's dress. Poor Fanny, thought Agatha, very much the mother, drooping over a child in each arm. ·

"John is like Edward, but Eddy takes after me," she said brightly.

"Do you want them to be missionaries, Agatha?"

"I don't know. Of course it's the highest . . . but then a doctor's is a very noble profession too. John is dreadfully upset if an animal is hurt, just like Edward, but he can't do anything about it, he only runs away and is sick, actually sick, so I don't know that he would really make a doctor. Edward wants him to be an artist and he has an idea of drawing, but I don't think I should quite like that. It doesn't seem real work for a man, does it? And there would be so many temptations."

Eddy suddenly snuggled his head against her waist, and, freeing John, she caught the younger boy in both arms and kissed his duckling fluff.

"Eddy is going to be mother's own boy," she said, with all the opinionated note gone from her voice. It was suddenly warm as Fanny had never heard it. John slipped away and took possession of Blue-Ribs once again, and Eddy,

catching sight of him, set up a wail and struggled to be
free.

"Of course he's only a baby yet," said Agatha, letting
him go.  Once again she and Fanny sat staring across the
arid spaces where no conversation flourished.  They were
saved by Selah, appearing, as so often in days gone by, as
the bright angel of information.

"Tea?  Oh, thank you, Agatha.  I have had it with
Colonel Sladen, but I don't mind. . . . I have been hearing
such news.  His Excellency the Viceroy is coming to see
Upper Burma, and I have been chosen by the Colonel and
the Ministers of the Hloot Daw to help at the reception.
The Glass Palace is going to be used; you will feel quite
at home, Fanny.  My aunt and I are to make the list of
the ladies to be presented to their Excellencies, and of course
I shall include you.  Julie, too, and the d'Avera girls, but
only the important ones such as the wives of Ministers will
shake hands, you others will just bow.  What a time I shall
have differentiating the rank of the ladies!  There is to be a
pwè with the famous actress Yindaw Mahlay appearing, and
I shall translate her songs . . ."

Agatha was quite excited by the news.  Many were the
tales of the charm of Lord Dufferin and his wife.  Burma
had been sadly neglected by successive Governor-Generals,
this was to be the case no longer.  She would go round to
Julie's and see about some silk for a new dress. . . .

Fanny made her farewells and left, leaving Agatha and
Selah to discuss the difference in her.  She went back to
the Convent by the edge of the moat.  Several soldiers
were walking along, looking about them curiously, laughing
and joking.  There never was an invading army that behaved
better than the British in Upper Burma, there had been
nothing on either side to arouse angry passions, and a sort of
amiable facetiousness held the air.  The Burmese themselves
were blandly unaware of having been conquered, they knew
that they were the supreme work of existence, nothing disturbed that happy conviction.  Here and there under a
mango tree was a soldier laboriously addressing a Burman as
Kinbya—meaning "mate"—according to instructions, in-

stead of as Hi, Johnny! as his fancy would probably have directed. Already the town was full of traders, Shans, Kachins, Chinese, Persians, Indians; and a caravan was even now passing along by the moat to the tune of jingling mule-bells. Fanny noticed nothing of all this life.

When she came to the road where she had to turn away from the moat, she paused, and looked back at the high red walls, the floating lily-leaves, the golden seven-tiered spire.

Suddenly there flashed into her mind with a pang sharper than she had felt for weeks, the memory of her first day in Mandalay, when her father had stopped to let her see just what she was seeing now. Once started, picture memories came crowding into her mind. . . . The time she and her mother had gone to visit Sinbyew-mashin, the time she had heard of that disaster in Zululand and returning along this road had met Bonvoisin. . . . And the time she had gone stumbling back in the new dress and hat, choked by her sobs. . . .

She had never met Pierre Bonvoisin to speak to since that day. She had only seen him once—when she had been down at the mail-boat when he and his young wife left to seek elsewhere the fortune that had vanished like a pierced bubble in Mandalay, its peacock colours gone into the empty air. She had caught his eye and had felt her own face stolid, yellow, blank, just as she was aware that his was livid and fretful. Her triumph she had savoured by keeping it close behind that blank stolidity. Sandreino caught her eye and winked at her; she had stared at him with the same refusal to understand.

That was the first time she had left the Convent. The second time she had come across Maung Yo, very important and bustling, a portfolio under his arm, going off to meet the Chief Commissioner, for the Kinwoon Mingyi, philo-sophical as ever, had placed his knowledge and his powers at the disposal of the new Government. Maung Yo had looked at her and laughed. Fanny understood that sort of thing so much better than the difficult articulations of Europeans; she knew he meant that after having a bad scare at what he had done for her, he considered everything had turned out for the best. Instead of being clerk to a Minister very much out of favour at Court, he was now assistant to the member of the old administration most in favour with the new powers. Fanny was no longer an exciting miracle to Maung Yo, she seemed to have lost her sparkle, but he was grateful to her.

Fanny looked long and hard at the golden spire and suddenly it swam before her, its edges ran into the shining field of sky, it flickered like a flame and her eyelids burned. She began to sob a little, like a hurt child, standing there at the edge of the moat, staring at what had been to her the centre of the Universe.

CHAPTER IV

## TEA TABLE

IT seemed to Agatha that though the House of Alompra
had fallen, everything was so unchanged that it might have
been the old days, except that Edward instead of her father sat
opposite her at tiffin, and that it was generally Selah or an
officer's wife who came in to have tea with her, instead of
Fanny.

Edward was acutely aware of differences; Agatha, of
the things that were alike. He found himself regretting
that old deplorable atmosphere, the collection of scoundrels
of every nationality, the processions of swaggering notables
on elephants, the yelling lictors, that had gone to make up
the old kalā town, and regretting still more the sense of
menace, of violence and arrogance and fairy-story wealth
and power that had emanated from the hidden Palace. . . .
This bright, clean efficiency . . . how admirable and how
unexciting! Adventure was gone from life in Mandalay.
A series of moral values now held sway, instead of a fantastic
caprice, and it was his job to preach the moral values. He
had preferred to do so when he might have suffered for it.
He knew he was wrong, of course, he could understand how
to young officers, civilians and soldiers, the great adventure
was making Mandalay into a decent, safe place to live in . . .
but something gorgeous, incongruous, sordid, strange, that
had not its match upon the earth, had gone.

These matters did not trouble Agatha. In the old days
she had looked at her own figure against a background of
Mandalay, not directly out at Mandalay from within herself;
and now she did the same thing, as she would through life,
and it followed that changes did not strike her nearly as much
as similarities. There she sat, pouring out the tea in the

long room, the green and golden glow from without filling it like a tide, the birds calling, and various visitors—" the gentlemen "—those creatures who always had talked amongst themselves and always would, sitting round Edward.

Occasionally a polite " I'm afraid this must be very dull for Mrs. Protheroe . . .," or perhaps even the compliment of " Let's ask Mrs. Protheroe what she thinks. Woman's intuition, you know, what? " . . . otherwise she sat and sewed when her tea table ministrations were over, and just listened. She didn't really like being asked for her opinion, because so often she knew it was quite different from Edward's, and yet she would hear herself trying to say the sort of thing he would agree with, because she so wanted him to think her brain capable of understanding his. . . . She didn't like doing that; Agatha was honest in so far as she knew how to be, and yet she did so want Edward to think she had been the right wife for him, that other and finer soul made for his!

In the old days it had been the quiet, dry Shaw or the kind, young Phayre who had sat with her father, now it was one or two brilliant and keen, young Civil officers who came to see Edward, to hear what he knew, to tell him what they thought. Even Sandreino came in sometimes now that he was an enthusiastic supporter of the British . . .

And, just as in the old days, Agatha only touched the world of action and administration through what she heard. She was as far as Fanny, that unimportant little widow, from mingling with the great figures that were making history. Mr. Bernard, Sir Harry Prendergast, no more came into Agatha's life, except for a few polite words at the Club or a dinner party, than they did into Fanny's. She heard more because people came to talk with Edward, who had known the old days and could give useful advice, that was all.

Fanny heard nothing, because the social change in Mandalay was that what had been the Court circle had become a mere tradesmen's circle. . . . Supaya-lat's friends, who had made the power and the aristocracy of Mandalay, would for evermore be but on the fringes of gentility. . . . Julie and

her father, with true French acumen, were very busy with
their weaving, had taken a dozen or so pupils into their own
house, and were selling silks to the officers' wives. But Julie
and her father were now tradespeople, not Court favourites.
. . . Fanny, once supreme as European Maid of Honour, was
now just nobody. Agatha, as wife of the Chaplain—for the
visit of Dr. Marks was not to be of long duration—had a
certain definite and, especially in her own mind, very good
position, but that didn't enable her to penetrate into the high
places unless she were asked.

Of course the great subject of talk, the matter she heard
bandied back and forth perpetually, was what was to be
done with the Kingdom of Ava now it had been conquered
. . . was it, in short, to be treated as the Kingdom of Ava or
as Upper Burma? A protected monarchy or annexation?

Annexation, of course, said Agatha sturdily when she was
asked, for once heedless of what might be Edward's opinion.
But she only sent the conversation off into fresh arguments.

Mr. Bernard had always maintained, in his correspondence
with the Government of India, that the British had no right
to annex Upper Burma or even to interfere with it, because
of purely internal mal-administration. Thibaw was an
ally of England, not a good one, but still an ally, with whom
ran unbroken the treaty made with his father, King Mindoon.
Neither barbarities to his own subjects nor the fact that
British trade was suffering in consequence of his misrule,
made Thibaw a proper object for armed interference, and as
long as those two matters had been the sum and front of his
misbehaviour, the Chief Commissioner had set his face
against any action on the part of the Government of India.

It was France, with her efforts to establish a Protectorate,
that had brought about the crisis. Even Edward, who
pointed out mildly, much to Agatha's annoyance, that
France had as good—or as bad—a right in Burma as the
British—what was the difference morally between the
French from Indo-China and the British from India?—
admitted that, things being as they were, England could not
allow that any European Power save herself could be tolerated
along the frontier.

" Granted the principle of colonization or conquest at all, we can't let anyone else get in here. That would not only be stupid, but would let the Burmese in for a worse mess." Agatha listened to Edward with a mixture of relief, that he was as far orthodox as he was, and anger. Of course the English had a better right anywhere in the world than anyone else . . . everyone knew that.

He saw her buttoned-up face, and continued placidly, to the men :

" You mustn't forget that the Chief's political opinions are the same as Lord Ripon's were—the real old-fashioned Liberal. He believes in self-government. When Ripon was Viceroy he trusted him absolutely. He can think himself into the skin of the people he rules. Ripon's term was short and his own countrymen reviled him, but the Indians worship him. Mr. Bernard has the same traditions and the same beliefs."

That, of course, would be how Edward would talk, thought Agatha, jabbing the needle into a minute pair of John's breeches with some violence.

" Yes, all that's true," said the Chief's secretary, " but Bernard's a strong man as well as an idealist. He hates show and fuss, he's come down into the highways and byways in a manner that's not possible for a Viceroy. He would never have sanctioned an Ilbert Bill, not for years to come, at any rate."

" All this talk about people being fit to govern themselves makes me sick. . . ." This from a Major of violent opinions. " They're only children and the sooner we take them over the better, and when they're troublesome smack their little bot—— " He remembered Agatha and hastily took a long drink of whisky and soda.

" Well, it's a pretty odd situation now," broke in the young secretary. " We've got Prendergast in supreme command, Sladen as chief civil authority; while Bernard, the Government of India and the Secretary of State discuss what's to happen to the country. Meanwhile, we poor devils are trying to be constitutional and to carry on as much as possible on the old lines. There's the Hloot Daw

still functioning, with the place of the King taken by Sladen.
. . . And how he, of all men, must enjoy that! The only
important difference is that Mr. Bernard is over the lot, and a
very good difference too.    We've put in district officers to
carry on with the old Woons of each town, and most of the
old régime are pulling their weight and behaving splendidly.
But it can't go on like this.    I suppose when Dufferin comes,
he and the Chief will decide on something.    If only the
Nyaungyan Prince hadn't died, there'd have been no question.
As it is . . ."

When Dufferin comes . . . a new constitution for Ava,
new frocks for Agatha, for Fanny, for Selah, for the wives
of the Ministers of the Hloot Daw.    When Dufferin comes
. . . and Lady Dufferin, such a lovely woman and so charming.    Life in the Palace again.    And for Selah a place of
importance . . .

"I am having pink," said Selah to Agatha, as they heard
the men, who had duly bowed over their hands, descending
the verandah steps, " what are you? "

Agatha had wanted pink too, and felt annoyed.

"Blue," she said shortly.    "I always think one should
dress to match one's eyes—that is if they happen to be blue,
otherwise it's hardly worth while, I suppose.    Brown's such
a dull colour for frocks."

Out on the verandah Sandreino lingered with Edward
after the others had gone.    The mask had fallen from his
face for a short while and his Latin cynicism showed itself
for a moment in the twist of his lip.

"I am glad the British have come, Protheroe," he said,
" and I think on the whole you will make a good job of it.
But to think that this is all because of one silly little woman! "

Edward stared at him and wondered whether the pegs
had gone to his head—indeed, they had relaxed his guard
and made him forget, or rather, let slip as unimportant,
his promise to Fanny.    What was a promise to such as
she, anyway?    Sandreino looked sideways at Edward and
his moustaches lifted in a smile.

"You don't imagine that this has been because of the
Bombay-Burma, do you? "

"No, of course not. It was the treaty with France that someone got copied and sent down. They say it was you, Sandreino."

"Oh, so it was, so it was, in a way. But who do you think told me about it and got the copies made?"

"I can't imagine."

"Little Fanny Bagshaw . . ."

"Fanny . . . but why on earth . . .?"

"Ah, there it is. Jealousy, revenge."

Edward blinked.

"But why? Whom . . .?"

"Little—not that she is so very little now, eh?—Fanny had an affair, oh, but an affair . . . of the most intense— with Bonvoisin, the man who got the concession for the Ruby Mines. He went to Paris and came back with a wife, one of those little fair innocent bourgeoises, straight from school. And so——" Sandreino waved an expressive though not over-clean hand towards the Palace. He gave a little laugh at Edward's puzzled face. "She had an admirer in the office of the Kinwoon Mingyi, and so she got the copies made and she brought them to me. Result— the French are kicked out of Upper Burma and the British come in. And the fine M. Bonvoisin is ruined."

Edward stood silent. Little Fanny—for, as to every man who had known her in however slight a degree, she would always be little Fanny to him—he could not connect such violence, such directness, such important matters with Fanny.

"You did not think she could do it, eh?" said Sandreino shrewdly. "Well, let me tell you it is the British part of Fanny that pushed her to do that, yes."

"Surely not. Passion . . . revenge . . . all that sort of thing . . ." began Edward.

"You think that is Latin? You are wrong. We Latins do not think love worth all that. We enjoy love much more than you Northerners, we may kill others and our- selves because of it, when you would only go to law, but we would never throw away a solid business proposition, a really practical important thing for it, like you all do. You are the sentimentalists.   We are not sentimental.   You dress this thing up to yourselves, and when you find it is not at all what you think it, you break up everything that is really much more serious.   We think love is a personal thing; it is worth a life or so, because we do not rate life as high as you, but we are never sentimental."

He stopped abruptly and looked sideways at Edward.

" You will keep this that I have told you to yourself?   Not even to Madame?"

" Of course," said Edward rather stiffly.

He was still standing on the steps when, after Sandreino had gone, Agatha and Selah came out together, hatted and gloved, to go and buy silks at Julie's.   Agatha gave him the information as they passed.

" . . . and look after the little boys, won't you, Edward? If the dirzee calls, tell him I expect to have the stuff for him to-morrow.   Oh, and Fanny asked if he might make up hers too, as she can't have him at the Convent, so of course I said ' yes.'   There'll be two dresses, tell him."

" Fanny ! "

" Yes.   Her dress for the Viceroy's reception.   Oh, Edward, you know.   You've heard all about it."

" Fanny's dress for the Viceroy's reception . . . I see."

He heard the voices of Agatha and Selah drifting in little chirps through the trees as they disappeared.   " . . . a dreadful dress, of course, but it seems those plain skirts are coming in, and one might use it as a pattern.   After all, I am lending her my dirzee."

" Yes, indeed . . ."

## CHAPTER V

# FANNY AND EDWARD; AGATHA AND EDWARD; EDWARD AND EDWARD

THE reception was over. Agatha in blue had buzzed hither and thither, where Supaya-lat and her butterfly Maids had flitted; Selah in pink had been here, there and everywhere, introducing the Burmese ladies to Lady Dufferin, who had been just as charming as everyone had anticipated. As Selah said afterwards, it was indeed a magnificent spectacle, because of the Parisian mirrors and gilt furniture and the plush couches that had not yet been removed. And because of the Burmese ladies themselves. . . . They did indeed compare rather favourably with the European. Little delicate creatures, smiling and shikoing, diamonds in their ears, about their necks and wrists, on their fingers, diamonds pinning the flowers in their hair.

Selah only presented the most important of the Burmese ladies, and with these the Viceroy and his wife shook hands, but the others merely shikoed and passed on. Fanny was of these latter, in spite of her new silk European dress. She was only the widow of a steamer captain, or an ex-Maid of Honour, whichever way you looked at it she was not one to have her hand shaken. Agatha was sorry for this, but then she had not had the arranging of these matters, and herself, as the wife of the official parson, was high in the official world for one day. With Selah, she was amongst the twelve ladies who were presented with tea made by her Excellency's own hands. The others just had tea made in the usual way.

After tea came the pwè. Fanny, Agatha noted with compunction rather than surprise, had disappeared. Poor Fanny . . . it must be rather dreadful for her after she had actually lived in the Palace and, by all accounts, been quite an important person in it for so long. . . .

Edward, who did not attend the pwè, which was for the ladies only, ran into Fanny as she too was leaving the Palace. She was walking along, head down, rather stumblingly, her new yellow silk skirts held up in one hand. She had on, he noted idly, a little straw hat with yellow flowers in front of it. He would, conscious of his knowledge, have avoided her if he could, but she had already seen him. He took off his hat and greeted her. She responded absently, and for a while they walked on together because it was the obvious thing to do.

They passed out of the Western Gate, as it was so much the nearest to the kalā town, and suddenly she stopped and looked at him. Edward, searching his brain for something to say, asked if she had heard the story of the Taingda Mingyi, whom the British, distrusting with reason, had sent into exile.

" You know, Mrs. Bagshaw, when he got as far as here, the cart was held up in a block, there was a lot of traffic. He looked out and saw where he was, where he'd sent so many people to their death, and of course he didn't believe the British were going to give him a decent home somewhere in India. So he said: 'Is this where you are going to kill me?' Just like that . . . he'd never thought it could be anything else."

Fanny looked at him absently. She would not have minded if the Taingda Mingyi had been killed ten times over, and the point of the story escaped her.

" They ought to have killed him. He had killed so many people," she said, giving her due meed of attention to Edward's remarks and then at once going on with her own thoughts: " Do you know where Supaya-lat is? "

" Supaya-lat? She's with Thibaw. They've been sent to India with their attendants. They're being given an allowance. They're all right."

He felt a fool as he said it. All right . . . The flame of the last real arbitrary conscienceless royalty on earth, in a bungalow, with so much a month doled out by Government!

Fanny said no more.  Her mind was a blur of unhappiness, so that she could not distinguish which part of the unhappiness was about herself and which about Supaya-lat. But she did know that it was the vision of Supaya-lat, not that of her own form—as for so many years she had envisaged it—that had haunted her that afternoon in the Glass Palace, and that was much for Fanny.  They walked on again and Edward broke the silence.

"Tell me, Mrs. Bagshaw, what are your plans?  You see, you have always been such a friend of my wife's, that you must forgive me for asking what may seem an impertinent question.  What . . . where . . ."  He trailed off.  If she had a broken heart, what use to speak to her of plans?

Fanny wrinkled her brows.

"That's just what has been worrying me, Mr. Protheroe. You see, most of my first—I mean my husband's—investments seemed to vanish after King Mindoon died.  And I'm not clever . . . not at working.  I have met someone who says do I think I can help in a shop."

"What sort of a shop?"

"An antique shop in Bombay, like there used to be at Brighton.  You see, the English like buying old things, they are not like the Burmese, who like the new.  And now there will be lots and lots of old things, with everything the town women stole from the Palace and more that people will make.  And I know so many people in Burma that I thought yes, perhaps I could do that."

Edward, appreciating the simple intricacies of her speech, thought it was very likely that she could, but thought also that Bombay was a long way off.

"My friend thinks I should be good," said Fanny, " and I want to go far away.  And in Bombay there will be all the tourists coming who will want to buy things."

"What is your friend like?  Is she nice?  Has she got a connection already?"

"No, not yet, but he soon will have, because he has the same thing at Rangoon and done very well.  This is to be a branch and I am to be put in charge . . ."

" Oh, I see. You are sure this . . . this gentleman is all right? "

" Oh yes, Mr. Rawlinson introduced me, so as to help me."

They were at the parting of the ways and Edward held out his hand. Fanny slid her plump little kid-gloved fingers into his grasp. Looking up at him, she grudged this Mr. Danvers to Agatha, though she knew he wouldn't have been any good to her. Pale indeed beside Pierre . . .

" You are kind . . ." she said impulsively.

Edward's heart bled. He thought of the afternoon just over, when she had been nobody; of what Sandreino had told him, it seemed to him he knew what her life must have been.

" Fanny . . ." He paused, holding her hand, to try and express with perfect precision the love of her and of all helpless, battered things that swelled in his heart and sometimes threatened to choke him.

And then he caught the look in her eyes, the look that came there in spite of her surprise, the look that always would come there, the look that, with a sickening truth, he could only describe to himself as coquettish. He shook her hand tepidly and let it drop. What was the good? He loved her the more, poor helpless creature, for the very vulgarity of her reaction, because it made her the more pitiful, but it was not a love that Fanny could have understood coming from a " gentleman." All he took away with him, besides his aching pity, was the wry knowledge that she imagined, for one moment at least, she had " interested " him.

" I was so sorry for Fanny this afternoon," said Agatha to him at supper. " But, after all, it isn't as though it were one of us. I mean, the King and Queen being in exile and Fanny having been a Maid of Honour and now being no one. I mean, you somehow can't feel they were real. Not *really* real, not like people one knows."

" We didn't know the King and Queen, but we know Fanny."

" Oh yes, in a way. But . . . Well, Edward, as you

know, I'm not a snob, but poor little Fanny couldn't have been a Maid of Honour anywhere else in the world, could she? A weaver's daughter! You see, these Burmese people didn't know the difference."

"Perhaps," said Edward, "it's like it is with art. Look at the Chinese and Japanese. The finest art in the world. They can't go wrong, but directly they touch the West they make mistakes. Do you remember that Chinese millionaire we knew in Rangoon? With the lovely Chinese things all mixed up with Goss china with the arms of Bude and Buxton on it, and the stuffed head and neck of a giraffe growing out of the middle of the drawing-room parquet like a palm tree? Well, if it comes to that you have only to think of the Palace—the horrible gilt mirrors, the plush sofas, all stuck about amidst the lovely Burmese carving and lacquer."

"Yes, that must be it," agreed Agatha, though privately she thought Chinese and Japanese art painfully bare and their pictures very badly drawn; "you see, poor little Fanny isn't really a *lady*. They're none of them even *ladies*. Not as we count ladies. Imagine Fanny at a tea party at home! She'd never have been to the Academy, and couldn't talk about it if she had. And as to the latest Seton Merriman or Marion Crawford! And they're all the same, Ministers and their wives and all."

Edward said nothing. He let Agatha go up to bed, promising to follow soon. He wanted to be alone for a while. He felt that Agatha was lacking in imaginative pity for these flowery Burmese children suddenly abandoned amidst the punctual machine-like crashings of the West, and yet he was aware, guiltily, that he knew what she meant. Take this conquest—no bloodshed worth mentioning— for these things are not computed by a few heartbreaks, but by statistics—nothing but the pathetically quick collapse of a childish pomp brought up against iron facts. Yet that childish pomp had been the whole of the lives of these little brown people . . . were they of less importance than their paler conquerors?

To Agatha, horrified though she would have been had

she realised it, the answer would have come affirmatively.
Their souls, of course, were equally important, in the eyes
of God each soul counted as much as any other. But the
*happiness* of these little brown people who knew nothing,
who had got hold of life and civilization all wrong . . . it
couldn't matter as much as the happiness of people who
went back and forth to England by the P. & O., and
had sons at public schools, and knew about things like
trains and the Civil Service, and being Conservative, or even
Liberal. . . .

Perhaps even Edward was not quite sure of this, except
theoretically, but then Edward had all the medieval theo-
logical impatience of the idea of happiness in this world as a
blessing. He even had a stern distrust of it. It was not the
happiness or otherwise of the Burmese that he worried over,
his unease was deeper. Like a refrain through his head ran
*Small Eastern nations and great Western powers.* . . .

The splendid mood of thanksgiving he had experienced at
the first Morning Prayer held in the Lion Throne Room
had not sustained its exaltation. Glamour, success, the
triumph of the thing for which he had lived, had taken him
out of himself that day, had raised him on its high crest,
borne him along, filled the furthermost corners of his soul
with light. But it is not on such eagle eyries that the mind
of man can rest, and ever since, amid all the talk of daily
organisation, amid the jokes and satisfactions of the younger
members of the conquering party, he had mislaid his pearl
as he had been wont to mislay it amid the little sordid satisfactions and jealousies of mission life. He was perhaps no
good, had no spiritual strength or staying power except when
he was alone, he told himself sadly.

Of course it was better for the Burmese to be conquered—
Edward was too practical and truth-loving a man to side
with those sentimentalists who denied that even as far as the
actual welfare of the natives went, it was better to leave
them alone—but wasn't there something else, something
intangible but perhaps more important than physical and
even moral welfare? Naturally it was better for famines
and fevers and leprosy to be dealt with properly, naturally

it was better to be decently governed, not to be squeezed
dry . . . But—but——

In the passion of his own wish to belong to himself, Edward
could sympathise with a nation that was no longer free.
Agatha looked after him so well, he was darned and patched
and fed and medicined and shepherded . . . and yet . . .

It sometimes seemed to Edward that he had drifted into
marriage with Agatha just as the Kingdom of Ava had
drifted into submission to the British. It was true that he
hadn't indulged in cruelties and outrages, but wouldn't it
have been better if he had, if he and Agatha had sometimes
glared at each other like a couple of tiger-cats, if they had
occasionally hated and feared each other?

He remembered that evening by the moat, when he had
tried to express to old Marks something of what he felt
about the overpowering female quality of Burma and how
that quality had always terrified him. It was the tamein
that had conquered Edward, the silken swaddling femininity
of it, just as it had been the cause of the downfall of Ava.
Although men it was, men of the Civil Service and the
Army, who had actually taken the Kingdom, yet to Edward
the whole march of events at Mandalay was as a dance of
women, some gaily-coloured, some sombre, woven on a
golden ground.

Strange and grotesque pattern! He saw them, caught
each of them in the arrested action of a characteristic pose—
Fanny, as he had first known her, tiny and supple, fluttering
with ribbons, her eyes sidelong; the thin brown Supaya-lat,
with a graceful but minatory gesture of her fine hands, her
lithe hips swathed in her bright tamein; the old Queen,
once so dominating, but of late years broken and anxious,
creeping along behind; the flower-like little Maids of Honour
bowing and smiling; the pale ghosts of the murdered Queens
and Princesses, drifting along lightly as on the finer clearer
air of another space, from which they only reflected into this
gold background as into a metal mirror. . . . Julie, dim-
eyed, peering forward, but always marching steadily ahead;
Selah, prancing firmly, her flowered muslin bustle waggling

as she went, her hat tipped forward over the bright roundness of her face. The nuns, patterns of black and white, their hands folded in their wide sleeves, their heads bent, their lips moving—joining so quietly and demurely in the dance. The invincible American Baptist ladies, striding along, singing the hymns of Moody and Sankey; Agatha, the thin English girl, straight and a little angular in her long softly-falling garments, her mouth a little pursed, Agatha, who had stood to him as a precious symbol of the old known world in this strange company. The Hairy Woman, whom he had seen when Sladen arranged for her to be sent home to her village, ambling along with her nice dog's head bent upon a sorrowful hand. The young French bride, blonde and passive, innocent cause of that wild, final quickening of the dance.

And Fanny again, Fanny as she was now, bringing up the procession, dancing viciously, angrily, that strange and horribly jocund dress twisting about her plump little form, her black hair straggling from beneath an absurd hat decked with yellow flowers, Fanny beating time, faster and faster . . . urging all the feet on to that last flurry that had brought the mazy pattern of strange steps to a sudden end. None of those feet would ever dance again, but would wander down dusty ways in quietness.

Fanny already, though she had been at the reception that afternoon, had dropped entirely out of the life of the new Mandalay. This antique-selling friend of hers—she hadn't told Agatha anything about him—he felt guiltily sure that Agatha hadn't yet shewn much interest in what Fanny was to do. All by herself Fanny had been trying to build up a new life, a very different one from any she had known hitherto, and, being Fanny, was naturally building it round a man. Edward felt that none of her old friends would ever see Fanny again save from a distance, that even if you were in the same room with her you would get no feeling of nearness. Completely unimportant, she was already disintegrating, as it were, no one was conscious of her any more, save perhaps the seller of antiques. Some day she might marry again, a worthy tradesman, probably.

Not of the stuff of great drama was any one of the people

of the show made, thought Edward; no stern Roman passions animated either the women or the men. The Kinwoon Mingyi had not fallen on his sword but was serving the British Raj. His eyes were the saddest eyes, it seemed to Edward, that had ever looked out of human face, as sad as the eyes of a monkey, dark in the yellow, wrinkled leaf of his old countenance, but he still lived. Supaya-lat still lived and would go on living, a common scold, a senseless spendthrift. Thibaw would drink and sulk and grow maudlin over the sacred writings he had so long neglected. Fanny would not take the veil, she would take instead her place as a little shopkeeper. Agatha and he would not agonise over having lost their way in what was supposed to be the loveliest of life's gardens. No, they would make the best of things, realise they were not of the stuff of which the great lovers or the great workers of the world are made, they would get along somehow. People did. That was life and that was what people were like. Hardly ever a great final gesture; even Fanny, who alone of any of them had been capable of a great gesture, had survived it—it had not ended her.

Yet Edward felt that, had he but saved himself for that high endeavour for which he had surely been created, he might have touched something which now was lost to him for ever. But how, in the hot heavy insistence of that female quality in Mandalay, that like a fragrant but too-heavily embroidered coverlet, had lain over the whole of life, could he have escaped?

Edward's resentment was not against Agatha, it was against his own weakness, embodied in his wife. That he should have. . . . That he should not have been able to steer clear! But he was too just, too pure in his mental processes, to blame even fate, he blamed perhaps the parents and pastors who had brought him up and taught him nothing of man and woman; but he blamed still more his own compliance with the needs of his physical nature, for he was one of the born ascetics to whom concessions to human weakness —or acceptance of human strength—are indeed sin. These things might be, he never denied it, right for others, he was profoundly aware that for himself, the chosen of the Lord, they were wrong.

Christ! thought Edward, for the first time in his life using the sacred name as an expletive and not as what it had always stood for to him—and it gained as an expletive from that fact and gave him a deep inward satisfaction that otherwise he couldn't have derived—Christ! what have I been doing . . .? And, when it was too late to alter it, he looked back on those swift-rushing years between the early and late thirties—those years that hold all the balance of a life, and marvelled at his own incompetence and blindness. As Mr. Lumsden had done, as inarticulate Fanny had done, but as Agatha could never do.

I am *I*, Edward Protheroe, and I see now not important or vital and yet the only *I* that I can ever really know. . . . A missionary, a Church of England clergyman. . . . I have always seemed somebody because I have lived in circles where a missionary and a Church of England clergyman was somebody . . . whatever he was like. I have been more than most, because I am what I am, fairly attractive, good family, all the rest of it . . . what has it all rested on? Where are those high hopes, those golden visions, those ecstasies of faith and spiritual ambition that used to make me alive as fire? I am the father of a family, my life has been permeated by the odour of drying baby garments, by tins of patent food, by a thousand domestic necessities that there is no avoiding. Somehow when one is young even such things as these seem lovely in the light of illusion. . . . One imagines a young mother bending over the tub before a leaping fire, the smell of violet powder, the dancing reflection on soft sweet flesh. It isn't like that really, not unless one is just a visitor, an uncle, or a friend who has been mildly attached to the young mother, brought in to see the sacred rites of baby-in-his-bath. This everyday business, especially in the tropics, is ugly, squalling, smelly, even dangerous . . . the poor little brutes, with all these swift diseases. . . . Lovely to look in occasionally and partake of these sacred intimacies as a visitor . . . wearing and sordid to have them forced on one as part of daily life.

Lyric ecstasies . . . why are we all brought up to expect them, why is the whole convention of the book world, a convention accepted by the world of living beings, based on the idea that sooner or later life is transmuted by something wonderful that is supposed to make everything different? Life is never quite round like that . . . it's all sorts of funny shapes, not enough here, too much there. . . .

Edward, carrying the small oil-lamp up to bed, and hearing the derisive chuckle of a lizard on the wall, envied for a moment the complete roundness of the emotion that must have been Fanny's in her love-affair. She would " get over it " because, so it seemed to him, simple and violent sensations are more easily eliminated from the system than more complicated and half-false sensations. Lack of roundness, of completeness, is the curse implicit in a higher civilisation. But, even as he thought that, he realised it had its compensations. He would always have books and his own thoughts, no such blessings could be Fanny's. How dead she seemed compared with the bright, shallow, little creature they had known!

Edward sighed as he went into the bedroom and saw Agatha kneeling at her prayers. And Fanny, turning over impatiently in bed at the Convent, reflected that in Bombay she must find a boarding-house. Convents were really too difficult.

## CHAPTER VI

# THE CLUB

EDWARD went to the Palace to hear the news. He heard it
with many variations, but the main facts were the same. Of
course the Viceroy and " the Chief" had been conferring
together, and the results came through in gossip inevitably
coloured by the views of the retailer. Yet certain truths were
unmistakeable. Edward recognised them by his own knowledge of the Burmese people. He knew it was true, as Lord
Dufferin said, that the mass of the people were indifferent to
what the future form of government might be, provided it
protected them; but that all the same there was an enormous
amount of reverence for the royal blood, and that any
Alompra Prince who could have presented himself would
have gained a following, no matter what his record. If the
pious and intelligent Nyaungyan Prince had still been living
there would have been little doubt what course should be
adopted. But there was no one; save a few Princes stained
with crime, or one or two who had for many years been
supported by the French. . . . The Nyaungyan Prince had
indeed left a little son, but if he were placed upon the throne
it meant that the British would have to administer the
country for him till he came of age; and, to put it vulgarly,
would have all the trouble and none of the profit.

The country was so disorganised since Thibaw's rule that
dacoity flourished everywhere, and it would, as the English
were realising, in any case take several years to pacify it.
Mandalay had fallen almost without a protest, but the
civilising of a wild and mountainous country, where criminals,
and those men who had been forced into being criminals,
had taken refuge for many years, was likely to be a long and
expensive business. Neither—and this was flying about to

358

the accompaniment of wry twists of face and low whistles of dismay—was the difficulty likely to be less because Prendergast, the gallant and splendid, the " Happy Warrior," had made a dire mistake in allowing the Burmese soldiers to disband with their rifles. . . . That would mean months or perhaps years of vagrant armed bands, marauding and slaying . . . it had been a greater error than permitting women to pass in and out of the Palace on the night of the surrender.

In short, though both Bernard and Dufferin—the former because of his principles, and the latter because he had his hands only too full already, would have welcomed a protected monarchy, there was no possible monarch to protect, and annexation was the only way. They would go on threshing it out, but that was what it would come to. The great Bishop Bigandet, a Catholic and a Frenchman, had advised Dufferin, with the logic of his nation, that annexation was the only way to peace, and that any middle course would be fatal. The great ones were working as most of their critics at home had never worked in their lives, and would soon have a complete plan for the direction of the country, with its cost, ready to submit to London.

A week or so later came the news that the Secretary of State approved of the plan, which substituted for the arbitrary power of the Viceroy, more legal methods. The whole campaign was approved of, especially the fact that the total casualties on the British side had been four British officers, seven men, and ten Indian private soldiers. No Indian officers had fallen.

It was obvious to anyone with a mind capable of assimilating such affairs at all, that Ava had neither the elasticity nor the power of resistance necessary for a buffer state. It would always lie open to Chinese or French aggression if left to itself. A puppet king would prove himself a very expensive and troublesome fiction.

No one, reflected Edward, certainly not the Radicals in England, or the French, would believe in the real regret of Dufferin and Bernard—men whose characters ought to put them beyond suspicion—that they could not place a Prince

of the House of Alompra upon the throne.   But Edward
knew Mr. Bernard well, and Dufferin all men knew by
repute.   That the latter especially would regret the dying
out of the royal idea in Burma, he was sure.   The prestige of
the House of Alompra—of whom Mindoon had been the
only good and conscientious King—was yet enormous in the
land, and that was the sort of idea that a Dufferin hated to
die out.   He would have loved to use it in the cause of
order, for the sake of its old-time beauty.

And beauty did seem to have died already in the arbitrary
changes that had perforce been made.   True, the Palace of
old had been sordid enough, the litter of empty tins and
foul waste had grown beneath the gilded rooms, there had
been amongst the whole feather-brained, cruel, gay, respectable gang of them, no active sense of loveliness, no " taste "
as that word is understood. . . . But unconsciously the old
Palace life had stood for beauty, for a something artless and
barbaric that was now lost.   On a green baize board in the
Lily Throne Room were pinned notices of polo matches,
on a long deal table were the illustrated papers from England.
A portrait of Queen Victoria hung upon the red-painted
wall.   The whole construction showed up somehow for the
cheap affair that it had always been, though in the old days no
one would have known it.   Where the Moguls had built in
marble, these people had built in wood, where the Persians
had had inlays of precious stone, these had glass imitations;
instead of old Eastern carpets, there were modern Aubusson
and Axminster.   These were people who lived for the
moment and who built for the moment, of wood, or corrugated iron;   leaving unfinished edges, using gilding instead
of gold. . . . Now, past the Bee Throne, where the King of
Ava had shown himself in wedding array, the Duck Throne,
where the King had reposed to receive foreign ambassadors,
the Deer Throne, where King and Queen had every month
offered gifts of yellow robes to the monks, the Peacock
Throne, where the King sat to inspect his elephants and
horses and review troops, past the very Lion Throne itself,
whose occupant had been Lord of the Life, Head and Hair
of all beings, the new authorities came and went, and sober

conferences took the place of pwès, while on the Lily Throne
of the Queens of Ava, young subalterns sat and swung their
legs and jested about " Soup-plate " and laughed over the
jokes made by *Punch* at the expense of the fallen dynasty.
And ladies, not only wives who had to be in Mandalay, but
eager American and English tourists, who knew somebody,
who knew somebody, who could help them to get to Mandalay, sat on the Lily Throne so as to imagine what it was
like being Queen. . . .

And the Thrones appeared somehow cheap and tawdry
under this treatment, only the imperishable loveliness of
their lines and design, and the beauty of the whole proportion
of each room survived. The actual fabric seemed to shrivel
and fade. Yet they were less tawdry, thought Edward,
than the jokes written by complacent stay-at-homes in
London, over which the young men made merry. To
him these jokes did not appear particularly funny. He
even had an uneasy feeling that in time they would seem
vulgar.

He sat one day at a long table in the Lily Throne Room
and turned the pages of *Punch*. Not much attention was
paid to the Annexation of Burma in any of the English
papers—as news it was so much less than the fall of Khartoum
—but what Edward did read was apt to fill him with a rising
sense of shame. There was, for instance, the skit called
" Thibaw's Diary."

*Monday. Glad it's all over. Cost me a pang giving up
Mandalay and the entire army, especially as I had settled a grand
military execution for next week. This invasion has put out all
my arrangements. The Cabinet Torture I had fixed for the 15th
postponed indefinitely. These Barbarians don't know how to
govern. Why, they have been in the capital for at least twenty-
four hours and haven't killed anybody—not even impaled a Prime
Minister !*

*Tuesday. They are beginning to understand me and my
little ways. A dish of live snakes at breakfast this morning,
capital ! Had an interview with the Chief Barbarian. He*

*was very civil but refused to scald my late Privy Council to death in boiling oil.*

Of course it was true that Thibaw had killed and tortured, it was true that his rule had been bad . . . but this seemed somewhat smug and unworthy all the same. . . . Edward went distastefully away, only to run into a group of young officers twanging a banjo, and trying to make a tune to a poem of which the inspiring refrain was: " He must cease to be a King . . ."

" ' *King Thibaw's a shocking fellow,*
*Far too long has had his fling,*
*Drinks and gets extremely mellow—*
*He must cease to be a King . . .* ' "

The youth who was picking out a suitable air upon his banjo paused when he had sung thus far, took a pull at his peg, and started again:

" ' *He is crueller than Nero,*
*Like a tiger he will spring,* '

tum, tum, tum, tum. . . . Now I've got it!

' *Not by any means a hero,* '

all together, you fellows—

' *He must cease to be a King.* '

All sing the next. . . .

' *Now he'd stop all British trading,*
*Unto bankruptcy would bring*
*Folks who deal in bills of lading—* '

What the devil are bills of lading? The chits you get at the end of the month for all you've taken on board?

' *He must cease to be a King.* '

Now, last verse. All together.

' *All his subjects gladly gather*
*Underneath the British wing,*
*Off with Thibaw then—or rather,*
*He must cease to be a King* . . .' "

Edward, feeling outraged and yet a good deal of a prig, walked away.

## CHAPTER VII

# LOST SHWAY DAGON

"I THINK it's disgusting," said Agatha firmly, when news was brought—of course by Selah—that Fanny was to marry her seller of antiques. " To marry again at all always seems horrid for a woman, and to marry an Indian! "

" He's not an Indian," said the conscientious Selah, " he's a Zerbadi—his mother was Burmese."

" It's all the same."

Selah began to laugh.

" Do you remember when Fanny married Captain Bagshaw and sneered at me because she said I was happy to live among crows? Mr. Mahboob is a darker crow than any Burman! What fun it will be to remind her of that! "

But no one had the chance to remind Fanny of anything. The next thing they heard was that she had gone to Rangoon without so much as leaving a note of farewell behind her, and that when she arrived there, she had married the dark but presumably devoted Mr. Mahboob. A very nice respectable man, though not always very lucky in business, little Rawlinson said. . . .

Rumour, coming back to that sadly-abased circle that had once been the fringe of Court, declared that Fanny had, on her way to Bombay, called in at Madras and seen Thibaw and Supaya-lat. Fanny never wrote to anyone to say how the visit had passed off. She had slipped out of Burmese life as though it had never known her, and so had Supaya-lat. The new order of things was established.

The padauk trees broke many times into their golden showers, the rains into their silver, before bands of robbers ceased to range the land, and Pierpoint and young Phayre were amongst the first to be killed in skirmishes with dacoits.

The pacification of a people so full of contradictions as the Burmese took far longer and claimed more lives than had the easy conquest. For here were folk among the kindliest and the most wantonly cruel of the races of the earth, who would cherish the mendicant and the stranger, or torture, rob and slay. They had a contempt for pain and death and yet ran away if a cracker went off. The curious quality of restlessness inherent in the Burmese easily developed into crime, or could be led into ways that were all goodness.

Their religion of pessimism and humility did not prevent them from being great gamblers, merry-hearted and conceited. Neither, reflected Edward, did Christianity, also a religion that taught this world was a shadow show, prevent those who professed it from having just such qualities. The Burmese were intensely superstitious, but was there really much difference between believing in the Holy Coat of Treves or in the Footprint of Buddha?

Edward admitted humbly—and without the distaste his father-in-law would have felt in the admission—that it was to the Catholic and the American Baptist Missions that the Government of Burma owed much during the difficult time of pacification. Tribes that had always been despised, such as the Karens, had taken to Christianity, whatever its particular brand, with honesty and enthusiasm. Edward learned to admire both Jesuits and Baptists—a far more difficult matter than admiring Buddhists and Mahomedans.

All Edward knew of life—and it was considerably more than he had known on first coming to Mandalay—he had learned in Burma. He had known marriage and fatherhood; it had been borne in upon him, in spite of his abiding passion for the Christ idea, that there was much of the truth in other religions—indeed, in every religion. There was one dreadful season of the rains when the first realisation of this cost him hours of torment.

He had come from Kilburn to convert the heathen who worshipped idols. It was in terms of idolaters he had thought of the Hindus and the Burmese. Now he discovered that the thousands of figures of Buddhas venerated all over the country were not idols at all. No one worshipped them, such a thing was expressly forbidden by the Buddhist religion. No one even worshipped the Buddha. The "idols" were only to help the devout mind to concentrate on the idea of the Buddha, the just man made perfect.

Even the Hindus did not worship their statues of Vishnu, Siva, Krishna and the rest. They worshipped the gods behind them. They no more worshipped "stocks and stones" than the Catholics worshipped the actual crucifix or the statues of the Virgin. The Mahomedans allowed no images at all, and were as outraged by the Trinity of the Christians, as the Christians by the multiplicity of the Hindu gods. For purity of doctrine, the Mahomedans surely had the palm, for spirituality, the Buddhists.

It was, so Edward at last perceived with a curious mingling of relief and shock, in matters practical that Christianity was so immeasurably superior to other religions. For with all its austerity, its high ideals, Buddhism remained a selfish creed. The good Samaritan might have passed on with a reflection on the transitoriness of human happiness had he been a follower of Gautama. Negation as the highest good did not lead to active kindnesses. These people were kind, not only because they were by nature among the most charitable of races, but also because Buddhism enjoined charity and abhorred cruelty, but to refrain from active cruelty is not the same thing as to practise active kindness.

The good King Mindoon had been the cause of the deaths of hundreds of bullocks that dropped by the wayside, worn out by the heavy loads they dragged for the building of the Yankeentaung Pagoda. With broken legs they were let. to die of hunger and thirst because Buddhism forbade the merciful taking of their tortured lives. What matter . . . they were only expiating the sins of a former existence.

In short it didn't matter what happened to animals because they had souls, just as in Latin countries it didn't matter what happened to animals because they hadn't souls. . . . And Edward thought miserably, not for the first time, what a thousand pities it was that the Founder of Christianity had not seen fit to lay down a teaching on this sad matter of the animal world . . . you had to do such hard work with a

few pitiably thin sentences such as the one about the ox or
ass that fell into a pit on the sabbath day . . . or about not
muzzling the ox that trod out the corn, or that one which
said that not a sparrow fell to the ground without the Father's
knowledge. . . .

Edward, whose life was a misery to him every time he
saw a pi-dog with its back sticking through its skin like a
series of reels of cotton, tried to go with eyes as averted as
possible through this implacable Eastern world. Doubtless
the men who drove the oxen, so beautifully commemorated
on the towers of Laon Cathedral, had urged the wretched
beasts with goad and whip up that hill. Small good did it
do the oxen that their services were commemorated in the
sculpturing of the stones they had dragged. They knew as
little of that as Mindoon's beasts left to die under the Burmese
sun. Edward thought sadly that the truest text in the Bible
was the one about the whole creation groaning and travailing
in pain. . . . He started a hospital for dogs and drugged
himself with physical labour. But he never succeeded in
quite forgiving the Almighty for the pain of the helpless.
To him, cruelty or even unintentional disaster was so much
worse for children and animals than it was for grown men
and women. The children and animals could have no
philosophy with which to meet suffering. They couldn't
say? " We brought this on ourselves," or : " It was only an
accident, it wasn't meant," or : " What, after all, will it
count in the tale of the centuries or the measure of the stars? "
No philosophy could be theirs. Animals couldn't do anything but just suffer. It was a spectacle to which Edward
could never accustom himself.

Little John . . . what wouldn't he have to go through?
Eddy would always manage all right . . . but John . . .
the living, breathing expression of all that he, Edward,
might have been, of much that Mr. Lumsden might have
been. It was odd that he so often in the lonely tracts of his
thoughts, found himself meeting the wistful figure of his
dead father-in-law, and recognising how alike in many
things their minds had been, though Agatha's was so entirely
different.

John . . . the chance for John to be an artist. . . . But,
from Agatha: " A good public school for the boys, and, of
course, Sandhurst for Eddy. I'm sure he's a born soldier."

The time had come when the boys would be better in
England, and Edward himself had malaria in his system.
Yet, like many men whose best years have been passed in
the East, he saw the end approaching with dismay. But it
had to be England for Edward and Agatha . . . Cheltenham
or some such sink of morality, he supposed drearily. And
reproached himself for lack of trust in God when he was
offered a good country living near Chichester. The boys
could go to Lancing when they were old enough, a good
Church tone there. Agatha could go to London occasionally
to see the Academy and attend meetings of the Poona
Mission, of the children's branch of which both John and
Eddy were members.

The real Burma was over for him, anyway, Edward had
felt at the time of the annexation. Ridiculously he felt it,
for he knew that the Alompra dynasty and the Palace had
never been really in his life. And yet it had been those
early years at Mandalay during the lifetime of Mindoon and
the first perilous months of Thibaw that he had felt Burma
in his bones, as it were, and had loved it. He had known
ecstasy then and only then. Absurd as it might seem now
to him, he had known it on that evening when he had
walked by the moat with Agatha—poor dear Agatha!
after the first massacres. He knew now that it had been an
ecstasy based on wrong premises, but did that make it any
less real? Certainly it had not done so at the time. He
had first thought ecstasy was only to be found in religion,
then that it was born of the relationship of one person to
another; and when he had found how that latter had
betrayed him, he had for a while denied ecstasy entirely.

When he had returned to Mandalay on that first Sunday
in the Palace, some measure of truth had been vouchsafed to
him. There was ecstasy, but it was in ideas, especially in
the idea of beauty apart from any moral implication, that it
lay. That was why he had minded about the fall of the
Kingdom of Ava. An idea had been wiped out of the

world. The idea of royalty that had held romance and magic for men since the beginning of the world, but which the world seemed to be growing out of, as a child discards its toys. David, Solomon, Charlemagne, the Black Prince, Henry of Navarre, the Roi Soleil . . . all the schoolroom list of them swam up at him. It was an idea that seemed to be dying off from the face of the earth, not because it was a bad idea, but because the world had gone past it. You couldn't call the modern constitutional monarchy the same thing. . . . Here, in Ava, it had survived, in all its pomp and arrogance and unreason. That was why something had definitely been wiped out at the conquest of Ava. Not a people—far from extinguishing a nationality, the annexation had moulded the country again into a coherent whole—but an idea.

But would Ava be happy in the long run, as part of the Indian Empire, Ava that had nothing in common with India, and had always regarded everyone save the Chinese with contempt?

These things, he knew, were in the future, though men already murmured of them. It was the past that Edward unreasonably regretted, deplorable as he knew it to have been. He felt that he alone in all Mandalay knew what Fanny must have felt, and except for endowing her with more power of thought than she possessed, he was right.

Not that even in his mind, and still less, he knew, in those of others, were either Fanny or Supaya-lat often present nowadays. What had seemed at the time such great events had now fallen into the perspective a few years bring about. But on the last few days in Rangoon sight of Selah made the old days live again.

Selah was about to be married to a tall, handsome Armenian cousin—and married in the English Church, since the marriage of cousins was forbidden in the Armenian community. She came down to the steamer at Rangoon to " see Agatha off." There were also many friends from the Mission. Edward was touched by their kindness, he wanted to be alone with himself and his own youth, and went below.

When the yellow froth of the Irrawaddy was churning

away from the screw, Agatha leaned over the taffrail, waving mechanically, but her eyes were fixed on the pure flame of the Shway Dagon melting into the past. . . . She might not always have liked Burma, but she was leaving her youth there.   And it seemed to her only the other day that she and Fanny had sighted that suave contour.   Fanny . . . she had quite ceased to count.   Not only that, but little Fanny, once so full of her own triumphs, seemed to have ceased to exist since the British had taken Upper Burma, even while her dimmed semblance had yet lingered there.

Somewhere a stout Fanny rocked in a bentwood chair and ate too much curry, but it wasn't the Fanny who had come from Brighton to Mandalay with Agatha.   And Agatha, who was not usually imaginative, had the odd notion that the strange secret life of the Palace and Fanny herself had ceased at the same time, so completely had the breath of the English blown both away.

# EPILOGUE

It had happened—Edward was a Canon. Agatha was happy. Chichester, that grave and reverend place, acknowledged Edward as a Canon. The boys had long left Lancing —Eddy having done well and John badly—when their father was, so to speak, canonised.

Agatha had not liked England when they returned to it. She found herself as strange in the London of the nineties as Fanny in the Mandalay of the British Government. Oscar Wilde, The Yellow Book, Aubrey Beardsley, that startling playwright, Mr. Pinero, these things bewildered her. Not that she and Edward, in lodgings in Pembroke Square, Earl's Court, meeting other clergy at the Army and Navy Stores, which they used as a sort of club, were really any nearer these strange *fin de siècle* phenomena than Fanny had been near the world of Barnard and Prendergast, but, read the *Strand Magazine* as much as you would for your literary pabulum, there was no getting away altogether from this other strange disturbance in the air. Agatha took it out in visits to All Saints', Margaret Street, or, if she could not get so far, to St. Cuthbert's, Earl's Court, but she had out-distanced Edward. . . . More and more he reverted to the Church of George Herbert and Bishop Ken—that Church of a pious and grave beauty which seemed to him truly English in its simplicity and tolerance.

Sussex was not much better than Pembroke Square, thought Agatha. No one seemed to know what she was talking about when she began: " When we were in Burma . . ."

When we were in Burma . . . when we were young . . . when such much more exciting things were happening than have ever happened to you, who think you are *fin de siècle*

371

. . . when we might have been murdered in our beds . . . what is all your modern stuff you make such a fuss about compared with what we went through in Mandalay? No good . . . it conveyed nothing to their minds. And then, just as country people might have begun to be interested (through much hearing of it) in the missionary career of that wan spiritual-looking woman, Mrs. Protheroe, wife of the Vicar of Lemmings, near Chichester, came the Boer War. . . .

Another of those things that had happened to the British Empire ever since Agatha could remember. Disaster after disaster, of course . . . and then the old Queen dying. . . . The end of the world . . . but after all, they say the Prince has been doing all the hard work for years, only she was so jealous of him. . . . Anyway, he's terribly ill, this new-fangled disease invented by Frederick Treves. There's always been the saying—Mother Shipton or somebody—about him being " King but never crowned . . ." But another saying on which Agatha had brought up the boys warred with this one: " When Seventh Edward on the throne doth reign, Sixth Edward's Mass shall be said again." That meant that the first prayer book of Edward the Sixth, for the restoration of which all " good " churchmen prayed, would be in use once more. So Edward the Seventh had to live. And he did, but the first prayer book of Edward the Sixth didn't come into use all the same.

But Edward became a Canon, and John, spurning the University, insisted on going to Paris to paint, and Eddy, spurning the Army, insisted on going into the City. Money was what was going to matter nowadays. Motor-cars. . . . Some day soon everyone would simply have to have a motor-car and you couldn't do that without money. John didn't care about money any more than Edward and Agatha had ever done, but then they had never envisaged it. Every-one took it in as a factor in the new generation. How terribly soon one had to leave off not being *fin de siècle*, and had to be afraid, with a superior smile, that one wasn't twentieth century!

Burma—Mandalay—where were they? They lived in

letters from the people still working and sweating ·out there
while Edward with—very often—despair in his heart at his
own comfortable life, trundled about the Sussex lanes.
Sometimes, walking to the crest of the Downs, he would
stand and look across the fair country to the sea.   Pale
downlands, dark rings of trees, saltings drained of tide or
brimmed with it like liquid silver. . . . Pattern of pale
colours, of broad shining spaces, that for all the essentially
English quality of it, yet brought back to him the reaches of
the Irrawaddy and the pearly colour of spring along its
shores.   And he would think of the Gem City and see
splashed across the faint Sussex landscape the arrogance of
scarlet and of gold.

The memory of that violent colour was kept by Agatha
also, but with a difference.   To her it was not lost beauty,
but lost self.   To Agatha, Ava was primarily the background
that gave her own figure interest and significance in a world
that was fast going past her, and great was her grief and
amazement when she had found that no one knew where
Burma was upon the map, and that only a few widows and
mothers bereft of sons knew what she was talking about.

Agatha, elderly, knowing she had never been the figure of
romance that every woman, however unfitted, feels she
ought to have been, consoling herself for the children that
were growing away from her, with the dependence of a
husband whom life had tamed and brought, if not to her feet,
at least, to her side . . . that something wild in him which
she had always mistrusted and feared, conquered by the
Church and by life—those two opposing forces which so
often have the same result—what had she been at best but
the spectator of a brightly-coloured puppet show?

She was actually glad when reality was given to her
memories by the arrival of a letter from Fanny, terse and to
the point, not long and discursive like the letters of Selah.
Bombay had proved a fairly good venture; she was tired of
it, yet she didn't want to go back to Burma.   So they were
going to try England.   They could get over Indian and
Burmese things that were good and cheap.   Buddhas,
lacquer, silks, poongyi chests of red and gold, inexpensive

rubies, moonstones, silverware. . . . Of course it would be Brighton, where Fanny had only too good reason to remember the curiosity shops. They had heard of one in East Street going very reasonably. . . . Fanny would run it, and Mr. Mahboob go back and forth taking things with him. People in India were so glad to pick up old English things that they thought dated from the days of John Company.

The Great War, that made Burma seem a small thing even to Agatha, broke upon the world, and everything else ceased to matter. John went into the Flying Corps, and Eddy into the Army Service Corps, and Agatha went carefully all her days, as mothers did, and made many bargains with the Almighty if only her boys could come through all right. She would have sacrificed all the other children in the world for hers as lightly as Supaya-lat had sacrified the other children of Mindoon. In far away Burma, Selah was a member of the Armenian Refugee Fund and of the Society for the Prevention of Infant Mortality in Rangoon. In Europe mortality of infants went on apace.

Fanny and her Mahboob came near starvation in Brighton in those early days when antiques were not selling, but Fanny did not write and complain of poverty, and gradually normal values, which rule that accessories are more vital and valuable than necessities, re-established themselves, and trade looked up.

John lost a leg in the first year of the war, and thanked God it wasn't his eyes or his hand, and Eddy, the prosperous, the safe, picked up an undesirable wife in Havre, one Poppy, a wife who almost reconciled Agatha to the sin of divorce. It was Eddy who drove the new Canon and Agatha over to Brighton to see Fanny. During the first two years of the war Agatha could have gone but had not, there always seemed something so much more important to do. Girl Guides, or swabs, or one of the boys coming home on leave. What was Fanny's life during that time? Agatha did not know, it was more hidden from her than the strange days in the Palace had been. Did Fanny go to the whist-drives, the supper parties of oysters and stout, which her fellow-shopkeepers gave amongst themselves? Agatha had heard that she did, and that the darkness of Mr. Mahboob was considered rather romantic. Did Fanny ever look back longingly to the old days in the City of Gems, as she handled her lengths of ribbon woven by Julie's pupils and sold them to Brighton schoolgirls or dashing young women staying at the Ship or the Metropole? Agatha, in her Chichester fastnesses, wondered, but she did not know. Then the war became more of a settled habit, and when one day a letter arrived from Fanny, at a time when Eddy, on leave, was at the Metropole with the startling wife, Agatha suddenly felt a wish to see Fanny. Eddy drove over to fetch Agatha and Edward in his little car. They all had lunch together and Agatha sat and wondered what would have been thought of young women in her day who had made up their faces and dressed like that? Edward rather liked Poppy. He was under no illusions about her, but he liked her. She drank too much, she had certainly not been a virgin when she married Eddy, and she was not what is called good style. But there was something about her that was a sort of relief and rest to Edward.

After lunch she frankly went upstairs to sleep it off, and Eddy followed her somewhat sheepishly, while Agatha and Edward walked about Brighton and Agatha showed Edward where she had been at school, and where Constance Kent had lived. Then they turned up East Street, arm in arm. Agatha caught sight of them both in a long mirror in a hairdresser's window. That wasn't Agatha and Edward, not that dowdy woman and lean, rather bent man, both with a drooping air. . . . No, no. That couple were old, Agatha and Edward were still quite young. This hat . . . I only got it last year in Kensington High Street, they said it was a Paris model. It couldn't look all wrong like that. Fanny . . . what will she look like?

Agatha, that thin, old, grey-haired woman. . . . Fanny that squat, brown, little old woman, with the gold-rimmed glasses pressing across her flat nose and giving her the air of a be-spectacled toad. .    Her dark husband—Selah's crow! —hovering at her shoulder, bland and smiling. . . . Edward could imagine him selling or not selling, with equal impassivity, the Staffordshire figures, the imitation Chippendale, the Burmese trifles of gilt and glass mosaic, the lengths of silk from Mandalay, the imperturbable Buddhas in stone and gilded wood and brass, that crowded the dusty shop.

They had tea in the back part of the shop. The two women talked—Agatha most—Edward said little; Mr. Mahboob, beyond expressing the opinion that the weather was frightfullee cold in England, said . nothing. Agatha faintly condescended, though unaware of the fact. She had always had the knack of condescending over a tea-pot, and when with a social inferior she could do it even over a cup. Yet she was honestly glad to see Fanny, that Edward knew. Isn't it always ourselves we are meeting, thought Edward. She's meeting her own young self in the old Fanny, and so am I.

The years had made Fanny almost mulishly uncommunicative. That was the greatest change in her. True, ever since the fall of Mandalay she had been a different creature. She had never chattered since. But then it had seemed that shock and disappointment, the loss of everything she had held by in life, had rendered her quiet for the time being, it was impossible to believe that gossipy little Fanny was going to be so dead for ever. Now, though she talked, because there was much to say, she gave a curious effect of being rusty in her speech, as an unused lock is rusty. It was as though she had lost the habit of words . . . Edward glanced at the bland Mr. Mahboob, who sat gazing at Fanny with genuine admiration in his kind, brown eyes, and reflected that however odd their married life might be, as the married life of people very different from ourselves always appears, at least Fanny had a man whom she had managed to keep fond of her.

Fanny had enquired politely after the family life of Agatha and Edward, after the welfare of " the boys." No, she herself had had no children. Selah had had a daughter who was married. It was to a letter of Selah's that she turned for her news. She held it close to the gold-rimmed spectacles and read out portions of it. Julie, it appeared, was now quite blind, had been blind for some years. She still kept on her ιooms and sold the silk in the house with the courtyard. She was more *dévote* than ever.

Agatha, listening to the letter, relaxed in her chair and sat with her hands folded in her lap. The shop grew dim but no one thought to turn on the lights. The Buddhas sat and smiled faintly through the dusk of sky-shutting-in-time. Agatha and Edward saw Julie, old and blind, sitting fingering her silks anxiously between critical fingers as her girls placed them there. Julie, entrenched for ever in the dark tower of her blindness. . . .

Selah, too, more cheerful vision, in the bungalow that she described, full of china ornaments and little pictures and Christmas cards from her friends, Selah busy and bustling.

And then a third figure crept in, a figure that Selah's vivid letter conjured up. For Supaya-lat, a widow, was back in Rangoon, to end her days there in a house by the lake.

" You will not be surprised," (wrote Selah), " to hear that I have been asked to go and see the ex-Queen, now that Thibaw being dead, she has been given a bungalow in Rangoon. Julie, although she is blind, has also been all the distance from Mandalay to visit her. I agreed with a double object, to be of use to the Government and to convince her of the unjust treatment we had at her hands. I took with me many presents of fruit and flowers. She has a fine bungalow in a large compound, and the furniture is all from Rowe & Co., European red plush chairs and gold mirrors. She also has a new and expensive bed got for her by the Chief of Police, all brass. The house and compound she lets get dirty like the Palace. She feeds lots of dogs and poongyis. She feeds many dozen poongyis every day and gives them presents of the Eight Necessities. The Government has paid her debts several times but she is always spending, though now it is on religion.

" I meant to reproach her for her treatment of me, but on that memorable meeting I found I could not for very pity. She is totally subdued in spirit, calm, affable, looking miserably old and toothless. A totally different person from what she was when exercising her power. I thought of her with

her graceful body and her black glittering eyes that used to
be as those of snakes at the attack, darting this way and that
and scanning everyone in determination to command and
defeat every opposition, and I fell a victim to pity and my
anger vanished.

" She always wears now a white tamein, jacket and pawa,
and is very religious. She tells her beads all day just like
the Catholics. At first she just stared at me and said: ' I
thought you were dead and your youngest sister only was
alive,' but I said, ' no, all my sisters are dead and I am alive.'
Her surprise and chagrin at my still being alive having
abated, she said she was very pleased to see me. Our conversation then turned to the pleasant olden days in the Palace.
She said that now she would stop all intrigues and jealousies
such as had existed then, and said how she had always prevented the use of filthy jokes and dresses, after the manner
of the late Queen Victoria. She asked what my husband
earned, and when I said what a good salary he gets from
Government, she said at once: ' Your husband is rich, can't
you lend me money?'

" She is like what she was in the old days, when you know
she never had any money for always spending it. Being
caught between the upper and nether millstones I had to
extricate myself tactfully from this uncomfortable plight,
so I said my husband had to keep all our poor relations and
also we had our position to keep up, and that all our property
and jewellery had been confiscated. She seemed quite
surprised and said who by, and I said by her Minister, the
Taingda Mingyi, at her orders, and she said that was what
Ministers were always like, doing wrong and then blaming
it on the King and Queen."

Edward laughed and Mr. Mahboob joined in very heartily.
Agatha did not laugh— she was back in the old days. Fanny
at once laid down the letter on her lap, and would not read
any more. She had shrunk back into herself in some odd
fashion, and when she switched on the light the faces of the
Buddhas were not more impenetrable than hers. She would
not promise anything definite in reply to Agatha's request

that she should come over to Chichester—"It's a nice trip on a fine day."

Fanny took out some bundles of wide, heavy, silk ribbon and Edward dutifully bought whatever Agatha chose.

Fanny accompanied them to the door. She seemed to soften again suddenly as she bade them farewell.

"Good-bye, Agatha. I do not think I will come. I am soon going away. But I am glad to have seen you. Very glad."

"Where are you going?" asked Agatha.

"I am going out to Supaya-lat. She has sent for me."

"Fanny! But the shop?"

"We shall sell it. Or my husband can keep it on," said Fanny, as though he were not there.

"She is always veree devoted to the Queen," said Mr. Mahboob. "It is tiresome the Queen has no money for the fare and I have had many expenses lately, so we will have to go third-class, which we have never done before, and of course there are the enemy submarines, but Fanny wishes to go."

"You must let me know if you have a sale here," said Edward quickly, "I am moving house soon and shall want some furniture."

Mr. Mahboob bowed politely. Agatha and Fanny kissed suddenly, moved by a common impulse. They had only shaken hands on meeting.

Edward, well wrapped up on the dickey-seat motoring home, was glad to be alone. On the darkness of the heavy hedges and night sky he saw a pageant of the past, a frieze of gaily-coloured figures. He was glad of the fresh English air upon his face, he had felt oppressed in that little shop by the insistence of the past. The tragedy of the Kingdom of Ava had enveloped him once more.

True, it had been but a surface tragedy, compounded of bright pigments, of barbaric embroideries; the deeps, except the deeps of jealousy in Supaya-lat and Fanny, were never stirred. Even the Kinwoon Mingyi, that wise and infinitely sad old man, had been too much of a philosopher, too much of an accepter of whatever happened, to be a tragic figure.

A bloodless conquest had followed on a tragedy of the nursery, a nursery of vicious children. It was the pathetic impact of ignorance against material knowledge, and ignorance was bound to lose. Children playing with toy soldiers, but with real lives, had become so vicious that the grown-ups had to step in and take charge; it was not a real tragedy, it was the re-shuffling of a pack of coloured cards. Edward sometimes felt as though he had dreamt it all, as though, as in " Alice," the highly-coloured protagonists had changed into playing-cards and suddenly rained about his head.

Even to him, to whom the players were and would always be, real human beings, common as bread, the march of events at Mandalay had always held, and always would, the coloured inconsequence of a show. The whole thing had been so pitifully childish . . . one forgot the danger to life, which at the time had brought the heart leaping into the throat. . . . The truth was, these Burmese people had not been the fit matter for tragedy, too gay, too care-free, too tolerant, too bumptious, they were not revengeful or fiery like Maho-medans, of a slow, deep burning like Hindus, nor enigmatic as were the Chinese. Theirs was not the intolerance of any of these, nor had they the sturdy obstinacy of the Protestant or the zeal of the Catholic. They had still their toys, the pleasantness of their daily lives, their family loves, their coloured wear, their consciousness of superiority; the gay bubbles of their souls still flew against a painted sky in the golden glow of evening.

The oft-quoted " mystery " of the East was not to be sought in these pleasant, violent children, any more than mystery, because of her sex, was inherent in woman.

Woman . . . the resentful Edward was back at that again —impossible to get away when you thought of the Kingdom of Ava. Woman . . . the thing that had conquered him and that had conquered Ava. Agatha had happened to be the soul, informing a particular guise of flesh, that had ruled his life; Fanny, little Fanny, so limited in all her appre-hensions, a shallow-brained, little creature of mixed race, had changed the history of a kingdom.

He had never told Agatha about that, never would.

Sandreino had asked for secrecy and Edward had promised it. But now, rushing through the sweet, dim, Sussex lanes, he thought of Fanny, whom he would in all probability never see again, with a peculiar tenderness.

He admired her for a loyalty that, in spite of her act of treachery, was truly hers. She at least had never bowed the knee to the British in Burma. For, thought Edward whimsically, you 'couldn't count the awful afternoon of the Dufferin's reception; that was a mere transitory and parlour politeness. Agatha might have pointed out that Fanny was not likely to wish to stay on in a place where she had had a " good position " and would now have none, but Edward knew he judged more fairly in granting Fanny different motives. She had not been able to live on with the ghost of the dethroned Supaya-lat. With the actual Supaya-lat she could and would live—it was for the Queen, that lost symbol of royalty and romance, she was returning now. She would travel in danger and discomfort and probably live in worse discomfort—for it would embrace a spiritual unease—when she arrived.

He pictured a sullen, nagging Supaya-lat—who had, just like disappointed European women, " got religion "— spending too much money and always clamouring to her friends and to the Government for more; he pictured Selah with a satisfactory husband in a bungalow full of ornaments; he pictured Julie Delange, old, blind, suspicious of her workers and anxious for the good name of her manufactures, in the old French house in Mandalay. And he knew that Fanny, Selah and Julie would always cherish for Supaya-lat that curious devotion that not all her acts of injustice had been able to destroy. That the Queen still wanted them was their pride. That was why Julie had gone down from Mandalay, why Selah had visited her, why Fanny was throwing up the life she and her Mahboob had made. Supaya-lat was the symbol of beauty in their lives.

Perhaps, thought Edward, if Agatha had known the Palace life as they knew it, she would have felt the same. But, more probably, she would have considered herself, and rightly, above such tinsel notions of romance. . . . Yet

Agatha was very quiet and somehow subdued that night
when they went to bed, as Edward wandered in and out of
the dressing-room, which, as a Canon, was now his, intermittently discussing Fanny and the Queen.

A few weeks later Agatha met the postman in Chichester,
and he handed her a picture-postcard in friendly country-
town fashion. It was from Fanny and had been posted at
Port Said. "Do you remember Mrs. Murgatroyd and
when she would not let us go ashore to buy things here?"
wrote Fanny in her large round script, that of a little conscientious schoolgirl.

Agatha remembered. She had remembered so much that
she had never forgotten, since the tea party at Brighton.
Now, pursuing her mechanical household shopping in
Chichester on a grey and windy morning, her face buttoned
itself up in the old way, as though she were disapproving of
something. But she wasn't. She was merely feeling—not
exactly envious of Fanny (that, of course, would be absurd!),
but a queer sort of little left-out sensation. . . .

For to Agatha, just as to Burmans, the seven-tiered pyathat
would always be in an odd way the Centre of the Universe.
It stood to her for that something strange in her life which
alone had redeemed it from the ordinary; that something
strange which was, more and more, all she had. . . . It
wasn't as a missionary she regretted the Kingdom of Ava,
it was as a romantic.

Fanny was commonplace; Julie, Supaya-lat, all the
players in the drama were commonplace—even she herself
might appear so to outsiders; perhaps everybody was
really commonplace when you knew them, but the idea of
the whole thing had somehow been romantic and satisfying.
. . . If she had only known it, she had that conviction in
common with Edward, after all.

But she didn't know it, and neither did he. She only was
painfully aware that the young Edward of the past, whom
she had really never possessed, was yet more hers than this
apparently tamed, elderly husband, because for a brief space
she and her young lover had imagined they shared a dream

of life together.   The grown John and Eddy would never be hers as those far off pale, little boys had been, and still were.   That was, after all, the best of children; their infancy was always yours.   And Chichester now seemed faint beside memory of Mandalay.   That golden ghost of a city, unsubstantial as it should have seemed amid the solidities of Sussex, was yet touched with perpetual sunlight.

And of this something strange, this glowing ghost-city, Fanny was inescapably a part.   Supaya-lat must have felt that when she sent for her.

The Queen had sent for Fanny. . . . Agatha, turning her steps homewards, saw the spire of the Cathedral stand up against the cloudy sky like a drawn sword.

Never again for Agatha, but soon for Fanny, would the Shway Dagon, like a tongue of flame whose still music is for the ears of the spirit, burn in the golden bell of evening.


**THE END**

# F. TENNYSON JESSE

was born in Chislehurst, Kent, in 1888. On her father's side, she was the great-niece of Alfred, Lord Tennyson. Her mother's family, until her grandfather made a fortune in coal, had been Cornish seafarers. After studying art, she began a career as a journalist in 1911. Writing for *The Times* and the *Daily Mail* in London, she became one of the few women journalists to report from the front at the outbreak of the first world war.

In 1918 she married the playwright H. M. Harwood, and throughout their long married life they collaborated on several plays. All seven of her own plays were produced in London's West End. In addition to her plays and novels, Fryniwyd Tennyson Jesse published three collections of short stories, numerous poems, belles lettres, and a notable history of Burma. A brilliant criminologist, she edited six volumes of the Notable British Trials series, and her *Murder and Its Motives* has been acclaimed by authorities in the field.

Of the nine novels she wrote, *A Pin to See the Peepshow* (1934)—televised in 1972—is perhaps the best known. *The Lacquer Lady* is considered by critics to be her best work. The breadth and versatility of her prodigious body of work distinguish her as one of the most talented British writers of the period between the world wars. She died in London in 1958.